Pr

Maredith Ryan

TABLE OF CONTENTS

DEDICATION

For Kendal, my greatest solace.
For Olivia, my biggest advocate.
For Jack, my favorite writer.

PROLOGUE

The Kingdom of Zion stretches far and wide. It's famous for its incredibly beautiful forests and breathtaking mountain views. It's infamous for its hot, desert regions and its dangerous, stormy seas. The mainland is home to large cities such as Glimmer, Lockwood, and Astrid and smaller villages like Frostfire and Dramer. Off the southern and western coasts of the mainland are several small islands, sporadically arranged throughout the Sequestrian Sea and the Floriz Ocean. The Glacial Sea is the northernmost landmark of Zion; cold, forgotten waters frozen in many areas during the winter and bitterly cold any other time. Northern cities of the mainland only know the winter season and its icy tundra. Both mainland and islands are home to various people of all shapes, sizes, and cultures.

The kingdom is a monarchy, ruled by the king. For centuries, there has been one family in dominion of the land. The long line of Alwyn kings has been widely known for their wisdom and generosity. For just as long, there has been a king on the throne with a queen to rule alongside him; she maintains less power but is still highly revered as one of the top royals of the kingdom. Even still, the Queen can never be head monarch of the kingdom. If something happens to the king, the next male heir is to be crowned immediately. This is the way things have always been done. King Windenmeyer, the founder of Zion thousands of years ago, built the kingdom from the ground up, starting with the brilliant, shining city of Glimmer; his pride and joy. A city flourishing with trade ports, farmland, and people; and widely known as the City of

Perfection. The laws of the land he put into motion continue to thrive with the royal leaders of Zion present day.

King Bronze, the fifty-seventh and current king of Zion, and his wife, Queen Rose Alwyn, have three children—two boys and a girl. The eldest is Jeb; the people of Zion—specifically Glimmer—know him by his tenacious smile and boyish looks. The now twenty-five-year-old heir to the throne has trained long to one day receive the blessing from his father as the sole ruler of Zion. This right comes by two means. Either the heir-to-be comes of age at forty and, therefore, takes charge of the throne. Or the current king is rendered incapable of completing his task as king, whether by means of illness, paralysis, or death. Jeb is being raised with this knowledge in mind. Shade—who's the star of this particular Zion chronicle—is the next eldest, eight years younger than his brother. Amberle, the youngest Alwyn, is only a mere nine years old with blonde hair just like her mother and a shy, sweet demeanor.

Shade's best friend for as long as he can remember has been Lady Erin Sansa, daughter to Duke Gregory and Duchess Minerva Sansa. It's rather fitting that the Old English meaning of "Sansa" is "unyielding"; for the duke's daughter is a rather suitable owner of that title. Prince Shade has found himself on the cross end of Lady Erin's attitude on more than one occasion, and the girl never backs down from a fight. She has three younger siblings; the twelve-year-old twins, Eliza and Eleazar, and six-year-old Edith. The Sansa family lives within the castle grounds in a separate house built behind the castle itself. However, with how much time Erin spends adventuring with the young Prince Shade, she might as well live within the castle walls.

All of Zion adore the royal family and their loved

ones.

At least, at one point, that was the consensus. But there is far more to the beautiful kingdom than meets the eye. Because for many long years now, there has been a growing unrest, a festering darkness whose deep tendrils have spared no part of Zion. Threats of treason, anarchy, and mayhem run rampant. Threats that continue to grow in number and strength. All it takes is one moment, one catalyst to jump start the movement and send the kingdom into a downward spiral of confusion and chaos.

King Bronze has spent several years—at least fifteen now—trying his best to quell the pulsing darkness and, ultimately, dispel it altogether. He's traveled across Zion seeking support and quieting revolts. This support, at one time unanimous, has started to decrease as the traitorous voices grow louder. He has kept this darkness a secret from his beloved home of Glimmer, and *especially* his beautiful Windenmeyer Castle and the loved ones she protects.

But the darkness cannot be silenced forever. It won't be. And it has slithered its way into the City of Perfection, past the royal gates, and into the prestigious halls of Windenmeyer. It has snaked by all of King Bronze's extensive, secretive, protective measures and into the very heart of Zion herself.

And within that pure, pulsing heart, enters the catalyst. One little speck, one little tendril of darkness that will forever taint the land of Zion.

CHAPTER 1

Eighteen-year-old Shade had always been a troublemaker. If ever a quarrel occurred, you could find Shade right at its center; duking it out with the best of them. If food mysteriously disappeared from the kitchen, you knew who was behind it. Skipping classes to ride on horseback far from the castle grounds and deep into the dark forest just to perform mischief and create chaos among the commoners was right up Prince Shade's ally. The young, thrill-crazed, second in line to the throne didn't have a responsible bone in his body. He was a good liar, an amazing thief, and an even better warrior. Now, he did have his times of kindness and even those actions that showed he had the potential to become a great king. But, overall, he was conniving, somewhat cocky, and every girl's heartbreaker.

As you can see, Prince Shade Alwyn of the kingdom of Zion, with his midnight, chin-length mop of black hair was many things…But he was not a murderer. And, certainly, not the murderer of his father, the king.

It happened so fast. One moment, the family had been enjoying a lovely lunchtime meal around the table (Shade had actually been pestering his sister, Amberle, beside him by poking her with a fork), when suddenly, King Bronze gagged on the food he'd started eating.

Things got serious when Shade's father had fallen from his chair, strewn across the floor. Queen Rose (Shade's mother) and a nearby guard dropped beside him, tugging at his robe.

1

"Poison!" The guard had bellowed after a moment. Poison.

King Bronze, ruler of every land, animal, person, and rock in the Kingdom of Zion, had been poisoned.

Prince Jeb, heir to the throne, had bolted to his feet, Shade following, at the sight of their dying father. From deep within Shade's cloak, a small flask with just a few drops of liquid had tumbled to the ground, echoing loudly off of the polished floor.

All eyes had turned his way. Shade knew what was in the flask, knew it was what had poisoned the king, but had no idea how it had gotten to be with him. The look of desperation on his face was out of place as he had looked to his older brother, "I—"

Guards were upon him in a flash, Prince Jeb looking on with cold fury.

Pushing aside the fact that his own brother didn't trust him, Shade concentrated on escaping with this life. His home for eighteen years had suddenly become his nightmare.

Shade had jumped on top of the table, the forgotten food attracting unwanted attention by the house flies. From there, he'd searched for a way out of the Dining Hall. The hall's main doors were left unattended, every guard near rushing to the table to stop him.

Now, Shade thinks fast, shoving a boot into the chest of one guard and kicking mashed potatoes into the face of another. The clanging of dishes and such erupts as Shade barrels down the length of the table, towards the main doors and freedom. A hand clasps around his ankle, almost sending him sprawling to his stomach, but a firm jerk and he is on the move again.

Shade is dimly aware of his mother yelling for the guards to stop, yelling that Shade has to be innocent.

Her voice goes unheard by most, as they claw frantically at Shade.

Someone manages to grasp hold of his cloak and it is wrenched from his shoulders. He keeps moving, though, determined not to become a prisoner in his own home. The home that now looks as if he isn't welcomed to.

Several guards have by now clambered onto the table and hurried from behind.

Shade reaches the end of the table, front flipping over the three guards awaiting him there. Just like that, Prince Shade's escape is in sight. But right as he reaches the doors, a figure skids into view, blocking his path.

Erin is a tall, long-haired blonde; her attitude mirrors closely that of Shade's. Shade's heart falls and he stumbles to a halt; he and the duke's daughter have been friends since birth, the duke and his family forever loyal to King Bronze. Shade is devastated at the sight of Erin turning on him, too.

But she points with her bow away from the Dining Hall. "This way, Shade!" In her other hand, she holds Shade's sword, case and all. She throws it his way.

Shade leaps into action, ashamed that he'd thought his friend would ever betray him. He catches his sword and clips it around his waist on the run.

Erin's eyes flit past Shade, taking in the room behind him, "Hurry!" She urges, before taking off.

Shade blows through the doors, takes a sharp right, and sprints after Erin, quickly catching up to her. "Well-well, is someone slowing up in their old age?" Even in the dire situation, Shade manages a tease.

Erin snorts, "Where's your cloak, young prince?"

Shade feels the sting of that one, grinning as they

continue their escape through the castle. Alarm horns sound inside the castle, alerting the entire castle of their break away. They pass separate hallways branching off from the main one they are on. Guards in those hallways catch sight of them, screaming for them to surrender. The two ignore every shout. They are in the clutches, the very heart of the allies-turned-enemies. Every way out is blocked by guards wielding swords and spears. Erin has an arrow notched on her bow and Shade's own sword is drawn, both of them hoping they won't have to use them.

"Is it just us? Alone against all odds?" Prince Shade asks, breathlessly, "Where's your father when we need him most?" The duke is always finding ways to get the two friends out of trouble. Life-long friend to the king, Duke Sansa has always been like another father figure to Shade.

Erin grabs hold of his arm, dragging him to a stop. She stares at Shade with a look of anger and terrible sadness on her face. "My dad's dead, Shade. Poisoned, just like your father." She relays to him quickly how her mother found him at their kitchen table only minutes before, head face down in a bowl of oatmeal. Duchess Sansa, understandably beside herself, suspected foul play and was on her way to warn the castle guards when word of the king was quickly and frantically passed throughout the castle. Erin had only just risen from bed when her mother bustled her out of the room with a hurried warning. "She told me to come find you. That you needed help."

Shade looks down in sadness at this news of the duke. "Erin…" He wants to apologize; but how does one do that for the death of their father? Instead, he takes her hand and squeezes it.

She speaks first, all trace of sadness leaves; replaced with anger and determination, "We'll figure out who is behind this. And, when we do…"

There is no need to finish. Shade meets her gaze and nods once.

Shouts arise down the hall, "There they are!"

Shade and Erin take off once more. "The Western Tower." Shade says, aware that, for the moment, they really are alone, "Get to the Western Tower."

They book it to the far western side of the castle, having to take a few detours and even knock some guards senseless a couple of times. Shade doesn't remember the hallways being this long before now. They seem to stretch on forever, doorways flying open on either side as servants and maids poke their heads out to find the source of the commotion.

At one point, he races around a corner and topples into a guard, whose arm makes to raise the bow in his hands. Shade grabs its wood with both hands and pulls hard, yanking it from the guard's grip, then elbowing him in the face. The guard stumbles back just enough for Shade and Erin to run past him.

Shade glances down gleefully at the new-found weapon in his grip. He slips the bow over his shoulder and continues running. Finally, they come upon the doorway leading up the stairway that will take them to the top of the tower.

Without slowing, the two athletic youths dash up the stones, arriving shortly to the climax of the look-out tower. Shade slams and bolts the door, locking them inside.

"So, this is your brilliant plan, prince? Shutting us away in a tower, with only one door? The door you just bolted. You do realize we are trying to *escape*, right?"

Erin huffs at him.

Shade doesn't answer, walking to the one opening in the tower, a window that overlooks the land a mile west, emptying into the Sequestrian Sea. This particular tower is about sixty feet high. Looking directly down from the window, Shade spies what he knew would be there all along. Erin must have forgotten.

She is still ranting.

"Erin, please *do* shut up," He states with dripping sarcasm, "And, come see what my *brilliant* plan consists of."

Erin stalks over to join him at the window. The two look down at the rushing water of the Sanctum River.

Erin grins, "Prince Shade, I do believe I could just kiss you, right now." She lets out a deep breath, eyeing the rushing waters closely.

Shade smirks, "Pucker up, Lady Erin; the pleasure would be mine." He leans towards her mockingly. But, to his surprise, his heart actually catapults in his chest at the thought of meeting her lips with his own. It had been doing that more as of late.

Erin shoves his head, with pursed lips, away, "You're so full of it."

A banging on the other side of the door informs them that the guards have arrived.

"Alright, prince," Erin beckons at the window with an arm, "This was your idea. Lead the way."

"Ladies first."

Erin glares at him, "So, now you resort to chivalry?"

They argue back and forth, unaware of the happenings on the other side of the door; until all they hear is silence. Shade silences Erin with a hand across her mouth. The look in her eye is fierce, but when Shade holds a finger to his lips and looks at the door, she stops short. The prince drops his hand and turns as if to face the door head on.

"Um…what—" Erin is cut off as an explosion blows the door from its hinges and sends Shade crashing against the tower wall. Erin is thrown out the window, glass shattering. She grabs hold of the ledge at the last second and hangs there against the wall.

Large cracks appear along the walls of the Western Tower and the structure shakes violently. The guards and knights who had caused the explosion, stumble with the shaking of the tower just inside the doorway, obviously surprised by the weakening structure.

There is no time to think. As the tower crumbles around him, Shade jumps from the window, crying for Erin to let go. Shade falls, arms and legs pinwheeling. The water comes closer, eager to meet with him. The exhilarating drop threatens to drag a shout from his lips he knows would sound anything but manly.

Erin screams his name. He understands enough to look up. A giant chunk of collapsed tower streaks downwards, straight above him. Shade angles his body to where he'll be entering the water at a dive. Now, the water seems to recede in fear as it sees what follows the young prince. He notes the reflection of the giant structure in the water and fears it may be too big to avoid.

Shade closes his eyes and hopes for the best, as the cold water envelopes him.

Everything is silent.

And then Shade is propelled downwards by the force of the tower wall crashing into the water. He has enough sense to pump his arms and barely get out of the way as the wall sinks rapidly past him. The current of the Sanctum River shoves him along. And to his dismay, Shade realizes he has failed to draw in a deep enough breath for the plunge. The surface of the water seems too far, and he has a dismal thought that he may not make it.

But a different thought pushes the first out of the way.

Is Erin okay?

This encourages him onward, determined to find the answer to that question. And, hopefully, a good answer.

Just when his lungs feel as if they will burst for lack of oxygen, Prince Shade breaks through the surface, gasping. Far above, guards gesture down at him from the large hole in the side of the tower. Their shouts can't be heard over the rushing water. The river takes him further away from the castle and the overarching limbs of the beautiful trees obscure him from view.

If they can get to the stables, sitting towards the outskirts of the castle grounds, they can grab a couple of horses and hit the road.

"Erin!" He shouts. The waters around him are choppy and devoid of his lifelong friend. That means one of two things: she has already made it to shore or…and he can't bear the thought…she is *underneath* those choppy waters.

"Erin!"

And then a pair of hands are grabbing him from behind, dunking his head back under the water. He resurfaces, sputtering and flailing his arms, as a tinkling laugh greets him.

Erin, next to him as the river takes them downstream, is smiling; her voice is the source of the laughter.

Shade glowers at her, pushing her away, as best he can in the water.

"Did I have you worried, dear prince?" Erin teases.

"Come on," He grumbles, paddling hard for the bank. The current is strong but they pump forwards and are soon pulling themselves from the river. Shade's sword is still in its case at his waist and the bow resting over his shoulder and across his chest; Erin's bow is still intact, although she has lost several arrows to the river.

All Shade wants to do is lie down and rest. The raging, brisk waters have drained him of energy. Erin is feeling its effects as well, but Shade pulls her to her feet and they run, ignoring the weight of their water-logged clothing.

Erin still has her light green cloak on. Each cloak of an owner holds a certain sentimental value to them, as the cloak is often the family's heirloom, passed down from their elders. Erin's cloak was handed down to her by her father and is, therefore, the heirloom of the Sansa bloodline. So, even though it weighs her down, she isn't about to leave it behind.

Watching her pull it protectively around her shoulders, Shade has a sudden twinge of sadness, thinking of his own cloak that was torn from his torso in his escape. His cloak was blue, like the ocean. His father had given it to him when he was ten. Shade had been so proud of it. Now, seven years later, he frowns at the memory he so wishes he could go back to.

"The stables. Hurry." Shade says. Erin follows him at once.

They are in the forest, away from the castle walls. Here and there are small cottages where the servants and maids, of Shade and his family, live. He and Erin make sure to stay out of sight. These houses are still within the castle grounds and inside the outer wall.

On the other side of the outer wall, the largest and capital city of the Kingdom, Glimmer, thrives. Glimmer and its Windenmeyer Castle, named long ago after the first king of the land, sits along the Sequestrian Sea. Glimmer's ports flourish with trade and the majority of the city prospers in its riches.

Soon, Glimmer will be warned of his and Erin's so-called treachery. They need to get out while they can.

The castle grounds are huge, but the stables aren't far from their position. The two reach the stables and hurry to the entrance, still dripping wet. Shade opens the stable door, and in his haste, runs smack into someone who had been coming out.

Greaver. The gray-haired stable-hand. He cares for the horses on a daily basis. He and Shade only speak on rare occasions and usually, it's about their fascination with horses.

"Prince Shade," he says, surprised. He bows his head in respect. Greaver is a thin man with a hunched back and a tanned face lined with wrinkles. He has always been kind and grandfatherly to the prince. "I was not aware you were riding today. And directly after your shower." His eyes take in Shade's wet clothing. Then, Greaver notices Erin, "Ah, hello, Lady Erin. Riding as well? You know, they say going out with wet hair causes illness. I'm sure it applies even more so for sopping wet bodies."

Greaver has always been easy going and funny. But Shade doesn't have the time to share a laugh. "Greaver, we need two horses, right away. Please." He adds.

Greaver sees the desperation on their faces, "Prince Shade, is something the matter?"

As if on cue, the alarm bells of Glimmer sound, now alerting the entire city that a traitor is on the loose. Greaver glances around the forest, listening intently to the sound of the bells, then looks back at the two in front of him.

Shade sees understanding dawn in the older man's eyes and is about to plead for him to trust them, but the man speaks first.

"I see," He stares hard at Shade, his dark eyes scrutinizing. Shade stares back, tensing to run. Erin's hand rests on Shade's arm as if preparing to pull him into action.

Greaver surprises them both by winking. He clears his throat, "Well, right this way, Prince Shade and Lady Erin, I believe there are two horses patiently awaiting your presence." Greaver turns on his heel and starts off towards the horses.

Shade and Erin share a shocked look, then practically run after him.

Greaver gathers two knapsacks, loading each with food, a blanket, a water canteen, and a knife. He hands one to Erin. The other he continues to load, adding to it a compass, a map of the kingdom, and some matches. He gives this to Shade along with a brown, somewhat tattered, cloak. Greaver then sees to the horses, tightening saddles and altering stirrups.

"Now, you be good to these kids," He says softly to the horses, one black as night, the other caramel in color, "I think they could use some help." He turns to Shade and Erin, "I apologize, there's no time for you to change out of your clothing. Winter is approaching, so the night will be chilly. Let's hope you dry before then. Alright, you two, go out the back. Get out of here. Stay clear of the main gates. They'll have those heavily guarded."

Shade dons the cloak, slings the knapsack over his shoulders and hurriedly mounts the majestic caramel steed. Erin hops up on the black one.

Shade reaches down and grabs Greaver's arm "Wait," He says, "My father is dead." The words seem to echo around the stable, even with the wailing alarms outside.

Greaver frowns sadly and bows his head for a moment, before returning his gaze to Shade, "I feared as much. There have always been enemies of your father. I had only hoped they would remain silent. It seems my hope was in vain."

Guards' yells are heard from somewhere nearby.

Greaver glances towards the outside voices, then back at the prince and his companion, "You must get out of Glimmer. It is not safe. Go to Lockwood. There are people there you can trust. Tell them it was I who sent you. They will help." He pauses, then adds, "I hope. But, be careful, there are many disloyal to the throne, as well."

"How do you know so much?" Shade asks.

"Just as there are enemy spies within the castle walls, there are also spies loyal to the king. Your father was a good man, seeking to protect his Kingdom and all who resided in it. But the knives of evil run deep. King Bronze was not dissuaded by them. But I fear Prince Jeb will not be as strong in resistance. The Kingdom of Zion needs *you*, Prince Shade, to someday restore it back to its former glory like your father was trying to do. But that day is not today. You must go."

"My family," Erin whispers, staring pleadingly at

Greaver. Aside from her murdered father, Erin has a mother and three younger siblings; twins, a boy and a girl, age twelve, and a little sister who recently turned six.

Greaver stops her with a hand on her shin, "I will take care of them, Lady Erin. You need not worry. You either, young prince."

Shade looks down at the stable-hand, "Sir, I…" He can't seem to find the words to express his gratitude.

"I know, Your Highness," Greaver nods to show he understands his thanks, "Be careful. And may we see each other again someday. Perhaps, in a more positive time, yes?" He winks and then is gone. Out the stable entrance, ready to lead the guards astray.

The horses, the black named Riot and the caramel named Cracker, shoot off out of the back doors of the stable; fellow horses neighing wildly as if pleading for Shade to take them with him.

The forest is a blur around them. Shade looks over his shoulder; no guards are following.

Yet.

So, Greaver is a part of some secret group that Shade's father had formed? Did his mother know about this? And, if she did, was she safe? Shade almost turns Cracker around to race back and save her and the rest of his family. What will happen to them? Will Jeb really turn against his brother? And, what will become of Amberle, his younger sister, only nine years old?

Shade doesn't want to think that any harm could come to them, but the thought is ever-present. It is imperative that he and Erin get to those who can help. He pushes his horse to go faster.

They speed past the main gates, guards hurrying around in a frenzy. A few hop up onto horses of their own, giving chase to the two youths.

"Shade!" Erin gives a shout of warning.

Behind them, one of the guards is pulling back a bowstring. Shade has seen these guards in training. They are incredibly accurate on the backs of moving horses.

The guard lets the arrow fly. It embeds itself in the trunk of a tree next to Shade's head as he zips past, startling him.

They are aiming to kill. Which means Jeb had given them that order. Even if Queen Rose trusts Shade didn't betray his father, she has no say in the matter. There must always be a king on the capital's throne. For reasons unknown to Shade, the rule made many years ago was that women were not fit to rule in Windenmeyer Castle. He thinks it has something to do with the way things have always been done and change being frowned upon. He has, no doubt, been taught every in and out of the history of Zion throughout his schooling; but who wants to learn when there's fun to be had?

Erin whips out her own bow and takes aim behind her, she lets loose an arrow that sticks in the leg of one of the guards who hollers out and topples off his horse.

Shade has watched Erin in training, as well. He admits she can beat him any day with a bow and arrow. But as far as sword fighting and hand to hand combat go, Shade has her every time.

"Head to the Shadow Gate!" Shade yells. The Shadow Gate is a gate not known by many. Erin nods and leads the way, since she is one of the few who know its exact location (the duke had built the gate a couple of years back…Erin was supposed to keep it a secret, but had told Shade about it). Erin tosses Shade her case of arrows.

Shade lithely turns full circle in his seat, and faces the chasing guards. He hopes his horse will follow after Erin's. He raises his own bow, trying to hold it still. When he shoots, the guards on their horses scatter, and the arrow flies past harmlessly. Erin's arrow case now only holds five.

The guards realign in formation. This time, two of them take aim with bows.

Shade slips the arrow pack and bow across his back, then pulls out his sword. The guard to his left fires first, followed a second later by the one on the right. Shade has little time to react. But quick reaction time has always been one of his strong points.

As the arrows zoom towards him, Shade notices they will likely soar straight past him on either side, nailing Erin. He isn't about to let that happen. He holds his sword in his right hand, and brings it over to block the first arrow. The arrow 'pings' loudly off the strong steel of the weapon. After blocking that arrow, Shade uses the same motion and arcs the sword to the right, cleaving the second arrow completely in two as it tries rocketing past.

Cracker makes a sudden left turn that almost sends Shade tumbling off. He sheaths his sword, muttering to himself about Erin's crazy driving, and turns back to face frontwards. Then, he ducks low on his horse to pick up speed. Erin is already far ahead, her wet, blonde hair and cloak billowing out behind her like a cape. Soon, he is on her tail, or rather, her horse's tail. She initiates a few turns here and there, probably to lose their pursuers.

Not, however, to lose Shade. Which is exactly what happens. His horse turns one way, but, unfortunately, he does not turn with her. He lands hard on his back, the breath escaping his lungs in a "humph!" Without a second's delay, Shade jumps to his feet and scrambles up the nearest tree, hiding deep in its dark boughs. He squints through the heavily foliaged branches but can't find Erin.

A horse neighs loudly and Shade's head whips in its direction. It's Riot. Erin has pulled him to a stop and is staring back towards the rushing guards intently. A riderless Cracker shuffles nervously at the dark horse's side.

Shade can pick out the conflicting look on Erin's face. Should she go back for Shade, or trust he can find his own way?

She doesn't have long to decide. The guards on horseback stampede under and past the tree Shade is hidden in. Much to Shade's relief, Erin frowns and takes off once more, Cracker following.

Shade may not be very familiar with the Shadow Gate, but he knows the rest of the forest like the back of his hand. He only hopes Cracker is smart enough to circle back around for him or to stay with Erin.

He starts off across the branches, jumping from tree to tree. The loud stomp of horses running fades as the steeds draw away. Shade doesn't falter, though; he only picks up the pace. He runs flexibly, as if the treetops have always been his home. As if the winding branches of old are like smooth grass beneath his feet. Soon enough, he catches up to the guards as they try to force their horses through the thick briars of the forest. The horses whinny in protest.

Shade runs silently above them and without another glance, leaves them behind. He readjusts the pack and the guard's bow across his shoulders. The branches begin to spread out and Shade has to start jumping from limb to limb. It is no different than running.

When Shade was younger, starting early in his years of childhood, Jeb used to bring him out into the forest and teach him to climb the trees. Shade wanted to learn how to run across the treetops so badly like Jeb; he wanted to be just as brave as Jeb. But, for the longest time, Shade was terrified of falling. Falling and getting hurt.

"Shade," Jeb had said softly one time, placing a comforting hand on his younger brother's shoulder, "What is fear?"

Shade had looked up the trunk of a tree, holding back the threatening tears. This. This was fear, he was convinced.

Jeb had smiled softly, "It is nothing but an emotion of our own creation. Whether we let it control us, or we ourselves control it, is up to us. Fear is only what you make it." He led Shade to the base of the tree and stared up into its beckoning limbs, his eyes glittering doggedly at the challenge. "So, little brother...what will you make it?"

Shade sprints faster, running for his brother, his family, running for his father who was so suddenly no longer here to run for himself. His arms pump, his chest heaves with exertion, but Shade doesn't slow. It is now his responsibility to get to safety and one day, return to his kingdom. Isn't that what Greaver had said? The only hope left for the Kingdom of Zion was Shade himself. A whole kingdom resting on his shoulders.

Shade stops, doubled over, trying to calm his beating heart, his labored breaths. He is afraid.

17

"Fear is only what you make it."

Shade stands, nodding to himself. He will not let his fear control him. He hears a *neigh* beneath him and a quiet "shhh" follows soon after. Shade drops to his stomach and peers through the trees to the ground below.

Erin sits atop her horse, peering back the way she had come. One hand holds tight to Cracker's reins, the other caresses Riot's mane.

Shade grins. He swiftly maneuvers his way down the many branches until he is directly above Erin. She doesn't scare easily, but now Shade will finally get her back for the countless times she has waited patiently in a storeroom and under tables for Shade to walk by. He would never admit it, but Erin has scared the pee right out of him on more than one occasion.

He starts the countdown in his head, tensing to drop on the unsuspecting girl. Five, four, three, two—

"Quit lollygagging and get down here before the guards catch up." Erin says.

Shade is so surprised he loses his balance and topples backwards off the branch. For the second time within the hour, Shade lands roughly on the hard ground. He wheezes painfully and stumbles to his feet, "How…?" But he can't get the other words out due to his breathtaking fall.

Erin rolls her eyes, "Just get on your horse. Time is a privilege we don't have."

Shouts and neighing draw their attention back towards the direction of the castle. The guards haven't given up. They are close.

Shade jumps atop Cracker right as she takes off after Riot, the two steeds used to running together.

When Erin leads them through an especially briar-filled and bushy part of the forest, the guards fall behind for good. Riot and Cracker, horses bred to run through the wild, are akin with the crowded forest. But the guard horses, trained to walk the beaten paths of the castle grounds, are in unfamiliar territory and buck in resistance when their riders attempt to force them through.

Erin and Shade ride another mile, zigzagging through the forest, until coming to a stop. They and their horses are breathing hard.

"We've lost them, for now." Erin says. Her cheeks are rosy and her hair dry, both thanks to the wind. Shade can't hold a chuckle in at the sight of Erin's long hair, stuck in all different directions.

She smirks back at him, "You should see yourself, prince."

Shade reaches up and tries patting his wild hair down, but to no avail. It hangs in wild waves just past his ears; he runs a hand through it to brush it back off his face. He shrugs, laughing.

Erin looks at him, "I'm glad you're okay." Her eyes linger on him a moment longer, her smile almost wistful, then she kicks Riot lightly and trots off, "Come. We're close."

The Shadow Gate is exactly what it sounds like; dark and hidden in the shadows. Thorn vines wind its way through and around its bars and, after dismounting, Shade has to cut some away just so Erin can find the handle that will open it up. Beyond the gate is more forest; these will lead them away from Glimmer and further into the countryside of Zion.

"I've never been here." Erin states. "This far, I mean."

Shade looks at her. She is biting her lip like she

does when she is nervous or frightened. "Me neither." He says gently. The alarm bells still sing, but they are more of a background noise now. "But...there's nowhere else for us to go. Not right now, anyway."

"My family...it makes me sick to leave them behind." She lowers her gaze to the ground ashamedly.

He feels the same about his family, too. Shade places a comforting hand on her shoulder, "Greaver will take care of them. And, we'll be back someday. When we're stronger. The traitors won't stand a chance. It's going to be okay."

Erin looks up into his eyes and Shade is all at once struck by how beautiful she is. Her vivid green eyes stand out against the blondeness of her hair. The dip of her nose and how it blends perfectly into the skin above her lips. And her delicate, full lips. He has noticed her beauty before; more and more over the last few years. But, at this moment, he sees it plain as day. A little smile forms on her face/

Shade feels a tug on his heart at the splendor of her smile. "We're in this together." He squeezes her shoulder once, before letting his arm drop back to his side.

Erin shoves him playfully, nodding. "Well, then, prince...will you lead the way, or shall I?" She asks in a haughty voice.

He leers, handing her arrows back to her. "Come now, Lady Erin. You've already led us to the Shadow Gate. I can't let you have *all* the fun, can I?" He grabs the reins of his horse, pushes open the gate, and walks into the unknown.

CHAPTER 2

The forest beyond is alive with wildlife. Shade's ears are humming with the calls of birds, deer, and other animal species. At every turn of his head, he spots a different animal jumping into the trees and foliage. The setting sun is able to break through the thick canopy of trees in some areas, alighting the brilliance of the forest.

Shade's clothing has almost completely dried, save for the thin sheen of sweat that is beginning to seep through. He and Erin have been on horseback, moving at a brisk pace for an hour or so. The castle already seems so far behind. Every time he thinks about stopping, turning around, returning to the castle, he's reminded of the cold, vacant look in his father's eyes as he lies on the floor. So, he steels his nerves and continues onward.

Shade takes out the map in his knapsack and studies it. He knows what the Kingdom of Zion looks like, but he is embarrassed to admit even to his best friend of forever that he is unequivocally lost. Glimmer's sister cities to the east, Sparkston and Fry are both almost a hundred miles away from the outskirts of Glimmer. Countryside laden with small towns and villages here and there sit separating the cities. After Sparkston and Fry, there isn't another big city for two hundred miles. Only mountains and forests. Lockwood is on the other side of those cities and is close to four hundred miles from Glimmer. They still have a long way to go.

North of Glimmer are the all but forgotten cities of Pire and Klepton, cities once run by wealthy traders and marksmen, but have fallen under the powerful hands of greed and desire. The cities are basically overrun with criminals and no-goods. Shade's father had been trying to restore those cities to the brilliance they had once been; at least, until he was murdered.

Glimmer's west is occupied by the Sequestrian Sea. Its body stretches far and wide and contains countless small islands, most of which are uninhabitable. The more southern one goes into Zion, the more they find deserts and dry lands. They eventually become cut off by the Gargantuan Mountains and one of the Silent Sisters. Once the mainland ends, there are more oceans and islands. Truthfully, Shade does not know very much about that area of the kingdom. Anything off of the mainland is somewhat out of the king's jurisdiction, so he's never really cared to learn about it. Shade wishes now that he had spent more time in the library and less time in trouble.

"You're lost."

Shade narrows his eyes, "Just because I am consulting a map, does not mean I am lost."

"Yeah, but you are."

He sighs, and looks up at Erin, "Well then, perhaps, I could use some help. We're still headed East, which is the direction of Lockwood. But it appears there are some obstacles in our way."

"Like what?" Erin asks, leaning over to eye the map.

"Like the Gargantuan Mountains."

Erin's lips form into the shape of a silent "oh". She peers down at the map. "That is quite an obstacle. Any way to go around it?"

"Not unless we want to go four days out of our way

and venture through one of the Silent Sisters." The Silent Sisters are two separate forests on either side of the long outstretched Gargantuan Mountains. One forest is filled with creatures of the night, the other, creatures of the day. Both are very dangerous.

Before Shade completes his sentence, Erin is already shaking her head, "No, bad idea. And we can't go back." She crosses her arms and lets out a long breath. Where Shade is impulsive, Erin is calm and calculating.

Shade stares off into the distance, "There's no going back. Forward is the only way."

"Through the Gargantuans, then." She says plainly.

They continue on their way, this time at a slower pace. The horses, although trained for long days on the road, are tired from their exciting morning. Shade is tired as well and can tell by the slight slump in Erin's shoulders, that she is too. That could also have something to do with her family back at home. Shade thinks of the twins, Eliza and Eleazar, crazy pre-teens with hair just as dark as their father's and robust, infectious personalities. Both are athletic and easy-going, always up for a good time. He thinks of Edith; sweet, shy Edith; with blonde hair as beautiful as Erin's, both she and Edith nearly carbon copies of their alluring mother, Duchess Minerva.

Shade looks away from his friend, realizing he's been staring too long and she's bound to look over and notice. He makes a promise to himself that he will see Erin and her family to safety. If that means he has to fight the entire kingdom, he will. If that means he has to take the throne at this young of an age, he will.

Take the throne. When he thinks of it that way, it sounds like he's committing some sort of wrongdoing.

"*Claim* the throne." He mutters to himself. Yes, that sounds better. After all, didn't Greaver basically say Shade would be the better king for Zion? He shivers slightly at the thought of being king. Is this something he truly wants?

Want or not doesn't matter. If this is what Zion needs then Shade will do his absolute best to see it through.

For the past fifteen miles, they've been riding through open fields and country, sticking to forgotten dirt paths and weeded areas. Shade searches as far as he can, over hills and beyond small country houses, but can't seem to find any sort of forest coverage for miles and miles to come. The night is approaching fast; soon, they won't be able to see at all.

He doesn't like being out in the open like this. He squints into the semi-darkness, away from the path they've been traveling. It looks like there's a small rock outcropping not too far away. He encourages his horse towards it. Erin follows. It doesn't take them long to get to it. It's enough coverage to hide themselves and the horses behind for the night. They dismount and begin preparing the horses to settle in for the evening. A feeling of gloom settles across the shoulders of both human and horse. Shade's stomach growls loudly and Cracker '*hmphs*' as if to say, "Tell me about it." They rest with their backs against the rock. The night is cold and Shade knows it won't be long until winter is upon them; perhaps even a few weeks' time at most. Still, neither one of them dares start a fire.

"What's today's date?" He asks.

Erin leans her head back against the rock, gazing up at the many stars. "November 20th. Your birthday's not for another month, Prince. But nice try."

Shade smiles, but it doesn't reach his eyes. "Too bad." He sighs. "If we're going to make it to Lockwood, we will need to find some help along the way."

She's quiet and, in the darkness, Shade wonders for a moment if she's fallen asleep. But then she says, "As in, people?"

"Perhaps. I was thinking about warmer clothing, since the temperature will drop soon. However, people would be nice. Preferably, trustworthy ones. But, you know, beggars can't be choosers. After all, I ended up with you." She slugs him in the shoulder and he laughs.

He grows somber quickly, unable to turn his mind away from the horrible day for too long. Both of their fathers–dead. Poisoned. By whom? And why? Shade is grateful for Erin's presence. He shifts slightly to where their shoulders are touching and is pleased when she doesn't pull away. Maybe she needs him as much as he needs her right now. With their horses huddled close, shielding them from some of the cool air, they slowly drift off into a dreamless sleep.

CHAPTER 3

Just as the day is beginning to lighten, Shade is awakened by the sound of horses neighing and not their own. Sometime in the night, Erin had slouched over, her head on his shoulder. But, now, she jerks away at Shade's quick movement. He holds a finger to his lips. She watches him with questioning eyes, blinking away the drowsiness.

The sound comes again. It's definitely horses, coming from the direction they had fled last night. Erin is on her feet, crouched down, clutching the separate reins of Riot and Cracker. Shade tip-toes to the edge of the rock and carefully peers around the edge.

He counts eight riders, all of them wearing the soldier's uniforms of Windenmeyer. They're no more than forty yards away, eyes scanning the landscape. They must be looking for him. His only comfort is they do not seem to be in the mood for stopping. They're moving quickly, soldiers on a mission. Still, it won't be long before they're far enough beyond the rock that one look over the shoulder would reveal Shade and Erin's hiding spot.

He turns back to Erin. "Guards from the castle. If we're careful, we can shift around the rock as they're riding past and they won't spot us."

Erin pulls Riot and Shade follows with Cracker in toe. Thankfully, their horses are well-trained enough to recognize a tense situation. They obediently follow without a sound. Shade doesn't dare breathe until the soldiers have disappeared from view, southeast of their position, over another hill almost two hundred yards away. Even then, he waits several more minutes before relaxing and leaning against the rock.

He lets out a long breath. "They're looking for us. And they've likely sent word to any nearby village or city to be on the lookout. I wonder what the bounty is on us." He eyes Erin with a smirk, "Millions of dollars, no doubt. And gold, obviously."

"For you, maybe. If I'm lucky, they don't even know my name."

"Yeah, right. You're best friends with a prince of Zion. You're going to need a lot more than luck to help you out of this sticky situation."

"Ugh, I'm renouncing you as my best friend."

"On whose authority?"

Erin looks him in the face and says in a deadpan voice, "Mine." But after a moment, she smiles.

If only she realized the amount of authority she could have over him if she wanted. He shakes his head, "Keep dreaming, Lady Erin. Come on, let's get out of here."

They start off east, making sure to avoid going the same direction as the soldiers. The day is long and, as it continues, foreboding. Clouds cover the sky and it grows dark much sooner than the night before. They are tired, hungry, and thirsty. Riot and Cracker take wobbly steps, fatigued and parched. Rain has started to fall in a lazy, depressing drizzle. The horse's hooves squish into the soft earth, the chill seeps through their clothing and into their bones. Shade is certain he's never felt this miserable in his entire life.

Eventually, they trot over a rise and their horses pull to stop. Below sits a quiet, secluded village. One that, if a rider blew past in a rush, would never spot it. The village has homes and barns, small storefronts and a pub; all of which contain lights starting to flicker on with the forthcoming evening.

"An outer village of Sparkston?" Erin asks.

Shade watches people meander from place to place. Some are returning on horseback or horse drawn carriages, and it is safe to assume they are returning from work in another town. "Possibly." They had missed Sparkston's city limits by a couple of miles not too long ago. Shade is almost certain that city was on the soldier's list.

"Do you think they're friendlies?" Erin asks, looking down at the little village.

Shade hesitates. There is no way of knowing for certain at this time. He thought he could trust his own castle, but that has proven dangerous. "All I know is night is closing in, I'm wet, and we need rest."

Erin lifts her hood over her head. "There's a barn on the other side. Let's crash there for the night. Maybe the horses could find something to eat."

Shade pulls his hood up also. He tugs on the reins. They make a path around the town and descend on the other side, near a lone barn away from the bustle of town. It appears empty, but Shade hands his reins to Erin, hops from the horse, and sneaks around the edge of the barn. The closest building is a small farm house with a chicken coop behind it. There are lights on in the house. Shade hears a door bang closed, and stops in his tracks. But it is just someone leaving the front of the house. The man walks away from the house, towards the middle of town.

Shade takes a breath and continues along the edge of the barn. He comes to the entrance, and peeks in through the cracked door.

The barn is dark, but it is very much alive. From noises alone, Shade can tell there are several animals within. He places a hand on the door and starts to slide it back enough for him to slip through, but stops short to look in one more time.

"You gonna go in?"

Erin's voice comes from behind, startling Shade so bad that he jumps. "Good *Glimmer*." He hisses, looking over his shoulder.

Erin stands there, a reign in either hand, eyebrows raised. "Whoa, there. Little jumpy, aren't we?"

Shade puts a finger over his lips, giving her a quizzical look.

Erin shrugs her shoulders, mouthing, 'What?'

He just shakes his head and enters the barn, opening it wide enough for Erin and the horses to follow. What little light is left outside streams into the barn, illuminating 3 horse stalls, a pig sty, and a few chickens who now scatter in alarm.

Shade closes the door behind them.

The horses *whinny* quietly and the pigs go on with their sleep. The barn smells of animals and manure, perfect for masking a prince and his best friend. Small light streams in through cracks along the barn.

Shade feels his way along the wall until he bumps into the table he had seen when the door was open. The table has various tools and objects strewn across it. He brings his hand above his head and bumps into the hanging lantern, sending it swinging. It knocks into the side of his head and he grunts, annoyed.

"Shade, little help, eh?" Erin bumps into him slightly from behind and he can imagine she's waving a hand around her, searching in the dark.

"I'm trying." He replies.

"Really wish I could see."

"I can't find the knob." On the last word, he locates

29

it and twists. A flame ignites within the lantern and the inside of the small barn is bathed in soft light.

"There it is," Erin says dryly, rolling her eyes at him, "Thank you, prince."

Shade turns back to look at the desk, muttering, "Couldn't find the knob," under his breath. He stops short at the sight that greets him from the desktop. What he thought at first were tools and objects are actually stacks of various sorts of swords and weaponry. "Whoa." He says.

Erin finishes tying off the horses on a nearby post and joins him at his side. "Holy Windenmeyer. This guy's got a whole arsenal."

"Wonder what he plans to do with it..." Shade says, tinkering with one of the knives. It has an arched blade and a brown rubber handle. Some of the rubber flakes off in his hands, but the tip of the blade is as sharp as any sword. There's a part of him that wants to stow the knife away in the satchel his horse is carrying, but he shakes his head and sets it back down. They aren't thieves.

"Come on, let's get settled in the loft above and hope no one ventures back out to the barn tonight." Erin says. She reaches to turn the light back off, when there's the sound of a twig crunching underfoot behind them.

"Who the Zion are you?"

Erin's eyes widen in alarm. Her hand moves to the short sword at her side.

"I wouldn't." The voice warns.

Shade looks at Erin from the corner of his eyes, then stares at the arched knife on the table in front of him. He knows his next move.

"Turn around slowly." The voice says.

Female. Her voice is steady, unwavering.

Shade closes his eyes, breathing deeply. He mustn't harm her severely, just enough for them to get away. Prince Shade is many things; but a murderer is not one of them. His eyes snap open at the same moment he grabs the knife by the arched blade. In the next, he's spinning, blade in hand, and launching it with expert marksmanship towards the girl wielding a crossbow behind them. But before the knife ever finds its mark in her right shoulder, she fires an arrow that shoots the blade right out of the air.

The arrow glances off of the knife and Erin ducks as it sails over where her head had just been. The knife ricochets harmlessly to the ground.

Erin straightens, eyes the arrow now embedded in the wall behind her, gives Shade a withering glare, and faces the girl.

Shade watches the girl carefully, shocked at all that has just transpired. Almost comically, he now raises his arms in surrender.

"Another move like that and it'll be your last." The girl says. She's short, maybe four inches shorter than Erin, with dark hair that's almost completely shrouded by a hood. Strands of it peak out from behind the hood and curl around the sculpted features of her face.

Shade's eyes widen slightly at her beauty.

Her eyes are stark blue against the shadows surrounding them. Her skin is tanned, kissed by the sun. Even the dirt smudges on her cheeks and forehead are cute. She wears gray riding pants and a dark jacket spattered with holes here and there. Black work boots don her feet and the brown crossbow she holds looks similar to many of the weapons lying on the table. She looks to be around the same age as Shade and Erin.

She takes in two of them and her eyes narrow. "Throw your weapons over there." She jerks her head to the side.

Erin glowers at her, anger seeming to come off of her in waves.

The stranger glares back, unflinching.

Shade is the first to speak again. "We don't want any trouble."

The girl finally looks from Erin to Shade. He notices something in her eyes, but it is gone before he can fully understand what.

"Then I suggest you do as I say."

Shade swallows and eventually nods. He unclips the sheath holding his sword from around his waist, careful to cover up his family crest burned into it. "Do it."

Erin wants to argue, but finally obeys, nostrils flaring. Shade throws his sword and sheath to the side and begins taking the knives on his calves from their holsters. He throws them in the same pile as his sword and Erin's bow and arrows.

The girl eyes the weapons curiously. "Interesting choice of weapons. We don't have many bows around here. Unless of course you're from Glimmer. Which would also be interesting." She trails off thoughtfully.

"We don't want any trouble." Shade repeats. "We were just looking for a place to stay for the night. But I can see this has caused some issues. So, if you'll just let us get out of your hair…"

"That means move, Peanut." Erin says.

The girl inclines her head. She lowers the crossbow to her side and lets one hand drop away from it. "So, are you of importance, too?"

Erin's startled by this question, but covers it

smoothly with a scoff. "I've never been important. Neither has he. Why do you think we're running away?"

"You're definitely running. I can tell that much. I am curious, though." She stares hard at Shade, an eyebrow raising. "What on earth would a prince of Zion have to run from?"

Shade's stomach drops. She knows. How does she know? Of course, she knows. Shade's face is plastered across billboards and posters; along with the rest of the royal family. It's customary for the royal family to be displayed consistently throughout Zion. Only now his face likely frequents "Wanted" posters as well. On the inside, he is panicking. But a calm smile spreads across his exterior. "An intriguing question asked towards one clothed in rags."

"A disguise." The girl says without missing a beat. "You are, indeed, running. But, from what, I wonder? Prince Shade, isn't it?" Her blue eyes glance between the two of them, before landing on Shade with some finality. She shifts the crossbow in her hands slightly, but only so she can step closer.

Shade's teeth grind together and Erin stiffens beside him.

The girl rolls her eyes, "I may look homeless, but I'm certainly not daft. I know who runs my country. And considering you are not at the Windenmeyer Castle, I believe it is safe to assume you are not the prince to be crowned come morning."

At this, Shade tenses. Alarm streaks his and Erin's faces. There is no use hiding it anymore. They've been found and are now at the mercy of the small girl standing before them.

"How?" Erin asks.

"News travels fast in these lands." The girl says. "I don't expect royals stuck behind guarded walls to understand how things out here work. Soldiers came to our doorstep not an hour before you arrived." She sighs, "King Bronze is dead. Prince Jeb is to take the throne. And everyone in Glimmer is to be on high alert for Prince Shade who poisoned his own father." She points a gloved hand at Shade, "You're a wanted man."

There are several seconds of tense silence.

Erin bends almost imperceptibly, coiling her legs in order to spring forward and attack. Shade knows they're in deep with no clear path of escape. How could they have been so stupid? They hadn't even made it a hundred miles from the outskirts of Glimmer.

"My father and I are the only ones left." The girl finally speaks. "Mom died two years ago from Cypher Fever. The sickness almost took Father last year but our town nurse saved his life. Now they're a thing, or whatever." She says almost as an after-thought, rolling her eyes. "Anyway…there's been talk of treason within the castle walls. But, just as news travels fast out here, so do rumors. Until recently, I thought that's what they were." She raises her crossbow once more. "There's opposition to the throne and the royal family even within this very town."

She swings the crossbow to rest in a strap on her back. "Lucky for you, my family isn't one of them. You hungry?"

Shade blinks, confused by the sudden change in atmosphere. "Uh…you don't think I killed my father?"

The girl's nose scrunches in thought, then she shakes her head. "Nah. You don't look like you'd have the guts to start a rebellion."

Suddenly, a chuckle escapes past Erin's lips. She

quickly covers by clearing her throat, then asks, "How can we trust you?"

The girl shrugs, "I guess that's for you to decide. But Dad's making ham and beans, and Juliett, his nurse *friend*, is coming over. They won't mind the extra mouths to feed. Although you should probably be gone by light. I, for one, do not want to be executed for housing the treasonous prince and his girlfriend. Oh," She says at Shade's small cringe, "You're not dating, then?"

"Well, I," Shade tries to say, "We're not, I didn't—"

Erin, arms crossed, huffs, "No, we most certainly are not dating. Just good friends." Her glare towards him sends chills down Shade's spine.

He hadn't meant to make a face, it just kind of happened. And he wasn't trying to imply that he wouldn't want to date Erin. He had already realized there were some sort of deeper feelings building up for her in his chest; but that wasn't something *she* needed to know. Was she upset that it seemed he didn't want to date her, or that the girl thought they were?

He shook his head. Girls. So confusing.

"Well, in any case, I would greatly appreciate it if you joined us for dinner. It would make things less awkward with the two who *are* dating. But it is up to you whether you want to eat tonight. Feel free to bring your weapons, but Dad prefers they be left in the parlor just off the great room." She steps toward the cracked barn door that she must have slipped through to get in. Her hand on the door, she turns back one last time. "Oh, and my name's Dru." She tilts her head, "But Peanut works, too." Then, she disappears into the night.

They stand there quietly. Shade realizes his hands are still raised and slowly lowers them. A *whinny* from the back causes Erin to jump.

She turns to him, the question out before her lips have hardly formed the words. "What just happened?"

CHAPTER 4

"Get back here." Erin hisses. She grabs Shade's shoulder and wrenches him back behind the barn door. "We can't just walk in there and believe they won't send a call out. Soldiers will be upon us in minutes!"

"Erin, she's not going to turn us in."

"No?" Her eyebrows raise, "And how do you know that? Because she told us she wouldn't? What—did she bat her eyes at you? Well, dear prince, despite what you think, not every girl fawns over your every move."

Shade sighs and lifts his hands in annoyance, "I don't know, Erin. I just have a feeling, okay?"

Erin opens her mouth to say something, frustration and anger crossing her face in waves. Her mouth closes, as if she doesn't know what to say next. Shade watches her amused. Erin has always known what to say; but now, it seems, she is at a loss for words.

"You have a feeling." She says flatly. Her face falls into a mask of sadness, her eyes drop to the floor. "Our families' lives are hanging in the balance, and they are counting on us to save them and you base your actions on *feelings*."

Shade immediately feels guilty, and he quickly places his hands on either side of Erin's face. "Hey, hey," He lifts her face to look in his eyes, "I promise you, we *will* save them. And the rest of the kingdom."

Erin's eyes glisten with tears and Shade is struck by how vulnerable this strong, powerful, woman can be.

Shade continues, "Whoever these people are, maybe they can help us. The first sign of danger, we'll get out of there. She let us have our weapons back, so that means she has some sort of faith in us." He pulls her into a hug. "But if you really are uncomfortable with it, we will stay out here for the night and leave before they know. It's up to you."

Erin hugs back, takes a deep breath, breathing in his scent, and then pulls away. "No, come on. Let's go in there. Other than being annoying, she doesn't seem so bad. Besides, I'm hungry. Although she does seem rather skilled with a crossbow."

Shade's brow furrows, "That is a bit alarming." Or encouraging, depending on whether or not they can recruit her as an ally.

"But nothing we can't handle." Erin heaves a sigh and peers out the doorway. Darkness has fully descended, the moon the only light aside from the few houses and barns that are lit. She eyes the night warily. "Stick close, prince. I'd hate for you to die before the plan to retake the throne hardly manifests."

"My hero." He says, a hand to his chest.

They slip into the night. The house isn't far from the barn, but there's a bit of open land to cross before then. They slink close to the earth, carefully navigating the hole-filled ground. Erin reaches the house first and flattens herself along the wall, sneaking along its edges. Shade follows suit and the two edge around to the front until they come to the door. There are two steps leading up to a quaint wooden porch. A wooden swing sways softly with the breeze and the porch is lit by a single lamp hanging from the ceiling in the center of the porch. The door is also wood and light from the inside escapes through the small cracks lined along it.

Erin falters on the first step. "You first."

Shade starts, "Me? What happened to 'stick close'?"

"You're close, aren't you?"

Shade pushes her aside and steps in front. "I prefer to lead anyway."

Erin rolls her eyes, "Oh, whatever—"

"Shh." Shade steps to the door, places a hand on its wood, and slowly pushes inward.

The door opens with a creak and the two quickly step into the house, shutting the door behind them.

They're standing in a hallway, but almost directly to the left is an open living room with a ratty brown couch and two armchairs that look as if they have seen better days. The hallway continues forward and dead ends but not before it branches off three more times to the right and once to the left. The house has a warm glow about it and a glorious smell penetrates his nose.

Erin latches the door shut and then looks at him expectantly.

A room sits to their right and Shade spots muddied boots, coats hanging from hooks, and several weapons, some of which are similar to those in the barn.

"That would be the parlor." Dru says from a doorway further off the living room. She has taken her brown jacket off and underneath is a cream-colored tunic tucked into her gray pants. Her dark hair is shorter than Shade first realized, just barely past her shoulders. "You can leave your weapons and cloaks in there. Supper's waiting in here." She smirks, "I was beginning to think the soldiers had found you after all." She ducks back into what Shade assumes is the kitchen.

"I don't like this." Erin murmurs as she sets her bow in a corner of the parlor. She hesitantly slides the arrow pack off her shoulder and sets it beside the bow. "At all." She starts to pull a knife from the hidden pouch on her thigh, but decides against it.

Shade unsheathes his sword and pulls only one knife off his calf. The other will stay, just as Erin's had. He leaves the guard's bow—he supposes it's his now—next to Erin's. He unties the cloak from his neck and hangs it on an empty hook, then pulls the satchel over his head and sets it down beside his weapons.

Erin squeezes the neck of her cloak, shaking her head. "I will not take this off."

"You don't have to." Shade says gently, then starts towards the kitchen. The brush of a cloak hitting his leg tells him Erin is following.

As they draw near the doorway, voices can be heard from within.

"And you're sure it's him?" A male voice inquires.

"Positive." Dru says.

"Well, should we stand? Do I need to bow? I wish you would've told me sooner; I'd have put on something a little nicer." A third voice, this one female, says, exasperated.

"Honey, you look fine. I'm sure the prince won't care what you're wearing. He's on the run, after all."

That's when Shade steps around the corner and all talking ceases.

The kitchen is small, like the rest of the house. A table with four chairs sits in one corner. At the table is a man and a woman. The man looks like an older male version of Dru, with his handsome features, dark hair, and blue eyes. The woman is tall and slender, her red hair covering one shoulder in a braid. The two stare at him, equal faces of surprise and wonder. Dru leans against a counter away from the table.

All at once, the man and woman spring from their chairs and both put on a display of awkward bowing.

"Your Highness." The woman breathes, at the same time the man apologizes for being dressed so poorly. He then throws the woman a guilty smile. They continue their awkward bouts of bowing.

Dru snorts, "Dad, Juliett—don't embarrass yourselves. There's no need to bow, it's not like he's *the* royal highness. He's hardly a prince anymore."

Juliett gasps.

Dru's father gives her a placid glare, "Watch your tongue, Dru, this is a prince of Zion you're talking to."

Dru waves a dismissive hand. Shade finds himself smiling at the girl. He is so used to everyone—what was it Erin said—fawning over him, that the blatant indifference is actually a welcome affair. "No, it's okay." Shade speaks and all eyes turn to him, "Please, treat me as one of your own. It is an honor to be invited into your home. I understand this is a risk you're taking and I am very grateful."

"The honor is ours, Prince Shade." The man says.

"Call me Shade, Mr…?"

The man grins, the act lighting up all the handsome features of his face. "Call me Roy." He stands fully, hardly coming to Shade's own height, and beckons to Juliett. "This is Juliett, she is the nurse here in the village. And my girlfriend."

Juliett, easily taller than Roy, bows her head, "Hello, Pri—uh—Shade. You are younger than I expected."

There are several more seconds of silence, until there's a melodramatic throat clear from behind Shade. He steps aside, smiling slightly at his friend's forwardness, and Erin steps into the kitchen.

She nods at Dru and acknowledges the other two before smelling the air pointedly. Her eyes glance

41

around the kitchen. "I was told there would be food?"

A short time later, they're all seated around the table, Roy having pulled another chair in from a different room. They enjoy a wonderful meal of ham and beans, cornbread, and a sweet cream they claimed came from their goat.

Shade had never heard of such a drink but he was fond of it, and even Erin's eyes widened in pleasant surprise. Although there is little talk while they eat, after the table is clear and the dishes in the sink, Roy turns to them solemnly.

"So, we have heard the terrible news about your father." He looks down sadly, "I am sorry, Shade." Roy goes on to explain the palace soldiers that appeared on his front step shortly before Shade arrived. They spoke of acts of treason and murder committed by the young prince.

Shade nods, swallowing down the sadness. He will mourn his father later. Now is not the time. "Erin's father was also murdered." He glances sideways at his lifelong friend, who's confident gaze only gives away a slight flicker of sadness. "And our families' whereabouts or status are unknown. We are determined to find who has committed these crimes."

"Juliett and I share my daughter's opinion…you did not kill your father, nor did you order him to be killed." Roy glances at Dru, "I don't know how much Dru told you, but there are traitors to the throne in this village. Only a few remain loyal. I'm sorry, but you cannot stay here long. For your sake and for our own."

Shade and Erin share a look. "Of course," Shade says, "We understand. We will be gone by morning. We happened upon your barn and were looking for a place to stay for a few hours."

Roy leans back and crosses his arms, looking thoughtful, "You're very lucky it was our barn you came to and not someone else's. It is difficult to tell anymore who can be trusted."

"Dad," Dru says impatiently, "Tell him." She's upright, leaning once more against the wooden cabinet structure. Her arms are folded across her chest, making her appear even smaller in stature.

Shade looks between the two of them curiously before settling on Roy.

Roy leans forward and lowers his voice, "We can help you. Long before the attack on your family, a treacherous rebellion started out here, throughout Zion. You've heard of Pire and Klepton, cities lost to greed and fleshly desire?"

Shade and Erin nod.

"The rebellion originated in Klepton and quickly spread to Pire. Men who wanted power and more money than they knew what to do with. Soon, talk of treason was whispered in alleyways and secret gatherings. It didn't take long for the cities to fall, the leaders escaping in a rush of fear as their citizens became too powerful for them to manage." Roy's eyes take on a distant look as the story progresses. "This all started around fifteen years ago. They've only recently become powerful enough to break through the protected walls of Windenmeyer and potentially wreak poisoned havoc into the City of Perfection." He grimaces slightly at his poor choice in word and glances quickly at Shade, who gives nothing away. Roy continues, "But, as you can see, the reach of treason stretches far and wide. All across Zion. There are very few cities that remain completely pure and loyal to the king. Lockwood, *maybe*. Greenbriar, doubtful." He looks back to Shade. "What are your plans?"

Shade considers this question, still unsure if he should trust these strangers.

Before Shade can respond, Roy continues, "It's okay, you don't have to answer that. My only hope is you plan on finding allies, reinforcements, so that you can someday retake the kingdom. Right now, it has fallen into the hands of some very powerful, dangerous, evil men and women. And, if you plan on saving our land, then like I said, we can help you."

Juliett stands and grabs a pitcher of the white cream off of the counter. She refills their cups. "Do you have a map?"

"It's in my satchel." Shade says, as Erin leaves the room. She returns moments later and hands the map to Roy, who spreads it across the table.

"So, we are here." He says, pointing to a tiny dot in between Glimmer and the Gargantuan Mountains. "We're about an hour and a half horse ride from Glimmer. Is there a particular direction you're heading?"

Shade looks at Erin next to him who hesitates before finally giving him a grim nod. His eyes travel to Dru. She appears thoughtful and curious, wearing the same look as her father. He doesn't even know these people. Yet, they could have easily called for soldiers and sent them packing and they haven't.

Shade takes a breath, deciding that their need for help outweighs their fear of trusting them. "We're actually heading to Lockwood. A friend who helped us escape the castle told us there are people there we can trust. Allies who will join our fight to take back the kingdom."

At first, Shade wonders if this has been a mistake; because there is silence in the small kitchen and the three strangers share passing glances. But then excitement and pride shine in Roy's eyes. He lets out a breath and nods, his smile widening, "Well, then, Prince Shade, you've come to the right place for help." His finger runs across the sketched mountains. "There's a mountain pass that will take you towards Lockwood. It isn't the easiest way, but it is the fastest; and time is certainly of the essence. Luckily, the mountain pass is exactly where we were going to suggest you go. Juliett has some family in Frostfire, a village at the top of the pass. It's been a while, but I have visited that village before and have some deep friendships there, myself."

"They will help you." Juliett assures, "My brother is the village leader and I have other family members there as well. They moved there years ago when the village was dying. My uncle and brother helped save the village and then took on the roles of leadership. My uncle has since passed, but Bane still leads there. And the village is very strong. You can trust them." She looks sad, "I only wish we could come with you."

Roy nods, "But our place is here. If we leave, people will start to suspect. You have your mission and we have ours. We may be able to win back the people here." He looks at Juliett who nods in agreement.

"You sound as if you've really prepared for this." Erin says, her eyes narrowing suspiciously. Leave it to Erin to be the critical, logical one. And, thank Zion for that, Shade thinks to himself; her logic has saved him from countless lashings in the past.

Roy expects her suspicion and responds genuinely. "Just as the traitors have prepared, so have the loyal.

45

We knew this day would come. However," Roy chuckles, "we had no idea the prince would show up on *our* doorstep. After you reach the pass and whatever help Juliett's family will provide, you can continue on your way to Lockwood. I have *heard* it is one of the pure cities, not yet tainted with treachery. I hope that is true."

Roy continues, "From here to Frostfire is about seventy miles. Factor in the winding pass of the mountain, that's more than a day's worth of travel. You'll need to head out first thing tomorrow morning. Shade, I offer up my bed to you tonight, and Erin, you may have Dru's—"

Shade holds up a hand and says, "Erin and I would prefer the floor. Do not give up your beds for us. We insist. Your hospitality, protection, and help are more than enough."

Roy starts to shake his head no, then must think better of disagreeing with a prince of Zion. "Fine, then. One can have the couch, the other the floor. We will bring you blankets for the night. Tomorrow, we'll send you off with food and water."

"I'll write a letter addressed to my family and sign it, so they know to trust you." Juliett says. She starts rummaging in kitchen drawers for pen and paper.

"Thank you." Shade says to both of them.

"Of course. Forget lineage, *you* are the rightful heir to the throne. Why? Because you have not betrayed Zion. And we will follow you, Prince Shade." Roy bows his head.

Shade smiles softly, grateful to have met this family. "Thank you." He whispers again, overcome with gratitude.

Roy clears his throat, "Now, a good night's rest and

you'll be ready for your journey." He holds out a hand towards Shade. After a moment, Roy closes his hand, thinking he has overstepped. But Shade quickly throws out his arm as well and the two grasp in a friendly handshake.

Dru steps away from the counter and walks to the table, arms still crossed. "Good, now we have a plan. But before any of that can commence, I think we have some more important matters to attend to." She looks Shade up and down, "Like your attire. You can't *possibly* hope to travel unnoticed in that garb."

Shade stares down at his clothing. In all the craziness the day had brought, he had completely forgotten he was dressed in royal apparel. His cream tunic, lined with strips of blue, is tucked into brown trousers. His fancy boots look off against the old wood of the kitchen floor. The arms of his tunic fluff at the end. Shade smiles sheepishly, almost embarrassed by his clothing compared to the others.

Erin also has on a tunic, but this one is less royal and formal and not as brightly hued. Her light green tunic mashes well with the quiet tan of her pants. Even her green cloak looks like it could belong in a village like the one they are in.

"I may have some old clothes Shade can wear. Dru, will you check on something for Erin?" Roy asks.

Juliett is already heading toward the door before Dru can respond, "I actually believe I have just the thing. An outfit of my sisters she left a long time ago." She pauses, glancing down, "May she rest in peace." Then, she's gone from the kitchen. They hear the front door open and close.

"Oh, and one more thing," Dru says, her nose scrunching up in distaste, "The bathing room is right through that door," she nods out of the kitchen and to a door in the hallway. "You two should put it to good use. It's nothing like the palace bathing rooms, I'm sure. But—"

"Beggars can't be choosers." Erin repeats the line she had said only a little while ago.

Dru looks at her, pleased. "I do believe you and I will be fast friends, Erin."

"Whatever you say, Peanut." Erin mumbles, looking none-to-pleased at Dru's comment about friendship. "Now, where's this bathing room?"

Dru raises a brow at Shade, then directs Erin down the hall.

* * * * *

An hour later, Shade, hair wet, is seated on a pallet on the floor of the living room. Water beads sprinkle his neck every time he shifts. The warm shower was refreshing. And Dru had been right...Shade *really* stunk. He shifts awkwardly in the clothes Roy had given him: navy farmer's trousers and a light gray tunic with a navy belt tied around it. Work boots sit by the door where Roy had left them. Right after, Roy had taken Shade's royal clothing and disappeared out the back door, mentioning something about a burn pile.

The hallway creaks, alerting Shade that someone is coming down it. Erin rounds the corner, her hair wet. She wears burnt red trousers with a crème top almost identical to Dru's.

She nods at Shade, smiling slightly. "You sure you don't want the couch, prince?"

Shade shakes his head, "It's all yours." He watches her recline back into the cushions and eyes shut in exhaustion.

"Who wants hot tea?" Roy asks, carrying a tray in

48

from the kitchen.

Shade and Erin each take one. Shade is struck by how down to earth this man is. He definitely doesn't seem like someone who's made weapons like the ones in the barn. Shade wonders if the man can spare a few of them for their journey tomorrow.

Roy sets the tray on a table beside the couch and then takes a seat in the armchair. "I'm so pleased it's starting to get colder so we can enjoy this delicacy. Even in the warmer months, I've always enjoyed a good cup of tea. Warms the soul." He leans forward in the chair, "Prince Shade, Lady Erin, I just want to reassure you that we are the good guys. Although it may seem it, the entire kingdom is not against you. I should have shown you this earlier, but I wanted to wait until I gained your trust a bit more." He rolls up the sleeve on his right arm. Stretched up and down along his forearm is an etching of a two-inch tattoo with three circles, each a different color. Each circle overlaps the other and all three share a small space of skin together.

"What is it?" Shade asks, earning a sarcastic whisper of, 'It's a tattoo,' from Erin.

"Each circle represents a different portion of the kingdom, a separate section. Each section stretches horizontally from coast to coast." Roy points to the green, "The lively forestry surrounding Glimmer with its Windenmeyer Castle and Sequestrian Sea on the west coast. This little village I call home is also considered within this circle." The circle at the top of the triangle-shaped tattoo is blue. "This represents the upper stretch of Zion. The colder, icier regions: Pire, Klepton, Dramer, other northern cities ruled by snow and ice. And the last," He settles on the red,

49

"Everything below the green circle. The deserts and hotter regions."

The door opens and Dru enters, arms full of firewood. "It's a little chilly out there tonight." She notices her father's rolled sleeve and a smile forms on her lips, "Ah, telling them the story of our ancestors?" The wood in her arms has pushed her sleeve up and a sliver of the red circle in the tattoo peaks out. She makes her way over to the fireplace and begins stoking the fire.

"What does it mean?" Erin asks impatiently.

"Dru kind of stole my thunder," Roy chuckles, "But, yes, it was passed down from our ancestors.

"Hundreds of years ago, treachery already feared, a group of brave men and women banded together, making a pact to ward off any evil that may rise up against the king. As long as the king was found worthy. This has been passed down from generation to generation. My great-grandparents, grandparents, parents, me, and now Dru. Juliett derives from the mountains, her family passed it to her. We are spread out within the kingdom; new members being added often. Our pact includes the protection of the king and his family, support and aid given. This tattoo identifies us to our fellow protectors."

"How has it been kept quiet?" Shade asks.

"We are careful," Dru answers, her back to them. She finishes stacking the wood, picks a match from off a nearby ledge, and sets fire to the wood. "If one with the tattoo is found guilty or treasonous, they are quickly and efficiently dealt with."

Shade doesn't have to ask to know by what means she's referring to.

Roy nods at his daughter, looking at Shade with

sympathy in his eyes, "It's true. We don't mess around. And now the time has come for us to put our history and training to good measure."

"Training?"

Dru turns around and laughs at Erin's incredulous look, "Yes, training. Just because we were not trained in a castle does not mean we are any less capable of fighting. You saw all the weapons I made?"

"*You* made them?" Erin's face now reflects surprise that slowly dissolves into guarded respect. She leans back into the cushions of the sofa gives a dignified nod.

"She's already a better creator than I'll ever be." Roy says, "And she's nearly passed me in fighting skill as well. One day." He grins at Dru.

Dru shrugs, "I learned from the best." She steps back from the fire, now crackling softly, and joins her father on the floor. He hands her a cup of tea and she nods in thanks.

Shade sips his tea. They sit in comfortable silence for several minutes, Roy and Dru occasionally talking in soft tones about their day. As the warmth spreads through Shade, the stress of the day begins to weigh on him. He rubs one eye, suddenly very tired. This is all such big news; he needs a little time alone to process it. Protection pacts, tattoos, and an enemy of the kingdom. All in one day.

Roy takes their silence as fatigue as well and stands, rolling down his sleeve. "You should get some rest."

"Thank you, sir," Shade says as Roy makes his way towards the hallway and disappears through another doorway.

Roy turns just before the room, bowing his head

respectfully, "No, Shade. Thank *you*." He leaves.

Dru brushes the dirt and wood off her hands, nods at the two of them, and leaves as well, dousing out the lamps along her way.

Erin turns to Shade, "What are you thinking?"

Shade tightens his lips, staring at her thoughtfully. "I think we can trust them. But let's not take any chances."

Erin unsheathes the knife from her thigh and sprawls across the couch on her stomach. She puts the hand wielding the knife under her pillow and shuts her eyes. "Have you ever known me to do such a thing?" A wistful smirk plays on her lips before her jaw goes slack and she's already asleep.

Shade scoots his pillow closer to the hearth and the warming fire. The sweet scent of burning wood permeates the room. As he lays his head down and pulls the sheet over him, countless thoughts run through his mind.

But his head has barely hit the pillow before he, too, is fast asleep.

CHAPTER 5

"Shade."

Shade groans, wishing away the nightmare. His sleep had been restless and filled with bad dreams about his family, Jeb with black eyes and a willowing frame, and evil running rampant throughout Zion. Thank Glimmer it is just a dream. He rolls over, still encased in sleep.

"Shade!"

His eyes flutter. Why does that sound so real?

"Wake up, you daft prince!"

Shade's eyes pop open. Not a dream.

Erin kneels over him, shaking his shoulders. Her hair falls into her face and her eyes are filled with frenzied worry. "They've found us." Is all she says. She jumps up and hurries to the parlor where their weapons still lie.

Shade stands and, shaking off the daze, joins her in the parlor. "How do you know?" He stumbles into the new boots Roy provided for him.

"Dru came running in only moments ago. Something about a meeting in the town square. There are soldiers and they're starting to go door to door, just like last night. Except, this time, they're dragging people into the street. Roy and Dru have gone to get the horses ready. Come on." Erin hisses in annoyance when Shade fumbles with his sheath. She whips it around his waist, buckles it together, and almost sutures him when she shoves the sword in its case. She shoves Greaver's cloak into his hands.

Shade kicks it into high gear, finally fully awake. His other weapons donned, he throws the old cloak around his shoulders and slips the bow over his head. Then he quickly laces up the boots and joins Erin at the door.

Erin goes for the handle, but Shade grabs her wrist and yanks it back. She starts to protest, when they both hear several *whinnies* outside.

Shade glances out the window.

Horses are coming up the road with soldiers sitting atop them.

"Back door." Shade whispers. He turns and shoves Erin gently, who obeys without question.

They sprint down the hall and out the back door. The sun has barely started cresting the horizon, so the nightly creatures still rattle their tunes. A rooster crows nearby. The grass is wet with melting dew as they high step it to the barn.

The neighing of horses grows louder.

Erin slips on the wet grass, but Shade pulls her up by one hand without missing a beat. She mumbles a quiet, "Thanks." They dash through the barn door.

Shade catches the satchel thrown his way, full of various food, drink, and medicine.

"Don't lose that, it's my favorite satchel," Roy says with a grin. He continues latching the saddle around the caramel horse's midsection. Shade empties the remaining contents of his old satchel into the new one.

Dru has finished readying Erin's horse, Riot. She hands her the reins, before hurrying over to her weapons table.

Juliett is there, too. She walks up to Shade and grabs his hand, placing an enveloped letter into his palm. "Our family crest is stamped on the inside. Bane, my brother, will know it's from me."

Shade nods. He slips the letter into his new satchel

and walks to his horse, grabbing hold of the reins. "They're close. At the front door of your house." His voice comes out in a desperate whisper.

Roy's smile falls, he nods, before disappearing to the back of the stable. "Hang on." He calls over his shoulder.

"We cannot thank you enough," Shade whispers to Juliett, "I will repay you someday." He looks down at her face, slightly wrinkled with a combination of age and worry.

Juliett only smiles, "Your presence and your courage to fight back is payment enough."

Dru hurries back to them with a separate bag, tied securely. "I'm sending you with some extra knives. A couple of throwing, a carving, and a gutting. Never know when you'll need to hunt for food." She holds out the bag with one hand, watching Shade closely.

"And hunt, you will," Roy says quietly. He is leading another horse into their midst. His smile doesn't reach his eyes, but he gazes at Dru with love.

Dru straightens, "Dad?" Her hand holding the bag drops to her side and her face takes on a wary look.

"Hurry, there isn't time to discuss." Roy hands her the reins and hugs her dearly. "It isn't safe here, Dru. You must go. You know the way. Lead them to the others."

"But, Dad—"

"Dru." He interjects, "Go. We will be fine."

There's the clomping of feet and shouts. They've broken down the door of the house and stampeded in. Several voices alert Shade that some are headed towards the barn.

The prince hops atop his horse, "We ride." He's always wanted to use that line; he only wishes it didn't mean leaving two newfound friends behind.

Erin grasps Juliett's arm tightly, then climbs onto her stead.

Dru gives her father a kiss on the cheek and hugs Juliett quickly. Then unwillingly, she pulls herself onto her horse; a charcoal-colored stead with white spots.

"Thank you," Shade says. "Please, be safe."

Roy turns, "Thank you, Prince Shade. We will meet again someday. And don't worry about us, we know how to handle ourselves." He grasps hold of Juliett's hand. "Now, go. Out the back."

Shade and Erin meet eyes. She nods. He tightens his legs around the mare and she takes off towards the back. Erin follows and, finally, Dru pulls her eyes away from her family and gallops after them.

The daylight hits Shade in the face as they exit the dimly lit barn. He squints at the sky. They lead their horses up the hill and out of the valley where the little town sits. At the top, Shade glances back once more to see the soldiers barge their way into the barn. None have spotted them atop the hill, but they shouldn't stick around long enough to allow them the chance. Dru shoots past him, refusing to turn. Shade turns away and they begin their trek across the grassland.

Shade hopes he will see Roy and Juliett again. The guards at Windenmeyer have always been hard-nosed. Stoic. If they suspect Roy and Juliett of harboring fugitives, they will show no mercy. His father was a gracious king—very few suffered at his hand. But, now that he's dead, and now that traitors of the kingdom have stepped into the light, there's no telling the kind of force the guards will use to get what they want.

Or, perhaps, even at the new king's orders. Shade shakes his head of the thought, refusing to believe ill-thoughts about Jeb.

Shade's uncertain how long they run. Long enough for the sky to glow pink and yellow. Long enough for the air to turn warmer and the secrecy of night to disappear with the light. In the distance, the Gargantuan Mountains loom.

Their horses continue in a steady gallop, afraid to slow down even the slightest. Shade spots other little villages scattered across the landscape as they travel. Eventually, the rolling hills turn into forestry and coverage. They don't stop until they're several paces into the trees.

Dru dismounts and tenderly runs a hand down her horse's mane.

"How long have we been riding?" Erin asks. It's the first words any of them have spoken for hours.

"We're not even halfway there, yet," Dru says. She takes a swig of the water in her canteen and passes it to Shade. "Don't hold back, there's plenty of freshwater streams on the way."

Shade drinks deeply, before passing it on to Erin. The sun, peeking through the trees, is well past the middle of the sky. It doesn't seem like it should be possible, but soon the sun will be setting once more. He stretches, sore from the consistent horse riding.

"The base of the mountain is still twenty-one miles away through forestry and then we have a 10 or so mile trek up the mountain. That's when the fun begins." Dru says it with a frown, her brow furrowed with thought; giving Shade the impression that the "trek" will be anything but fun.

Shade notes the sadness that crosses Dru's face. Erin hands him back the canteen and he walks over to Dru. He clears his throat, "Thank you."

Dru takes the canister without a word and goes to mount her horse again.

"You *will* be with your father again," Shade says, stopping her for a moment. "I promise you."

Dru looks up at him, her stone face taking on a whimsical smile. "I don't doubt that. It's only a matter of when." She hops onto her horse. "Let's keep moving. The sooner we get to Frostfire, the better."

They start back through the trees. Shade and Erin follow Dru as it seems she takes on the forest with random twists and turns. But as they continue further, Dru's confidence only builds; it is obvious by the way her shoulders straighten and her eyes alight with recognition upon passing various gigantic trees or large rock structures.

"What's Frostfire like?" Shade asks, trying to take Dru's mind off of her family.

Dru considers this question, tilting her head like she does when she's thinking. "Cold. No matter the season, it's always cold. Sometimes it feels warm enough to wear a light jacket. But usually, even now as autumn draws to a close, there will likely be snow on the ground." She guides their horses through a thick part of the brush, cutting down vines that are in her way with a short sword she pulled from her waist. Her crossbow is strapped along her back; sometimes the sunlight breaks through and glints off its shiny, black frame.

"It's high up on the mountain," she continues, "If you're not accustomed to it, it can be hard to breathe at times. But it is beyond beautiful. Wildlife surrounds it—trees, caves, brooks and streams, wolves, foxes, moose, hares, and more. There's a spot just outside of the town where you can climb up to a small cave jutting out of the mountain. You can see for miles and miles across the landscape beneath the mountain." She smiles, "I used to want to live there, I begged father to move us. He would take me to visit all the time when I was younger. It's a great trading outpost—furs and various clothing, shoes, game, even ice. Since I've gotten older, we don't visit as much; but we still come at least twice a year. It's always refreshing."

The area around them opens up into clearer land; the trees are sparse and their horses can trot smoothly.

"What about the people?" Erin asks.

Here, Dru chuckles, throwing a wink over her shoulder. "The men are strong and handsome, the women equally so. Everyone hunts, even the women and children. They're trained at a young age to fight in case their village is ever under attack. Which," She looks down sullenly, "has happened more times than you think. Frostfire is where I did a lot of my own training. It's where I learned how to shoot a crossbow and hold a sword. While their surroundings are mostly icy and cold, they themselves are warm and welcoming. That is, if they trust you. A strong emphasis is placed on family, blood relation or not— everyone is family. They take care of their own." She smiles. "They took me under their wing when I was very little. Frostfire is just as much home to me as anything." Dru shifts in her saddle and sheaths her sword.

"How big is the village?" Shade asks.

"The village itself with its trading posts, mess hall, school, and small stores are all within a half mile of each other. Homes within and surrounding that half mile perimeter stretch to no more than two miles. I would say there's about four hundred people living in all of Frostfire."

"Small village." Erin notes.

"But mighty warriors." Dru reminds them. She urges her horse to stop off the main path they've been traveling and down a short hill. From this position, they are invisible from the path, tucked behind the safety of trees and brush. "It's getting dark, we should rest. I don't like traveling the mountain in the dark." Her eyes take on an eerie look, but she doesn't elaborate any further.

They dismount for the night, tending to the horses. Shade rubs Cracker's neck and runs a hand along her back. He feeds her a handful of grain, kisses her nose, and then finds a comfy spot on the ground beside her. Dru comes from the trees, carrying firewood. She uses flint to start a fire, keeping it low in the case they need to quickly douse it. After settling down, Dru hands each of them a small loaf of bread. Between sips from their canteens, they enjoy a quiet meal in the dim light of the fire; their horses surrounding them in a safety cocoon of sorts. Shade uses the blanket Roy gave him. The fire warms them for a little bit; still, Shade is grateful for the warmth the blanket provides. He lays down but doesn't sleep. Through the darkness, he can just barely make out the blink of Erin's eyes and he knows she's awake, too. Dru is facing away from them, but he can tell by the stiffness of her shoulders that she isn't sleeping either. It seems none of them are able to truly rest tonight.

With morning light comes morning travel. Which quickly turns into afternoon travel. The journey has grown tougher because they've started a slight upward ascent that is rocky and somewhat difficult to maneuver.

Even still, Dru doesn't suggest many breaks. She urges them onward and then picks up the pace to a canter. "Let's get moving, I want to be there by dinner." Her eyes twinkle, "They make the best rabbit stew."

After a couple more hours of riding, they make it to the edge of the mountain. The mountain pass curves upwards and disappears in a descending fog, making this section of the mountain look particularly ominous.

Dru stares at the pass, worried but determined. "Stay close. This can get dangerous." That same eerie look is back.

"What's the danger? The steep climb?" Shade asks. Whatever has her worried is beginning to get under his skin as well.

She shrugs. "Yes, but that's not it. We don't like to travel the mountain at night because that's when the wolves are braver. They stay away in the daylight, for the most part. But when it gets close to dusk and the fog has settled in..." She shudders, "It's like I can hear their howls now."

Erin and Shade look at one another. Neither of them says a word as they follow Dru and her horse up the first incline. It is not very steep, more of a gradual rise that wouldn't be noticeable if it weren't for the terrifying drop that's constantly either to the left or right as they take the twists and turns upward. The path is no more than two carriage widths wide. Shade does not want to imagine having to venture this pass in a wagon.

As they climb, they eventually stop zig zagging upwards and are now climbing straight at a steady pace. The air gets thicker and harder to breathe, and a chill sets deep within Shade's bones. He shivers, wishing he had on more than just a cloak. Trees and bushes line the path and pockets of snow appear every once in a while. The fog gets thicker until Shade finds it difficult to see Dru or Erin in front of him, although they can't be more than six feet ahead. Cracker whinnies nervously and her steps falter.

After several minutes of this blind walking, she comes to a complete stop. Dru and Erin continue ahead.

Shade rubs her mane, "Come on, girl." He prompts her onwards with a gentle kick to the ribs. She shakes her head stubbornly, her whinnying turning to terrified neighs.

Shade hears the growl before he sees the wolf. It comes from his left and his horse jumps to the right, almost knocking him off. Shade squints through the fog, just as a dark shape leaps his direction, a deep howl escaping its bared lips. He has just enough time to whip his sword from its scabbard before the large wolf hits him square in the chest, tackling him off of the horse. His sword bounces uselessly out of reach.

Cracker rears up on her hind legs and takes off into the fog.

The breath leaves Shade's lungs in a *whoosh*, both from the hard fall on his back and the heavy wolf on his chest. It growls menacingly, its teeth an inch from Shade's face. The hot, rancid breath emanating from the wolf's mouth makes Shade cringe, turning his face away.

The wolf snaps at his jaw, clawing at Shade's chest to try and get closer. His arms almost buckle under the wolf's strength, but the prince keeps the creature at bay.

Erin cries his name from somewhere in the

62

distance.

Shade feels the claws tear through the fabric of his cloak, his tunic, and then pierce flesh. He lets out a muffled shout, before finding the strength to push back against the beast. It falls backwards, giving Shade enough space to scramble for his sword. He finds it in time to turn and point it toward the wolf. The wolf roars, jumps, and impales itself through his sword, crying out softly. Shade rips the sword from the dead animal.

Erin calls his name again, this time closer. He whips around, but still can't find her through the fog.

There isn't time to celebrate his kill, because several more wolves have joined the fray. Their snarls and growls come from all directions. He stands to his feet, picking the sword up with him. He turns in a circle, watching as one by one, beasts step from the fog and into view, hunched and hungry.

The haunted look in Dru's eyes now makes perfect sense.

Shade grips his sword with both hands tightly, glancing warily around to see which will be the first to attack. He is greatly outnumbered, but his father had taken him on plenty of hunting trips for him to know what to do in a situation like this. Each trip ending with the same lesson—survive. But on none of those trips was he injured and bleeding from chest wounds.

As if on cue, the pain in his chest ignites, consuming his torso in what feels like fire. He shakes his head trying to clear it of the black spots dancing on the edge of his vision.

"Come on!" He shouts impatiently at the creatures.

One of the larger wolves tilts its head, sizing the prince up. It snorts, as if laughing at Shade's bravery.

Then, it hunches its shoulders and leaps.

Shade swipes expertly, and the wolf falls. But another replaces it, and another, and another. They snarl and jump at Shade with never ending energy. One catches his outstretched arm in its mouth, and Shade stumbles from the weight. He swings his sword at one wolf, and kicks the face of another.

With the butt of his sword, he pounds the snout of the wolf clamped down on his left arm and it crashes to the frozen ground. But, in his haste to rid the wolf, he leaves his entire back exposed. Realizing his mistake too late, Shade can only watch over his shoulder as a wolf hurtles towards him. He spins, prepared to take another tackle.

But just before the wolf can reach him, it's shot out of the air. It lands in a stiff heap at Shade's feet, an arrow protruding from its chest. Shade turns, just as another beast falls with an arrow in its spine.

Erin bursts through the fog, her horse galloping, her bow having just released another arrow. Her braided hair whips around her face as she turns swiftly in the saddle, firing arrow after arrow. Like some glorious goddess.

Did that thought really just cross his mind?

"Hop on!" She screams at Shade.

He sprints alongside her horse, grabs the edge of the saddle, and hoists himself behind her, cutting down a wolf jumping through the air. They gallop away from the brawl.

Some of the wolves give chase, but eventually they all trail off, howling at the sky in dismay. Slowly, the fog dissipates and they are riding through clear air once more.

They round a large rock and Dru meets them, one

hand steering her horse, the other holding the reins of Cracker. "Are they following?" She asks, her eyes scanning over their heads.

Erin shakes her head, "But I would rather not stick around to find out." She looks at Shade over her shoulder, the look of focus turning to concern. Her eyes trail down to his chest, spots of blood seeping through the fabric. "Shade, you're bleeding."

Shade tries hiding a wince, "It's nothing." But it stings like fire.

Erin narrows her eyes, but the worry is still there. "You couldn't outrun a couple of animals?" The accusation in her voice angers Shade.

"My horse left me!"

"She was spooked!"

"Oh, and I wasn't?"

"Prince Shade," Dru interrupts, hopping from her horse. She strides to them and rips back the fold of Shade's cloak. Where it had seemed there were only a few spots of blood, underneath tells the real story. Shade's entire tunic is drowning in a deep red. "You are *very* injured."

Erin breathes in sharply. She grips Shade's arm. "How far is Frostfire?"

"We'll hit the outposts a couple miles from here. The guards will have to take us in. But once they see he's injured, they should move quickly." She opens the pack on her saddle and removes a roll of gauze from within. "This is all I have, but I'm worried if we don't attempt to slow the bleeding now, it will be a lot worse by the time we get there. And by a lot worse, I mean you'd be dead."

Shade snorts, feeling very light-headed. He smiles lazily, "Not one for mincing words, eh?"

Erin's frown deepens at his lazy response. She gets down and helps Shade clamber off. He removes his cloak and pulls his tunic over his head, biting back a groan.

Erin tries to keep the worry off her face. But Shade knows her face, her mannerisms like nobody else in this life. He stares into her eyes. They betray her. "Hold still." She says, caught between looking into his eyes and patching him up with the gauze.

"I'm not moving." Shade says, trying to grin. As Erin wraps the gauze tightly around his torso, Shade closes his eyes. A wave of pain ripples through his body, and he stumbles forward.

"Hey," Erin says firmly, catching him by the shoulder, one arm wrapped tightly around his waist, "None of that. Get on your horse and *move*. Dru, hurry." She wraps the cloak back around his shoulders and throws his tattered tunic to the side.

Shade does as she says and pulls himself onto his horse. They ride off once more at a gallop, this time Erin bringing up the rear. Shade keeps a careful eye out for more wolves, but Dru says they prefer the density of the fog over clear sky.

Nearing the end of the second mile, Shade's vision becomes blurred. He rubs his eyes but that mere movement hurts, so he sticks to grasping the reins tightly. Blood seeps through the gauze, runs down his stomach, and drips onto the saddle.

Erin rides alongside him and steadies him with a hand on his shoulder. She calls ahead to Dru, "I thought you said two miles!"

A moment later, Dru draws up short.

Erin and Shade's horses follow suit.

They're in a small alcove, surrounded by snow-encrusted rocks. Just ahead, the path continues. But Dru doesn't move. Instead, she glances expectantly at the rocks on either side; as if waiting for something.

Shade sinks forward, resting on the mare's neck. He's having a hard time keeping his eyes open. But he takes a deep breath and sits up again, determined not to let this injury get the better of him. To be honest, he is kind of embarrassed. To supposedly be some great warrior and future king of Zion, it is a slight against his pride to be taken so low by a mere creature.

Erin looks as if she wants to yell at Dru, but she bites her tongue, taking in their surroundings as well. They continue standing in the alcove, their breath creating little plumes of fog in the cool air. She glances again at Shade, who meets her eyes with what he hopes is a look of confidence. She grimaces back.

Dru waits a few moments longer, before saying: "You're getting better, but I can still hear your breathing."

Four figures, two behind each rock on either side, jump into view and land smoothly on the ground eight feet below. Boots smack the crunchy grass and white powder puffs into the air. They each wear tunics with hoods, two gray, one white, and one green.

The green hooded one flips back his hood, revealing brilliant red curls half pulled back in a ponytail. He holds a bow in one hand, and the other is clinched into a fist.

Erin slowly reaches for her own bow, tucked between her pack and the saddle. The slight movement causes the man's eyes to flick towards her. She stops in her tracks, her mouth just barely open in slight awe.

Shade recognizes that look. She clearly thinks this fellow is good looking. Shade narrows his eyes at the man, glancing back and forth between him and Erin's captivated look. He finally settles his gaze on the man, studying him with a glare.

So, he has good hair to match his green eyes and good body. Big deal. His face is handsome, his cheekbones strong and defined, his chin chiseled with a patch of red beard hair in the center.

Shade almost snorts; he bets the guy can't even handle a sword.

The man's piercing gaze settles on Dru. Then his mouth twitches into a quirky grin and he strides towards Dru, who has dismounted in a flourish.

"'Bout time you paid me a visit." The red-head laughs loudly, scooping Dru into a hug and spinning her around. His accent has a certain lilt to it, and some vowels are left out of certain words.

She hugs back, but then pulls away. "I came for the village," Dru states, getting straight to the point, "Call the elders to a meeting, tell your father it's important." She holds out a hand to Erin, who digs Juliett's letter from Shade's satchel. Dru hands it over, "From your aunt."

The man frowns, taking the letter, "Aunt Juliett? What's the matter?"

"No time for that now, we will discuss later." She stretches an arm in Shade's direction, "I'm sure, by now, you're well aware of the treason within the castle. I present to you, Prince Shade and his friend, Lady Erin." She talks quickly, almost impatiently, their growing concern making each of them antsy.

The young man glances at Erin once more, then settles his gaze on Shade. His eyes take in the prince's bent form and pained expression. "Hm." He mutters, "Much smaller than I expected."

Shade continues to glare.

"Dru," Erin warns, both hands holding onto Shade's arm now.

"He's injured." Dru says, "The fog crept in sooner than I expected and the wolves were hiding within."

The man ponders this, staring thoughtfully at Shade. Then shrugs, "We have a healer." He points at the gray-hoods, "Stay and keep watch. Nigel, come with me." He whistles and two horses trot around the left rock.

The white-hood, Nigel, hops aboard one and the red-head man aboard the other. The latter says, "Follow me, Father is going to love this." He grins at Dru, "Welcome back, Little Bow."

She rolls her eyes, "Just because I choose a crossbow doesn't mean it's less of a weapon than your full bow."

"No," He admits with a smirk, "But it *is* little."

"Hang in there," Erin whispers, squeezing Shade's arm.

They ride another two minutes up the mountain until they reach a large wooden wall that stretches across the entire path.

"Harper!" The man shouts., flinging his hood back once more

A large man appears, looking over the edge with narrowed eyes. "Baron," He mutters. Then he gives a short whistle and disappears once more.

"Good to see you, too!" Baron chortles.

Shade wants to punch the smile right off his face. But he doesn't have the strength, at the moment. What little he does have, he's using to grasp the horse's mane tightly.

Slowly and with a loud creak, the wooden gates

slide open. Dru glances back, worried as she takes in Shade's shivering form. "To the medic, Baron. And *do* hurry."

They dash inside.

Shade attempts looking around to remember their surroundings. The path is lined with sparsely placed log cabins. He notes several people stopping to watch as they barrel past. True to Dru's description, the ground is layered with a thin line of snow. Peaks of the Gargantuan Mountain Range surround the village, encasing it in a protective embrace. That's all he sees of Frostfire for now, because a fresh wave of nausea hits and he has to shut his eyes before he throws up. After another minute, the horse stops and Shade peers through blurry eyes.

A long, brown cabin sits before him, smoke rising from a chimney. Several steps lead up to its entrance. Shade can't see past the open doorway, but the inside appears dimly lit.

"What's the meaning of this?" An older, broad-shouldered man, with the same red hair and chiseled face as Baron, rides up on a white horse.

"Father," Baron greets, smacking Juliett's letter into his father's hand after they both jump off their horses. "From Aunt Juliett."

The man opens the letter, his tall figure seeming to tower over the large horse he just got off of.

"Lord Bane," Dru bows her head, "This man behind me is injured. And, as you can see, it is quite imperative he remain in good health."

Lord Bane's eyes scan the pages. Then, without a word, he beckons to the riders that are with him.

They jump into action, all converging around Shade.

"No!" Erin exclaims when some of them take her off her horse and pull her to the side. "Get off me!" She pushes against them, watching Shade desperately.

Shade weakly shoves off the men, but they drag him from his own horse. He shuts his eyes once more against a wave of nausea. But he swallows the pain and grunts out, "I'll cut off your hands for that." He means for grabbing Erin the way they did, but he can't elaborate any further than that. The threat falls empty to the ground, like the continuous dripping of blood from his chest.

"Careful!" He hears Erin cry from his left. That's the last thing he hears, before the darkness takes him under.

"Don't fight," Dru says, "They're helping us." She dismounts and squeezes Baron's arm in thanks. The red-head gives her a smirk in return.

"Could've fooled me." Erin spits, shoving out of the reaches of the men. The glare she sends their way could melt iron. She starts towards Shade, but the men have already begun carrying him away. "Where are you taking him?" She stops next to Dru, turning her icy glare on the girl.

Lord Bane nods towards the cabin, "See to it that he gets the utmost aid as necessary." The men carrying Shade nod in response. "Baron, with me, we must call a meeting." The lord continues, "Dru, you're welcome to come along. And you," He stares at Erin, his frame a good three feet taller than her.

She straightens, watching out of the corner of her eyes as the men lead Shade into the cabin. Her hands form into fists but remain stoic at her sides.

The stern look on Bane's face breaks into a smile, identical to Baron's. "You're a firecracker. I like that.

Come along with us. I promise, your friend will be well looked after."

Dru nods reassuringly at her. Erin doesn't feel convinced. Too much has happened the last few days for her to be separated from the prince. Still, she glances once more at Shade's unconscious form, who has been carried inside. Then, she turns to Lord Bane. "Where are we going?"

Bane's eyes twinkle and he looks to the sky. "We're calling a council of the elders. And, then, we're going to start a revolution." He laughs, "The true heir to the throne is alive!"

CHAPTER 6

Erin follows after them, quietly taking in her surroundings. The village is small, but beautiful. She glances up at the tall mountain peaks that surround all sides of the village, their white and blue layers beautiful to behold. Every log cabin looks relatively identical, with only the landscaping around it—rocks, snow, or grassy patches—to note any sort of difference between them. The ground is snow-laden throughout the town, and it's alive with the bustling of toned men and women. Children play in the streets, their eyes following the steady march of the soldiers, their leader, and an out-of-place girl with bright blonde hair, in stark contrast to their dark brown or deep red hair. She can't help but be reminded of history class back at the castle when they learned about the Viking warriors of old. Frostfire and its natives bear a lot of resemblance to Vikings of old.

Erin drops back to where she's walking in step with Dru, her eyes moving warily among the ranks of people, "Um, what does he mean the heir is *alive*? Shade was never *dead*."

Dru nods, "Word of the treachery to the throne has spread like wildfire. There were other rumors that spread as well. Talk of King Jeb being behind the murders, that the youngest prince had also been murdered, and that the Queen had fled the castle."

Erin didn't realize the rumors could spread that fast. She considers Dru's words, "For all we know Queen Rose is dead." She says quietly, "And Jeb might as well be. He won't last a month on that throne." Erin takes a breath, chastising herself for being so loose with her tongue. Prying ears could be anywhere. She clears her throat, "So, they thought Shade was dead. Are they so willing to place him on the throne without even knowing him?" She recalls how this Lord Bane had called Shade the 'heir to the throne.'

"All I know is this village does not support King Jeb. They don't trust him. Never have."

Erin shrugs, grunting in agreement.

"I take it you don't like him either."

They pass a building with a tall steeple on top and Erin thinks it must be a church. Another building, this one larger and differently shaped than the houses, has the looks of a school building. Then, she notes more changes in the size of the cabins as they continue walking. These appear to be more stores or blacksmith shops. She spots several barns brewing with loud animal noises. They haven't been walking long, but looking ahead, she can see the small village of Frostfire ends. The pathway angles left, taking them a different direction, past more homes.

Erin shrugs again. "Jeb was always jealous of Shade. He didn't used to be, but recently, he's turned selfish, desiring the throne with a fervor like never before. So, it makes sense that he might be behind all of this." Shade has always been better liked in the City of Perfection. He's smooth, handsome, funny, and kind. He's had the people on his side from the beginning.

Erin hopes he will be okay. She swallows a lump of worry, recalling his pale skin and deep wounds.

Dru continues, "Did you live in the castle?"

"Not inside it, but I lived with my family in a house within the castle grounds. We were within the walls, yes."

"Did you ever venture outside those walls?"

Erin smiles, considering all the many times she and Shade had snuck outside to the town of Glimmer below the Windenmeyer Castle. "Yeah, a few times. We never left Glimmer, though."

"The world outside of your castle life knows, for the most part, everything that goes down within those walls. Some things are kept secret—but if a royal birthday approaches, a scandal occurs, a big announcement is made, it doesn't take long for the rest of Zion to know. Messengers ride back and forth between cities, villages, and towns every day." Dru looks over to see Erin's reaction, "Whether they be rumors, truth, or flat out lies, we know everything there is to know about the royal family. Prince Shade has always been the beloved, favored son of the kingdom."

Erin's eyes widen and she lets out a small laugh, "What? Wait, you're serious?" She knew this of Glimmer, sure. But the entire kingdom?

Dru nods seriously.

Erin clears her throat, "Right, I mean, he's pretty cool, I guess. He'd make a great king, even if he doesn't see it."

"Exactly. Most of Zion agrees. Now, he does have his enemies. Thank Zion," They stop before a one-story log cabin that stretches at least fifty yards, and Dru turns to look at Erin, "This village is Team Shade."

"He's still smaller than I expected." Baron whispers, walking past and trooping up the outdoor steps and into the cabin.

Erin studies the structure before her. It's easily the largest building in town, larger even than the barns. Music can be heard coming from inside and out the open doorway. Her eyes widen as a new smell permeates her nostrils. This must be where they eat.

"Well, for the most part." Dru chuckles at Baron's comment. She beckons to the building. "This is the mess hall. Every meal is held here. Sometimes, immediate families will eat in their own home. But, more often than not, everyone enjoys a mass meal here together, three times a day. The cooks are four widowed women who take great joy in feeding the village."

Erin follows her into the cabin. It is open wide, several rows of birchwood tables are set up across the open space. The ceiling is high and dim lights decorate the cabin, giving it a homey glow. Over in one corner, several couches and rocking chairs surround a fireplace with a warm fire glowing within it.

Bane's loud voice carries over to her and she glances to the front of the room, near the kitchen. He is addressing a group of nine others, all seated at one of the tables.

"A village meeting." Dru explains. "I've had to sit in on my fair share of meetings," She says rolling her eyes, "Father and Bane are basically best friends, especially since Father is now dating Bane's sister." She leads Erin to a back table and they sit, watching.

Erin tries listening to the meeting. They're discussing Shade's arrival and what comes next. All of it is important, but Erin gets antsier the longer she is away from Shade. "How long will this last?"

"This one shouldn't take too long. It's mainly to let the village know that the prince and his girlfriend are in town." Dru says plainly, staring at the group of individuals in deep conversation.

"Oh, friend. Just friend." Erin assures, "Best friend. Brother and sister, really. We've grown up together." She dips her head and begins playing with a strand of hair, suddenly feeling awkward. This is the second time in the last few minutes she's said too much. "But I would like to check on him, when can I do that?"

"Dru, bring her forward." Bane calls back to them, arm outstretched.

Dru gives Erin a sympathetic look, "That'll have to wait. He's in good hands, Erin. No need to worry." She beckons Erin forward.

But Erin's temper rises, and she clenches her fists to her side. She grits her teeth and whispers through them, "You better hope you're right, Peanut." Frostfire is beautiful, but the people are sorely testing her patience.

Instead of getting angry, Dru tilts her head to the side, a thoughtful look on her face, "Is that a threat?" She starts towards the front and Erin, her anger dissipating like the fog from earlier, can do nothing but gawk at the girl's passive reaction and follow after.

CHAPTER 7

Shade blinks, the world slowly coming into focus. The first thing he notices is he's in a large room and it's morning. Light pours in from different windows and he squints against the brightness of it all. The second thing he notices is the pain in his chest; it's dull, much duller than initially, but it still aches. Thirdly, he takes note of a woodsy, manly, smell. There's the sound of movement and a slight wind wafts the smell even stronger. He blinks again, lifting his head.

Someone is sitting to his left. The person shuffles, stands, and draws closer to his bedside. A red streak covers the person's head.

Shade's sight finally fully focuses, and he stares into the icy green eyes of Baron. The annoying redhead they met outside the village limits. Shade recalls the memory vaguely.

"I hope you're stronger than you look," Baron states, "For the sake of, well, the entire kingdom."

Shade lets his head fall back, suppressing a groan. Not the person he wanted to see upon waking up.

Baron straightens, "Girls!" He calls, "The little pre-king is awake." He looks back at Shade once more, "That friend of yours is quite beautiful. And *excellent* with a bow. Tell me, how does she feel about redheads?"

Shade glares at him and pulls himself into a sitting position, wincing slightly. He leans his back against the wall behind his bed. "Why are you here?" He works his arms, shoulders. Everything hurts but at least it's all working.

Baron places a hand on his chest, "Me? Waiting for

you to awaken, of course. The three of us were instructed to take turns. Unfortunately, I drew the short straw and had to take first watch. Which now makes this my," He pauses, counting on his fingers, "sixth time *painfully* sitting on my barrel in that *extremely* uncomfortable chair."

Shade coughs, "How long have I been out?" He looks around him. There are several beds spread throughout the cabin and he assumes this to be some sort of medical ward. He remembers seeing various cabins and lots of villagers on their way in, but can't recall much else. And was there an enormously large man on an enormously large horse? He shrugs to himself.

"Almost three days." Erin whisks into the room from outside, her cheeks rosy and her hair falling from its braid, like normal. She grins and hurries to his side. "'Bout time you wake up, prince." She pulls the chair closer to his bed and plops down in it. "You've missed a lot."

Shade just looks at her, a soft smile settling on his face. He notes the healthy glow of her skin and that there are no longer dark bags under her eyes. Good, she has been resting.

Dru comes in through the outside door next, her dark hair pulled half back. She pulls the door closed behind her, closing out the cold. She sets her crossbow to the side and joins them at the bed. "How's the chest?"

"Better."

"Good." Dru says, "They told us the cuts were deeper than they first thought. Some only mere centimeters from causing permanent muscle damage, or from reaching the outer edges of your heart." She says all of this in one breath and the action makes Shade smile wider. Dru is a rather interesting young woman.

Baron snorts, "You heard him, he's fine. Now, can we quit sitting around and *do* something? I'm bored out of my mind."

Shade ignores him, having only eyes for the girls. "What have I missed?" They both sit watching him, almost expectantly. He realizes they must have both been worried sick because the relief at seeing him awake is evident in their features.

"The entire village has been in a buzz since you got here." Dru says, to which Baron quietly adds, 'Well, not the *entire* village.'

Dru goes on, "Training has picked up and supply runs have been doubled."

"Why?" Shade asks.

Erin grins wider, "Because they all want to join the revolution."

He blinks slowly, wondering if some of the medication still hasn't worn off. "The revolution?"

"He really is daft." Baron states simply, looking from Erin to Dru. He pulls his shirt sleeve up, revealing the 3-ringed tattoo like Dru's. "We're on your side, man." Then he lowers his arm and looks around impatiently.

"They desire to see you on the throne, and they want to do whatever it takes to get you there." Dru explains. "Including me." She looks down, a small laugh escaping her lips.

Shade thinks he notices a redness creep onto her cheeks.

"Speak for yourself." Baron mutters, staring wistfully at the door.

Erin's eyes shift between Shade and Dru, "Reel it in, Peanut." She sighs and turns back to Shade, "*Anyway*, the village is beautiful and the people are so kind. They are excited to meet you."

Shade takes all of this in. A revolution. A village on his side. An army in the making. A lot had happened. He raises an eyebrow, "Three days, you say?" He shifts and starts swinging his legs over in order to stand up.

"Whoa, hold up," Erin grabs his arm, "Where do you think you're going? You still need to rest." The hand on his arm tightens enough to stop his movement.

"I've been resting for long enough," He ignores her hand, "Besides, we need to get back on the road if we're going to make it to Lockwood within the fortnight."

"Fat chance that'll happen." Baron says, shaking his head. "Storm's coming in late tonight. You lot won't be leaving for another week at the earliest."

Shade just stares at him, his eyes narrowed. The dialect in which he speaks is different than anything he's ever heard in Zion before. Granted, he's never been beyond Glimmer. Still, he finds the way Baron speaks to be rather annoying. At this moment, Shade also perceives how Baron is eyeing Erin a little too closely for his liking. He doesn't think he likes this guy. "Duly noted." He speaks in a clipped tone, "But this *lot* will be leaving whenever I say so." The tension between the two is palpable. Baron folds his arms across his chests, eyes also narrowed. Shade holds his gaze, but glances away when he feels a foot kick his own.

'Be. Nice.' Erin mouths, her eyes drilling into Shade's.

81

"Actually, no we won't." Dru admits, unaware of the silent conversation between the two best friends. "The storms up here are pretty bad. The council is calling for a major blizzard."

"Blizzard? But it's hardly Winter." Shade groans.

"You think the mountain cares?" Baron shakes his head, one hand beckoning at Shade as if to say, 'Can you believe this guy?'

Shade takes a deep breath, trying to let his irritation slide away. "Got it. Who's in charge here? Surely, not you." He glances at Baron who is, once again, watching Erin closely. Baron catches Shade's stare and raises his eyebrows.

The irritation only deepens.

The door swings wide and a wash of cold air blows in. A large figure steps through the frame, blocking the outside world entirely for a just a moment. Then the man is through the door and closing it behind him. He lifts his hands to take off the green hood. Shade recognizes him as the large man with the large horse from the other day.

The man smiles, taking off his gloves and stepping closer. His burly red hair, and chiseled red beard frame an intimidating face weathered with wisdom. "Prince Shade. I am Lord Bane of Frostfire. It is an honor to meet you." He holds out a long, muscled arm, hand extended.

Shade is in awe of this man. He stands, humbled and grateful. "I assure you, the honor is all mine. Thank you for your help. These are troubled times, and I know that trust is not a thing to be taken lightly. Thank you for choosing to trust us. You will not be disappointed."

Lord Bane's eyes twinkle. "I believe you. Listen

well, youth is not a thing to be looked down upon, but *revered*. I see in you the desire to work wonders. If we are but a stepping stone on your way to glory, then it will have been well worth it."

Shade doesn't know what to say, so he bows his head. "Thank you."

"Now, come! The village wants to meet you. And we have a lot to discuss before the storm hits tonight." Lord Bane strides across the room to a chest in the corner. He opens the lid and digs around. "Here are some clothes for you to wear until we can find something more suitable." He tosses the clothes across the room to Baron, who catches them and throws them against Shade's chest.

Dru gives Baron a look, who shrugs his shoulders as if to say, 'What? Did I do something wrong?'

Shade ignores it all, nodding thankfully as if his chest isn't still burning in pain.

"Oh, and how fond are you of that tattered brown cloak?" Lord Bane asks.

Shade thinks back to several days ago when Greaver threw the cloak around his sopping wet shoulders. While the cloak was not his blue family crest stolen from him in his escape, it had been given to him in a time of need by a man who truly cared for him. Shade glances around, looking for the cloak now. "Greaver." He says, almost absentmindedly. He looks at Erin who's face falls with concern.

Lord Bane stops in his tracks. He had been wandering the room, looking for a pair of boots, but now turns slowly to look at Shade. "What did you just say?"

Shade notices the stiffness in Bane's shoulders and answers cautiously. "The cloak was given to me by a man named Greaver Estes. He's one of our stable hands. We didn't know he was on our side until he helped us escape the castle grounds. Why?"

"Greaver." Lord Bane whispers, sharing a look with Baron, "He's alive."

"You know him?" Erin asks.

Lord Bane nods, a smile spreading across his face. "He's a friend. I haven't heard from him in years, and assumed he was dead after the split that happened in Lockwood."

"He told us to get to Lockwood because there were allies there," Shade says.

Bane nods again, his eyes taking on a distant look. "Indeed. But unfortunately, there are enemies, too. You will need to be careful upon entering the city limits. The city's loyalties are divided ever since the change in leadership. Most of the town is loyal to the throne, but some desire to overthrow it."

Shade shakes his head in wonder, "How did we not know about the divide happening within our kingdom?"

"Your parents knew." Lord Bane states simply, "They likely kept it from their children as much as possible. To protect you not only from the outside world, but from yourselves as well. As you can see, they failed to keep Prince Jeb under close watch and now he has allowed his heart to be corrupted by evil men who whisper false sayings in his ear."

Shade is hit with a stab of guilt, sadness, and a bit of anger. "My brother is many things, but I find it hard to believe that a traitor is one of them. I don't know why he is acting the way he is, but I hold firmly to the notion that his hand is being forced. I believe my mother and sister, and Erin's family are all stuck within those walls. Jeb would never hurt them."

Baron snorts, shaking his head. "Those are the kind of thoughts that will come to haunt you. Pardon me, Prince Shade, but I don't care what you think you know about him, your brother is a traitor past saving. We have spies, like Greaver, on the inside who know things."

"Your devotion to your brother speaks highly of your character, Prince Shade." Lord Bane says sincerely, "But, I must warn you, some people have a way of hiding even the darkest parts of their souls. Don't let your grace be your downfall. Every leader must know when a cause is lost."

Shade considers this, fighting back the urge to lash out with a harsh word. He bites his tongue, his mother's words echoing in his ear: *One who is quick to anger is quicker to fall.* He would not win the loyalty of the kingdom by reacting out of frustration or stubbornness. "Yes, sir," is all he says.

"What spies?" Erin asks, eyeing Baron warily.

Baron waves a dismissive hand, "Spies like Greaver. But that's irrelevant right now. The council is waiting, a snowstorm is on the way, and I'm hungry— three matters that are currently of the utmost importance."

"I'm guessing the brown tattered cloak is somewhat special." Lord Bane says, nodding, "I'll see what we can do about patching it up. Baron, ladies, let the prince get dressed, then all of you meet down at the mess hall."

Dru stands and throws a light punch into Baron's shoulder, "It's been a while, but I bet I can still beat you there. Loser rakes the stalls tonight?"

Baron looks at her out of the corner of his eye,

shrugging. "Ah, I don't know, seems kinda childish now—" He takes off at a dead sprint out the door, Dru hot on his heels, laughing without a care.

Lord Bane watches them. A grin spreads across his face and his shoulders shake with laughter. "How does that saying go? 'Many things never change.'" He leaves, pulling the door behind him.

Some things never change, Shade corrects in his mind. But he says nothing to the big retreating form of the Lord of Frostfire.

Erin stands from the chair then and pulls Shade in for another tight hug. Almost just as quickly she pulls away, looking slightly embarrassed, and smacks him on the shoulder. "Good Glimmer, Shade! You can't do that!"

Shade can't help but chuckle. "Get attacked by savage wolves?"

"No. You can't get hurt in the process."

"I'll be sure to tell the beasts that next time. 'Excuse me, but I can't get hurt. No, seriously, I'm not allowed. I'll be in trouble—" He trails off into laughter.

Erin rolls her eyes and swats his shoulder again. She shakes her head, smiling. "I'm just glad you're okay." Her gaze wanders off towards the door, "These are good people, Shade. I think we can trust them. Plus, they'll help us get to where we need to be."

Shade takes a deep breath, letting it out slowly. Then, he nods. "If you trust them, then I trust you. Just don't ask me to like that Baron guy. He leaves a bad taste in my mouth."

Erin laughs.

Shade watches her laugh: the way her eyes almost fully close, the way her mouth spreads portraying

86

brilliant white teeth, and the way her whole face encompasses a beautiful, captivating joy. A look he has seen a million times, but only just recently has become extremely endearing. Like the small dimple that appears just under her left eye. Or the strands of hair so blonde, they appear white in certain lights. He's so intrigued that he almost misses what she says in reply.

"Do his extremely good looks intimidate you?"

Immediately, Shade's smile drops. "What?"

"Oh, come on, even you have to admit he's sexy in that rugged kind of way."

"I will never refer to a *man* as being 'sexy in that rugged kind of way.' Especially not," he stops himself from calling Baron a rude name and settles for, "him."

Erin just smirks. "Anyway, guess you better get dressed. We don't want to keep them waiting."

Shade waits for her to leave but she just sits back down in the chair. He shuffles back and forth on his feet awkwardly, "Um…are you gonna leave or what?"

"Oh," Erin stands once more, surprise crossing her face, "I suppose. I mean, it's not like I haven't seen you in your underwear before." She crosses to the door.

"Well, I just need some time alone to recuperate, really." He lies, the truth of the matter being that, although Erin *had* seen him in his underwear countless times before, *now* it suddenly mattered to him.

"Whatever, prince. I'll be just outside." She turns back once more, "I'm really glad you're okay." She gives him a once over, and seeing it makes him squirm, smirks playfully. Then she hurries out the door.

Shade stands there, an unspoken question on his lips. Did she really think Baron was good looking?

He then thinks: And since when did I really start caring?

He picks up the clothes Lord Bane had found for him. The shirt is cream-colored and long-sleeved. When he carefully pulls it over his torso, he finds that it is loose fitting, but soft. The left shoulder catches on his arm, and he feels a slight twinge. With all the pain in his chest, Shade had nearly forgotten the wolf bite on his arm. It is neatly stitched with a wad of gauze wrapped around it. He wonders how long those need to stay in.

He turns to the pants. They are the same fabric as the shirt, except thicker and charcoal gray in color. His boots stand at attention next to the bed, so he laces them on his feet. A warm winter coat, light blue with a hood, lays across the back of a chair a few feet away from the bed.

Shade picks it up. It isn't the royal blue of his family crest, but it will do. The outside is a wind-resistant material with the inside lined with what looks like sheep wool. He pulls it on, immediately warmed by the soft interior.

The pain in his chest has subsided and he begins taking in his surroundings a little better.

He notes again the many medical beds lined up in rows. The walls are made of logs and the fireplace in one corner is lit and welcoming. A few doorways branch off into separate rooms. Shade pokes his head into one and realizes some are private quarters. One room is a toilet room, with the hole in the middle of the floor dropping to the outside world, typical of most latrines within the kingdom, and then another room is a small kitchen.

Pulling the coat tightly around him, he ventures out the door.

Erin straightens from where she's been leaning on

the wall and hooks an arm through his, "This way, prince."

Shade pulls his collar up closer to his ears, "Gracious, Roy wasn't kidding about the cold." They take the few steps down from the cabin and Shade marvels at the world around him. The village truly is tucked in amongst the mountains; he thought perhaps his fevered mind had been playing tricks on him. And there are patches of snowing spread across the hard ground. According to the others, there will be lots more of that come nightfall.

Erin chuckles, shaking her head; but both of them trail off at the thought of Roy and Juliett. "I hope they are okay."

Shade just nods grimly. The soldiers definitely found them in the barn, but what happened next? He looks around. The area of town in which they walk is quaint, seeming almost uninhabited. He remembers Dru describing the entire village as such. "So, what's there to do around here? Anything fun? Dangerous? Any trouble to stir up?"

That makes Erin laugh and Shade smiles.

"Oh, but of course," she says, "there's hunting and training, work that usually involves meal prep, scouting outside the walls, or maintenance, and, yes, lots and lots of fun. Yesterday, a massive snowball fight broke out just before dinner and Trident fell into a pile of snow taller than him!"

Shade's eyebrows rose, "Trident?" He assumes she isn't referring to the old mythical tale of the staff belonging to a Mer-king deep in the underbelly of the sea.

"Right, you wouldn't know. Trident is the four-year-old son of the town blacksmith. Really, the whole family, the Blacks, are blacksmiths."

"The Blacks are blacksmiths? How original."

"Hush. They make the village's weapons and such. Then, there's the Blues; they are over the upkeep of the water lines and supply. You see, each family has their own jobs to fulfill within the village."

She continues informing Shade of the various families and their specialty as they walk along. Shade takes note of the simplicity of the buildings and barns. However, upon deeper inspection, one can find the hidden nooks and crannies contain secret doorways, or perhaps hidden weapons, and each building is strongly fortified by steel linings along the walls. These aren't just normal log cabins; they're strongholds, bunkers even, built to withstand the trials of time, weather, and, no doubt, war. He recalls Dru telling them about how Frostfire has had to face different raids in the past.

"…they look after any and all animals; tame animals, that is." Erin is saying, "Nothing like those crazy beasts you faced the other day. And, of course, I can't forget the teachers! The Whites work together to educate the village, and not just the children; they work with any and all!"

"It's been three days." Shade interrupts before she can continue, "I know you have a brilliant memory, but you're talking like you already know these people. Have you met every single one? And what's with the last names? What—they have a 'no acceptance' policy if your name isn't a color?" They pass two small children making snow-angels and Shade waves at them. They stop, give him a curious look, wave grandly at Erin, then scamper off.

Erin gives him a sidelong glance, her arm tightening around his as she answers his questions.

"There are no last names! Isn't that crazy? They are grouped in families by the color of their family crest. You know how we have cloaks? Well, they have hoods. The color of their hood is how they are identified. I mean, they obviously have first names, too."

"Obviously." Shade says, as confused as ever. "So, hang on. Who are the Blues again?" They've been passing small houses up to this point, but now they come to a beautiful church with a steeple stretching to the sky. He cranes his neck to follow its ascent.

Erin rolls her eyes at him, "Keep up, will you?"

They stroll along, passing villagers here and there who throw Erin a polite wave or smile, and stare at Shade in fascination. He begins to take notice of their hood colors while Erin continues her explanation of the village and its customs.

"The Blues deal with the running of the water system. The Blacks are the blacksmiths, that's kind of a no-brainer, shouldn't trouble your little mind *too* much. Grays are basically security. Everyone in the village is a warrior, but Grays spend the most time outside the camp, on guard duty or something like that. We met a couple of them when we first arrived. Although Nigel isn't very kind. In fact, he seemed to be very cross the last time I spoke with him." She waves a dismissive hand, "Anyway, Reds are the nurses, medics, and healers. Whites are educators. Browns look after the animals, as well as take care of the food supply. That means meat, wheat, and veggies, so they look after gardens and such. The Greens are the head-leaders and care-takers of the people as a whole. They make the decisions with advice from the council. Yellows focus mainly on maintenance or upkeep of the village. Groundwork, building repair, etc. Purples are the messengers; they are in constant communication with other cities near and far. The council is made up of every leader from each of the families."

Shade nods, trying to follow along. Erin is very talkative and forthcoming, two characteristics typically not associated with her. He imagines this has come from spending so much time around Dru who, in the short time Shade has known her, he has learned is very open, honest, and bubbly. "So," he says in response to Erin's spill, "No wonder the red-head's an arrogant oaf, he's *entitled*. Now I understand."

Erin stops walking and wrenches her arm from his. She looks exasperated, "*That's* what you got from all of this? You're unbelievable. Come on, we're here, anyway." She stomps towards the Mess Hall.

Shade, unable to hide a smirk, trudges after her. "Hold up, there's only nine families in the entire village?"

Erin sighs, talking back at him over her shoulder, "Originally, yes. But over the years and generations and marriages, the families have grown tremendously into what we see today of Frostfire."

Shade nods thoughtfully. "I see. He *is* arrogant, though."

Erin throws up her arms and turns to face him. She's standing on the top step of the Mess Hall porch, so she looks down at him disapprovingly. "And you *aren't*, prince? Come now, get down off your high horse and show a little humility for once."

Shade is taken back by the hostility in her voice. He watches as she turns briskly and strides into the building, before gritting his teeth and following after. Was it something he said?

The mess hall is buzzing. But as soon as Shade steps inside, the voices fall silent. All eyes turn his way. There have to be at least seventy people gathered in this cabin. Some are sitting at tables, others are standing and mingling in groups. Even the kitchen crew behind the counter pauses cooking long enough to give Shade a good look.

Then, as if by some secret cue, they slowly push up the arm of their sleeve (some with the right, some with the left), to reveal their tattoos.

Shade can't help the relief from spreading across his features. They are loyal to his father; they are on his side. He and Erin do not need to fear danger in Frostfire. Even still, he knows they must always be on their guard.

"Frostfire," Bane's voice echoes. He steps out from around a group of people, "Prince Shade, rightful heir to the Windenmeyer throne of Zion."

Before they can do something embarrassing—like bow—Shade speaks. "I owe you my life. Thank you, to any who helped heal me. Thank you for your aid in housing us. And thank you for your devotion to my late father. If only he could see you all, could have met each of you...He would have been so honored, as I am now." He bows his head.

Smiles spread across faces and nods are shared.

Then from the back someone shouts, "Get that boy some meat! He's like a beanstalk!"

Laughter erupts and the hall is, once again, loud with voices. Shade inclines his head, smiling genuinely. He has never in his life been referred to as a beanstalk, toned as he is. But, as he continues to notice the consistent, muscular bulk of seemingly every Frostfire resident, he admits even his tall, lean build somewhat pales in comparison to many of the men and women before him.

Bane places a hand on Shade's shoulder and steers him to a table already laden with plates of food. Delicious food. Beef tips, potatoes, corn, vegetables, and large rolls. Shade's mouth waters at the sight. He sits and Erin sits beside him. Baron and Dru sit across the table. A few others join them.

"Get some food in ya, boy." Lord Bane bellows, taking the open seat beside Shade, "You'll need your strength for what comes next."

Shade doesn't have to be told twice as he has already begun filling his plate. He picks up his fork and begins eating, mulling over Bane's statement in his head. What *does* come next?

As if reading his mind, Bane continues, "Frostfire stands with you. You have our weapons and our provisions as you go forward on this journey. Erin filled us in on the heavy stuff. Now, what's your next step?"

Shade takes his time chewing and swallowing the hunk of meat in his mouth. Partly because he hasn't eaten in a couple days and doesn't want to upset his stomach, and partly because he has no idea of his "next step."

"Sir," He finally says, "Aside from seeking allies in Lockwood, I don't know where to go from here?" The sentence is phrased more as a question than a statement. And he wishes immediately he can take it back. Some of the gumption at the table seems to dissipate. A couple of the guys lose interest in the conversation and turn to their plates, almost disappointedly.

Baron stares at him quizzically, one eyebrow

raised, "You want to take back the throne, defeat an unseen enemy, and you have no game plan?" He looks at Erin, "You willing to die on that bridge?"

Erin looks down.

This angers Shade. He hates the flash of fear that crosses Erin's face; she shouldn't have to worry. Doesn't she know he will take care of her? He hates the disgusted look on Baron's face as he watches Shade in pity. But, most of all, Shade hates that Baron is right. What's a rebellion with no course of action?

What's an army with no one to lead them?

Bane waves his son off, "Shade, listen to me. You don't have to take on the entire weight of the kingdom right now. Nobody is expecting that. And, quite frankly, it would not be wise. Take it day by day, moment by moment. In this moment, or perhaps, the next few moments, what is it that you need?"

Well, that's an easy answer. He needs the one thing he left Windenmeyer for; the one thing Greaver told him to find in Lockwood. Help. Allies. Lots and lots of allies. He looks around the mess hall at the numerous people talking, laughing, and milling about. They believe in *him*; they are willing to follow *him*.

And he doesn't even know their names.

His decision has been made. "I want to get to know my people."

Bane smiles, obviously pleased with this answer. "Well, young prince, you're in luck. A blizzard's coming in. There's not much else you *can* do."

That pretty much settles the itinerary for Shade's next five days. He spends long hours in the mess hall, meeting new friends, learning more about their way of living, and building relationships. He comes to really enjoy Frostfire and, further, to love its people. Each one of them has unique perspectives and talents that, combined, help make running Frostfire a relatively smooth operation.

For instance, the Reds—medics—most enjoy the company of the Whites—educators; they are similar in the fact that they each deal with children most often. Because of this, they are also heavily involved in the lives of the children's' parents. It's a small town, so everyone knows everyone; however, Reds and Whites know personal details and deep family values.

Blues are well-kempt and tidy. They work with the fresh water and must also think it necessary that they themselves stay looking fresh. They are easily the best dressed in the town. Of course, their idea of "best dress" is wolf skin, as opposed to rabbit, and leather hide boots instead of fur. Baron also tells Shade they like to keep to themselves, stay within their own faction. By the look of disdain on Baron's face, Shade is willing to bet he doesn't care much for the Blues.

Grays are more introverted and, well, loners. Probably because they spend a lot of their day outside Frostfire protecting it. There is one Gray in particular that Shade connected with. A lean, thirty-one-year-old with blonde-dreads named Ryker. Shade vaguely remembers him being among the ones outside the town limits when Erin and Dru had all but dragged his near-corpse into the village. Upon introducing himself, Ryker didn't waste time beating around the bush.

He'd given Shade a firm punch in the arm. "Ryker." He gives his name, "I'm a watcher on the wall, working my tail to keep you safe from what's out *there*," He'd pointed out the doors, referring to the whole of Zion, "I expect you to do the same for me with what's in here." His pointer finger moved to touch

Shade's temple, and then poke him in the chest. "I've got your back; now, I need you to have mine, Your Highness."

Shade liked him immediately. The two spent an hour chatting.

The two largest groups, Browns—livestock—and Yellows—maintenance—tend to be the big, beefy men and women. They aren't overweight by *any* means. Just *big*. One woman Shade met towered over him by at least two feet. The muscles in her arms rippled when she crossed them.

Purples are hard to get any face time with; they are always on the move, going somewhere. Purples are smaller and seemingly quicker. One young lady, younger than Shade by a couple of years, weaved in and out of people like a leaf blown by the wind. Her steps were light and her movements smooth.

"Messengers," Baron sighed, when he followed Shade's eyes, "You never can quite catch 'em."

Shade watched the pretty girl disappear out the back door of the cabin and figured Baron had probably tried "catching" her at one point.

Blacks are usually bone-tired and muddy. There is always something new to work on. Still, they made time to sit down with Shade and share their stories. One man, named Afton, talked his ear off about what wood worked best when stabilizing a home in the cold temperatures.

Shade did his best to follow along and nod when necessary. He decided he liked the man when a toddler boy ran into Afton's arms. Afton scooped him up and spun him around, eyes crinkling with laughter, "There's my lad! What have you been up to?"

Baron and Lord Bane were Greens Shade had

already met. The rest of the Green crew was made up of only nine others. They were the smallest group of Frostfire. One woman was strong-willed and determined. She strode over to Shade with no qualms about her and gave to Shade what seemed like a chastisement. "You listen he'e and you listen well. We won't coddle you and we won't kiss your boo-boos. You're the heir to the throne and we need'ya to act like it."

"Charlene, don't berate the boy." Lord Bane guffawed.

"It's not berating. Just a stern talking to. So we have our stories straight." She winked. Shade didn't understand but went along with it.

He found out later Charlene was Lord Bane's mother-in-law, at which time he asked Dru, "Is there a Mrs. Bane around here somewhere?"

Dru's eyes flashed with sadness and she leaned in, "She was killed in a Renegade raid seven years ago. Not just her, but several were killed that night and many more were kidnapped. And the town itself suffered greatly; buildings burned, livestock stolen, lives ruined. Lord Bane went crazy and would've tried killing every Renegade within a hundred miles of here if Baron hadn't stepped in." Dru looked over at the redhead fondly, "He talked him off the ledge."

Shade had so many questions. "Renegade raid? What are Renegades? And why are they raiding Frostfire?"

"Renegades are what we call ones disloyal to the throne. Basically, we believe they're the ones who have now seized control of Windenmeyer and your throne. Every once in a while, they pillage villages here and there just to show their dominance and strike fear in the hearts of Loyalists. Frostfire hasn't been attacked but that one time. Since then, security has been so tight, a Renegade wouldn't dare *think* about raiding it."

Shade felt heartache for his newfound allies and vowed to make sure Frostfire would never face that kind of trial again.

Of all the people he met, Shade's favorite was a White named Kressida.

"But you can call me Kress," She stated matter-of-factly. Her hair was gray, powdered with white specks; but she couldn't be a day over forty. Her sing-song laugh and beautiful smile reminded Shade of his mother, and he couldn't help feeling a pang of homesickness. "I teach most of the hooligans you see running around here," She had continued, "I don't have kids of my own, so they are my own. What about you?" She asked, "What life do you come from?"

Shade blinked. She was the only one to turn the question back on him. So, thus started a back-and-forth conversation that lasted long past most of the other ones. They discussed his upbringing and palace lifestyle. His hopes and dreams for the future of Zion. Kress even shared with him some of her own ideas about implementing education in such a way that all can have the opportunity to learn—no matter their rank or status. Shade left the conversation liking education a little more than before.

Now, Shade sits on the front porch of the Mess Hall, rocking slowly in a wooden chair that looks as if it has been around quite a while. The blizzard that has been raging for the past several days has lightened for the time being, and an easy snow falls. Shade has been bunking with Baron in his room at Lord Bane's house;

and, to be honest, Shade finds he prefers the medical cabin. Nothing like waking up in the middle of the night to Baron flexing butt-naked in front of the mirror.

Shade shudders.

The movement sends a twinge down his arm where the wolf bit him; not pain, just discomfort. The stitches were removed earlier that day and the wound seems to be healing nicely. The stitches across his chest will supposedly fall out when the wound is fully healed; he suspects that will be within a day or two. The medic had informed him he was released back to normal functions: hunting, running, bathing—all of which Shade has already been doing with Baron and the girls.

He laughs to himself, thinking of how this would blow over in the castle. Everyone would be waiting on him hand and foot, doting over why he should not be out of bed, and so on. The day after waking up, Bane had invited him along on a hunting trip...*in* the blizzard. Shade had gracefully declined, noting that these people had no sense of recovery.

He can't blame them; they're used to living on their toes, ready at the slightest crack of a twig. Besides, Shade is starting to realize his preference for this lifestyle over his old. He enjoys the calm, slower pace of Frostfire. He likes the way his chest feels, somewhat loosened from the heaviness of responsibility this lifestyle seems to entail.

Erin stays with Dru in a guest bedroom just down the hall from the boys. Aside from when Shade was talking it up with townspeople, the four had spent a lot of time together. Trudging through the blizzard for breakfast, lunch, and dinner, braving the weather for exploring Frostfire, and playing cards late into the night by the fireplace. Shade knows this won't last forever. Sooner or later, reality will come crashing back in and the weight of an entire kingdom will retake its place on his shoulders. But, for now, Shade is enjoying the peace.

A breeze shifts the fall of snow and some of it scatters across his coat and settles in his hair. Despite being bundled head to toe, he still shivers. But the fresh dusk air is welcoming; and besides, the Mess Hall is especially crowded tonight. Groups have gathered around to play cards, drink coffee, and talk. Lord Bane has a crowd around him in another corner, singing old folk tunes while he plays a guitar.

The night is approaching and soon everyone will head back to their respective homes. Baron says the storm will clear up through the night and normal Frostfire life will resume tomorrow. Shade guesses it will finally be time to mount a trek to Lockwood.

The cabin door opens, allowing the raucous singing of the people to carry out on the wind and across the town square. Then, the door shuts just as quickly as it opened.

"There you are, prince." An exasperated voice says.

Shade turns, a smile forming on his lips. "I needed a little alone time."

Erin's hair glows as the light from the hanging lantern on the porch catches it directly. "I can leave you to it—"

"No," Shade assures quickly, "I'm fine with being alone together."

Erin nods and leans against the railing by the stairs, her back to the falling snow. She sighs, her breath coming out in a puff of white. "Tomorrow, we head out." She states what Shade himself has been

101

considering.

He rocks in the chair, and links his hands together behind his head. "That's what I was thinking." He muses, "To Lockwood. Greaver told us there would be friends."

"And, Bane warned us there would be foes." Erin adds, "We'll have to be careful."

Shade looks at her. His best friend. The only one in all their years to have complete and utter faith in him; as a friend, as a comrade, and now as her future king. "Thank you." He says suddenly.

She raises an eyebrow, a smile threatening the corners of her lips. "Zion's future, thanking *me*, a mere peasant? Whatever for?"

Shade laughs, shaking his head, "Wow, I take it back."

Erin's laugh joins in with his, her eyes closed, head tilted back, breathing in the chilly air. She takes a seat in the rocking chair next to him. They sway gently back and forth, quiet for several moments.

Shade catches himself watching her and quickly looks back towards the falling snow, "Thank you for being here," He goes on, "For trusting in me. For standing next to me and bravely facing this road. I couldn't ask for a better companion."

She ducks her head, "Well...you're my best friend. *Of course*, I'm with you. How are you feeling?"

"Is that a blush I see creeping up your neck, dear Lady Erin?"

"Please, I don't blush. You'd know that if you paid mind to anything but yourself." She teases, rolling her eyes. "How are you feeling? Answer me before I grow bored of this conversation and leave you for the singing." She jerks her head to the mess hall behind them.

"Oh, top notch. Never better. I could take on a whole herd of wolves."

"Herd? They aren't cattle."

"Flock."

"That's sheep."

"Tribe."

A sigh, "No."

"Pride?"

Erin rolls her eyes again, "Okay, now you're just being dumb."

Shade grins smugly at her.

She punches him in the arm, laughing. "I'm starting to wish that *pack* of wolves had carried you off and claimed you as their own." Her smile settles and then fades altogether. Erin tucks a strand of hair behind her ear, turning towards him slightly in her chair.

"Uh, oh." Shade says with mock fear, "Getting serious."

"Ha. Shut up." But she can't keep another flash of a smile off her face before saying, "You've had a few days of team-building under your belt. Thoughts?"

"You've done your fair share of friend-making. You first."

This elicits another sigh, but then she begins. "These are good people. Great people. Their value on life is so high, and yet they manage in such simplicity. They don't need marble floors or fancy clothing. They have each other and that's enough for them."

Shade agrees. These are some of the most genuine people he has ever met. Aside from Baron. He rests his elbows on his knees. "What was it Lord Bane said after they'd carried me inside the Med Cabin? 'We're going to-"

"'Start a revolution.'" They finish it together.

"I think it's already started here," Shade continues, "Before we even arrived. They've been ripe for an uprising of loyalists to the throne for a while now. Dru told me about when they were raided by Renegades and Baron's mom was killed. That was seven years ago." He shakes his head, "How long has the kingdom been suffering and I've not even realized it?"

"It's not your fault," Erin says quietly, "It's not like your parents kept you in the loop about those things. I mean, you weren't the…" She trails off.

"Rightful Heir." Shade says grimly, "Yes, I'm aware."

"Forget lineage." Erin leans forward to rest on her knees like Shade. "You are the rightful heir. You want the best for the kingdom. *Your* kingdom. Can you honestly say you believe that's what Jeb wants?"

Shade considers this. There was a time when Shade was young, he wanted to be just like Jeb. He watched his older brother's every move; the seven-year age difference allowed for Shade to grow up, basking in Jeb's shadow. Oh, how he longed to be just like him. Jeb was the pride of Windenmeyer Castle. Every noble and messenger wanted to shake his strong, teenage grip. Any women of noble stature who visited the castle hung on his every word. Every child wanted him to lift them in the air and spin them around. Shade can't recall many times this happened outside of the walls, in the city of Glimmer. But surely, it was the same out there, too.

Jeb *was* right for the throne.

But, in recent years, Jeb had grown distant, conceited. Every decision made was purely selfish. He never visited the city; he rarely left the castle walls. He even stopped giving Shade the time of day. Shade doesn't remember the last time Jeb simply hung out with him.

"If you had asked me five years ago, the answer would have been yes." Shade finally says. "But, somewhere along the way, that all changed." Shade thinks back on the conversation with Lord Bane, and how he had stuck his neck out for his brother. He sighs, "I don't know, maybe he is a traitor after all."

"Or, maybe you're right, and he's found himself in the wrong place at the wrong time. Remember what Greaver said? Something along the lines of he didn't think Jeb had the ability to resist inside him." Erin says, "Maybe Greaver means that Jeb is easily influenced and persuaded. But maybe, there's hope for him, yet."

Shade only stares out at the snow.

"Whatever the case," Erin goes on, "*You* deserve the throne. All of Jeb's failures over the past few years, *you* have nicely cleaned up. Glimmer loves you. And I know that once they get to know you, the rest of Zion will too. I mean, look at this place." She beckons to the town, "We've been here a week and the people adore you; they're willing to go to battle for you."

A spark of hope settles in Shade's chest. She's right. With the right aid, Zion can be saved.

"And," Erin draws the word out, causing Shade to look at her expectantly. "Dru seems to like you. A lot."

Shade starts at her words. He's thankful for the dim lighting, masking his surprised expression, "Like, *likes* me?" There have been many girls who have liked Shade in the past. Two weeks back, Shade would have been pleased. Now, he hardly has time to consider such trivial matters, "There's no way. Surely, she and Baron are a thing?" He asks this hopefully; unsure if he actually believes it or if he wants it so badly to be true because then it would mean Baron doesn't have feelings for Erin.

Shade sits back, embarrassed by the thought, even though he knows Erin can't hear it. Shade has had crushes, love interests in the past. Again, there have been many girls before. Sure, he's been fond of a one or two here and there, but nothing ever consistent or deep.

Erin, apparently, is not pleased with his response. Several emotions flash across her face. Confidence to confusion to frustration within a second. She stands in a huff. "So many girls like you. Why is it so hard to believe she could, too?"

He stares at her, his mouth slightly ajar in confusion. "I don't…" Understand is what he wanted to say. She is being very confusing.

But at that moment, the door opens and Baron comes strolling out. He throws an arm around Erin's shoulders. "Hey, you. Wanna take a stroll? I know a great spot if this snow clears up." He glances at Shade, as if only just realizing he's there. "Well, hey there, Shady. Enjoying the weather? You won't mind if we're back a little late tonight, will you? Just leave the lamp on for me."

Erin's eyes find Shade's whose are flitting back and forth between Erin's face and the muscled arm around her shoulders.

"Um…" Shade mumbles. He's at a loss for words. Which never happens. Except now when it comes to Erin, it seems to be happening more and more often.

Erin looks away. She shrugs out from Baron's grasp but nods, "I'd love to come. Shade, would you and Dru like to join us?"

Shade finds his voice, glaring at Baron's arm, and then his face. Before he opens his mouth, he takes a breath. His kingdom is what is important right now. Whether Baron and Erin are a thing or not, is something he can't afford to think about. And, Baron is a solid fighter. Shade knows that if he wants to keep Baron on as an ally, he will have to hold his tongue.

So, instead of jawing off at the red-head like he wants to, Shade calmly stands and puts on a smile, "I'm a little tired tonight. But I'll go find Dru and see if she'd like to join you."

Erin crosses her arms and turns away.

Shade feels a little frustrated now as well; maybe because Erin didn't press for him to come, maybe because of the hurt he thinks he saw on her own face before she turned. He swallows hard. But then he shakes it off; there is no time for him to dwell on this. He stands and goes inside without another word. Behind, he hears Baron tell Erin to follow him.

Dru is sitting at a far table, telling some extravagant story that has her listeners hooked. Shade waits for her to finish, and can't help but smile when she ends with a loud noise, her hands reaching to the ceiling.

The table bursts into laughter.

"What'd I miss?" Shade says.

She turns and her smile widens, "Shade!" She jumps off the table and holds up a fist, which Shade bumps. Dru is such a nerd. "Ah, you didn't miss much. Just the really hilarious story of how I found out Dad and Juliett were dating. It's PG, I promise."

"Alright, alright," Shade waves it off quickly, "I'm not sure I *want* to know!"

Dru shrugs, "Eh, suit yourself." She raps the table with her knuckles, "Night, fellas!"

The group waves and hollers, giving her various send-offs. Shade waves bye, before being whisked away by Dru, her hand grasping his arm.

"I've got something I wanna show you."

"Well, actually," Shade starts, "I'm a little tired. The others wanted to know—"

"Nonsense. Come on, it'll be awesome. You can sleep later." She says without letting him finish and tightening her grip on his arm. She grabs her toboggan from the hat rack, pulls it on over her ears, and leads the way out.

Shade sighs but follows after, pulling his coat tighter across his chest, as if that'll staunch the brisk bite of the cold and the pang of confusion in his heart.

CHAPTER 8

A short while later, they're staring at the opening of a cave. A light snow is falling, and if Shade looks really hard, he can even start to see stars through the clouds. Cracker shuffles her feet, clearly not pleased with having been dragged from her sleeping quarters to venture into the chilly night.

Shade wasn't too thrilled about it at first either, but Dru's breezy attitude and intriguing stories have lightened his mood. They had only traveled half a mile into the trees. Now, waiting before this cave, he's all in, his curiosity peaked. "What is this place?"

Dru stares into the darkness of the cave. "Frostfire's greatest treasure." She breathes. Her voice holds a sense of awe. "We'll go into the mouth and tie off the horses. The rest we do on foot."

That's what they do. Shade gives Cracker a sugar cube to tide her over until he returns. She whinnies lightly and rubs her head against his chest.

In the five days, Shade's chest has healed greatly. He is still incredibly sore and moves slower than normal, but with the strong, fast-acting medicinal methods of Frostfire (the likes of which Shade has never seen) the cuts are beginning to scar and haven't had to be restitched at any point. His arm, where one wolf had latched on, is healing a bit slower since the arm is getting more use out of it than the chest; but it is looking better each day. Shade hardly registers the sting anymore.

"Get your torch," Dru says, pulling hers off the pouch along her back.

Before they'd left, Dru had insisted they grab clubs

that could act as torches to light their way. Shade now understands why. The cave before them is pitch black.

They go to work sparking a flame and, before long, have both torches lit with fire.

"Ready?" And, without waiting for a reply, Dru treks further into the cave.

Shade chuckles. The women in his life are so domineering. He obeys without question. "What if I'm afraid of the dark?" He asks, traipsing after the girl.

In the light of his torch, he can spot the sheepish look she gives him over her shoulder, "I'd tell you to buck up, little prince. And if that didn't work, then I'd leave your sorry rump for someone braver."

Shade believes her. He smiles in the darkness.

The cave is cold and dark. They have to climb over rocks and around bends. Pretty soon the mouth of the cave is no longer visible because of all the twists and turns. Shade begins to think Dru is pulling some sort of prank on him. "Is this some elaborate scheme to kill me and take the throne for yourself? You could have just asked, Peanut."

"Oh, contraire. If I wanted that thing, trust me, I'd already have it."

Finally, there's a little light ahead. As they draw closer, it grows brighter; and soon, their torches are almost unnecessary.

"What is this, more torches…?" He trails off when they come out into an open space. A very big open space. "Whoa." He whispers.

The cave is hollowed out in a wide-open space, about seventy yards in diameter. It stretches just as high as it is wide, and a large opening in the center of the rock ceiling reveals the open night air. Stars twinkle through the clouds. The cave is big, but that isn't the best part.

"Are those…?"

"Solar lights." Dru answers. At his vacant look, she continues. "Oh, of course, you wouldn't know what those are." She trails off, tapping her chin in thought. "Basically, the rocks within this cave have crystals inside them that harvest the sun's light." She points at the hole in the ceiling, "Enough sunlight is able to reach the rocks within this cave. The crystalized rocks keep the sunlight, store it, if you will." She looks at him, her eyes alight with wonder, "Then at night, when the sun has set, the crystals having stored up all that energy, *glow*."

Lining the wall around the whole cave and illuminating the pathway circling it are rocks, lighting up with a blue glow. Solar lights. They're beautiful and cast a welcoming glow on the water in the center of the cave. Even in the dimness, Shade can tell the water is clear and the prettiest of blues. The bottom stretches far below, but not a creature seems to abide within.

"It's a natural hot water spring." Dru says, grinning from ear to ear.

How intriguing, Shade thinks. He finds his voice, "It's beautiful. Frostfire's greatest treasure." He says, echoing Dru's statement from earlier.

She elbows him in the ribs, "Fancy a swim?" Without waiting for a reply, Dru sets the torch in a hook along the rock wall of the cave and begins taking her clothes off.

Shade nearly blanches and knows his face turns red, "What are you doing?"

Dru throws him a look, "Uh, swimming, duh. Come on, don't get cold feet on me now!" She strips to her undergarments. "Can't you tell the temperature here is much warmer than outside? The water keeps it heated."

Shade, looking anywhere but at Dru, nods quickly, "Um, yep, yes, I can tell." Out of his peripheral, he sees her throw her hands on her hips and imagines she's rolling her eyes.

"It's like a swimsuit, Shade. Be mature." There's laughter in her voice, and she takes off towards a higher point along the cave edge, where a section of the rock juts out over the water. Her stride doesn't slow and soon she's launching herself over the edge into a dive, a cry of joy escaping her lips. The splash echoes off the walls, soon replaced by her gasp of laughter upon resurfacing. "Come on! Surely, someone in that castle taught you how to swim."

Shade can't help smiling. He isn't going to lie, the water is very inviting. The lights cast the place in a peaceful glow, and it would be nice to drop a load off for just a little while. His parka and shirt are off before he realizes and when he gets to the jutting rock, he's only in his underwear. His feet slap the rock beneath and with a few long bounds, he somersaults off the rock and into the pool. The water envelopes him and it's nothing like the river he dove into two weeks before. On the contrary, this water is calm and warm.

His recent injuries invite the welcoming warmth of the spring. The stiffness in the muscles of his back and arm begin to relax. He resurfaces, spewing water in Dru's face, who was already shielding her eyes, as if expecting this exact thing. She shoves water at him with the palm of her hand. He ducks under the water and opens his eyes.

Such beauty. The rocks at the bottom of the pool are painted with vibrant colors. A sunset, grazing horses, and beautiful landscape; just to name a few. The water is pure and clear and, the farther down he goes, warmer.

Shade resurfaces. "The paintings at the bottom..." He begins, breathless.

Dru shrugs, as best someone can with their shoulders submerged, "Were here long before Frostfire was formed. Your guess is as good as mine. The mysteries of this mountain never cease to amaze me."

"Like magical healing herbs and oils?" Shade says, looking down at his chest.

Dru nods, "Amazing, right? That substance will be of use when the war begins."

Shade's swimming catches. He knew there would be battles; but he hadn't considered a full-on war until this moment. There is a long road before him. Before all of them.

They tread water for a bit, sharing small talk and taking in the hot spring's environment. At some point, it starts snowing heavily again; and white flecks float through the opening in the ceiling, only to melt into water droplets a few moments later.

"Thank you for bringing me here." Shade says, still in awe. "It's one of the neatest places I've ever been. If not the neatest."

Dru blushes, her eyes lingering on him. "Of course, anything for the future king of Zion." She treads a little closer, looking mischievous.

Shade is uncertain how to react. Should he swim away or close the distance? He's saved from the difficult decision when a long whistle sounds throughout the cave.

Then, the voice says, "Sorta scandalous, wouldn't you say?"

Shade turns in the water. Standing at the entrance to the pool is an amused looking Baron and an Erin glaring daggers.

Shade silently berates himself. He had told them he was tired, which he is, and couldn't join in the adventure; but then Dru had literally dragged him along. He hopes Erin understands all of this in his gaze.

"Hey, guys!" Dru shouts with excitement, oblivious to the silent exchange between Shade and his best friend. "Join us—the water's great!"

They oblige, Baron with barely contained joy, and Erin somewhat stiffly. Eventually, the four of them tread water together around the pool. Erin has loosened up, and her neck cranes around to take it all in.

"This is amazing," She breathes.

Shade still feels a little awkward about earlier. While Dru and Baron see who can hold their breath the longest, he apologizes, "Listen, Erin; I really was planning on going to bed. I went to Dru, to tell her what you said, and then she roped me into this. Honestly, I didn't even think about it."

Erin narrows her eyes, but she doesn't look upset; only thoughtful, and maybe...hurt? Resigned?

Shade really doesn't like that look on her face. He starts back tracking in his head, trying to figure out what wrong thing he had just said. "I mean, not that I didn't think about you! I just meant I didn't think about my fatigue because Dru was so adamant."

Erin is shaking her head.

"I'm sorry," Shade says.

She looks at him finally, sighing. "You're fine, Shade. I shouldn't be upset. I just miss spending time with you. The last few days have been," She laughs a little, "Really busy. And I just miss quality time with my best friend."

Guilt washes over him anew. "You're right, Erin. I've missed you, too." He wants to pull her in for a hug. But the water makes it difficult, and Baron and Dru, having grown tired of their game, are watching the two with interest.

Baron interrupts, challenging Shade to a diving contest.

Shade declines, "Not tonight. It's getting late and tomorrow will be a long day." He starts towards the edge of the pool, still not quite satisfied with the conversation he had with Erin.

"Lame." Baron says, but he follows as well. "Lord Bane is sending quite a handful with you. Including yours truly. There's nothing to fear." He beams at the girls, his wet red hair billowing out in the water, giving him the impression of a wooly creature.

Shade lifts himself onto the rocks, fighting down his frustration. How did Dru put up with this guy? But when he turns, a smile is plastered on his face, "Thank you, Baron, young Lord of the Green. Your loyalty is inspiring." Shade gives a dramatic bow in mockery, bending low at the waist and rolling his arm out with a flourish.

The odd look on Baron's face is enough to make Shade question his sarcastic response. But, then, out of the corner of his eye, he notices Dru and Erin smothering their laughter. Or, rather, trying to. That makes it worth it.

Baron sputters, clearly not used to being mocked.

The girls' laughter finally escapes, echoing around the cave once more.

"Oh, come now, Baron. If you're gonna dish it, you've gotta be able to take it." Dru splashes water his way.

Erin swims to the edge, and Shade reaches down to give her a hand.

She squints up at him, "Do I look like a damsel in distress, prince?"

"Never," He admits, chuckling, "Just a pretty girl whose hand I wouldn't mind holding." As soon as the words leave his mouth, Shade wants to take them back. He hadn't meant them the way they sounded. Or had he? He doesn't know. All he knows is if the other three keep staring at him the way they are, his ears might turn red in embarrassment. And, again, Shade never gets embarrassed, so that would be quite a sight.

Erin's eyes are searching his. Her mouth opens as if to speak, but then a voice calls out, cutting her off.

"In some towns, ignoring curfew is punishable by death." Lord Bane stands in the cave entrance, his arms crossed.

The four of them scramble out of the water and stand at as much attention as they can in their undergarments.

Lord Bane's eyes narrow, but then he laughs. "In this town, it just means there's fun to be had!" He slaps his knee, as if he has made a joke. "I remember those days." He adds, almost dreamily.

Shade clears his throat. "Actually, sir, we were just headed to bed. Tomorrow will, no doubt, be tiring. We need our rest."

Creases form on the skin between Bane's eyebrows and he nods solemnly, his smile fading. "Indeed, Prince Shade, it will be." He looks between the other three, "Head on to bed, I need a moment with the prince."

Baron shakes his hair out, and Shade again is

116

reminded of an animal. He grabs his clothes, salutes his dad happily, and wanders out of the cave, whistling without a care.

Shade hopes he freezes to death.

Dru and Erin are slower, but they also grab their belongings and attempt to dry off as quickly as possible; then, they don the rest of their clothing and head toward the exit. On her way out, Erin gives Shade a wink. A warm feeling spreads from his chest, seeming to take the chill away.

He is left standing there with the Lord of Frostfire, who raises an eyebrow at the young prince's appearance. "Feel free to dry off, Little King."

Shade scrambles for his clothes, embarrassed. "Yes, sir. Sorry, sir."

Lord Bane guffaws with laughter, this sound somehow louder than all four of theirs combined had been. "Do not look so patronized. Surely, I'm not as scary as I look? When you're finished, come sit with me."

A minute later, Shade joins Bane next to the water, their feet dangling over the rock edge. His clothes are damp against his skin, but the heat of the spring is already drying them.

Lord Bane lets out a long sigh. "Things are about to get a lot harder, son." He claps a hand on Shade's back. "But I'm not telling you anything you don't already know. I'm sending ten warriors with you. The rest will remain here with me, training."

Shade nods, avoiding the urge to stretch out his back where the sting of Bane's hand still smarts. "Thank you, sir. You have no idea how grateful I am."

"It's not as many as I would like to send, but it's enough to help you get to Lockwood, while remaining discreet. I wish I could join you, but Frostfire needs my guidance for now. Baron will go in my place. He's a knucklehead, but a gritty warrior. He'll not let you down."

"Yes, sir, I understand."

"Call me Bane; I am at your service. Lockwood is several days' trek from here. You should make it by the next full moon, no more than two or three weeks at the latest. Greaver is right, there are many allies there. But, Shade, listen to me." Lord Bane turns Shade's shoulders to face him, "Be careful, son. Trust no one without the Loyalty Mark, the tattoo. It's time to start building your army, and Lockwood is a good place to start."

Here, Shade gives a slight shake of his head. "In all respect, si—Lord Bane, I have to disagree. *Frostfire* was a good place to start. Thank you. I will do my best to make your fight, your sacrifice, worth it."

Bane's eyes twinkle. "I know you will. After Frostfire," He continues, "Lockwood will help produce great help. Do you remember Drake?"

Shade recalls a skinny Purple with dark, long dreadlocks and one line shaved through each of his eyebrows. He nods.

"He's going with us. When you make it to Lockwood, he is to report back to me. From there, I hope to know our next move. If nothing else, Frostfire will come to you."

Shade doesn't fully understand what he means by that, but he nods anyway. Is Lord Bane planning on leaving the mountain and bringing the entire town with him?

"Trix is one of our medics and among our greatest fighters. She'll accompany you, along with Ryker and

118

Fray—both Grays—a feisty Brown named Vision, my adopted nephew, Hagen—he's a Green—and a few others you can meet in the morning."

Lord Bane sighs again. This time, it seems heavier. "Can I tell you a story?" He already has a far off look in his eyes, and without waiting for a response, begins talking. "I was 14 when I became leader of Frostfire. It wasn't by choice. My father was on a hunting trip with several other men from the town. They got caught in a snowstorm that caused an avalanche." His gaze lowers, "After a week with no return, we eventually accepted their deaths. I turned 14 on a Tuesday and became lord of Frostfire the following Saturday."

"Oh, wow," Shade whispers, unable to keep the sorrow out of his voice. "I'm sorry."

"I learned a lot that first year, and I lost a lot," He admitted, "The wolves got some of our horses, bandits stole lots of our goods, and the mountain claimed some of our lives. As leader, I took every single loss to heart. I saw them as proof of my inability to lead. But you know what drug me out of that selfish thinking?"

Shade shakes his head, waiting.

"That amongst all of that loss, there was more I gained. Respect from my people as they saw me surging through the trenches alongside them. Strength to find the light when the world was plunged in darkness. And the willpower to never stop fighting for what is good and right." He points at Shade's chest, "Frostfire knows a good fight when it sees one. And you, young prince, have what it takes to make it worth it."

Shade smiles, some of his nerves dispelling. "Thank you. I have to say though, it would be nice to leave tomorrow with you at my side." Shade would feel very confident with the 8-foot warrior riding with him.

Lord Bane chuckles, "Well that'd leave old Briar in charge of Frostfire, and I'd rather come back to a town in one piece."

Like most of the man's comments, Shade is unable to follow because he knows nothing of this Briar fellow. But he laughs along with Bane.

"Besides," Bane adds, "Every bird must first fall if it's going to learn to fly. This is your kingdom. Now prove it."

CHAPTER 9

Prove it.

The two words bounce around in Shade's mind as he lays in bed that night. The pressure that comes with those words isn't exactly suffocating. Instead, it helps to keep him focused. He is after one thing and one thing only: the defeat of the Renegades and the simultaneous restoration of Zion. Until that happens, all else must take a back seat.

Even whatever weird feeling has developed for Erin. He shakes his head, what is wrong with him? Erin is his best friend. When did he find her unabashed beauty so intoxicating? When did a single look from her cause his insides to melt?

He rolls onto his side. Holy Zion, when had he become so mushy? Unbelievable. Falling for her was sudden; as sudden as the death caused by the poison seeping into his father's heart. Of course, these feelings could just be because she's the only lifeline to his past, to his family, that he has left. Yes, he loves Erin. She's his best friend, his closest confidant. But, perhaps, that's as far as the feelings go and he's only fooling himself.

Shade's thoughts transition to his mother, who lost both a son and a husband that morning not long ago. One to death, one to hiding. And Jeb might as well be gone if he really is as corrupted by the enemy as Bane believes him to be. He wonders how his little sister, Amberle, is holding up. She's only nine. Nine and without a father. Nine and her world, her future, are under attack.

Then he wonders about Erin's family. The twins,

Eliza and Eleazar, both in the midst of scout training in school, both young and lively—now facing a world without their father. And little Edith.

Shade swallows, willing away the worries.

His thoughts are interrupted by the raucous snoring across the room. Good to know Baron seems unbothered by Shade's looming existential crisis. Shade throws the pillow over his head and shuts his eyes, desperately hoping sleep will come.

At some point, it must. Because he wakes to the loud crow of the bird just outside his window. Having been accustomed to the bells and whistles of the castle alarm clock, Shade is still thrown off by the authentic way in which the townspeople of Frostfire arise.

Baron doesn't budge.

Shade shakes his head and slumps out of bed, stretching wide. He pulls on his trousers, dons his weapon, and laces up his boots. Then pulling Greaver's cloak around his shoulders, he slips out the door, leaving Baron to his snoring.

The village is peaceful on his walk to the Mess Hall. The world is just beginning to lighten with the rising of the sun. Early risers greet him quietly as he passes. For the most part, he sees Blues and Browns, checking water movements or feeding animals.

Erin is on the porch of the Mess Hall. Shade sees her from afar and flashes back to the last thing that happened between them the night before.

Just a pretty girl whose hand I wouldn't mind holding.

Erin sees him approaching and offers up a small wave. He smiles in return and joins her at the rocking chairs. "Since when are you out of bed before ten?" He teases.

But her face is stoic. "Since the survival of the kingdom rests on us." She seems distracted, looking around warily at passing villagers and the morning noises.

He searches her face. There was once a time he could read her like a book. "What's wrong? You seem upset."

Her eyes dart around, and Shade catches the slight shake of her head.

What had happened since last night to cause her alarm? She looks anxious.

No, Shade thinks, *she looks* scared. He glances inside a window of the Mess Hall. Some of the cooks are up and about, preparing breakfast. Other than a few other stragglers, no one is yet awake. They have some time before departure.

"Come," Shade holds out his hand, "Walk with me?"

Erin looks up, her eyes lingering on his hand, then his face; perhaps thinking back to last night, like Shade is. Some of the tension seems to leave her shoulders and she smiles. But she still swats his hand aside, "Since when are you so chivalrous?"

"The steps are still a little icy, I didn't want you falling." He says casually.

"Oh, please, prince. You just wanna hold my hand." She brushes his hand aside again and stands. She jumps down from the steps and joins him.

Shade grins cheekily, batting his eyes dramatically, "This is when you say 'just a pretty boy whose hand I wouldn't mind holding.'"

She laughs, "Yeah, where did that one come from?" She asks, referring to his response from last night, "Real smooth, prince. I'm *positive* that's the line you used on Mary Lou from the kitchens."

They start off behind the Mess Hall. A nature trail winds off through the trees and over rocky gorges of the mountain. Shade has wandered this trail many times in the past few days; but never with Erin by his side. He already likes it better.

Mary Lou was a girl who worked in the kitchens back at the castle. "Mary Lou?" Shade cocks his head, "Nah, I just used her for the extra roll she'd bring me after dinner."

Erin gasps and shoves him in the shoulder, "Shade, you did not! Please, tell me you didn't lead that sweet girl on?"

Shade is laughing now, watching Erin's face, "They were the flaky rolls with the cinnamon butter. You remember, right?" He laughs louder when she tries punching him in the arm this time. He dodges it nimbly. "No, Erin, I did not lead Mary Lou on. We were friends, nothing more. She brought me extra rolls, and I taught her how to write. Pretty fair exchange, if you ask me."

This must catch Erin off guard, because she stops walking, staring at him in awe. "Wait. All that time, you were teaching her to write?"

Shade stops walking then, too. He rubs the back of his neck, smiling ruefully. "Yes. What did you think was happening?"

She lets out a breath, looking slightly embarrassed. "Well, I thought…I just thought…" She throws up her arms, "I thought you *liked* her. So, of course, I assumed the two of you were snogging to your heart's content."

Oh. There's a moment of awkward silence and then Shade roars with laughter. He doubles over, hands on his knees. Erin stands there, arms folded, trying, and failing, to hide the smile on her face. He finally straightens, holding his stomach from all the laughter. "I did like her, but not like *that*." Shade finally says, once he's caught his breath.

Erin shakes her head. She appears to be relieved about something. "And you were teaching her to write. Honestly, Shade, that's incredible. That's really sweet of you." Her eyes twinkle with pride.

They continue walking. "Mary Lou was a dear friend." He says after a moment, "I hope she's alright." He thinks about her kind heart and genuine curiosity to learn and hopes Jeb is treating her well.

The walk is peaceful and for a little while after that, they stay silent, letting the beauty speak for itself. Eventually, Shade leads them to a spot he had found the other day. It's a spot where the trees break, allowing for a breathtaking view of the land far below and out beyond.

They stop and Shade sits, patting the ground next to him. Once Erin sits, he points out into the open. "I think Lockwood is somewhere way over there." There isn't much that can be seen. Miles of open land and then land covered with countless trees and dips and hills. Lockwood is somewhere buried within those distant trees.

Erin sighs, "That's a long way. But just look at this view. Amazing."

Shade nods, "I could stay up here forever. Away from the world. Away from the responsibility."

"You wouldn't be alone." Erin says.

Shade feels good about that statement. "So, what's up? You were acting strange at the Mess Hall. Stranger than normal, I mean." He's trying to make a joke, but Erin doesn't laugh. Doesn't even smile.

"Dru received word about her dad and Juliett." She says, "A messenger arrived early this morning. The Renegades broke down the door, dragging them into the street. Along with several other families. Some were killed, others taken. There's no news of Roy and Juliett, whether they be taken or worse."

Shade lets his head fall into his hands. "Oh, no. Is Dru…?"

"She's upset. I mean, who wouldn't be? But she wants to continue the mission with us. There's nothing she can do for them now. All we can do is win this war."

All we can do is win. Shade swallows down a wave of nerves. So much is riding on him. Truthfully, leading the kingdom has never been one of his desires. Even now, he wonders at the terrible luck, seeing as it may be the only option. He sets his jaw, then. Zion needs him and he will answer; whether it's something he wants or not.

"But that's not everything." The look of fear has resettled onto Erin's face. And she glances around again.

Shade follows her eyes. They look behind them, at the path they took to get here and the snow-covered trees. "What is it? No one followed us."

"I think there's a spy here."

Shade's blood runs cold. "What? Why?" A spy in Frostfire? Of course, how stupid could be? Nowhere is safe; not even the seemingly perfect mountain village.

"On our way back to the house last night, Dru and I were on one side of the Mess Hall and overheard an...argument, I guess you could call it." She continues, "Two voices. Men. One said, 'Does Storg know about this?' To which the other replied, 'That the

126

prince approaches Lockwood? Yes'." She looks at Shade worriedly, "We stayed to listen as long as we could. One was a messenger, I think, because the other told him to leave immediately and send word to the 'others. Whoever the 'others' are. That's all we heard before Dru knocked over a bucket and we had to flee."

Shade nods, not allowing his own fear to show. He must be brave. "They could have simply been inquiring whether a fellow townsperson was aware of our plan."

"Dru said there is none named Storg in the whole village."

Well. This certainly is something to grow fearful about. But Shade nods, forcing a determined look, "Right then. I guess it's a good thing we're leaving these traitors behind."

"Unless they're going with us." Erin says quietly.

Shade nods, "Then, we will deal with it accordingly. Does anyone else know about this?"

"No, I don't know who to trust. I didn't recognize the voices, but that doesn't mean we don't know them. I just don't know, Shade."

The way she says his name, in a breath lined with worry and fear, causes his heart to ache. He wants to wrap her into a protective hug and never let go. He settles for a shoulder-bump. "Hey, we're going to be okay. I'll mention this to Lord Bane. He needs to be aware of this. Otherwise, let's keep this between us and Dru. I'll not let anything happen to you two."

Erin nods, her eyes losing focus somewhere off in the distance. "What if this is all for nothing? What if, in the end, we still fail? I mean, we're just kids."

Shade sighs. Her thoughts mirror his own. Instead of answering immediately, he follows her gaze. The

127

stretch of land before them is beautiful and speaks of wonders and mysteries. He wants to explore its rolling hills and hidden valleys. He desires to know more of his kingdom. But he is well-aware of the many obstacles that stand in their way.

"Yes, we're young," he says finally, "a wayward prince and his faithful friend." He smiles at her, earning a smile in return, "But, we're not alone. And anything worth fighting for, is also worth dying for. So, whether we win, or we fail miserably...I'll fight to the end."

Erin bumps his shoulder, "I'll follow you to that end, prince. Just don't make me regret it. If we die, I'll kill you." She's smiling but Shade knows her enough to think there might be a little bit of truth to that statement.

They sit quietly, watching the sunrise pierce the land like an arrow. Then, without another spoken word, they stand and walk back to the little village. The Mess Hall is much busier when they arrive. Dru greets them, her eyes lingering between theirs, silently asking if Erin had warned him.

Shade only nods, squeezing her arm, before ducking past her and into the building in search of Lord Bane. Villagers bus around, carrying equipment, trays of food, or children. The village is awake to see off the small battalion. Shade is grateful for each of them and their assistance; but he still glances warily at them all after what Erin told him.

Shade hears a loud voice and follows it back to the kitchen. Lord Bane stands speaking with one of the cooks, making sure she is providing the battalion with plenty of food. He turns at the approaching footsteps and welcomes Shade with a grin.

Shade waits until he's finished, then nods towards the back door. He doesn't want to appear concerned in the case that someone is watching, so Shade says, a little loudly, "Can you show me that knife trick again? I want it perfected before we leave."

"Certainly, Shade." Bane looks a bit confused, but follows him out the door, "I feel like you had it down fairly well, but if you'd like—"

Shade isn't one to interrupt, especially a lord, but he doesn't have many options, "I'm not pleased with my stance just yet." He holds the door open and they step into the growing daylight on the backside of the kitchen. The tree line is several feet ahead. There is no one in sight, but he isn't taking any chances.

He pulls a knife from the belt on his hip and squares his shoulders.

"Your stance looks good. Are you sure it wasn't in the release, maybe?" Lord Bane asks. It is obvious he thinks Shade is pulling his leg, considering once Shade learned the trick two days ago, it was as if he'd been doing it his entire life.

Shade balances the blade between his pointer and middle fingers, his thumb carefully tracing the sharp tip of the blade. "What was it you said? 'Keep it loose, draw back swiftly—'"

"Flick the wrist and hold the follow-through." Lord Bane finishes, "Really, it's quite simple."

"Right," Shade says, his eyes scanning the trees. No one appears to be around; he's fairly certain it's safe to warn Bane. "Keep it loose. Draw back swiftly. Flick the wrist." He begins muttering each phrase under his breath. To anyone watching, it would appear he is simply trying to memorize each step by repeating it to himself. But Shade is merely creating a distraction, for Bane was correct, Shade knows every step to perfection. "Hold the follow-through." He lowers his voice and puts emphasis on the next words, "*There is a traitor here.*" He whispers, before reciting the steps again, "Keep it loose. Draw back swiftly…"

If Shade hadn't noticed the slight tense of Bane's shoulders out of the corner of his eye, he'd have thought Lord Bane hadn't heard him.

"Flick the wrist. Hold the follow-through." Shade goes on, "*Answers to a Storg*. Keep it loose. Draw back swiftly."

Bane nods slowly. Then, "Well, go on, lad!" He bellows, "Either let her fly, or hand the blade over."

Shade twirls the knife once in his hands, takes a spinning start, then flings the blade into the nearest tree. It holds true in the bark, the handle wobbling slightly. A perfect throw.

Lord Bane claps him on the back, "You're ready." Then he faces him head on, "And we're ready, too. We'll be watching…" He pauses, "for when you need us. We will meet again, Shade."

He'll be watching out for this traitor. He is going to be on high alert. Shade hears the meaning behind the words.

Fifteen minutes later, they are gathered in front of the Mess Hall.

Baron stretches dramatically, his belt and weapons lying in the snow next to him. "Are you ready for this trek? Nothing like endless hours on the back of an animal." He grins and winks at Dru, who waves a dismissive hand.

"Light work." She says. Her hair pulled back in a high pony-tail today, the tips of it just barely brushing her neck.

Erin eyes Shade as he and Bane approach the gathering. His lips tighten, but otherwise, he gives her no sort of indication. She turns away, tightening the bow string across her shoulder and the arrows in the pack across her back.

A group of ten stand before them, all donned with various supplies and weaponry. Ryker gives Shade a slight nod, his long dreads tied back into a low ponytail. Drake stands beside him, just barely rising up to the blonde man's shoulder; his much darker dreads hang loose and long. Shade begins to recognize some of the others Lord Bane had mentioned the night before.

A woman with a dark, jagged haircut to her shoulders is lacing up a pair of tall boots. She's skinnier than most people here; meaning, she appears to lack the kind of muscle common in just about every Frostfire native. But the scar stretching across one eyebrow and the fire in her eyes makes up for anything lacking. A red hood pokes up from the coat on her back. Trix.

A tall man with a large club and a gray hood stands on Ryker's other side. A striking spider-web is tattooed across his bald head. The man cocks an eyebrow at Shade, who offers a wave. The man doesn't return it. Fray.

The broad woman Shade met the other day looms in front of him, her muscled arms just as menacing as before. "Vision." Is all she says, before taking his arm and shaking it in greeting. Shade has to grip his arm with his other hand or risk it being pulled out of socket. He decides against reminding her she had done this very same thing the other day, and only smiles in gratitude.

Hagen stands next to Baron. Shade has had a couple of conversations with Lord Bane's nephew. But where Baron is incredibly arrogant and full of himself, Hagen has appeared relatively meek and mild. Even now, he glances over Baron's dramatic stretching with disinterested calm.

Afton, the blacksmith with the son, smiles at Shade and offers him a thumbs up. A part of Shade wishes he wasn't coming; he has a family to take care of. But guiltily, Shade realizes that all of these individuals before him have someone they're leaving behind.

Someone worth fighting for. Inadvertently, Shade spares a sideways glance at Erin.

"Perez. Risa." Bane calls, holding out an arm.

Two Blues step forward, identical stances and nearly identical faces. Other than the fact one's clearly female and the other's male, they could almost pass as the same person. From their beautiful faces and long brunette hair, to their fancy rubber lined boots with exotic fur and formal posture.

The man places a fist over his heart and bows his head to Shade, "Perez. At your service, Your Highness."

Shade stares. Since leaving the castle, few had referred to him as such; and, even then, it was mainly in mockery.

Baron shuffles closer to Erin and Dru, "Blues," He says, his voice laced with sarcasm, "Always so haughty." He nods at their stiff attitude and regal appearance.

The woman casts an eye towards Baron, having clearly heard his comment, yet appearing to have taken no offense. Her eyes return to Shade. She, too, places a fist over her heart and bows a low head; her dark hair falling around her face, the gleam of an ax visible just over her shoulders and donned upon her back. "Risa. Your Highness," she adds the last bit as almost an afterthought. Shades notices her eyes, resigned and guarded, and guesses these two have a troubled past.

Once again, he finds it natural to compare the siblings to the likes of Vikings. They seem so formal and, yet, so domineering at once. "Shade," he says, clearing his throat. "Just Shade is fine. Thank you."

"Twins," Bane says, as if that isn't already obvious. But he smiles nonetheless, looking proudly at his people. "You serve your village great. And your kingdom greater."

And as if by some cue, the other warriors follow the Vikings' lead, placing a fist over their hearts.

Even Baron. For the first time Shade can remember, there is no mockery or joking look in his eyes. Baron stares intently at his father, unwavering. Simultaneously, the warriors pound their fists once against their chests.

Dru watches them with excitement. Shade is certain she has seen this before. She looks at he and Erin and pounds her chest twice, ending with a 'peace' sign thrown in their direction. Erin's mouth twitches, holding back a smile. That is not at all what the others had just done.

Shade returns his gaze to the warriors, understanding this must be some sort of sacred ritual for this village when sending off troops. Or, perhaps, it is something the citizens of his country do as a whole. He is reminded again of the importance of learning more about his people.

Lord Bane nods once at the warriors, who drop their fists and turn their attention to Shade. "They are loyal to me. And, now," Bane addresses Shade, "they are loyal to you." Behind his eyes, Shade thinks he notices a warning; perhaps, Bane is not as confident in the loyalty of his people as before.

Does Storg know about this?

That the prince approaches Lockwood? Yes.

Shade blinks away the words Erin had shared and eyes the warriors with what he hopes is a look of confidence and bravery. Even as his insides coil with indecision.

They are heading to Lockwood in search of allies, knowing traitors will likely be found as well.

But Shade can't help thinking he might be bringing one of them with him.

CHAPTER 10

Shade doesn't expect the goodbye to be as hard as it is. He has never been a crier but will admit, his eyes get a little misty when Afton's son hugs his father and then wraps his arms around Shade's legs as well.

And sweet, wholesome Kress, her white robe shining blindingly amid the white of the snowy world. When she touches a palm to Shade's cheek, saying something in a language he can't understand, Shade longs for the moment he will see her again.

Other than Charlene, who all but throws him out on his rear-end, muttering something about "goodbyes are for sissies," Shade feels the love from every villager who comes by to see the caravan off. Even Lord Bane offers him a quick, encompassing hug.

"Stay alert, young prince." Bane's eyes wander past Shade's shoulder. He leans in, mouth next to Shade's ear. "I would say trust the Mark," To anyone, it might appear Bane is giving him some motivational words, "but I fear those disloyal might have taken that from us, as well."

With those encouraging words, Shade and his caravan canter off into the mountains. Shade looks back once, catching sight of Lord Bane's outstretched hand high in the air, his village spread out behind him.

Then, Shade lightly squeezes Cracker's ribs with his knees, and she carries him away. Will he ever see these people again?

My people, he reminds himself.

They travel in relative silence for a long while. Occasionally, some of the members toward the back speak in hushed tones; but never loud enough for

Shade to hear what they are saying.

Ryker leads the cohort, his hood pulled up, hiding his stark blonde dreads. A large shield rests across his back; it's silver and blue and looks heavy. But the Gray carries it with ease. The large brute of a woman, Vision, and Drake ride directly behind him. Fray rides at the back, alongside Afton and Hagan. The others are spread anywhere in between. Shade assumes there is some sort of method to the pattern, as he recognizes himself to be in somewhat of the middle of the cohort; along with the group's only medic, Trix. The twins stick close together, but their eyes never stop wandering; checking every crevice, dip, and hidden corner of that mountain.

To Shade's relief, Erin is also nearby. Although, he finds himself wishing it was just she and him, like it was at the beginning of this journey. He wants to talk to her; he desires to know everything about her.

He ducks his head, laughing to himself. Doesn't he already know everything about her?

"One might say that is a sign of madness."

Shade's jaw clenches. And then there's that guy. He gives Baron a sideways glance, who is smiling ruefully. "Is there not some poor, lonely girl for you to comfort?" He asks drily.

Baron seems to ponder this, placing his chin on his hand, elbow resting against the saddle. "Hmm. Trix is too old, Vision, too scary. Risa enjoys her own company too much."

"Sounds familiar," Shade says, thinking he and the twin might actually be perfect for one another.

To his right, Trix makes a noise of disdain at Baron's comment. Shade thinks she can't be older than 30.

Shade doesn't mention how the wrinkles under her eyes, and the specks of gray in her hair do not help her cause. He admits, Trix is pretty; but it's really hard to see past that thick, intimidating scar. He wonders what her story is and considers asking, but stops himself when he sees her growl in frustration at a drop of dew that falls from a hanging branch and lands on her forehead. She wipes it away, huffing loudly. Someone has a temper.

"Dru hates red-heads," Baron continues.

"Not true." Comes Dru's voice from a few paces back.

"Dru doesn't *like* red-heads."

A pause. Then, quieter, "Kind of true." She admits.

"I suppose Erin *has* seemed a bit lonely lately." Baron says, easily loud enough for Erin to hear.

This captures Shade's attention; but he keeps his face as blank as possible. He focuses on running his hand through Cracker's mane. She *neighs* softly at his touch, grateful for the gentle brush. He fights the urge to glance back over his shoulder at Erin's face, a little worried to see what her response might be.

Shade expects Baron to continue and even, perhaps, drop back a couple of paces to walk alongside Erin. Instead, Baron saunters his horse closer to the prince and says. "*Kiertunyazi.*"

Shade almost says 'bless you,' but then realizes he recognizes the sound. He looks at Baron, a question in his eyes.

"*Kiertunyazi.*" Baron repeats, shrugging his shoulders at Shade's look. "That's what Kress said to you. It means 'True King.'" He snorts, "Not sure I would agree, but...I figured you might be curious."

Shade *has* been curious. In fact, up to this very

moment, he had wondered if he had made up the whispered word from Kress altogether.

"It's the language of our ancestors," Baron continues. "Originated from Old Zion. We don't really use it anymore. But Kress says it's important to remember where we come from, so she still teaches it in school."

Kiertunyazi. The word plays over and over in Shade's mind. Is it a true statement? Is he the True King?

He straightens his shoulders, sitting up higher in the saddle. If he *is* to be the true king, it is time he starts acting like it. He encourages Cracker forward leaving Baron still babbling about random "naughty" words in their ancestor's language.

Shade slows when he gets next to Ryker, who looks at him, a bit surprised to see him at the front. But Ryker just bows his head. "Good morrow, Your Highness."

"Ryker." Shade says, "Please, bowing is not necessary."

A slow smile stretches across Ryker's face. "Ah. You are a prince, yes?"

Shade doesn't answer, which is answer enough. Ryker nods, as if finalizing it. "Then you shall always receive my bow." He falls quiet and they ride the next mile in silence.

Shade recalls something Ryker mentioned in Frostfire; his curiosity causes him to broach the subject, "The other day you said something that caught my attention. What did you mean by you're a 'watcher on the wall?'"

Ryker gives a knowing smile, his eyes never leaving the road ahead. "Us Grays are commissioned with the safe-keeping of the village. If danger befalls

138

Frostfire, it's on us. We spend time outside the village gates, yes; but we also physically sit atop the entry gates, watching for any and all who approach the village limits. We look out for danger, raise the cries of alarm if needed." He glances Shade's way, "We are watchers on the wall. If we don't warn the village, if we don't keep it safe, who will?"

Shade considers this deep thought. He is thankful to have this watcher on the wall by his side; he deeply hopes Ryker can be fully trusted. Shade glances behind him at the girls, wondering again about the treacherous conversation they overheard.

The morning is cold; Shade can see his breath hang in the air, almost seeming to crystallize into ice. They have slowly begun a downward descent; although, because of the consistent loops and turns of the mountain range, it almost feels as if they are walking in circles. There is little fog accompanying them on their travel down—much to Shade's relief. An entanglement with wolves is not how he wants to spend the first day of their journey.

Eventually, they enter a larger part of the mountain pass, with a forest on either side of them. Far into the woods, Shade can see the wall of the mountain still rising up around them. He has enjoyed their time in the mountain, but is looking forward to being on level ground once more.

"It will take us all day and night to get down the mountain. The Gargantuans are true to their name," Ryker offers. "We will make camp before then. This part of the kingdom is no stranger to Renegades. The higher elevation will give us coverage and sentry points." He goes on to explain how Lockwood is still around 200 miles away, once they factor in the off-road traveling conditions they will have to endure. They will pass several smaller cities before then. "Some will be friendly." He stares forward, grimly, "Some will not." He explains a small village they will seek aid in for a couple of days; a village not near as big as Lockwood, perhaps the size of Frostfire. "Yagar. We are familiar with some of the blacksmiths who live and work there."

A loud, guttural noise sounds to their left and Shade realizes, trying to hide his repulsion, that Vision has hocked a loogie, and spat off to the side. "Yagar street-rats."

That same slow smile spreads across Ryker's face. It's the look of someone who knows too much, but never tells his secrets. "Vision doesn't like the place."

"She got kicked out of a bar there one time," Drake says, appearing out of nowhere. Shade finds his incredible ability to sneak somewhat alarming. The messenger is short, so Shade peers down at him in the saddle curiously.

"I don't drink," Vision adds, sending a glare in their direction. "And I don't appreciate those who do." The horse she rides on seems too small for the large woman. Shade can almost see the horse's grimace as he carries her.

"A fight broke out between two drunk guys and she got in the middle of it," Ryker explains, "She was only trying to break it up."

Drake laughs quietly, "By shoving one's head up the others—"

"They had it coming." Vision growls, spitting again. "'Sides, it's not just the bars I hate. It's the food, it's their manners, their latrines, their hostels. It's their General. It's the entire place. The people deserve better."

Ryker's eyes take on a far-off look. "Ah, yes. General Saipan can be a handful."

Shade opens his mouth to ask about this leader of Yagar, but is interrupted by Ryker's sudden stop. The Gray signals for the rest of the cohort to stop with a low whistle. His eyes scan the trees. "Hold." He whispers.

The scarring wounds across Shade's chest seem to tingle. He eyes the forest, suddenly on edge. "What is it?" The trees appear fairly harmless, standing stock-still in the quiet of the day. There isn't any wind to rustle their snow and ice-laden branches.

Ryker doesn't speak. He just holds a finger to his lips, then lifts his other hand in a closed fist into the air.

There's the sound of a soft patter of hooves hitting the ground and then Fray and Hagan are beside them.

Ryker looks at Hagan, "Probably nothing," he says.

An unspoken word seems to pass between the two and Hagan nods almost imperceptibly. "I know you well enough to know it's *rarely* probably nothing." When Shade had first heard Hagan's voice, it sounded different than he had imagined it would. Shade figured the Green would sound similar to Baron, cocky and proud. But the elder cousin's voice is deeper, more wizened. Hagan turns to Fray, "Check it out. A clean sweep, take the twins with you."

Without another word, Fray, Risa, and Perez canter ahead, weapons at the ready.

"Afton, Baron, circle back." Hagan directs. They obey as well, weapons drawn as well.

Shade notes how easily Hagan gives the orders,

and how efficiently they are followed. If Shade is to be king, he must carry himself with as much authority.

As if by some silent cue, the rest of the cohort arms themselves as well. Shade draws his sword. He is acutely aware of Erin's sudden presence beside him and another chill runs across the scars on his chest. He and Erin have been in danger before. Danger of receiving a reprimand for talking during class or training, never the kind of life-threatening danger they have faced over the past couple of weeks.

"Probably nothing." Ryker repeats, "But let's get off the main road just in case." They urge their horses into the forest, not stopping until they are well hidden from view of the path. Once at a safe enough distance, they dismount and duck closer to the ground, their feet making soft indents in the snow. As they have traveled down the mountain, the feet of snow have turned to inches. In some places, it has started to melt altogether.

"What raised concern?" Hagan asks in a low voice. He holds the reins of his horse in one hand and steadies himself against a tree with the other.

Ryker bends down next to him and studies the road, "Buck rubs on some trees twenty yards back. Wolves run this area of the mountain range. Deer and other herbivore wildlife usually stay as far away from this land as possible. The only reason they'd come this far north is if—"

"They've been spooked." Vision finishes, nodding. "Something down the mountain has them running up it. I saw the rubs, too. Didn't think anything of it until I also noticed this." With one arm, she moves aside an overgrown bush, a motion that would've taken both of Shade's arms and potentially a leg to do.

On the ground is a rather defined pile of feces.

"*Lorgada.*" Vision says.

Baron leans towards Shade and translates, "Crap." Shade didn't ask. He ignores the Green.

Dru makes a face. "Gag." She mutters. She pulls her coat tighter around her and steps further away from the pile of poop.

Vision glances around the group grimly, "Now, I'm no scientist, but I am best friends with the animals. And *that* didn't come from no animal."

Hagan turns immediately, "Drake—"

"Already on it, sir." The messenger jumps aboard his horse and takes off through the woods, back in the direction of Frostfire. He's off to warn them of this unseen threat.

Or, is he off to betray the kingdom further? Shade shakes his head.

Ryker turns to him. "Hunker down, Your Highness. We may be here a while."

143

CHAPTER 11

As it turns out, they don't have to wait as long as expected. Afton and Baron return within the hour, and the other three follow shortly after.

Nothing was amiss further down the mountain— aside from more signs of recent wildlife. And after retracing their steps, neither Afton nor Baron found any oddity either. But it was clear someone had been around; and recently, judging by the freshness of the—

"*Human* poop?" Baron asks, not trying to mask the laughter in his voice, "Someone dropped a deuce on our land? Took a dump near our home? Laid a log on—"

"Okay, can we stop now?" Dru asks, shaking her head in disgust. "Clearly someone has been here. But who? And why?"

"And how have our scouts missed it?" Trix asks, throwing an accusing glance in the Grays' direction.

Shade expects them to jump up in defense and start making excuses, like he most certainly would do. But Fray and Ryker seem unbothered by the glare. They continue a quiet conversation with Hagan. Trix, however, appears rather perturbed; she stomps away from where they've made a temporary camp.

"Someone's got an attitude." Erin whispers, watching Trix's dramatic departure. "Reminds me of your sister."

Shade smiles, "Trix's flourishing exit *did* have a bit of Amberle's iconic flair." If she didn't get her way, nobody did. He misses his sister. They've buried Father by this point, no doubt. After a moment, he asks, "What do you think they're doing right now?"

An almost haunted look passes over Erin's face. "I'm not sure I want to think about it." Shade understands completely.

"Then don't. Just hold your breath, the smell will pass." Baron interrupts, shoving his way between the two. "Besides, whoever did that is long gone. Not a trace of anyone for miles around. Drake should be halfway back to Frostfire by now. He'll warn them and they'll send out consistent patrols."

"Even still, we should keep moving." Perez says from a few feet away. He's bent down on his haunches toying a thin weed idly through his fingers, watching the Grays and Green with interest. Fray, Ryker, and Hagan still stand huddled in conversation.

Risa stands nearby, arms folded, leaning against a tree truck. A bored expression rests on her face, but her eyes never stop scanning the forest. Shade wants to know what's going on inside that head of hers. Intriguing individuals, the twins are.

"Yes, we should keep moving." Hagan says, as the three break apart and rejoin the others. "Drake will find his way back to us. If we want to maintain efficient timing, we've got to bust it the rest of the way down. Stay vigilant." He looks directly at Shade, "Perhaps, stay in the middle of the pack this time, 'eh prince?"

This is the first time Hagan has spared Shade so much as a bit of eye contact. Shade's so surprised, he almost misses the condescending tone with which Hagan speaks.

Disappointment festers within Shade's chest. So much for Baron and Hagan being different; maybe Greens were all the same. Shade squares his shoulders, not breaking eye contact with him. "With all due respect, Hagan, I'd like to remain up front. The view is

145

better." He adds, almost testily.

Hagan holds his gaze, a challenge flaring up behind his eyes. Then, he gives an almost begrudging nod of his head. "As you say."

Shade fights back a smile of triumph, turning to Erin. But she and Dru are both rolling their eyes and shaking their heads. 'Men,' he sees Dru mouth. Beside her, Baron is grinning, eyebrows raised.

"Little prince has a bit of fight in him after all." Baron whispers, as Shade walks past to mount Cracker. "Give him a solid punch, and I might even like you."

So, Baron and Hagan may not always get along; that's something to take note of. Shade jumps aboard his horse, already pulling at the reins. "Ryker?"

Ryker glances his way, a handful of crackers paused halfway to his mouth. His eyes raise in question. "Uh...Your Highness?" He appears surprised to be addressed by Shade with such an authoritative voice.

Shade fights back an indignant grunt. Earning their respect might prove more difficult than he first thought. Once again, he recognizes the importance of taking bigger strides into a leadership position. "Carry on." He says in reply to Ryker's surprise.

Ryker looks at Hagan.

Hagan, arms crossed, says nothing, only watches Shade with mild interest. Then, finally, he grunts. "As he says. Let's go."

Ryker jumps to, then, bowing at Shade. "Of course."

They canter back onto the main path. Shade, true to his word, stays at the front with Ryker and Hagan flanking him on either side. Vision has dropped to the back of the pack with the twins and Erin.

As if sensing the tenseness in the air, the horses pick up the pace, and maintain a steady canter for most of the remainder of the day; which, as it turns out, is uneventful. They stop twice more for water for the horses; but never lessen their quick pace. Hagan has not spoken again, but Shade can feel the pulsing frustration coming off of him in waves. Meanwhile, Baron hasn't stopped talking—to Erin, to Afton, and even to Trix, who spends a majority of the time in brooding silence.

Ryker answers all of Shade's curious questions about Yagar or the kingdom as a whole. Many of the smaller cities and towns remain loyal to the throne; however, some of the larger cities like Astrid—a town located in northeastern Zion—and Greenbriar—not far from Lockwood—are either faltering in loyalty or are completely disloyal to the throne.

"I would venture to say about half the kingdom has given over to the enemy." Ryker says grimly.

At another point in the journey, Vision adds more reasons—and phlegm—for her distaste of Yagar. Apparently, years ago General Saipan had been the sole cause behind the deaths of some of her relatives. Saipan had been visiting Frostfire on what was then an annual trip in which trade occurred. A group had gone out hunting. General Saipan, unfamiliar with the mountain terrain, had unknowingly ventured from the safe path and found himself at the edge of a cliff. The fog was thick, the wolves attacked, and he and his horse fell over the edge. The general landed several yards below on a portion of the cliff, jutting out away from the mountain. His horse had not been so lucky. Neither had three of the Frostfire natives who had come to his rescue. One was maimed to death by the wolves; the icy edge of the cliff split from the mountain and disappeared into the abyss off the mountain, taking the other two individuals with it; both of which were kin to Vision.

Eventually, Lord Bane and several others were able to rescue the general without any more casualties. But the damage had already been done. General Saipan's stupidity cost the lives of three loved individuals that day. Not many have yet to forgive Saipan for this mishap. Especially Vision.

Even still, Ryker assures Shade that, although a pill to work with, General Saipan is loyal to the throne through and through.

By the time nightfall is upon them, the horses are fatigued. Shade feels Cracker's shuddering legs with each step. He rubs her neck affectionately, "'Atta girl." He murmurs. The sky is a dark shade of blue, as the last bits of remaining light dips further and further below the horizon. Stars numbering in the millions begin to blink into focus. Just as Ryker suggested earlier, they have stopped just before the bottom of the mountain, on a well-forested hill that looks out across the landscape. To their left is a steep cliff face and, at their backs, the road they have traveled.

The trees make the world seem darker. Shade pulls up to one with a particularly thick trunk and dismounts, still murmuring soft words to Cracker. She dips her head in response and nuzzles his hand softly. He gives her a treat, ties her around one of the low-hanging branches, and begins helping the others set up camp.

It doesn't take long. The Frostfire natives are very efficient and Shade finds himself almost useless, standing to the side while the others start a low fire, feed the horses, and set the poles for the tents.

Embarrassingly, he realizes he has never actually made his own camp. He always had servants to do it. And, on the occasions he and Erin would sneak off, they normally took pre-lit torches or a fire-starter.

Thankfully, Dru saves him from his awkward standing, by grabbing his hand and pulling him towards the edge of the cliff. "Come."

Shade has no other option, but to obey. You'd think he'd be used to being dragged around by these girls by now.

Dru stops at the cliff edge and sits, patting the ground next to her. Her eyes scan the land. "We need to chat."

When Shade hesitates, she rolls her eyes, sighing, and adds, "*Your Highness.*"

"No, that isn't..." That isn't why he hesitated at all. He hesitated because Dru isn't exactly the one he wanted pulling him to the side. He looks back towards the camp. Erin is speaking with Baron and she laughs at something he says.

Shade stiffens, suddenly frustrated with himself and his feelings; and done with the entire situation. Whatever the situation even is. He'd been hesitant to sit because of appearances. What would Erin think? Then again, why does it matter? He plops down next to Dru, bumping shoulders playfully with her.

She grins and shoves back with enough force to almost knock him over the edge. It wouldn't be a long drop, maybe twenty feet. But it would hurt. Dru steadies him with her hands, laughing. "Easy there! Weak." She adds the latter word under her breath, teasingly.

Shade smiles, eyeing her out of the corner of his eye. "Maybe. At least I'm man enough to admit it."

Then, he sighs tiredly, "I don't even know how to start a fire." Let alone...lead a kingdom. But he doesn't say it aloud; no use in a pity party.

"Tomorrow we'll leave the mountain. Ever been on this side of the Gargantuans?"

Shade ducks his head. Up until two weeks ago, he had never even been out of Glimmer. "That's a negative. I assume you have?" It seems as if Dru has been everywhere in Zion.

She nods once, a quick movement that shakes loose the strands of dark hair curling against the sweat on her face. "Pretty country. Ugly people." She chuckles, "Well, most of them at least. And I don't mean physically; although that is also the case. Lockwood isn't so bad."

Shade recalls his earlier conversation with Ryker. "Yagar. Ever been?"

A far-off look crosses Dru's features. "Once. A long time ago. Dad and Bane were friends for many years before Juliett came along. Frostfire had some sort of trade business involving Yagar's horse industry. Baron and I went along for the ride and got a whole lot more than we bargained for." She shivers but Shade gets the feeling it isn't the cold. "As a child, the place was terrifying; dark, cold, the people were rude and scary looking. Fights break out everywhere and the crime rate rivals even that of some of Zion's northern cities. Which is crazy, considering this village is hardly bigger than Frostfire. The leaders could not have cared less about those they led. We barely made it out of the village alive."

Shade lets out a breath of air. "Wow. Is the place still under the same leadership?"

Dru turns to him with a relieved expression.

150

"Thankfully, no. They had huge turnover in leadership some ten or so years ago. I've heard the town's up and coming…ish. But, even still, Frostfire doesn't trade or even speak with Yagar unless absolutely necessary anymore."

"This is all very encouraging." Shade states dryly. "Seeking aid from a rampaging city."

"Oh, take heart. Even in the darkest of places, there can be hope." Dru flashes a smile that quickly fades. "So, Erin told you about the other night? What we heard?" She asks quietly.

The traitor. Shade nods. He watches Dru's face and gets the sense there's something she isn't saying. "Do you have more information?"

Dru shakes her head grimly, "But I have my suspicions. The Greens have run Frostfire for as long as I can remember. In recent years, I know there are some other families who haven't particularly liked that."

Shade gives a low whistle, "Ah, shoot." He mutters, "The last thing we need is in-fighting. Anyone in particular?"

Dru shrugs, glancing over her shoulder at the others making camp fifty feet away, "Some of the Blacks, maybe the Blues."

Perez. Risa. Afton. Two Blues and a Black with them on this very journey.

"But again, I'm not trying to make something out of nothing. This is all hearsay, anyway." Dru says, getting to her feet, "I think we've got a long trip ahead of us." She heads back towards the others, calling over her shoulder, "Eaten anything, Shade? Grub's going fast."

CHAPTER 12

He doesn't sleep well that night. And the morning of the next day is just as bad. Perhaps it was the incredibly steep twists and turns that led them off the remainder of the mountain. Maybe it was last night's rabbit stew not settling well in his bones.

Whatever the case, Shade is left in a sour mood. And, it seems, so is the rest of the coalition. Drake had arrived sometime in the night, having returned from his impromptu trip to Frostfire. Bane, of course, had not been surprised by the warning, but would increase security forces and combat training nonetheless. He sent Drake back with an encouraging message that he would meet us soon in Lockwood.

"S'pose everyone got as much rest as me then." Afton says, his voice a low rumble in the quiet of the morning. He rubs one eye blearily.

Shade watches the older man and thinks about the son he left behind. He wishes Afton has not agreed to come.

Why *had* the man decided to come along this journey? Perhaps, he is under orders from whoever this Storg character is?

Shade sighs. Again, this is all speculation. He glances around the crew and has to agree with Afton. It does appear that everyone is considerably more tired today. The slump of shoulders, the weary drag of the horses' feet. Everything points to the idea that this journey might be doomed from the start. This notion is further supported the moment they reach the base of the mountain.

Ryker's whistle is barely past his pursed lips, when

the arrow strikes home. He's launched backwards off his horse, the arrow protruding from his chest.

Shade, having been riding alongside him, immediately ducks, a second arrow whizzing past his head. A cry from behind indicates the arrow has landed a hit elsewhere. He spares a moment's glance and sees Dru at the back, clutching her arm. The arrow must have skimmed it. Blood seeps through her fingers and she ducks down behind her horse. She pulls at the reins, seeking shelter.

And then Shade's eyes find Erin's, and her mouth starts to form his name, but then Afton's burly form on horseback blocks Shade's view of her.

"They're in the trees!" Afton hollers, as more arrows come flying from the front, somewhere deep within the forest. Shade can't see the enemy, but he knows they are close. One arrow lands next to one of Cracker's hooves and she rears back in fear. He settles her quickly and turns back to find Ryker is still grounded. Shade doesn't think, just jumps from the horse, and falls to his knees beside Ryker. He whacks Cracker on the behind to send her into the coverage of the trees. A deep grimace masks Ryker's face, but the Gray is alive.

The world is in chaos around them.

Someone is shouting for Shade to retreat into the woods. Another shouts a command to return fire. He glances up, to the harrowing sight of Risa swinging the large ax from her back. She and her brother kick their horses and race *towards* the screaming arrows. Trix looses arrows in their wake; they streak past the twins and meet their marks somewhere in the trees with satisfying "thunks."

The enemy is still unseen, but their arrows are

becoming less. Shade hopes this is a sign of them falling, and not them regrouping only to hit them harder from another direction.

"Your Highness," Ryker says through gritted teeth, pulling at Shade's jacket, "Get out of here!" Blood seeps out from around the arrowhead in his chest. However, it's not a terrible amount, so Shade thinks this to be a good thing. Ryker attempts to shove him away, but the man is weak and his arms fall helplessly to the ground.

"Save your energy." Shade demands. He grabs the shield and lifts it over Ryker's shoulders. Then, he ducks behind it, protecting Ryker as well, just in time to lift it in defense. Two arrows embed themselves on the other side. Shade feels the force of them pelt the hard steel. He keeps it there, watching Ryker's heavy breathing and tightly closed eyes. "Eyes up, soldier." Shade says, repeating a phrase he once heard one of his trainers say to him.

Shade recalls that memory. *It had been a hot day. Very hot. And, beyond that, Zion summers along the western coast were also very dry. So, it didn't help that dust of the earth was constantly disturbed with their quick movements and floating up to prohibit their breathing and sight. Still, Tollux, captain of Shade's royal guard (yes, every member of the family has a royal guard devoted entirely to him), was finishing up a long training session in which he taught Shade the basics of sword-fighting. Shade was young—no older than seven. Tollux didn't care. He was just as hard on the prince as he was with the soldiers he charged.*

Shade parried one of Tollux's blows and, getting ahead of himself, stopped to marvel at his good block, staring at his sword in wonder. That's when Tollux

*swiped the little prince's legs out from underneath him
and Shade found himself breathless, flat on his back,
dust billowing up around him.*

*Tollux stood over him with a look of disdain, "Eyes
up, soldier." He had said, "The enemy is still at hand."
It was a lesson on never getting ahead of himself. The
fight is never over while the enemy still stands.*

Now, Shade is hoping the phrase will keep Ryker
conscious until he can receive proper aid. It works, the
Gray cringing softly, but meeting the prince's eyes.
"As you say." He whispers.

Once Shade is fairly certain no more arrows are
flying their way for the moment, he throws the straps
of the shield over his shoulders like a backpack, puts
his hands under Ryker's armpits and begins dragging
him backwards, towards the coverage of forest and
away from the flying arrows. Ryker cries out in pain.

"To the trees, *hilcipe!*" A gruff voice and even
gruffer hand shoves him aside, taking Ryker from his
grip.

Shade watches Vision heft Ryker over her
shoulders, careful to avoid pushing the arrow in any
further. Shade notices Ryker's bow where it has fallen
from his hand to the ground below. This reminds Shade
of his own, which he stupidly left strapped to his pack
on the back of Cracker. He grips Ryker's bow tightly
and stands. Several arrows have struck trees nearby;
Shade rips one of these from a solid trunk, stretches the
bow's string, and scans the trees ahead for signs of
enemy life. A bow and arrows are not his strong suit,
but he can still cause some damage.

Vision glances down at him, as if surprised to still
see him there. She makes a disgruntled noise and then
shouts, "Go!"

He doesn't budge, still waiting for an enemy to show its face. But then, the choice is stolen from him, as Afton and Hagan both grasp under each of his arms and heft him into the woods. He's barely able to keep hold of the bow, before he's launched to the ground in the safety of the trees. He takes the impact smoothly, rolling from his back to his knees in a low crouch. Shade growls low, "Let go of me."

His spiteful words bounce harmlessly off of Hagan, who's face remains impassive. He's crouched behind the frosted shrubbery, eyes watching the now empty road. "Come on, Fray, what do we know?"

Shade turns quickly, his heart suddenly in his throat. Risa and Perez went after the enemy; sounds of battle echo from their entry into the fight. Hagan and Afton were the ones who shoved him into the trees. Vision has followed them and now carefully lowers Ryker to the ground. She then tends to the horses, who are all well-trained enough to follow the group calmly into the woods. Vision begins tying them off at various trees. Shade spots Cracker among them. Trix has taken shelter near the edge of the woods, her bow still trained and firing sporadically. Drake, seeming to appear from nowhere as usual, relieves her, his crossbow at the ready.

Trix now darts down beside Ryker and goes to work, assessing his injury. The arrow sticks out of his chest and Ryker coughs lightly, clearly in some discomfort. Drops of blood paint the snow pink. Shade notes there are only a few areas of snow remaining as they have reached the bottom of the mountain.

"You lucky snot." Trix says, breathing a sigh of relief. "Aren't you glad you wore chainmail...like I said?" She adds.

Ryker breathes out a strained laugh. He tries to stay still while she pokes and prods around the injury.

Shade continues searching. He can't find the others. Where's Baron and Dru?

Where's Erin?

"Small group. Probably renegades." Fray responds to Hagan. His voice sounds from the foliage somewhere to Shade's right. "Untrained. They're already retreating." Sweat gleams across his bald forehead, giving the spider-web tattoo a strange, glistening appearance.

"Where are the others?" Shade asks, trying very hard to keep the panic from his voice. They are more than capable of taking care of themselves, but he doesn't like their disappearance any less.

"They were at the back," Comes Hagan's calm reply, "Baron and the girls. They may have retreated into the trees on the other side of the pathway." There's a moment of quiet and then he adds, "They are not our priority."

Almost absentmindedly, Shade is grabbing the older boy's collar and standing, their eyes now level and he vaguely recognizes the slight difference in their heights. Shade is taller; Hagan stands on tip-toes, eyes blazing. "They are *mine*." Shade says firmly. Erin is his best friend. She's the only family he has right now. If something happens to her, he will never forgive himself.

"Easy." Afton says, voice low. He balances in a squat, his arms spread out wide in an attempt to calmly diffuse the situation.

Hagan's hands are at his side, fists tightly clenched. He stares hard into Shade's eyes, nostrils flaring. "Their lives mean very little in comparison to yours,

157

hilcipe." It's the second time within the last-minute Shade has heard this word of Old Zion spoken. "I have my orders and you would be hard-pressed to prohibit me from obeying them."

No more enemy arrows have shot into the clearing. Risa and Perez are still gone, but the shouts and sounds of war have halted. The only noise is Shade's breathing, as he barely manages to suppress his anger. His thoughts are scrambled, but his hands, still clutching Hagan's collar, remain steady. He knows he shouldn't be doing this; his frustration is not with Hagan. He dislikes how they *all* are treating him, as if he is fragile or incapable of protecting himself and those around him; still, that gives no excuse for his sudden expression of outrage. Some part of his mind tells him that altercations with his own people will not help their cause. Nor will it manifest a unified coalition of warriors to retake the kingdom. Hagan is on his side.

But although Shade knows all of this, his worry for the others is squashing any sensible thought. And, besides, the Greens can be so blasted haughty. Someone needs to put them in their place.

Thankfully, before Shade can make a mistake he'd end up regretting, a voice sounds to his left, further back in the woods. Back towards Frostfire and the mountain they had just traveled.

"Aye! Gone for two minutes and missed all the action. Okay, boys, let's go." Baron comes into view, shoving up his sleeves and throwing his fists up, a sly grin on his face.

Erin and Dru step into view behind him, their breathing quick, their horses trailing obediently behind. Dru's crossbow is lowered to her side and Erin's short sword, too. Shade notes the tip of it is red.

Then he searches her face for any signs of distress or pain. He finds only a hard set of her mouth.

It takes him a moment to realize her disappointment is directed at his current state of holding Hagan at the throat. Shade looks back at Hagan, who's eyes have not left the prince's face. Then, he releases the Green and takes a step back, shaking out his hands as the anger suddenly leaves him.

Hagan drops to his heels and clears his throat, still glaring at Shade. He fixes his cloak around his shoudlers.

The tension in the fifteen-foot radius around them dissipates. Hagan turns, already barking orders. "Afton, Fray, locate the twins. Vision, scour the area for any stragglers. Reconvene back here in five." He kneels down beside Ryker, "Condition?"

"I believe the word was 'lucky,'" Ryker mumbles.

Trix shushes him with a snap of her fingers, "Quit squirming." The arrow is no longer stuck, it lies beside her on the ground. She must have pulled it during Shade's moral crisis. Her hands work quickly, almost blurringly so, while she mops up the little amount of blood with gauze. She then pours some sort of cleansing liquid over the small hole in Ryker's chainmail, and the Gray sucks in a breath of pain that turns into a laugh. "This woman's going to be the death of me."

Shades recognizes the playful banter between Trix and Ryker and realizes they must be a thing. He notes the gentle, yet deliberate care Trix takes in cleaning his wound.

While Vision, Fray, and Afton follow their orders, Shade picks up the discarded bow and returns it to

Ryker, leaning it up against a tree beside him. He re-situates the sword at his side and steps away, giving Trix room to work. His anger has left, replaced with a small amount of shame at his thoughtless outburst.

Baron groans, letting his fists drop. "I'm in dire need of a good fight." He sighs, as if perturbed by the dissipating tension. "Well, anyway, we got a guy. Nasty looking fella with yellow teeth and a foul odor. He was circling around, trying to surprise us from behind."

Hagan stands, turning to look at his cousin. "Where is he?"

Baron leads the way back from whence they came. Hagan follows, hand signaling for Drake to remain with Ryker and the medic.

Dru slumps against a nearby tree, gripping her upper arm. Shade watches her in concern and touches her other arm lightly. "Stay here, Trix can help you soon. Close call, eh?"

She scoffs, eyeing her wound. Trickles of blood drip down her arm. The wound will likely need stitches; it has cut deeply into her upper arm. She grimaces tiredly, "Nah, prince. Nothing but a bee sting."

"She saved my life," Erin says pointedly, "That arrow was coming straight for my heart. Dru urged her horse to shove mine aside." She doesn't meet Shade's eyes, and he notes her slightly clipped tone. She's angry with him about his little display with Hagan.

Shade nods gratefully at Dru then asks, "What does hil-cee-pay mean?"

One corner of her mouth raises in a smile. "'Prince.'" She translates, "In some parts of the kingdom, Frostfire being one of them, it also means

160

'protector.'"

Shade considers this thoughtfully. Vision could have certainly meant it as either 'prince' or 'protector.' He's certain Hagan meant it as a slight, now that Shade is more aware of the arrogant attitudes the Greens' possess. "*Hilcipe.*" He says quietly to himself. Then he beckons Erin to follow him, and together they traipse after the Greens. "Remember to keep an eye out." He says once they're several feet away from the others.

She falls in step beside him, "Have you seen anything suspicious?"

Shade sighs frustratedly, "No, nothing. Be careful." He beckons to her weapon, "Where'd you stick him?" He asks, pointing to her weapon.

Her short sword still hangs limply at her side. "Stomach." She says sullenly. "It wasn't very deep." Her voice drops, "But I guess it was deep enough."

Shade glances sidelong at her, the seriousness of the situation settling across his shoulders like a lonely shadow. "You did what you had to." He says simply, trying to keep his voice light.

Death is anything but light.

Erin shakes her head, "I *killed* him, Shade." Then, as if forgetting her frustration with him, she grabs his arm, pulling him to a stop. "He came at me. I killed him. *I* killed him—"

Shade cuts off her whispered voice with a quick shake of her shoulders, "Erin, it was you or him. And, if we're being honest, this probably won't be the last time we have to kill."

She searches his eyes, then, slowly, looks away, "But it is the first."

Yes, it is the first. Shade, himself, hasn't even had to kill anyone, yet. He reaches down, his fingers closing around hers on the hilt of her sword.

She glances quickly back at him, a question in her eyes. But when she realizes he is taking the weapon from her grip, she jerks away, her brow furrowing. "And, what was *that*? That, that...show of *arrogance*?" She hisses, wrenching the weapon from his hands and pointing it back in the direction of the others, "Is enough chaos not already happening without y'all's egos getting in the way?"

Shade ignores her quip, because, in truth, he probably deserves it. He gently takes her wrist, and pulls the sword from her hand. Her wrist is warm and he can feel the pulse of her heartbeat under his thumb.

All the while she glares at him, demanding an explanation; her brilliant green eyes striking, her blonde hair, once again, falling from its braid in loose strands around her face.

He doesn't want to look away from her stark beauty, but he does anyway and begins cleaning her weapon, using the moss of the nearest tree. "You're right."

She sucks in a breath, gearing up for another argument, but stops suddenly, her head cocking to the side. "Wait, what?" The tension leaves her shoulders and she gives him a confused look.

Shade smiles softly, "You're right," He finishes cleaning the weapon, turns Erin around with one hand, sheaths her sword across its case on her back, rights her once more, and lets her go. "It is essential I learn how to better control my emotions. Hagan is no enemy of mine or the kingdom, infighting will only weaken us. I'm sorry. You were right."

She stares, at a loss for words. Her look of surprise shifts then, subtly, to exasperation. "You aren't supposed to agree with me and be all apologetic and sincere. You're supposed to argue and fight back and tell me all the reasons you had every right to be in his face, because he's a Green and 'all Greens are just the worst.'" She says that last part in a deeper voice in an attempt to imitate him. Her gaze searches him expectantly.

And now he is truly stumped. First, she's upset because he lost his temper. Now, she's upset because he recognized he was in the wrong and apologized?

Shade can't win. Instead of responding, he turns and continues walking after the other Greens, reminding himself of their current situation. Let Erin wallow in her own anger for a while.

Now, who attacked them and why?

Erin doesn't follow. A glance over his shoulder shows her retreating form, hands clenched at her side. For a moment, he considers turning around and finishing their conversation on a more positive note. But, no. He has more pressing matters.

Hagan and Baron are bent over the body when Shade arrives.

"No one I recognize." Hagan is saying.

"Do you normally recognize Renegades?" Shade asks, trying to keep the accusation out of his voice. Immediately, he's on edge as he looks at the body. The man is big, but clearly underfed, malnourished. His hair is dark and stringy, his eyes look up past the treetops, staring but not seeing. This is the first dead body, aside from his father's, Shade has been exposed to. Sure, he had attended funerals of nobility and such in the castle plenty of times. But never had the body still been warm at the touch.

Baron uses his hand to turn the man's head to the

side, revealing a large, red welp on his neck. It takes a closer look for Shade to realize it's a burn.

"It signifies a northern Renegade, from one of Zion's cooler regions. By the looks of his calloused hands and unkempt hygiene, I'd say Klepton or Pire." Baron glances at Hagan, "Wouldn't you?"

Hagan nods, "Klepton. Pire is more of a ghost town anymore. Klepton still has groups of Renegades ruling various sectors of the city." He shuts the man's eyes and bows his head, eyes closed.

Beside him, Baron searches the man's pockets, revealing only a folded piece of parchment; then he bows his head like Hagan. After a moment, both stand and turn to Shade, who gives them a questioning look. "You honor the enemy?"

"We honor the dead," Hagan replies, tone clipped. "Whatever side they are on; enemy or not, they still fight for a cause they believe to be right."

Baron sighs, shrugging, "They just happen to be wrong." He unfolds the parchment paper, stiffens, and hands it to Hagan whose reaction is similar.

"What is it?" Shade asks. He reaches for the parchment, but Hagan ignores his hand.

Instead, Hagan reads the paper out loud, "'The men are restless. We tire of tracking the prince. He's headed somewhere with resources. Maybe Lockwood.'" Hagan looks grimly at Shade, "We're lucky he never got the chance to deliver this. I do wish we knew where he was headed, though."

Baron shakes his head and follows Hagan, who has started back towards the others.

Shade walks side Baron., mulling over the note. Where *had* this man been going? Is he in league with whomever Dru and Erin overheard in Frostfire?

164

Suddenly, Shade's acutely aware of Baron's presence next to him. Could this Green be involved with the traitors somehow? And what about Hagan? Could they both be against the throne?

Shade stops that kind of thinking right there. He needs proof, evidence. Without it, there's only speculation.

"*Drengskuerpo*: it means 'Honor in Death.'" Baron says, "Learned that one my first year in school. Can you believe that? *First year*. I bet you didn't even know how to read at that age, little prince."

"You're right. I was too busy learning how to rule a kingdom."

"Ouch. Bit touchy this morning, eh? No one to pamper your hands and clip your nails out here in the real world?"

"Despite your ill-advised beliefs, my upbringing was not all comfort and ease. I spent time away from the castle, training, learning from my people, and seeing the world." In truth, this had only been once or twice that he remembers and never even outside the city limits of Glimmer. But he's not going to tell Baron that.

Baron's eyebrows waggle sarcastically, "Oh, you know all about roughing it, do ya?"

"As if you do?" Hagan interjects from ahead. "Quiet, Baron. We know nothing of a difficult life. Especially compared to a majority of the kingdom."

That seems to shut Baron up. Shade is silently grateful, finding it harder and harder to keep his hands off the younger Green's neck. Who does he think he is? To question Shade's motives?

Shade may have been raised behind the safety of heavily fortified walls, but King Bronze and Queen

165

Rose had raised their children to look beyond themselves—to serve others. Sure, Shade had his moments, and still does. But if there's one thing his father's death has taught him, it's determination to set right that which has been wronged in Zion.

He's reminded of his family. Are they safe? His mother and sister? Has Jeb completely lost all sense of right from wrong? Is he holding the Queen and princess captive? Was Greaver discovered for helping them? How many executions have there been since Shade fled? What's become of Erin's family? And Dru's?

Shade blinks away the questions and the wave of fear rising from the pit of his stomach. One move at a time.

Fear is what you make it.

And Shade will make it his strongest weapon.

They reconvene with the others. Everyone is there. Even the twins, who sit cleaning their weapons. Apparently, they had some luck in their pursuit of the enemy.

"So, an attack from the north? Is it safe for us to assume they are tracking *Kiertunyazi*?" Afton asks, nodding in Shade's direction, at which time Hagan presents the letter they found on the fallen Renegade.

Shade can see sweat gleaming on Afton's forehead and the older man wipes it away hastily. It seems everyone's' adrenaline is still running high from the recent attack.

After reading the letter, Fray says grimly, "Indeed. I was uncertain what else it could be." He hasn't left his position near the edge of the woods, eyes always watching.

It must be a Gray thing. To be on constant alert.

166

Shade has no doubt Ryker would be right there with him, had he not just been shot in the chest. He sits, back against a tree trunk, with Trix close by; she straightens the red hood around her neck and moves to recheck Ryker's bandaged chest; but he waves her hand off. He makes to stand, "We must continue moving. We stay here much longer, and who knows what'll happen. I'm sure reinforcements aren't far."

"If I may have your attention," Shade speaks suddenly, drawing everyone's attention. "It's true, I have little experience outside my home and I won't pretend to know what you have suffered in your lives." He realizes in saying this, he is confirming all their hesitancies towards his leadership. At the same time, he knows strong relationships are built on the foundations of honesty and trust. So he continues, "I am a prince of Zion. But I would appreciate not being treated as such. How am I to fight for this kingdom if you lot won't let me fight at all? Despite what you may think, I can hold my own. I value your loyalty and protection. I know without a doubt, that each of you would give your life for Zion. I would too." He eyes Hagan, "I *will*, if necessary. So, I ask that you allow me to fight for your lives as much as you will for mine."

It is quiet for a few moments.

Then, Ryker chuckles. "He means it. You all saw him. Wouldn't leave my side out there for nothing." He nods at Shade sincerely, "I hear you, Prince Shade."

Hagan stands. There's a new look in his eyes. Respect, perhaps? He sets his feet, then places a closed fist over his heart.

One by one, the rest of the group follows suit. Even Baron. Dru and Erin join, as well. As one, they pound

167

their chests twice, then bow their heads. Shade nods in appreciation of their respect.

"Now," Vision spits to the side, "We've lost a lot of the daylight," She looks angrily upwards through the trees; as if the sun is to blame for their setback. "A nighttime arrival at Yagar is no fun."

A glance passes between Risa and Perez. Perez leans over and quietly whispers something in the other Blue's ear, and she smiles mischievously. She turns her head and catches Shade watching.

It's the first time he has looked her in the eyes...and he can't look away. Her gaze is almost magnetic, impossible to escape from. One of her perfectly shaped eyebrows lifts with a question, the smile still present.

"Let's ride, then," Hagan says. He mounts his horse quickly. Then, as if remembering himself, gives Shade a questioning look.

With only a moment's pause, in which he forces his gaze away from Risa, Shade nods at the Green.

"I think they live for chaos," Dru whispers at his side, having watched Shade's exchange with the warrior girl. She nods towards them, "They're like exotic birds. Beautiful, but odd." Her arm is bandaged and her face no longer pained. She blows a strand of dark hair from her eyes, shrugs, then leaves to find her horse. Shade watches her go, then glances back at Risa who is still watching Shade with obvious interest. They hold each other's gazes until Shade, feeling a bit uncomfortable, glances away once more.

Risa. Yet another mystery for him to solve.

Forests are few and far between as they finally leave the mountain range behind. Shade finds his eyes constantly dancing across the land. He doesn't like how exposed they are. Afton has already assured him that they will soon come to "greener, hillier, and tree-filled land" before too long. And that, by nightfall, they will reach the outskirts of Yagar.

By the sounds of it, Shade doesn't think he will like their stay. He steers his horse up next to Ryker and inquires more about the city.

"We used to trade with them," Ryker says, "Horses, vegetables, eucalyptus—things we can't grow or breed on the tundra landscape. But since the fall-out, we've turned elsewhere for trade. Drake would know how Yagar fares currently; we send Purples often for various news and messaging." He grimaces, the discomfort in his chest evident.

"They don't like outsiders." Drake says, when Shade approaches him with the question. "And they're heavy carnivores."

Shade isn't exactly sure what that means but he decides not to broach the subject. Instead, he settles in an easy trot next to Dru, who throws him a sideways smile.

"Why the long face?" She asks. Her dark hair is pulled back off her neck, in a tight bun. Shade studies her face with its dainty features. A little nose, small lips, beautiful eyes, her small stature. Every characteristic really does point to delicacy. He recalls some of their times of training during their stay in Frostfire and knows she is anything but delicate when it comes to combat. The girl can hold her own and then some. The smile Dru is giving him is contagious and he smiles back. He could stare at that face for hours—it's mesmerizing. Without preamble, Erin's face pops into his mind. If Dru is mesmerizing, Erin is intoxicating.

Shade blinks the thoughts away and his smile falls.

There is no time for these notions. He looks away from his friend.

A throat clears from behind and Baron saunters his horse between them. "That's the man's usual face, Dru. Drawn and forlorn. The weight of the world on his *mighty* shoulders. Say, prince, why *are* you always so down-trodden? Life's too short to live in gray."

Shade considers this thought. It wasn't always this way. He was fun and entertaining. The life of the party and the one with all the latest jokes and pranks. Lately, there hasn't been much time for all of that. And, maybe, there never would be again. He isn't going to fantasize about a peaceful future while he's in hiding, on the run, and seeking allies.

"He should tell you about the Astronomy Tower." Erin says from behind, interrupting Shade's thoughts.

He glances over his shoulder in surprise, meeting her eyes for the first time since the attack. She quickly looks away, but there's a small smile on her face. "Go on, Shade." She continues.

"Oooh, the Astronomy Tower," Baron whispers in mock awe, "Sounds prestigious." He leans towards Dru and out of the corner of his mouth asks, "What's an Astronomy Tower?"

"Oh, for the love." Trix complains from a few steps ahead. "Shut up and let him tell the story."

Shade notices the entire group is listening in, awaiting his story. Even Hagan, his shoulders stiff and staring straight ahead, has slightly turned an ear to hear.

A smile stretches across his face and, after an encouraging nod from Erin, he begins. "Well, truthfully, it's somewhat embarrassing."

The school day had been particularly boring.

Although, to be honest, every school day was boring for Shade. There was always something bigger and better to be doing, trouble to be creating, mischief to find. Besides, school just wasn't something Shade was good at.

"That was different, however, for Erin," Shade says, narrowing his eyes in mock annoyance, "Top of the class, teacher's pet, always looking for ways to improve." He meets eyes with Baron who gives a knowing scoff and shakes his head. "She loved school, thrived in it. Anyway, on this day, like many other days—"

"Like *every* other day," Erin interjects dryly from behind. She knows this story well enough to recognize when Shade isn't being entirely truthful.

"Like, *many* other days, I had grown tired of the mundane droning of the professor. It was time to high-tail it out of there. I had this satchel, you see."

"Oh, the satchel." Erin sighs. "He loved that thing."

"A satchel?" Baron asks, "Like, a purse?" He snorts. He shares a sideways glance with Perez who doesn't share in his humor one bit.

"It was *not* a purse." Shade argues, indignant. And, it really wasn't. He explains how it was more a backpack, something that could hold school supplies.

"Except, I don't think I carried one school item in that thing a day in my life," Shade continues, "It held my less academic supplies. You know...slingshots, knives, homemade stink bombs and fireworks, little things like that."

"Oh, no, I can see where this is headed." Dru laughs.

"It was meant to be small. Just a little joke that everyone would find hilarious, even our professor. It

171

wasn't even the biggest stink bomb I had ever made."

"But it *was* the stinkiest." Erin adds.

Shade glances over his shoulder at her, "Would you like to tell the story?"

She holds up her hands, feigning innocence.

"I was supposed to set it up near our professor's desk, in one of the drawers, if I could manage," Shade's eyes take on a glassy stare, as he recalls the day perfectly.

Their professor was a mean fellow with dark hair and even darker eyes. He had a small, pointed nose and spectacles that always hung off the end of it. But he loved astronomy. So much so, that he often spent nights, staring through his telescope at the stars. This professor was in the midst of a lesson—Shade doesn't quite remember which—with his back to the class. It was at this moment, Shade was sneaking forward with his satchel. Their professor often spent minutes on end writing on the large pieces of parchment in the front of the classroom, so Shade was unconcerned about being caught making his way forward. He caught the eyes of classmates as he passed, and they smothered their laughter with hands and cloaks.

Shade remembers Erin's face, lined with worry and frustration. The shake of her head in disapproval. The shape of her pristine lips mouthing the words, "No. Stop," over and over.

He just flashed her a cocky grin and continued forward, now right next to the professor's desk. All he had to do was quietly open the drawer, remove the bomb from his satchel, relieve it of its detonation pin, and sit back to watch the show. The stink bomb was set to explode within 5 seconds of its detonation. Shade had done something like this a million times; for him, it was fool proof.

"Or, at least, I thought it was." Shade admits, "My satchel was extra full that day, because after school, some friends and I were going to the cliffs to set off fireworks. In my excursion to the professor's desk, the objects inside must have shifted and something pulled the pin out early. I was unaware of this. That is, until it exploded."

Erin's laughter sounds from behind, as she, too, recalls the incident.

The stink bomb exploded still inside the satchel and the force of it set off each and every firework within.

"How many fireworks you think I had with me that day? Four? Five?" Shade calls over his shoulder.

Erin says, "At *least* seven."

Shade grins sheepishly at the group, "Well, anyway, everything exploded. I was thrown backwards into the first row of students. Think I landed on Harvey Dawson's lap. Never seen the guy so perplexed. Of course, weren't we all? Debris was raining from the sky, some of it my satchel, some of it items on the professor's desk. The explosion caused our professor to jump so high, he lost his footing on the way down and ended up face first on the floor, eyes wide." Shade is laughing now, "By the look on his face, you'd have thought the castle was under siege."

"That's exactly what he thought." Erin adds, "He started yelling for everyone to 'take cover, grab weapons, save the telescopes!'"

Meanwhile, the class was in chaos. Some students, having been startled awake by the blast, were just as terrified as the professor and chose to duck under desks and cower in corners. Others were laughing hysterically. A hole had been blown through one wall

173

of the tower and different parts of the room were on fire, the smell of smoke and burnt hair in the air.

"I excused myself from Harvey's lap. Dazed, to be quite honest," Shade says, "And noticed my face was tingling." Shade mimics feeling his forehead, hair, eyebrows. "That's when it occurred to me, has my forehead always felt this large?" He sniffs deeply, "And then I thought to myself, has the smell of burnt hair always been this prominent?"

"He had burned his eyebrows clean off!" Erin exclaims.

The group breaks into varying degrees of laughter. Even Hagan's shoulders shake and Shade thinks he must at least be smiling.

After a couple minutes, the group's laughter finally dies back down. They've finally reached some coverage with trees becoming more frequent around them. They've traveled some ways off of any sort of path.

"What happened next? Did you get in trouble?" Dru asks.

Erin snorts, "Are you kidding me? The prince thrives off punishment. There was hardly a day that went by where he *wasn't* in trouble."

"Hey, now, I seem to recall you spent your fair share of time in trouble as well."

"The curse I bear for befriending you." Erin mumbles, as if exasperated. "Guilty by association. That's always been my mantra."

"Don't let her fool you," Shade says, "The duke's daughter is no saint." He says it without thinking.

"Duke, eh?" Baron asks, throwing an impressed look her way. "You didn't tell us you're royalty."

Erin clears her throat, suddenly somber; all traces

174

of laughter gone. "Yes, well, it never came up, did it? Unimportant."

Shade is quiet as well, his own care-free, joyous mood souring quickly. He shouldn't have brought up the duke, his death still very fresh. Both of their families, still in danger. He sighs, upset at himself.

Small talk eventually picks back up. Fray has dropped back several meters behind to ensure they aren't being followed. Ryker still resides towards the front, but Hagan and Afton are there as well. Trix stays close to him.

They travel until they're surrounded by forestry and the sun hangs low in the sky, kissing the horizon like an evening goodbye. It can be seen in the cracks between the canopy of trees surrounding them. They have been amongst these monstrous beasts of nature for a few hours now. The terrain has shifted from grass and plains to rolling hills with the occasional rock outcropping.

"We are close. Ten minutes from the outskirts of Yagar," Hagan says, "But, Vision is right. We should wait until morning to go any further. Set up camp."

Shade is grateful for the fire that night. Although not near as cold as the mountain, the winter season of Zion, now upon them, provides a certain bite wherever you find yourself in her land, especially at night. He sits in between Erin and Dru, sharing a can of pork n' beans and a small loaf of homemade bread from the ladies in the kitchen at Frostfire.

"Mmm, they sure can cook," Dru says, eyes closed as she savors the delicious taste of the bread. "When I was little, I used to beg for this every day. I used to ask for it for my birthday and Christmas. I could live off this stuff."

175

"It's better than any bread I've ever tasted," Erin agrees.

"Oh, come now," Baron says, from Erin's other side. "That castle bread must be something to behold."

"Nothing like this." Erin assures, nudging him with her shoulder. Baron nudges back playfully, a sly grin on his face.

Are they flirting with each other?

Shade suddenly needs air. Cold air. Lots of it. He stands, pretending to stretch. Some of the others are also enjoying the warmth of the fire. Ryker and Hagan talk in hushed whispers. Trix and Afton discuss tomorrow and what the day holds. Vision is sound asleep and seems to be enjoying it based on the guttural noises she's emitting. Fray and the twins are on sentry duty to start the evening. Drake sits quietly, writing on something. Not only does he deliver messages, but he apparently likes to write them as well. Shade asked him earlier what he likes to write, but the Purple was very secretive.

"Sometimes I like to journal," was all Drake had said.

Shade can't stand the look of triumph on Baron's face any longer. "I'll be back." Is all he says, before leaving the fire in search of *anywhere* else.

He finds Fray first. The man has a woven toboggan covering his bald head. He stares into the night, daring it to show its face. He merely grunts in acknowledgement when Shade walks by him, but Shade feels the Gray's eyes on him the entire time he passes by.

Could Fray be the traitor? Shade shakes off the eerie feeling and continues.

The twins are rarely separated, but tonight they are

176

stationed at opposite ends of the camp. Both of them walk a similar pattern, being sure not to miss anything the night has to offer. He nods at Perez, who inclines his head back.

Shade isn't going to lie, that dude is wicked cool. But there's something about him that makes Shade's skin crawl. Maybe it's the eyes; their piercing glow that seems to reach the soul. Maybe it's the menacing weaponry the man has at his disposal. Maybe it's the simple fact that he's a huge Viking warrior.

Whatever the case, Shade hopes this guy is on his side. He doesn't stick around the man long and finds himself in the presence of Risa; curiosity causes him to step forward next to her.

She doesn't say anything, only scans the trees. Then, begins her stalk back closer to the camp, stares into the trees, circles out wide away from the camp, stares, and repeats these actions until she has checked all directions. Shade quietly does it all with her.

After the third or fourth round, a smile appears on her face. It's a haunting look; one that doesn't reach her eyes. In the muted darkness, lit only by the light of the full moon peeking through the trees, it's almost scary. Her braided hair brushes Shade's arm as she turns and faces away from the camp, breaking her routine. "You have questions."

It's a simple statement. One that catches him by surprise; but he hides it easily with the lift of one shoulder. "No doubt, you do as well."

Risa continues watching the trees. Shade does the same, determined not to meet her gaze until she does. "Questions lead to answers. And answers can be dangerous," she says plainly, "But, yes. I do have some for you. Trade? An answer for an answer?"

177

"You first." Shade says, "How did you end up in Frostfire?" It is obvious from their demeanor, their clothing, their lifestyle that the quaint, little village at the tip-top of the Gargantuans is not the twins' original home.

Risa is quiet. So quiet Shade almost glances her way. Then, "Many moons ago, our family migrated south. Frostfire is where we ended up. I was young, only 6. Frostfire is just about all we've ever known."

"Where did you migrate from?"

She tsks. "That is not the deal, Shade. An answer for an answer."

This is the first time Risa has directly addressed him. And without a title, too. Although he would prefer everyone use his name and not his royalty, he can't help wondering if there's a bit of malice in the way Risa chooses to leave the title off.

"Why should I put my blind faith in *you*?" The question does not sound patronizing; merely, concerned, curious even.

"Not one for sugar-coating, are we?" Shade breathes out a small laugh. "Your concern is valid, understandable. I do not have much experience leading a revolution—any, actually. I can't promise you that I won't make mistakes. But I *can* promise you that my loyalty to Zion and my determination to seek out the truth is second to none. We will take back this kingdom and I will lay down my life to do so, if that's what it takes. I will seek daily to prove to you and my people that these words are true."

"Mistakes can be fatal." Is all Risa says at first. After a moment, she adds, "But I appreciate your response."

"Where did you migrate from?"

"North."

"That's not an answer."

Risa turns her head to meet his eyes, a warning in her own. "That is the only one you'll get from me."

Shade chews the inside of his cheek, biting back a retort. "What happened to the rest of your family? Why is it just you and your brother now? Your demeanor and attire speak of prominence, wealth. From where you hail, are you royalty?"

Risa sighs, "You are not very good at this game." But she answers nonetheless. "My lineage is of no concern to you. They are futile titles with no meaning anymore. My family? Some were killed when Renegades attacked. The rest were captured."

Shade looks down solemnly. Awful. He will put an end to these murderers. "How many?"

"Our entire clan. There weren't many of us to begin with. Twenty, twenty-five? Our parents were part of those killed. Our sister," Her voice catches. She swallows and continues, "Our sister was captured. That was seven years ago. Perez and I have tried searching for her, in the hopes that she still lives. But she has disappeared. And hope has not boded well for us in the past." She turns to face him fully. "Which is why, you must understand, I am having trouble *hoping* in the success of your endeavor."

Risa is Shade's height. But her intense personality and toned exterior make her seem much bigger. Once again, those intriguing eyes bore into his. "How do I know you are not lying? A Renegade in sheep's clothing?"

She is very close to him. So close, Shade can feel the warmth of her breath and smell its sweet, peppermint scent. "You come from a family originally

179

located rather mysteriously in a northern region of Zion. Which is, ironically, the area of Zion most prominently noted for being the birthplace and residence of Renegade tribes. I could ask you the same questions, Risa."

Neither of them moves for several moments, as if by being the first to break eye contact was an admission of guilt.

Risa's mouth is set into a thin line, and her tone is clipped when she says, "That is not an answer."

"I could make you promises until I'm blue in the face. You'll never believe a word I say until I back it up with actions. Stick around and, at some point, you will find that hope you've been looking for."

Her eyes narrow. Finally, she turns away and they both resume watching the dark forest.

"I'm sorry about your sister." Shade says after a few tense moments.

Risa grunts. Then, almost begrudgingly, she responds, "I'm sorry about your father."

That seems about all Shade is going to get out of this conversation. It hasn't been a complete waste of time. He has learned the twins came from the north and were likely of royal descent; Risa does not trust him; and they have a sister out there somewhere who, despite her best efforts not to, Risa still believes to be alive.

Shade bows his head once her way. She looks at him with mild surprise, then inclines her own head in return. He turns and begins making his way back towards the camp. When he is almost out of earshot, he hears the faintest of whispers from behind where Risa still stands.

"I would like that."

Shade knows she's talking about hope.

Back at camp, most of the others have followed Vision's lead with the intentions of getting some much-needed rest. Dru, her back to a tree, sleeps soundly. Baron is leaned against her, his mouth wide open and breathing deep. Erin lies a few feet away, curled up under a blanket.

Only Afton remains awake. He gives Shade a nod from his position next to the fire. His hands are held out towards the flames, wanting the warmth to seep through his gloves. Shade is about to ask him to wake him up when it's his shift, but Afton speaks before he can.

"I don't sleep," the bearded man says, "I will keep watch. Fray and the twins will trade out with some of the others in a few hours. Please, get some rest."

Shade doesn't argue. He finds a spot next to Erin and lowers himself to the ground. There isn't much comfort in sleeping on the cold ground; but, he's too tired tonight to care. As he goes to lay his head down a couple of feet from Erin's, he catches the flash of her eyes standing out against the dark blanket. He looks at her in surprise and whispers, "You're not asleep?"

There's a movement like shoulders shrugging. She peeks her mouth out from under the blanket, her blonde hair following, "I didn't know where you went."

Shade feels guilty for leaving the fire like that earlier. Erin is family; the last thing they need to do is leave each other's side out here. "Went for a walk. Sorry."

She murmurs something unintelligible. Then, her voice thick with fatigue, she says, "Next time, take me with you."

Shade smiles at her in the darkness, already hearing

181

the evening of her breathing. She had stayed up, worried about him. He lays down, scooting a little closer to her, drawing peace from her nearness. One of Erin's hands sticks out of the blanket, palm up. Shade reaches across and rests his hand on it, closing the space between them.

He sleeps soundly that night.

CHAPTER 13

Shade doesn't know how it happened, but at some point in the night, Baron rolled from his position next to Dru and ended up all in Shade's space, legs and arms sprawled across him. Shade has to give the Green a well-placed jab to the gut to get him to move.

"Aye!" Baron cries, startled awake. One of his legs kicks Erin's bundled form and an annoyed groan emits from the covered lump. Baron is on his feet, eyes wild and fists up. He glances down at Shade, who is glaring upwards menacingly. "I was having a brilliant dream, you oaf." He drops his hand and his eyes take on a glazed look, a wistful smile passing over his lips. "A *brilliant* dream."

"Please, spare us the details." Dru mutters, already standing and stretching.

Erin groans again, coming out from under the blanket. "You *kicked* me."

"Don't look at me, I was rather rudely disturbed!" Baron exclaims, beckoning at Shade.

Shade ignores him. He rolls to his stomach and lifts himself off the ground. He stands, stretches. He must have been sleeping on a rock, for his neck has the most awful crick. They don their weaponry, feed their horses, and help pick up the camp; then they gather in a circle around the ashes of the fire.

"Yagar is no stranger to crime; we do not separate; we stay in a group." Hagan says, "Drake left in the night to alert General Saipan of our arrival. We are ten minutes away. Do not expect a warm welcome."

That is all that is said.

On their trot, Shade finds Risa riding beside him.

They don't exchange any words, but Shade knows that last night's talk has improved their relationship somehow. Almost a mutual respect or agreement between the two.

Despite their solemn ride, Shade is in awe of the beauty of their surroundings. Unlike those closer to the mountain, the trees here are tall, with brown trunks that stretch high and branches that don't start until well over fifty feet up. Unfortunately, this means there is very little coverage. The ground is rocky in areas, with various larger rock formations placed sporadically. It is also hard, frozen; similar to the mountain, but different in the fact there isn't snow to give it some cushion.

If he didn't have more pressing matters, he might have enjoyed spending his days exploring these woods for hours on end.

Ryker whistles from ahead, his closed fist in the air a now familiar sight. Someone is approaching.

Actually, several someones by the sound of it.

From ahead, just over the rise of a hill, a barrage of riders on horseback come into view. One of the front runners is Drake, his mouth pressed into a thin line. Although his face rarely gives much away, the stiffness of his shoulders indicates this is not about to be a pretty conversation.

The head rider is small, probably smaller than Shade, with a hooked nose and stringy hair. His large eyes bulge from his head, giving him a bird-like appearance. He wears a large, black trench coat and a black headband around his greasy-looking head. The men and women flanking him do not look much better; all of them wear matching headbands and trench coats.

Shade's entourage comes to a halt and waits as the

184

other riders pull up in front of them. They wait in an oval shape, with Shade at the front center. He notices this, grateful they are giving him room to lead. Hagan and Ryker flank him closely, with Afton and Vision nearby. The others must be behind.

After both parties have stopped, a stare down ensues. The man with stringy hair, clearly the leader, smiles without humor, his cheek working tobacco. "Well, well," he says finally, his voice the sound of grating metal, "Frostfire. Been a while."

"Not long enough," Vision mumbles, so quietly no one across the way hears.

"General Saipan. We seek aid." Hagan says calmly, looking bored.

The general starts to laugh, at first softly, and then louder and louder until his entire crew has joined in and their laughter bounces off the tree trunks around them.

Drake glances in Shade's direction as if to say 'See what I've had to deal with?'

Eventually, their laughter dies. Horses shift uncomfortably. Someone clears their throat from behind Shade.

"I don't work with traitors." General Saipan tsks sharply and begins turning his horse around, the others following suit.

"You consider the rightful heir a traitor?"

The general barely glances Hagan's way, snubbing his nose disgustedly, "Jeb is the worst of them all."

"I didn't say *current*." Hagan's voice stops them in their tracks. Once he has their attention again, he adds, "I said *rightful*."

General Saipan seems to notice Shade for the first time. Recognition lights in his bulging eyes.

"*Kiertunyazi*?" Comes a whisper of Old Zion language from someone behind the general.

The general gives a hard glance behind, which shuts up the whispering quickly. He turns back to Shade. "So, this is you? Our knight in shining armor? Our savior?" He scoffs, "Not so regal outside your golden walls."

"That's what I said," Baron whispers, earning a shush from Dru.

General Saipan's nose scrunches, eying Shade, "In need of a shower."

Shade would like to ask him when the last time he looked in the mirror himself, but instead bows his head. Humility has never been his strong suit; but, since haughtiness has never worked in his favor either, humility it is. "Our gratitude to you for meeting with us. We don't need much. Rations, weaponry, a couple evening's rest, and then we'll be on our way. I would be in your debt."

Several snorts of laughter escape the smelly crew across the way.

Drake shakes his head slightly, a warning in his eyes.

"What our prince means," Ryker says smoothly, nudging his horse forward, "Is we are just as loyal to the throne as you are. Our mission will only help the throne, not hurt it."

General Saipan grunts, as if agreeing that is something that can't be argued with. "You endeavor to reclaim the throne?"

Shade realizes the general is addressing him. "We do." He says, "And you could be a worthy aid in that endeavor."

General Saipan works the tobacco in his cheek,

mulling this idea over. He glances at Hagan. "Two days, nothing more. We will provide you shelter, rations for the road, and," He looks disdainfully at Shade's horse, "better means of travel. These poor things are in need of a well-deserved break." He 'tsks' at his horse and they turn back to the town, his entourage following.

Drake drops back and rides with them towards Yagar. "General Saipan is not a man you want to owe." He says, explaining their clipped response to Shade's discussion of debt.

"He has a way of twisting words, situations," Ryker adds, "Another reason Frostfire has refrained from trading with Yagar in recent years."

"He is not someone you want as an enemy *or* a friend." Hagan says.

"Or alive." Vision growls.

Shade almost startles at the sound of her low voice, filled with such hatred. He glances backwards at Erin, whose eyes are wide. They follow the general to Yagar; a town as beautiful as its name. Meaning, not at all beautiful, but dingy, crippled, and dark. They're greeted by naked, dirty children (and some adults) huddled in corners of broken-down buildings or laboriously tilling the frozen ground. Some of them look up long enough to wave, others ignore them completely.

General Saipan doesn't give a single one the time of day; even the smallest children who run up to grasp at the legs of the horses, begging for food. He ignores them completely, speaking to his men in arrogant tones.

Erin, next to Shade, makes a strangled noise in her throat; she has always had a soft spot for children.

187

Seeing them this way is difficult for Shade; he knows it's even harder on Erin.

"Why doesn't he help them?" Shade asks no one in particular.

"Most of the town is as such. That still doesn't excuse how Saipan and his lackeys can live in moderate luxury while the rest of his people suffer." Ryker says, "I think he enjoys their constant need for him."

Anger alights in Shade's chest. And when one of the children, a young girl with blonde hair so dirty, it's almost black slips in the mud and narrowly avoids being trampled by the legs of Saipan's own horse, Shade can take it no more. Especially since this little girl reminds him so much of Erin's sister, Edith.

He shouts for his horse to halt. His crew around him stops as well, in alarm or confusion, he isn't sure.

Shade doesn't wait around for their questions. He steps down from Cracker, his boots squelching in the cold mud loudly in the sudden quiet. General Saipan and the others have stopped, turning around to observe, with identical looks of boredom, confusion, and in Saipan's case, frustration.

"Something wrong, *Your Highness*?" General Saipan means it as an insult, but Shade isn't bothered.

He walks the few feet to the little girl, whose face is downcast, staring at her hands and arms encased in stinky mud. Shade bends down next to her, fanning his cloak out behind him to avoid getting most of it too dirty. He carefully cups the little girl's cheek in his hand and turns it to face him.

Tears streak a path through the grime on her face. She can't be more than five and her large hazel eyes stare up at him in wonder.

He smiles, hoping not to frighten the girl. "Are you hurt?"

She just stares, then shakes her head no.

Shade offers his hand. The girl glances around warily. After a few moments of hesitation, she takes it and lets him help her to her feet. Other townspeople have stopped in their tracks, watching the exchange. Shade sees women, their mouths ajar. Other children, staring wide-eyed and scared. Men, their eyes narrowed with concern.

Still holding the girl's hand, Shade turns expectantly to the general. "Do you have food we can give all of these people?" Shade knows he's toeing a dangerous line, almost questioning the general's authority. But he also knows that if General Saipan desires his people's need for him, then he will not let someone like Shade draw away the people's loyalty.

The general stares, a challenge in his eyes.

Horses shuffle in the muck, voices whisper, Shade feels dozens of eyes trained on him. "It is early, we are not yet fatigued from the day. Perhaps, we could go out hunting if needed?" He asks, keeping his voice light and innocent.

"That won't be necessary," General Saipan says quickly. He narrows his eyes menacingly, then turns away, a forced smile entering his features. "I was planning to send out a hunting party this afternoon," He announces louder to the crowd around them, "We'll have plenty of food for all. Pause your chores for a while, go back to your homes, and wait for some of my soldiers to provide you with your needs. In fact, take the day off to celebrate my humble provision for all of you!"

His soldiers send up a shout of jubilation, praising

189

the general for his generosity.

The townspeople do not make a noise. They are not watching the general or his soldiers. Their eyes follow the prince, as he bends down beside the girl, whispers encouragement in her ear, and sends her on her way.

They watch him turn and walk back to his horse. Watch him mount the beautiful steed, nod at his entourage, and follow after the soldiers, further into town.

They're so preoccupied with this curious individual, 'Who is he?', some whisper, that they entirely miss the look of hatred flash across the general's eyes, or the whisper he spits into the ear of the nearest soldier.

But Shade doesn't miss it. And neither does his team.

"I thought your goal was to make allies," Baron whispers, "Not enemies."

"General Saipan is not someone you want as an enemy," Hagan repeats through gritted teeth.

"No," Risa muses, so quiet they all have to turn their head to read her lips. "But I do believe our prince just made more allies today than enemies."

Shade follows her eyes to the townspeople. Almost imperceptibly, several of them bow their heads.

Are they honoring him? Supporting him?

He tries not to read too much into it and instead, waves one last time to the cute blonde-headed girl, lightly kicks his horse, and follows the others.

CHAPTER 14

The rest of Yagar is no different than the start. Most homes appear dilapidated and tiresome, most people even more so. What's more, there seems to be more functioning bars than upright homes or stores. They come to a town quad where a majority of the trade (what little there is) must occur. Raucous laughter emits from yet another bar; this one, the biggest. A crude sign hangs sideways above the entrance reading "THE BAR." How very original.

As they pull up beside it, General Saipan is giving orders to many of his soldiers who groan in protest. Shade hears one of them grumble something under his breath, which means Saipan is probably distributing hunting orders. He tries hiding a smug smile, but catches a grin from Baron and can't help but return it. They may not agree on everything, but both enjoy seeing "Saipan the Smug" displeased.

They follow the general's lead, dismounting from their various steeds.

General Saipan claps his hands, "Best bar in town, upstairs doubles as a hotel. We've got the best cooks in Zion, easily. Get settled upstairs. Brunch will be in an hour. Then we will talk about those supplies you need. I may not always like to give it, but you'll find I'm a most welcome host when I want to be. Highness," he says, loudly and with power. "A word before you go in."

Nobody moves.

Saipan rolls his eyes, "A courteous word. I mean no harm. Honestly, Vision, do you know me at all?"

Vision stiffens, then reaches for the sword at her

hip. Hagan stops her coolly with a hand to her hilt. "You must understand, sir, our hesitancy to leave the future king's side, yes?" He nods at our crew, "Inside. Afton and I will remain with the prince."

The others shuffle inside, glaring down soldiers as they pass. Erin nods at Shade, a stone look on her face. She must hate it here as much as he does. Soon it's only the three of them, Saipan, and several of his men. The general's cheery expression drops. "Never challenge me in front of my people like that again."

"Is that a threat?" Hagan asks tersely, his arms folded across his chest. Afton leans against a nearby post, glowering at the general.

"A warning." General Saipan states simply, his eyes never leaving Shade's. "We may not be enemies, Highness. But I think you'd find I'm better to those I like."

Shade's life has been filled with various types of training. Some in combat or strategy, taught to him by his father and brother. Others in compassion and etiquette, taught to him by his mother and her maidens. One thing both of his parents had taught him was devotion to that which was morally right; they had trained him to never compromise his beliefs or cower in the face of threats. General Saipan may not be a bad guy, but he certainly isn't good. "I'm not out here to make friends, General," Shade replies with a firm tone. "I'm out here to win back my kingdom, whatever it takes. You can either get on board, or get out of our way."

The general is shocked into silence. When he realizes no one else is speaking, he steps back, freeing the path inside. Afton straightens from his leaned stance and beckons at the door for Shade to enter first.

Shade steps past Saipan, but pauses before entering the bar. He turns back, "And, General," He says, looking past Hagan's curious stare to the general beyond, "I do hope you get on board. You'd make an incredible general for my army."

* * * * *

"You really think he'd be a good leader for us?" Baron asks, an hour later, once they're finally settled down at the tables for lunch.

Shade scoffs, "Absolutely not. But that man's cunning enough that if he thinks he will, he actually just might. Besides," Shade takes a drink from the canteen of water placed in front of him, "I really do need allies."

He, Baron, and the girls sit at a booth along one wall of the bar. The rest of their group is fanned out at tables around them, almost entirely enclosing them in a protective half circle. General Saipan and his men and women reside at the opposite end of the bar, some of them missing because they are out hunting.

Their rooms upstairs are not the nicest. But, Shade admits, it's nicer than sleeping on the ground. Ryker had wanted to give Shade one of the suites, a room with a king size bed that was just slightly less moth-infested than the rest of them. "A king for the King!" He had joked, halfheartedly. But Shade insisted the injured Gray needed his rest. He would take the king and Trix would stay with him on a cot in case his injury needed redressing.

Only four other rooms occupied the upstairs. Erin and Dru were allowed their own room, sharing a queen. Vision and Afton took two twin beds in another. Two sets of bunk beds occupied another room; Hagan, Fray, and the twins called dibs. That left the last room, another set of twin beds, to Baron and Shade.

Why he always draws the "Baron" straw, Shade is uncertain.

Drake would not be resting. In fact, he was already on the move, traveling onwards alone to prepare other villages for Shade's arrival. Shade feels he is not deserving of this royal treatment. He has so much to learn in so little time.

A large woman with the traces of a beard sets four glasses down in front of them. "What'll it be?"

It takes Shade a moment to realize she's the waitress.

"Well?" She demands, "Ale? Whiskey? Rum?"

"Water." Shade says, "We refrain from ale."

Baron scoffs, "What kind of a prince *refrains from ale*?" He asks, his voice altering to mock the prince's voice. Baron looks at the woman, about to ask for something alcoholic, no doubt.

But Dru elbows him, "Sober and vigilant. The last words your father told me before we left the village. They were about you, Bare."

"Bare" sulks back in the booth. Tangled strands of his red hair fall from its ponytail, giving him somewhat of a homeless look. Shade thinks he'd fit right in with the people of Yagar. "Water is fine." Baron mumbles.

The woman grunts and leaves, "Hey, Grizzle! We got any water back there?" She yells on her way.

A faint voice responds from a hidden room somewhere in the back, "Water? You mean that stuff we use for cleaning?"

"Aye, they want to drink it." The woman replies.

"Did you say *drink* it? Does he know this is a bar?"

Baron lifts his eyebrows at Shade and holds out an arm as if to say, 'Exactly.'

194

Vision stands roughly from one of the other tables, glaring around menacingly. "I loathe this place," She growls, "I'm going to get some air while we wait for the food." She leaves 'THE BAR.'

Hearing her complaint, General Saipan says from across the room, "Hunting party will be back before too long. They'll finish up distributing to our, ah, people before coming here." He stares pointedly at Shade. "My apologies, Highness. I know you aren't accustomed to waiting."

Erin makes an annoyed sound and fidgets with the empty cup in front of her. Shade recognizes this tactic; she fidgets when she's holding back a retort. Her eyes flick to his and away again, nostrils flaring. Shade can spot an Erin "angry episode" well in advance. He speaks before she can have one.

"Actually, it's no bother, General," Shade responds, unconcerned, "Gives us ample time to admire your fine establishment here." He brushes dust from the table and eyes the cobwebs in the corners where the walls meet. "I trust you are just as welcoming to all of your guests. Thank you for your service to this great kingdom."

The general is, once again, struck dumb by Shade's words. Perhaps he's never met someone willing to go toe-to-toe with him and, in the same breath, sound kind and praiseful.

The low murmur of voices resumes and the conversational chatter returns.

Ryker is telling a story to Trix and the twins, all of which seem only mildly interested. Afton and Fray converse. Hagan only speaks when it benefits him, so he sits quietly brooding.

"I don't care what you're playing at, that guy

would make a *terrible* leader." Baron says, nodding towards the general. "The only place he'd lead everyone is to their deaths."

Shade disagrees. He sees General Saipan rising to the occasion when necessary. This town, albeit down-trodden and gross, would be uninhabited if Saipan didn't have some sort of leadership quality that demanded people obey or respect him.

"I do not remember this place looking so…" Dru scrunches her nose, "*disdainful*."

"And that's being generous." Baron adds.

"We won't be here long," Shade replies, "Long enough to restock."

"Vision says we'll have to trade out our horses," Erin says, "Is that true? Riot has been with me since he was a foal."

Shade has already considered his loss of Cracker, who has been with him just as long. A feeling of sadness settles in his stomach at the thought of leaving her here, so he knows how Erin must feel as well.

"They will be well-looked after," Dru says. "My dad has called General Saipan many things over the years. But he has also been quick to mention the general's love for horses."

"If Vision, who hates the living fire out of this man, who loves animals more than breath itself—I'm pretty sure—thinks it's safe to leave them, then there's no safer place for them to be." Baron assures.

Shade is slightly taken aback by his response. "That might be the first compliment I've ever heard you pay anyone." He eyes Baron with genuinely and the red-head feigns hurt.

"Aye, little prince, I have a heart!" Baron says, grasping his chest dramatically. "It about melted when you lifted that child from the mud. Anyone else tear up or was it just me?" Now he's smiling, trying not to laugh.

"If he hadn't done it, I was about to." Erin says, smiling at Shade. Her smile causes his own heart to start beating faster. "That was very sweet of you."

"I loved it," Dru agrees. "These poor kids. Poor families. They are in need of better living. General Saipan can give it to them; but he needs to see that it's worth it. Maybe by being here, we can prove it to him."

They spend the next several minutes discussing possible routes they'll take and villages they'll visit on their way to Lockwood. Dru is convinced they'll take the river, a route that will lead them past waterfalls and beautiful rainforests that her father used to travel. She describes the many hours they spent fishing at the streams and admiring the views. Apparently, there's an exciting waterfall they would likely come to if they took the river.

Baron insists the more direct route is to travel further south where there are less hills and more plains. "Better for traveling." He says in a tone that suggests it to be common sense.

"Yes, but also better for getting, I don't know— killed!" Dru huffs, "There is absolutely no coverage in Drysdale."

"Drysdale, that's the desert portion of Zion, correct?" Shade interjects, interested. He recalls the map of Zion he brought on this trip and the ones he studied during Cartography class. The region of Drysdale is located Southeast of the southern Silent Sister. It is known for its hot, dry conditions. Shade is not aware of many desert towns that occupy the region, but he has heard of numerous desert Nomads claiming the land as their own.

"Yes, and completely free of coverage. We'd be sitting ducks for the sun *and* the bad guys."

Shade smiles at the way Dru says "bad guys," such a child-like reference. He watches her argue with Baron, her body fully turned and facing him in the booth chair to get her point across.

"I said *direct* route, not safe route." Baron quips.

"How is going south, *miles* out of the way, the most direct route?"

"Are you an expert traveler, Little Bow? No, I think not."

"My crossbow being little does not make it any less volatile than yours."

They argue like an old married couple. Shade and Erin watch the two of them with great amusement.

The hunting party returns and gives the meat to the cooks in the back. Soon, the smell of cooked venison fills the air and Shade's stomach growls loudly. It's been a few days since their last substantial meal. He almost hollers with joy when the bearded waitress appears with large stacks of meat, potatoes, and carrots. Even the bread is edible; delicious, in fact!

By the time they have finished eating, the late morning has turned to afternoon and Shade is pretty certain he won't need another meal for three days.

"So, was it really *that* good, or were we just *that* hungry?" Baron asks, one hand holding his belly. He belches loudly.

Dru makes a face, waving the air in front of her. "Stop that. Rude."

The rest of the day is interestingly spent. Hagan insists they train to stay fresh and in shape; so, they run for a couple of miles around the town and then participate in a strange fighting tournament Baron creates; it's a mix between wrestling and boxing. It is friendly at first. But then blood is drawn and the women excuse themselves from the tournament.

"I deal with enough blood to see my own," Trix says. Dru voices her agreement with a 'Hear, hear!' Erin points out that she could disarm each of them easily, but would hate to embarrass anyone; she, too, joins the others to watch.

Shade's first match is against Afton, who he is hesitant to hit at first. But when Afton starts with a left hook that catches Shade in the kidney and almost sends him to his knees, he decides taking it easy on the kind, burly fellow isn't an option.

It doesn't matter in the end; Fray wins with flying colors. The man feels no pain, Shade's convinced. He was taking blows left and right without giving so much as a grimace.

The tournament lasts a good hour. The women had left halfway through and Shade is curious to know what they are up to. He rubs the cut above his eyebrow with a handkerchief Afton had produced from his coat pocket. Hagan had busted Shade's brow with a jab in the second round.

Funny, none of them seemed too concerned about punching the future king.

But Shade doesn't mind. He lives for this kind of stuff; and he wants to be treated like one of the people, not as royalty to be pampered delicately.

"Next time, maybe you'll get a shot at me, eh prince?" Baron's voice echoes from behind Shade.

Everyone else has left the clearing and headed back towards the heart of town.

Shade scoffs to himself. Get a load of this guy; he

never knows when to shut up. Shade turns to face Baron, a snarky comment on the edge of his lips. Only to be met with a fist to the nose. He stumbles back a step, completely caught off guard. Baron stands before him, fist still raised. In the next moment, Shade's charging the Green and tackling him around the waist. They crash to the forest floor, a frenzy of flying fists and feet.

Shade lands a hard hit to the side of Baron's head, who then twists and flips Shade off of him. Baron bounces back to his feet, lunging. Shade, also finding his footing, sidesteps and grabs Baron's torso, then delivers a satisfying knee to the gut. Baron trips him and they fall to the ground once more.

Shade uses their momentum to flip Baron over his head. He scrambles to his stomach and back to his feet, fists at the ready. "What is your problem?" He yells. He spits blood, knowing his nose has to be broken.

Baron is laughing as he stands, wiping blood from a newly split lip. "So, you *haven't* been looking for a fight ever since that horse carried your sorry, injured, rump into the village?"

Shade had. He most definitely had. He's wanted to strangle the arrogance out of Baron since the moment he saw him, red hair poking out from under a green hood. "My fight is not with you, Baron."

"No," Baron agrees, bouncing on the balls of his feet. "But, admit it, this feels good, aye?"

It *was* nice to feel his knuckles break skin on the cocky jerk. Shade's fist drops and he sighs, "Did you have to break my nose?" Shade is still angry, but some of the fight has left him. Yes, Baron is incredibly annoying and in need of a good butt whooping; but Shade is thankful to have him as an ally. Although the

200

Green did just break his nose, Shade doesn't peg Baron as the traitor. Knowing this makes it a little harder to wish ill-will towards him.

But just a little.

The tension leaves Baron and he shrugs, "Actually, no. I was already swinging when you turned. It was meant to be a glancing blow." He tries a sheepish grin, "Water under the bridge?"

Shade picks the discarded cloth up off the ground and now uses it to staunch the flow of blood coming from his nose. "Don't do that again."

Baron raises his arms in surrender, "As you say."

Shade nods tiredly. He picks up his cloak, dons his weapons, and starts for the town quad.

Baron follows, talking some nonsense about various skills he had to learn through different years of training in Frostfire. They pass multiple townspeople on their walk, Shade attempting to smile through the blood and swelling. Baron waves casually at the men and winks seductively at the women. A few of the children run up beside them, walking with chests out and heads high.

Shade thinks this must be how they view them; tall and proud. He tousles the hair of one boy, who stares at him with wide eyes. The kid points to Shade's face, then runs off. The sight of his bruising eyes must have scared the kid off. But a few moments later, the boy returns with a clean cloth and offers it with a nervous smile.

Shade stops walking to gape down at the boy. Then, he carefully takes the fresh cloth. "Thank you." He bows his head.

The boy grins, clearly pleased with himself. He bows back, bending fully at the waist. Shade straightens him with a tap under his chin.

When they make it to the quad, the rest of their team are all waiting for them.

Erin stands quickly from a bench along the wall of the bar. "I thought the tournament was over." When Shade draws closer, she gently lifts his hand away from his nose and her face lines with concern.

Shade holds his breath; this is the closest they've been in a while. And never had there been such longing to draw even closer. He stares at her eyes, specks of gold floating in a pool of brilliant green.

Deep laughter fills the courtyard and Afton's smiling face steps up behind Erin. "It was." Apparently, many of them find Shade's appearance funny as more laughter joins in.

"Ah, but the prince got in a few licks of his own." Fray notes, eyeing Baron's split lip and puffy cheekbone. Baron shrugs and applauds the prince good-naturedly.

Shade notices the eye roll from Hagan who says, "I'll get Trix." He disappears into the bar.

Risa and Perez are nowhere in sight; perhaps patrolling the area, as they always do. A part of him worries about no one else knowing their whereabouts.

Does Storg know about this?

That the prince approaches Lockwood? Yes.

Dru is scolding Baron who's offended by her strong defense of Shade. "Excuse me, I'm bleeding, too." He says.

"You really are the worst." Dru says emphatically.

Erin carefully places the blood-soaked cloth back on Shade's nose. He reaches up slowly to take it back from her grasp. She blinks, as if realizing how close they are. He watches her swallow, notes how it travels

202

down her slender neck. She doesn't move, only meets his gaze and he thinks there's a slight catch in her breathing.

But, then Trix is there, complaining loudly about 'Men' and their 'constant need to compare sizes.' She trails off into something unintelligible, then takes Erin's place in front of Shade. She sucks in through her teeth, "Yep, that's definitely crooked. Get inside, let's set that thing before it's too late."

Shade is no stranger to a broken nose; he's had at least six in his lifetime and has been the cause of a dozen more on others. But setting a broken nose is never fun. He follows Trix's orders and they sit at a table just inside THE BAR's entrance.

Shade's team and a couple of townsfolk are the only occupants in sight.

It doesn't take Trix long. She settles in front of him, begins explaining her routine for this type of injury, and doesn't even give a countdown before she's pulled and shifted the nose back into place with a noticeable 'pop.' Shade hardly feels it. In comparison to the wolf injuries a couple of weeks before, this is light pain.

But there's the sound of someone sitting down hard in a chair. It's Dru and she looks very queasy. Her eyes are distant as she says, "I do not feel good." Then lays her head down on the table, her black hair cascading around her face like a fan.

"She doesn't do bones." Baron explains in the silence that follows. "Or, blood."

Trix stands and moves on to the next patient, Dru, already pulling a bottle of peppermint from her bag of supplies.

That evening, Shade lies in bed, staring at the ceiling. Or rather, staring at the stars through a hole in the ceiling. Baron snores obnoxiously loud one bed over, a sound Shade has, unfortunately, grown accustomed to.

He wonders what his family is doing. He hopes they are safe. Despite his best efforts, Shade can't help wondering if Jeb really has turned dark. Jeb, his brother, his biggest fan, his closest companion for many years. Jeb, who hated the slaughter of animals for food and loathed the sight of helpless individuals in need of aid.

Jeb would hate Yagar; he would bring the gates of Windenmeyer here to provide food and shelter to every townsperson.

Or would he? Does Shade even know his brother?

Shade rolls onto his good ear, hoping to block out Baron's snoring. He hasn't been able to fully hear from his left ear since getting blown out of the tower way back at the castle. Dull pain ignites in his nose from where it touches the pillow.

He ignores it and closes his eyes.

CHAPTER 15

The next day passes in a blur of activity. Training in the morning, restocking of supplies, and interacting with the people of Yagar. The town does not have much, but they do seem to enjoy the company of each other; and they share their friendly spirits with Shade and his crew. Shade is glad to see that most of what Yagar used to be known for—deception and crime—seems to be becoming less common. He spends a majority of the afternoon helping people reboard walls in their homes and fix broken fences for their animals. He notices Vision is particularly interested in this activity.

Perez and Risa create a pulley system in which water is leveraged above ground and can be transferred from a nearby stream right to the people's front porches. Shade isn't sure how they are able to do that with the little supplies provided, but is impressed nonetheless. It's refreshing to see the twins working in a manner that does not involve Risa's mighty swing of her full-blown ax or the cutting edge of Perez's large, terrifying hatchet. Trix makes her rounds at sick or injured houses; by late afternoon, she appears rather fatigued, but doesn't show signs of slowing. Afton spends time in the blacksmith shops, helping pick out weaponry that is well-molded and trustworthy. Ryker, still recovering from his arrow injury, doesn't do much lifting but is always nearby. Shade even spots the Greens helping carry laundry to and from, with Dru, laughing everywhere she goes.

Shade thinks she has a beautiful laugh. He smiles after her when she walks past and gives him a cross-eyed face.

That afternoon, they venture further outside of the city limits. They go south, but Saipan is quick to halt them before they go more than a mile. "We should take care in how far we ride. These woods hold many secrets." He looks around, speaking softly as if the trees can understand what he's saying.

Dru explains to Shade and Erin that many people find the area between Central Zion and Southern Zion to be mysterious and strange. "Lots of superstitions are born in this area where the trees meet the sand. Old folk tales and fables of creepy desert nomads, sandstorms, and sand creatures." She shrugs, "I've never found substantial evidence to prove the stories real."

"Nay," Baron agrees. He waggles his brows, "But have you ever found proof that they *aren't*?"

At this she shakes her head, looking thoughtful.

That evening, General Saipan calls a meeting in the great bar.

"Yens are out tomorrow," He says, nodding at Hagan, "We've provided supplies enough for the next week. That is more than generous. If you care anything about them, your horses should be left here for you to retrieve on your return...if you return," He adds as an afterthought, "We've got some mighty fine steeds to send in their place."

The general talks some more about his incredible generosity, how it is second to none in most of Zion; *all* of Zion, now that he thinks about it. Shade has started to doze off when Saipan says something interesting.

"I've done some thinking, Highness. About what you said. And I agree," He nods, looking around at his soldiers, "We agree. The army that you are building is in need of an incredible leader like myself."

"Oh, boy," Baron mutters under his breath, "Here we go." He shifts in his chair and leans forward with mock interest.

The tears in General Saipan's eyes must be fake. "It would be a disservice to this great kingdom if I did not set aside my own life to serve it. So, we have decided that we will accept your offer. We will join your cause."

Shade keeps his face neutral, listening to this melodramatic speech.

"There are some towns further southwest, similar in size and demeanor to Yagar. We will seek recruits there while you journey on to Lockwood. This will not be an easy feat, as these towns and villages have not always cared for the humble town of Yagar. But we all have our crosses to bear."

Shade sits up straighter in intrigue. The general wants to recruit more; this is exactly the idea he has had in mind when wanting to build a rebel army to retake the throne—recruiting individuals who would, in turn, recruit more. General Saipan is not a lovely fellow, but he just might be an ally. Shade stands, nodding his thanks, "That would be greatly appreciated, General Saipan. You are correct, we will highly benefit from a man of your expertise. Thank you for your hospitality. I look forward to future endeavors with you and your people."

That pleases the general and the remainder of the evening is spent in joyous celebration.

"To our exceptional general!" One of the soldiers exclaim. "Such generosity!" Another adds. They've been having similar toasts all evening.

Shade finds himself at a table with Ryker and

Hagan.

"This was quite the stop, Your Highness." Ryker says, his voice low. He always sounds equally interested and bored; Shade isn't sure how one manages such a tone. "Consider me impressed. I fear we have misjudged your persuasive powers."

Hagan doesn't look impressed at all, "The kid did good," He says, "But we've hardly begun. Seek my praise when the throne is ours." He pushes back his chair and leaves the table.

"I do not seek praise. I request respect." Shade says to his back.

He stiffens; the only sign he has heard him. Then, Hagan disappears up the steps and into his room.

"Hagan has a tough outer shell," Ryker says, "He will come around."

Shade wouldn't really care either way…if it weren't for the threat of a traitor in his midst. Could it be Hagan?

Does Storg know?

That the prince approaches Lockwood? Yes.

* * * * *

After another restless night of sleep, Shade stands outside the bar with the others. He nuzzles Cracker's chin, runs a hand through her mane, and finishes with a kiss between her eyes. "Be good, girl. We will meet again." She whinnies softly in response.

The new horse General Saipan has provided is a large steed with a beautiful brown coat. His caramel-colored eyes shine in the morning light. He snorts when Shade approaches, but allows the prince onto his back. General Saipan watches him closely and grins at the horse. "Don't make it easy, aye?" He whispers to Shade's steed.

Without further ado, Shade and his team leave Yagar. General Saipan turns away with a flippant wave and begins ordering his soldiers with the day's chores. He had informed Shade he would be seeking allies within the week. Shade hopes he follows through.

It turns out they are taking Dru's route. She looks around triumphantly. "I *knew* we'd take the river. It's safer."

"We'll be in these woods for days," Baron huffs, looking to the sky in frustration.

He isn't wrong.

Despite the rocky terrain and winding of the river, they travel quickly and efficiently for the next week, only stopping to rest at night. The river is cold, frozen in some areas; but for the most part, there is a consistent flow, a constant background noise to occupy their days.

Shade's new horse doesn't like him very much. He's convinced Saipan gave him a stubborn steed on purpose. The horse does not follow directions well; and when he does, it's at his own pace. Baron thinks it's hilarious, of course. He doesn't offer to trade, though, which Shade takes to mean the horse makes Baron just as nervous.

On the second day, Fray catches something on the wind; a scent, perhaps, that he doesn't like. So, they take another detour that only prolongs their difficult journey along the River Walk. At some point, Shade finds himself traveling beside Trix. She doesn't say much, but offers him a drink from her canteen when his is empty. He nods gratefully and she grunts in return.

"Not a woman of many words, I see." Shade says, his eyes crinkling with a smile.

She doesn't return it, only shrugs. "I have nothing of value to say at the moment."

Shade decides to find someone else to ride by, which is how he ends up beside Erin for a good part of the journey and in the evenings when they stop to rest. Since their argument in the forest several days back, they have been back to their normal selves. They talk, laugh, and joke with each other. They reminisce about enjoyable times back home and about what the future may hold.

At night, they all keep the fire low, able to be doused with one stamp of the foot. Ryker informs them they are nowhere near a busy road, let alone a road at all; so, it will be highly unlikely they cross paths with anyone. Still, they are careful.

Besides, they discover that, although this is true of fellow humans, the same cannot be said for creatures of the forest. They spend hours scaring off curious squirrels trying to steal their food rations and annoying mice rummaging in their packs. On the fourth night of their tiresome journey, they hear a low growl from the trees and a lynx jumps out at them.

Perez raises his weapon to strike it down, but Vision cries out for him to halt. She jumps in front of the Blue, arms out, cooing softly at the creature. It bares its teeth, but eventually calms down enough to merely tilt its head curiously at Vision's noises and then scamper off into the night.

Shade lets out a breath he hadn't realized he'd been holding. "That was something. I've never seen a lynx."

"Beautiful creatures. Wouldn't hurt a fly." Vision rumbles as she saunters past him. He watches her pass and then turns back to meet Perez's eyes.

"That's what I was thinking when it just tried

attacking me." The Blue mutters stoically.

Shade smiles. Perez just ambles off into the trees, probably to do some more scouting. Shade shrugs. Some of these people are a mystery and he doesn't know if he will ever truly get to know them. He hopes he does; it's his preference that his rebellion be built on trust.

Conversations stay at a minimum, especially by day five when everyone is tired and restless of traveling. Shade does finally have a quality conversation with Perez at one point, in which they discuss their upbringings. Perez still doesn't say much and what he does is only spoken in short, clipped phrases. Shade is trying to get more out of the twins about where they come from; but their stories are sealed tight. Risa throws Shade a smirk after he asks too specific a question about their homeland and Perez moves to the back of the pack.

Dru has been abnormally quiet. She's caught some sort of cough and Shade occasionally sees her shivering. It is cold, but nothing like the mountain; and they're on the move so much, their bodies hardly have time to rest enough to cool. He thinks she is fighting off an illness. Back on day three, he had offered her his cloak. She smiled weakly and shook her head, telling him she already had Baron's and would be fine. He hopes this is true. Erin sticks near her, concerned for their friend.

"I don't like this," Erin says quietly to Shade at one point. "She's only getting worse. Trix doesn't have the medical supplies Dru needs. If we don't get to Lockwood soon, things could get bad."

"Should we go back?" Shade asks. But even as he says it, he knows this to be a dumb decision. Going

211

backwards would likely take longer than trudging forward. Erin just purses her lips and they continue the journey.

The River Walk was beautiful at first, but now even Shade is ready to be out, ready for new terrain. Aside from the lynx sighting, the woods have been quiet; too quiet. In some ways, he's ready for a little action. A fight. His nose is healing and the bruising has gone from black and purple, to yellow. The swelling has almost completely subsided. He's getting antsy.

As if on cue, a memory comes flooding back from one of his father's many life lessons. *Sometimes the greatest strengths take the longest to build.* He was referring to the large maple tree in the middle of the castle gardens. Its overarching branches encompassed a majority of the gardens in a comforting embrace. But the saying can be applied to this revolution as well. Building an army, gathering troops, support, and allies is going to take some time. He takes a deep breath, telling himself to have patience.

On the sixth day, a new noise greets them, louder than the flowing river. A low roar that starts out soft and then grows in level the closer they draw.

"The Falls." Baron says. "I was not in favor of this route. But, I'll admit, The Falls are beautiful. They make it worth it."

Soon, they are standing at the edge of a great cliff, watching as the river cascades off and falls far below. Mist rises from the bottom, giving the area a foggy view. The sight is beautiful, with the rising daylight, the blue water, and the greenery around them.

Dru had praised The Falls at great length the other day and Shade turns to her now, ready to jokingly chastise her for undervaluing its beauty; but she isn't looking at The Falls. She isn't looking at anything at all. Her eyes are closed, and she is forward slumped against her horse's neck.

"Dru?" He says, worried. He reaches for her hand, clasping the reins. It's ice cold. "Trix." He calls louder, "I think she's really sick." He jumps down from his steed, already shaking Dru.

Everyone stops. Trix is next to him, feeling for Dru's pulse on her wrist. She waits a moment, looking thoughtful, then looks at Shade. "Get her down. Her pulse is low."

With the help of Baron, who has quickly appeared next to him, Shade pulls Dru from her horse, laying her gently on the ground.

"She was just fine," Erin is saying, "I was talking to her."

"Has she felt sick?" Hagan asks.

"Only all week." Baron says in an irritated tone, not looking up from Dru's prone form. "You would know that if you weren't so concerned about being the leader of everything." His voice lowers to a mumble, "And you talk about *me* being arrogant."

"It's Green Ghoul." Trix says, pulling an ointment from her bag and rubbing it on Dru's neck, behind her ears, and even under her nose. "I was hoping we could fight it off without stronger medicine, but it's worse than I thought."

Shade had not missed the sharp intakes of breath at the mention of the illness. He glances around, "What's Green Ghoul?" It sounds like something befitting for the nomadic, superstitious lands of Drysdale.

"Bad." Is all Baron says.

Erin looks at Shade in worry. "Bad?"

"It's a virus found in certain types of moss; it can

213

be fatal if not treated properly. It causes chills, a fever, an achy body. Untreated, the virus can reach the heart and cause it to stop. Not contagious." Tris says all of this while working quickly. Pulling out oils and spices. "I'd say she contracted it sleeping on the ground or maybe from Yagar's beds—I don't know. I can only do so much. She needs liquids I do not have on hand."

"What's the closest big city?" Hagan asks Ryker.

"Lockwood."

Hagan shakes his head, "Still too far. What's the next closest town in general?"

Ryker looks at him grimly, "...Lockwood."

Baron looks away, spitting something in Old English. Shade thinks it's the word he'd heard Vision speak once: *Lorgada.*

"Then someone takes her and rides ahead. It'll be faster with just one horse." Fray suggests.

"How far?" Hagan asks. He's rubbing the back of his neck in deep thought.

"At least another day," Ryker says, "I will do it." He is already rearranging the pack on his horse to make room for Dru.

"You are in no shape." Trix says, not looking up from her work. The growing concern on her face does not sit well with Shade.

"My injury's over a week old—I'm fine." Ryker insists. "Hoist her up here to me. We will ride quickly."

"Your injury has weakened you. Again, without proper medical supplies, I have not been able to nurse you to full health. Your body would not be able to take the heightened, quick journey necessary for Dru's survival." Trix says, leaving no room for argument.

Dru's survival. That sets everyone on edge.

Vision rubs the neck of Shade's horse. "This guy

214

is in the best shape. He's stubborn but he's fast. Whoever goes must ride him." The horse snorts proudly, as if understanding Vision's words. "Isn't that right, Poe?" She coos at him.

Poe? The horse's name is *Poe*?

"I will go. I'm fast. I know the way." Baron states, already standing to move his supplies from his horse to Poe. Shade makes to remove his own supplies, but suddenly the horse grunts deeply and steps away, pawing angrily at the ground.

"Whoa, boy." Vision settles him.

Baron goes to trade the supplies, but, once again the horse moves. He rears back on two legs and slams the ground. The horse seems to glare at Baron with a challenge. Shade just manages to jump out of the way.

"What's wrong with him?" Baron demands, incredulous.

Vision whispers something to the horse, who whinnies softly. She looks apologetically over her shoulder, "I do not think he likes you."

"Can't imagine why." Risa says. Then she looks around in surprise, as if shocked she said that out loud.

"We're wasting time," Baron growls. He steps towards Poe. The horse bucks his head, catching Baron in the chest. Baron stumbles backwards and lands on his rump.

If the current situation was not so serious, Shade would be laughing.

"Allow me." Perez says, stepping forward. But Poe neighs, and shakes his head again.

Vision sighs, "Stubborn, alright. It seems there is only one rider this horse will allow." She looks expectantly at Shade.

"Me?" He asks, a hand to his chest. "He hates me."

"Absolutely not," Hagan is saying at the same time Ryker says, "The prince cannot go." The two of them meet eyes in agreement.

"I have to agree, sending Prince Shade is not our brightest idea." Afton says, looking a bit alarmed.

Shade understands he's Zion's future; but he had no idea they'd be so protective of him. Almost controlling, in a way. He watches Afton's face as the man glances around the group quickly. He's been acting odd lately. Distant and a little forthright when it comes to certain decisions.

Of course, Hagan is always forthright and Baron is always odd so that isn't saying much. Vision is hardy, Trix rarely speaks, Fray is constantly brooding, and the twins are mysterious and cold.

They are an intriguing bunch, to say the least.

Shade rubs Poe's neck. The horse looks over his shoulder with one eye and makes a soft noise. Well, this is unprecedented. It appears Poe has taken a liking to him after all. Shade makes his mind up, then. Dru needs urgent aid and he will stop at nothing to get it for her. "Baron is right, we are wasting time." Shade says, sure of his mission. "We will get her the help she needs; the rest of you won't be far behind."

"I will go with them." Erin says.

"You'll never keep up. Nobody will." Vision says, gazing fondly at the steed. "He's masterful. I've known horses like him before. Such heart, such talent."

"This is why she is single." Baron says dryly. The Brown either doesn't hear his quip or chooses to ignore it, because she still gazes fondly at Poe.

Shade doesn't like this. He's leaving Erin behind with a potential traitor. At the same time, if he doesn't go, Dru could die. "We will be fine." Shade assures, looking at Erin, praying his eyes pass the warning: *Be careful*. He must do this. For Dru. Erin wants to argue; but she just bites her lip and nods once. Shade doesn't wait for anyone else to disagree. He climbs Poe, who doesn't give him the slightest issue. "I assume we are done following the river." Seeing as how the river has dropped off into a lengthy waterfall.

Ryker is nodding, looking unhappy but resigned, "Follow the cliff edge. It'll eventually bring you to a road that takes you away from the cliff."

"We didn't want to take the Stallion Road. Too many potential eyes." Hagan warns, shaking his head. He clearly does not like this idea.

"It's the easiest and quickest route." Ryker says. He turns back to Shade, "The road will take you all the way to Lockwood. Try to avoid anyone you may come across, especially since you are alone."

Afton and Fray have lifted Dru from the ground and are handing her up to Shade. He grips her under the arms and places her in the saddle in front of him. He loops his arms around her and grabs the reins. Her unconscious form slumps back against his chest.

"You may run into Drake on your way, he was supposed to report back to us. But if you do, keep him with you. And, Your Highness," Ryker grips his arm firmly when Shade goes to pull away, "Be careful."

Shade nods, looking at each of them. Everyone appears solemn, unsatisfied with the turn of events. The only one not watching him is Hagan, who is quietly seething to the side.

"When you get there, ask for Blair," Trix says, "He's the best medic in the city, arguably, the kingdom."

"I thought that title went to the medics of Yagar."

217

Baron says, trying for a laugh as the general had said these exact words just days before. Nobody does. Shade has discovered that, although Baron is always in a joking mood, it grows when he's under duress. The Green's concern for Dru is making him antsy. He meets Shade's eyes and the prince thinks they look almost pleading.

"They may not be very welcoming." Hagan says, still with a tone of warning.

"Tell them you know Greaver." Afton offers. "It's where he is from." The man looks grave. Everyone is worried.

Shade nods, suddenly nervous. Dru's life is in his hands. He is venturing through unfamiliar territory with a horse who, up until this moment, he thought had it out for him. And he's doing it alone. Shade lets none of these thoughts show on his face. "Right. I'll see you in Lockwood."

Then, he lightly kicks Poe in the side and they take off into the trees.

It's the first time the steed has obeyed without complaint.

CHAPTER 16

The terrain makes it difficult to travel much faster than they were before. But Poe is able to maneuver the twists, dips, and turns of the forest with an ease Shade hadn't realized he possessed. Really, all Shade has to do is hang on for dear life. Dru is limp, and Shade holds her with one arm and uses the other to remain balanced on Poe's back.

By the time the sun is over halfway through the sky, they've already traveled a distance of at least eleven miles. The journey has grown long and monotonous; but there is little else to be done than to continue onwards. They stop briefly for Poe to drink from a nearby creek and Shade to catch his breath. But then they're on the move once more. On what Shade guesses to be about the nineteenth mile, they reach the road Ryker had mentioned.

The sun is getting low, the light starting to dim. It'll be dark soon, and Shade assumes they still have a long way to go. The road is more of a large pathway, with dirt and rocks for a surface. Poe breathes heavily, matching Shade's own breathing. He pats his neck. "Good, boy. Ready?"

He neighs. And if horses could sound happy, Shade would say Poe seems to be enjoying this.

"Hang on, Dru." Shade murmurs in her ear. She doesn't stir. He readjusts her against his chest, holding her close, and then they start off once more, this time on the Stallion Road. Shade sticks to the edge of it, in case they need to dive into the coverage of trees. They don't pass a soul for several miles and Poe hardly misses a beat. Every once in a while, a faded road sign is visible on the edge of the road. He isn't able to make out what's engraved into it until the third one.

Lockwood: 40 miles.

At least the pathway makes the journey a little easier. The scenery has started to shift from the tall, stretching trees, back to Elm trees and thick bushes. The wind is biting and cold and causes his eyes to water; he wipes them quickly and stares back at the road ahead. He leans into the warmth permeating from Dru's sick form.

Darkness has settled, only the moon lighting their way, when she wakes with a start.

She flings up a fist, which Shade manages to catch just before it plows his nose. It would have, no doubt, put a quick end to its healing. She bucks from her position on the saddle, clearly confused and startled. Poe slows to a walk and calming Dru becomes easier.

"Dru! You're okay, it's me—it's Shade!"

She stops struggling, leans her head back against his chest, and looks up at him blearily. Her eyes blink slowly, trying to process what they're seeing. "What happened? Where are we?" Her words are warbled and drowsed.

In the moonlight, he can see the flush of red on her cheeks from the fever.

"You're sick." He says, "I'm getting you to a healer." His arms tighten around her protectively.

Confusion sets in her furrowed brow, "Where's my horse? Where's…?"

He thinks she's trying to ask where everyone else is, but her scattered brain can't form the words. "Shh," he says gently, as they continue riding once more, "Rest. You're going to be fine."

She smiles dreamily, her head bouncing lightly

from their movement. "I know. I trust you. You'll take care of me." She sighs, "Baron says you don't know what you're doing. He says you'll get us killed. But I think he's just saying that—he doesn't want you to know he actually doesn't mind you."

"He punched me in the face."

"Well, yeah," she laughs deliriously, "But that's just a guy thing. Proving his dominance or something. I think he trusts you. Like me." She smiles again.

He looks back at her with concern. She is very much out of it.

"I trust you. I like you." She whispers. Then, so quickly he has no time to react, Dru tilts her head back a little more and kisses him on the mouth.

Her lips are soft and smaller than he realized. And so very warm with the fever. She stays there a moment, and he doesn't move either; because, honestly, there's something sweet about it. He doesn't want to break the moment. Her eyes close and she leans in.

Then her lips release, her head lolls down, and she's unconscious once more.

Poe never falters in his stride, just grunts in almost a teasing way.

"Ah, shut it." Shade says, shaking his head against the creep of red that has lit his cheekbones. He's reminded of Dru's red face and the heat of her lips. He frowns and wraps his arms a little tighter around her. He will not lose her. "Come on, Poe. Get her there."

Poe kicks it into another gear and they speed down the road.

After about another hour, they see their first signs of an approaching wagon. Shade whistles, low and fast. The horse turns on its heel and ducks into the coverage of the trees. They stop moving for the first

221

time in hours as they hide behind large bushes that line the road.

A caravan of three wagons approaches, lanterns dangling from the sides. There's a driver on each one, bundled with clothing to shield from the cold. Two of the wagons appear to be carrying supplies. The middle one is enclosed and Shade assumes there must be people inside. The wagons are not particularly nice looking. Still, he knows that anyone with an enclosed wagon comes from money; currency for that type of transportation doesn't grow on trees. Shade slows his breathing and rubs Poe's neck for him to do the same. They are fully hidden behind the bush. Shade peers through holes in the shrubs at the passing caravan.

He stares particularly hard at the middle wagon, seeking any signs as to where it hails from. The rims of the wheels are a faded gold, encrusted with dried mud and grass. As it passes, something flashes in the light of one of the swinging lanterns, just above the back left wheel.

Shade does a double-take. Was it…? Did he just see what he thought he saw? His eyes scan desperately again for the symbol, but the wagon is past and the shrubbery doesn't allow for him to see much further. After a minute, the sounds of the caravan fade away and they are alone once more.

Had he imagined the symbol? It seemed engraved into the wood, but it could have just as easily been a dent or scratch in the wood from years of wear and tear. If Shade had seen what he thought he had, then that caravan might have been a potential ally. Because what he thinks he saw is a symbol of three connecting circles, all overlapping at one point.

There isn't time to dwell further on this. He steers

Poe back to the road and they continue riding.

They haven't gone another mile, though, when they have to take cover again. This time, it's just a lone rider on a horse. Shade watches as he draws closer. When he's certain of the rider, he returns to the road. The other rider slows, but seeing who it is, finishes the last several strides and stops next to Shade.

"Prince?" Drake asks in surprise, his eyes searching the woods for the others.

Shade explains the situation quickly. "They wanted you to continue with me; but I do not think that is best."

Drake hesitates. His breathing is shallow and he appears pale. Shade wonders if he is feeling ill. "Shade, I will not leave you to finish this journey alone. I am coming with you."

Shade shakes his head. "Truthfully, I have something else I'd like you to do." He explains the caravan he had passed earlier and his curiosity about the symbol he thinks he recognized.

Drake appears thoughtful, "Gold rims, you say?"

"Faded. But, gold, yes. Royalty of some sort?"

He smiles without humor, "Typically, not around here. Royalty is reserved for castles and kings. But Lockwood does have several prestigious families—dukes, duchesses, and such. They could have come from there. Why they are traveling at night is very curious. And you're sure it was the Loyalty Mark?"

Shade pauses, reluctantly shakes his head. "I am only certain of what I *think* I saw."

Poe shifts uncomfortably, eager to be back on mission. Shade knows his time is short, he must get Dru to the healer. "It is enough for me to ask this of you."

Drake nods, "Then that is enough for me. I will find

this caravan and report back to you in Lockwood. The plan was to be there several days, weeks even. I will find you." He looks at Dru, "Get her aid. Zion be with you." He places a fist over his chest and bows his head.

"And you." Shade says, before they part ways on their separate missions.

* * * * *

An hour later, Shade starts to see some activity ahead. Several road signs the past several miles have indicated various towns here and there with separate roads forking off in different directions. The most recent sign tells him he has reached the outskirts of Lockwood. Up ahead appears to be a checkpoint with two towers lining either side of the road and a gate stretching between the two.

Shade lifts the hood of his cloak over his head, shielding a clear view of his face. Then, he draws up in front of the gate. The towers on either side of the road are beautiful and sturdy with gray cobblestoned structures. Shade peers at the one on the left and yells, "We seek aid from the healer—Blair!"

A hatch opens at its top and the armored head of a guard pokes out. "State your business!"

Shade opens his mouth, confused. Had he not just stated his business? He doesn't have time for this. "I need Blair. For healing."

"Rocky," A voice from the other side of the gate calls up towards the tower. It comes from a man standing on the ground; he isn't wearing his helmet, but is still dressed in armor and a cloak. "Just get down here." Then, the man looks at Shade, his eyes shadowed, avoiding the blinking lights of the torches lining the gate. "You seek our finest medic. Must be important."

224

Shade swallows, praying these guards can see reason. "My friend is very sick. We've journeyed far."

The guard eyes him warily, still hidden from distinct view. His voice is low, husky. "A desperate, midnight ride. Who sent you?"

"That's a conversation for the morning. Please, she doesn't have much time." Dru stirs in his arms, emitting a quiet moan that makes Shade's heart constrict. The girl doesn't have long.

Still, the guard isn't convinced; standing casually, unconcerned. Several other guards join him. The one called Rocky, as well.

"You understand our hesitation." The first guard, the one who appears to be in charge, says. "Can't be too careful. There are less than savory individuals out there these days. And we've got a fine city with fine people to protect."

Shade is growing impatient. Poe, too, for he huffs angrily and paws the ground. "I admonish you for your loyalty. The city is blessed to have you as one of her protectors."

The guard laughs. "Here that, fellas? He *admonishes* me. We are a *blessing*." The laughter of the other guards' sounds.

First, the Greens. Now the guards of Lockwood. Shade is getting very tired of arrogant blighters. "Sir, my friend is very sick—"

"Who sent you?" The guard asks again, all traces of laughter gone. He's moved closer to the gate, eyeing Shade seriously. He is still concealed in shadow, but Shade notes how the man inclines his head, as if getting a better look at him and Dru with one eye.

Here goes everything, Shade thinks. "A man named Greaver."

The guards had been shuffling and conversing in small tones, but everyone stops with a sudden silence that does not go unnoticed with Shade. So, they *do* know him.

The first guard steps even closer to the gate, his face mere inches from one of its bars. Shade finally has a clear view of the mysterious guard. A kind face, but a current hardened expression. One eyes clear, the other clouded.

He's blind in one eye, Shade realizes.

"What did you just say?" The man says quietly.

"He said Greaver," Another guard says in shock. "But I thought he was dead—"

The first guard, with one good eye, hushes him with a fist held high. He glares at Shade. Then says, "Why won't you show us your face?"

Shade is done answering questions. He's been waiting outside this gate long enough and is starting to feel uncomfortable, being in the wide open. "I request privacy for the time being. You can ask all the questions and receive most of the answers after my friend has been taken care of."

The guard considers this, a far off look in his eyes. "That name has not been spoken here in a long time. Mighty brave of you to show up now and speak it so flippantly."

Have they believed Greaver to be dead? Did Greaver leave the city on good or bad terms? Shade is starting to think mentioning his old stable hand was not the best idea, when the first guard makes a motion towards one of the towers.

The gate starts to slide, splitting open at its middle. The guards do not move from their positions, but a new guard leads two horses into the road.

The first guard takes the reins of ones, still watching Shade. "We will take you to Blair. But then you will have a lot to answer for. Starting with why you ride a steed of Yagar." At Shade's look of surprise, he says, "I'd recognize a saddle of Saipan's from anywhere. Dingy, excessive." He swiftly mounts his horse, along with another guard beside him. "Follow me, stranger."

Shade nods his thanks and follows after them, ignoring the stares of the other guards as they pass. He hears the gate shut behind him. "Almost there. Just hang on." He whispers against Dru's hair.

She doesn't respond.

They pass quaint houses and a few storefronts. Dirt streets branch off left and right, with more buildings lining their sides. As they draw closer to the heart of the city, the streets turn to cobblestone and the buildings become more elaborate and closer together. Most look dark, asleep for the evening; but some have lanterns out front or the warm glow of lights and fires behind the windows. He sees guards posted at various stations; they turn to watch Shade's interesting entrance. They rise over a hill. A hundred yards ahead, past numerous houses and stores, sitting atop an elevated hill, is the nicest house he has seen within the city so far. Clearly an estate of someone wealthy and renowned. He spots a few of these prestigious buildings as they travel further into the city

It takes several minutes, but they eventually draw up in front of a nice establishment; bigger than some homes, but not near as big as the houses on the hills. It's an off gray color stone with brown wooden window shades. The windows themselves are lit by the glows of candles.

Shade slides off the horse, pulling Dru with him. He knew she was small, but now, in her weakness, she seems so much smaller; her form fits evenly in his arms as he tucks her close to his chest and follows the guards to the door.

It opens before the first knock. A man stands there, with glasses and warm eyes behind them. His hair is black, peppered with white and gray and tied behind his head with a ribbon of sorts. He isn't very tall, but his shoulders are set in a way that signifies a man well-respected. Shade imagines he was probably in very good shape back in his day. His eyes take in the situation quickly. "Take her to the back. Let me get my things."

The first guard leads the way, beckoning Shade to follow. The second guard lets him pass, then closes the door, staying outside to watch the horses.

The house is open as they step into a large foyer with a high ceiling. To the right is another room, perhaps a kitchen. To the left is a large living area with various furniture and a fireplace, currently dark. A staircase leads up, curving out of sight.

The healer, Blair, disappears into the kitchen as the guard leads Shade to the right of the stairs and down a hallway that takes them further back into the house. It's some sort of medical wing with empty rooms branching off here and there. They go to the furthest room, just before a closed door that must be a back door exit. The guard lights a lantern in the hallway and takes it into the room.

Here, he lights several more, lighting up the room.

It's small, with just one twin bed and two chairs. But it is welcoming and homey. Shade steps to the bed and carefully lays Dru down. He tries brushing the hair

228

away from her forehead, but it sticks to her sweat. She murmurs something softly in her sleep.

Shade rights himself and turns to the guard.

He has a sword pointed two inches from Shade's chest. "Who are you? How do you know Greaver?" His sword-arm is steady and his eyes are narrowed.

Shade doesn't back down, just stands there glaring. He hopes his hood is still doing a good job of hiding his identity. "Who is he to you?"

"You are not in a position to be the one asking questions. How do you know Greaver?"

"Would you believe me if I told you?" Shade's arms are at his side, but his palms are open in a show of good-will. He means this guard no harm, but will do anything he must to ensure Dru's safety.

The guard doesn't respond. At first, Shade had thought him older; maybe 50s. But in the light, he can see the guard is younger; perhaps in his late 30s. He has dirty blonde hair and that one eye that is glossier than the other. Shade wonders if being half-blind prohibits the guard from succeeding in his duty.

"Why did Greaver leave Lockwood?" Shade asks.

The guard is perturbed that he is not receiving answers. His hand with the sword does not waver. "It was not of his own decision. He was... *asked* to leave. By his brother, a Duke of Lockwood."

"So, he is not well-liked then?"

"Quite the contrary. He is loved, admired. Many believe him to be dead. He left years ago and no one has heard from him since. Duke Harvard Estes is a great leader, but Greaver was exceptional."

"What happened?"

"Greaver is younger, not supposed to be the outright leader. But he was always better loved and

229

respected than Harvard. As brothers do, they fought over this often. Eventually, it did not end well." He steps closer, bringing the tip of the sword higher to Shade's neck. "Your turn. I have sources who once told me Greaver had found a way to Windenmeyer. Was working within the castle walls, even. Reliable sources, stranger. I ask you again—who are you?"

Shade's fingers twitch to disarm the guard; he could do it easily. The guard wouldn't have time to do anything but gawk. But what would that prove? His skill with a weapon? Hardly important right now. Where is that healer anyway? He looks past the guard, hoping to see Blair coming. Dru cannot wait for aid much longer.

"Answer, *stranger*. Your final moment is fast approaching."

Shade makes a decision then. For Dru. For the kingdom. The guard is bound to discover his true identity at some point. If Shade learns he cannot be trusted, he will handle it swiftly and then deal with the healer as needed.

Slowly, he reaches up to his hood.

"Tyson, you know my rule. No weapons in the house." Blair is standing in the doorway, holding a tray with various medicine bottles and supplies.

The guard, Tyson, grits his teeth but lowers the weapon. "Show your face. I don't have time for this."

"That is no way to treat a guest. And a royal one at that." Blair says, stepping around them and sitting in one of the chairs, his back to the two men. He sits the tray on the bedside table.

Shade's gaze flicks to Blair once, then back to the guard. Tyson's eyes now scrutinize him in a new light. "With *that* cloak? No way he's royal."

"Surely you recognize Greaver's old cloak?"

Tyson looks again, mouth growing slack. "It is, isn't it? He always used the same fabricator. Cherish—no one else likes her sewing."

"And, your sources are correct. Greaver does work on the castle grounds. Or, at least, he did as of a month ago. A stable hand." Blair continues as he begins checking Dru's vitals.

Shade blinks, stuck between feeling anger towards Blair at exposing his secrets and being grateful he is helping Dru.

"That would mean," Tyson stares at Shade. In awe, he sits down hard in the other chair by the door.

Shade drops the hood. "Greaver is my stable hand. Was." He swallows, "He is the reason I am alive and here today. He helped me escape Glimmer after my father's murder and my brother took the throne. I owe him my life."

Tyson sighs, shaking his head. "Never in my life. That messenger informed me you would be arriving. I thought he was drunk off his rocker." Then, just as quickly as it had appeared, his surprise drops, replaced by embarrassed horror. He drops from the chair to one knee, looking a bit awkward, "Deepest apologies, my lord. I had no idea."

Shade tries to hide his own embarrassment, "I will have none of that. The love and loyalty you have shown me for your city is honor enough." He turns away to Blair, who has bowed low in his chair. "Sir, will she be okay?"

Blair leans back in his chair, finally looking Shade in the eye. A tiny smile plays at the corner of his lips. "We have waited a long time for this, Prince Shade. It is not our intention to embarrass you. You are lucky to have happened across the Western Gate of Lockwood. Others are not as loyal as Tyson and his cohort." He lifts the sleeve of his right arm, revealing the familiar tattoo.

Tyson does the same. He then stands to his feet, sheathing his sword. "I can't believe I almost stabbed the future king of Zion. You came through Yagar?"

"General Saipan allowed us a couple days' rest. Nice fellow, the general."

"I assume that's sarcasm. I've never known a person to particularly enjoy the general's presence."

"Your friend will be fine." Blair says, "You got here just in time. She is very sick. But with my medications and a few days' rest, she will be as new. Tyson, show the prince to another room where he can get clean. Find another change of clothes. It will be morning soon and he will need his rest. I have a feeling tomorrow will be rather interesting." Blair says all this and then turns back to his work, dismissing them with a wave.

Shade looks at Dru one last time. She looks serene, lying there with her dark hair against the white of the pillow, framing her face, glistening with fever sweat. He leans down and kisses her forehead once. He lightly touches the healer's shoulder in thanks, then follows Tyson from the room.

"I have more coming," Shade says after Tyson directs him to a room two doors up the hall. He stands in the room and takes different items of clothing as Tyson finds them in drawers and closets. "They are at least a day behind. Nine of them."

Tyson locates a fresh pair of boots, the last item of his search, and stands, nodding, "They will arrive at the Western Gate, too?"

"Yes. You're sure your men are trustworthy?"

"It is not my men you need to worry about," He assures, "There aren't many here who are disloyal to the throne, and those that are hide it very well. We have our suspicions; we watch them very closely. There has been recent strange activity with our trade posts, but nothing substantial we can get a jump on. For now, I think it best we try to keep your identity a secret. There are not many who know what you look like. But the leaders of this city get enough frequent mailing to recognize your face if they saw it. And it is a guardsman's duty to know those he vows to protect. You are one of them, my prince."

"Thank you for your service. I do not plan on leaving this house. At least, not until my entourage arrives."

Tyson nods, "Bathing's the last room at the end of the hall. Water should be warm if the pipes aren't frozen."

There's a loud banging on the front door.

Shade quickly draws the sword at his hip, as Tyson does the same, holding one finger to his lips. He enters the hallway and makes his way back towards the front of the house. Shade follows.

The banging sounds again and then, "Eh, Tyson, little help? This horse won't move!"

It's the other guard.

Tyson chuckles, relief flooding his features. They sheath their swords and Tyson opens the door. The other guard is standing there holding Poe's reins taut. The horse has *sat down* on his hind end, immovable.

"Are you seeing this?" The guard asks incredulously. He spares Shade a glance, "Your horse is—" He cuts off, looking back at Shade. "Why, you're—it's—" He looks back and forth between Tyson and Shade, sputtering.

"Close your trap, Marv," Tyson says, "This needs to be kept under the radar for now. Can you manage that or will I have to send you back to latrine duty again for a week?"

Marv closes his mouth. "No, sir, trap officially shut. I'm just surprised, that's all." He dips his head, and clears his throat, then quietly murmurs, "Pleasure to meet you, my lord."

"Lord" is a new one Shade supposes will take some getting used to. He smiles at the guard, then at Poe. "He doesn't listen well. Are there safe stables nearby where he can rest?"

"Blair has a few stalls of his own in his barn a couple doors down. Well hidden, well-protected." Tyson answers.

Shade pulls his hood up and steps into the street. He touches Poe's nose. "Let this nice guard take you to the stables." Poe whinnies in protest.

"Got a mouth, this one." Marv says.

Shade grabs either side of Poe's face, looking him in the eyes. This horse is ridiculous. It's like he's human. "Poe." Poe snorts and pulls away. But in the next moment he stands and steps towards Marv, who takes an involuntary step backwards.

Marv looks at Shade, unsure, "Will he bite?"

"No." Shade has no idea, but he pats Poe's side and watches as Marv leads him away to the stables.

"I must return to the Western Gate; but I won't be gone long. Myself and Marv will remain with you and the girl. We don't want to draw too much suspicion with heavy traffic coming in and out of Blair's place. Blair knows how to handle himself and those in his care. You are in good hands."

"Thank you, Tyson." And Shade means it.

CHAPTER 17

Shade's shower is cold, but it doesn't matter; it gets the job done. He is clean and has on a fresh pair of underwear. There is little more he could ask for. What's more, Blair's place has indoor plumbing using an underground pipe-system he's certain the twins could create if given the time and necessary materials.

For about an hour, he tries to sleep, but to no avail. So, he sits thinking in the chair beside Dru's bed. He wonders where the others are and when they will arrive. He marvels at his luck; getting to Lockwood in record time and arriving at the safest gate possible. He longs for Dru to open her eyes and tell him she's okay.

Shade sighs and leans closer to the bed, feeling Dru's forehead. Her fever has broken in the time Blair has seen her and she is feeling a little cooler to the touch. Her cheeks are not as rosy and her breathing not as rapid. Every once in a while, her eyes move quickly behind her eyelids and he thinks she must be dreaming.

Shade's younger sister, Amberle, used to have fever dreams; night terrors of screaming and flailing. She would think the dream world to be real and wake up in horror, eyes wild and unseeing. She was really young then, maybe four or five. Amberle hadn't had a fever dream for years, that Shade knew of. But he wonders if she's had any since he left; the events of the past few weeks have weighed on him. He wonders if it's weighing on her.

Their father is dead, of course it's weighing on her.

He puts his head in his hands and sighs. He doesn't know how long he stays that way. Long enough for morning light to peek through the drawn curtains of the lone window in the room. Long enough for the fire from the living room to seep its warmth down the hallway and into their room.

Tyson returns with Marv. They make their presence known but give Shade his space. He can hear them conversing in hushed tones in the living room. Blair has been to the room a few times to check on Dru; but also, to offer Shade a blanket and a warm cup of herbal tea, which he gratefully accepts. He still isn't hungry, so the bowl of oatmeal sits uneaten on the bedside table in the room. He wonders where the others are and figures they can't be too far. He hopes Erin is doing well. Then, because thinking of Erin makes him think of her beauty and her smile and her soft-looking lips, he then recalls the kiss he shared with Dru on the road. Which only further adds to the confusing mess of emotions inside his head.

Sometime after midmorning, they have a visitor to the house. Shade remains in the room, but stands close to the hall and listens carefully. It's the family member of a recent patient who, by the sound of things, is not doing well. Shade is unable to hear Blair's response, but quickly returns to his seat when the door closes and footsteps start towards the room.

Blair appears in the doorway, "I've got to see to this man. He's one of my regulars. Epileptic. I'll be doing a home visit. My assistant, Liv, will be coming in shortly. She can be trusted not to say anything," He looks away, smiling as if something has struck him funny. "If anyone else stops by, let Liv handle it."

Shade nods.

An hour later, a skinny woman with dark hair and thin lips walks into the room. She bows her head at Shade, checks Dru's vitals, and makes to leave again.

"Blair says your name is Liv?" Shade says, "Thank you for your help."

She smiles without her teeth and nods. She is pretty; probably in her thirties. Her arms are small, but strong, the muscles clearly defined. Liv points at the rags on Dru's forehead and arms.

Shade looks between them and Liv, "Um, they are old. She could use fresh ones." He's unsure of what Liv wants. Why doesn't she just tell him?

And then when Liv lifts her hands and begins motioning, it dawns on him. Blair's confusing laugh at the mention of Liv's trustworthiness suddenly makes sense.

Liv is deaf. She's signing to him.

Shade looks down, embarrassed. He shakes his head and uses great enunciation as he says, "I don't know. I'm sorry."

Liv's smile widens and this time, Shade does see her teeth, white and perfectly straight. She makes a fist and rotates it clockwise on her chest. She points at Shade and then does the motion again. "Sorry." She speaks, her voice coming out low and strange.

Shade understands. She is teaching him how to apologize in sign language. He copies the motion. "I'm sorry." He repeats.

She brings her index and middle finger to meet with her thumb, then brings together both hands to rotate the knuckles of her index and middle finger together once mouthing 'No problem.'

"No problem." Shades says, mimicking the motion.

Liv smiles, then garbles out, "New. Rags." She leaves the room then.

Shade stands there, staring at the doorway. He

makes a vow to himself to learn sign language. He wants to be versatile, to reach the needs of his people. How can he do that if he cannot communicate with them? Father always did say learning the languages of their ancestors was important. Shade agrees, but that includes the language of those nonverbal.

By late afternoon, Shade is getting worried. Blair has returned and checked in on Dru a couple of times, so he is not concerned about her health. Blair assures she will wake soon and continue growing in strength. Shade's worry is for his party. He's heard nothing of their arrival. Tyson was imperative that Shade would be the first to know and that Erin and the others would be brought directly to him.

Where are they? Has something happened? Shade closes his eyes, thinking about the potential traitor among them. He worries for Erin. He should have never left her there with people they've known for only a month.

He paces back and forth in the small room, hand rubbing the back of his neck. The boards creak softly underfoot. He's uncertain how long he does this, but after a while a voice speaks.

"Your pacing could wake the dead." Dru says drily, her voice a rasp.

Shade starts, and hurries to her side. He sits in the chair near her head. Breathing an air of relief, he takes her hand. "You're awake."

Her dark hair is unkempt, but the smile on her face is radiant. "You were making quite a ruckus." She rolls her eyes, but they're light like her smile. She takes in his face, his clothes, and then their surroundings, "What'd I miss?"

He snorts. "Plenty. I'll fill you in on everything.

First, how are you feeling? I can get the healer if needed."

She waves her free hand, "No, I'm fine. Got a pounding headache but I'll manage." She starts to sit up.

Shade grips her firmly and gently pushes her back down. "Dru, not yet. You're still unwell."

But Dru ignores him. "Didn't stop you." She's referring to when he woke up in Frostfire after the wolf attack. "Where is everyone? How long have I been unconscious?"

Shade quits trying to stop her and helps her into a sitting position. He places the pillow behind her back so she's leaning against it on the wall.

"Where are we?" Her eyes scan the room. She finally looks back at him. "What's going on?" Her eyes take in the room and Shade's clean clothing.

She stops talking long enough for Shade to explain everything, from the moment she passed out to their current situation at Blair's home. He even shares with her his encounter with Drake and how he sent him after the caravan of curious wagons.

"So, it's just you and me? Alone? In a massive city of strangers, any of which could be disloyal to you and your cause?" Dru sighs, "Things have been better."

Shade smiles ruefully, "But, things *could* have been much worse. I'm glad you're okay."

Dru looks at him, her blue eyes bright. "Thanks for saving me." Her lips turn up into a tiny smile and she watches him closely. She has delicate features; soft curving eyebrows and lips, perfectly angled cheekbones and a smooth chin. She and Erin both share in their beauty; but beyond that, they are vastly different. Where Dru is all graceful, Erin is cut, sculpted.

He catches himself staring and looks down, "Well, I couldn't have done it without—"

"Ah, yes, Poe. I thought he hated you."

"As did I. But he's an incredible creature." Shade thinks fondly of the horse. He hopes he's being well taken care of in the stables. Blair seems like a man of his word; Shade trusts him to have quality stables and stable hands to look after Poe.

Dru considers something, her head tilting to the side. "I think I remember…" Her eyes meet his and then she looks away as if embarrassed, "Something. It's all very fuzzy."

Shade thinks he knows what she's referring to. The moment she leaned up and kissed him. The moment he kissed her back. He opens his mouth, "Dru—"

The front door opens loudly and heavy footsteps pound down the hall. Shade stands and positions himself in front of Dru, his hand on the hilt of his sword, ready to swing if needed. It's Marv and he's breathing quickly, "Some people were just arriving at the Western Gate when Tyson sent me to find you. It could be your group."

Shade nods, relaxing a fraction to turn to Dru, words forming.

"I'm coming." She says immediately.

But this is one battle Shade is not losing. "No, stay here. Your weapons are in the closet behind me should you need them."

"She won't." Blair says from beside Marv. "Need them, I mean. But I understand the caution. She is in safe hands."

Shade picks up Dru's hand and kisses it lightly. "I'll be right back."

There's a fire in her eyes; she's not used to being the one rendered incapable. "I'll be fine." Is all she says. Stubborn as a mule. He's reminded that although grace incorporates her every feature, Dru is anything but soft.

Shade hurries after Marv. Outside, the guard has already got two horses ready. Poe whinnies when he sees Shade. Shade lifts the hood over his face. "Good boy," He whispers as he hops on Poe's back. Poe snorts in return, seemingly perturbed that Shade abandoned him for so long. The prince kicks lightly and they trot after Marv.

This is the first time Shade's truly seen Lockwood in the daylight, but he hardly notices much past the questions in his head. They pass several people along the way, who stop to stare after the guard and his mysterious partner.

The ride seems much longer in the day than it had the night before but eventually they arrive at the gate. Tyson and a few other guards stand at its entrance, the gates tightly closed, much like they did when greeting Shade and Dru. Shade looks past them and through the gate as they pull up alongside the other guards.

Relief floods him as he sees a familiar bald head with a spider web tattoo. "It's them." He says clearly. But then as he looks closer, he realizes some are missing. Shade jumps down from the horse, as Tyson gives the signal to open the gate. He watches, troubled, as only four horses and their riders enter.

Afton, looking grim. Fray, unsmiling. Ryker, one arm in a sling. And Risa, her eyes flitting around at their surroundings, as alert as always. They all look bedraggled and tired. Afton nurses a new shoulder wound and Risa has a cut on her forehead.

"What happened? Where are the others?" Shade demands.

"You are unhurt, Your—you kind sir?" Ryker asks, realizing almost too late to hide the formality.

"They know," Shade says quickly, "They are trustworthy." He meets eyes with Tyson, who gives a proud nod. "Ryker, what happened? Are the others—?"

"Dead?" Fray asks. He huffs, spitting red-ringed saliva to the side. "We don't know. We were separated." He glances warily around the entrance to Lockwood, sweat gleaming off the spider web tattoo.

"Attacked on the road," Ryker explains, he still glances uneasily at the guards, "Is there somewhere safe, more private, we can go?" He lets out a deep breath, grimacing.

They draw a lot more attention on their way back to Blair's. So much so, that Tyson begins sending some men off to keep the streets empty and quiet any rumors. When they arrive at the healer's, he's waiting just outside the door. Several townspeople have made their way to his doorstep.

Blair addresses Tyson when they arrive. "Duke Harvard has, no doubt, been informed of our visitors. He will likely be by tomorrow if not sooner. Can you pay him a visit, make him aware of the situation?"

Without a word, Tyson sends two other guards to gallop further into the city.

"What will the duke do?" Shade asks, jumping down and allowing another guard to lead Poe away. The others do the same, following Shade's lead and trusting his discretion.

"Duke Harvard is a good man, but he doesn't like secrets. I am almost certain he can be trusted but the more time we have to avoid him, the better. Simply because he is well-known and it is difficult to remain hidden in the care of such a distinguished individual. It's hard enough keeping you concealed here, as it is." Blair explains, beckoning for them to follow him inside.

"*Almost* certain you can trust him?" Ryker asks grimly.

Blair doesn't respond right away. Then, "He wants people to like him. In the past, that has blurred his vision of right and wrong."

Shade wonders if he could be referring to the decision to ostracize Greaver from the city. He hopes Harvard can be a powerful ally.

Inside, Liv waits patiently near the staircase. She bows her head when they enter. Dru has been moved from the back room to the living room where there is more seating and space for everyone to be. She smiles widely, until realizing Afton is the last one in and there are no more to follow. She looks between the four of them, a question in her eyes.

"What happened?" Shade demands, taking a standing position near the fireplace. Everyone has hardly gotten settled, but Shade jumps right to the point. He is going out of his mind with worry. Where are the others?

"We were about thirty miles out when they attacked." Fray begins.

"Who?" Shade asks.

"Renegades? Bandits? We don't know. It was still dark out." Ryker says, "There were far more of them than us so we split for a greater chance of survival. Us four took to the trees one direction, I didn't see where the others went. When we felt we had lost our

244

attackers, we made our way back to the road and continued on."

Shade's eyes drop to the floor, as he fights for a calm demeanor. "Was anyone hurt that you know of?" Clearly, Shade means more than the obvious wounds they've received. He means something tragic.

Ryker looks at the others in question.

After a moment, Afton clears his throat. "Vision took a hit. Fell off her horse. I didn't see her get back up." He's looking at the floor, fatigue written on his features.

"She did get back up." Fray says, "With great difficulty, I might add. Perez helped her. That's the last thing I saw before the woods. It was dark."

Risa is quiet, watching the exchange. Again, Shade wishes he could see inside that head. For nothing more than to know the secrets of this intriguing woman. He gets the feeling she and her brother would be great allies, and not just because of their incredible skills in combat.

"Where did they come from? Was no one watching?" Dru asks from her position on the couch.

"Of course, we were watching," Ryker says softly. He sighs, rubbing a hand across his face. "Whoever this was had more training than most enemies we come across."

"Which is why I don't think it was bandits or Renegades," Fray says. "These people knew what they were doing. They were trained."

"Did you get a good look at any of them?" Shade asks. "Their horses? Their clothing? Anything?"

"That's just it. They weren't on horses," Ryker says. "They came from the trees."

"The trees, you say?" Tyson speaks up from the

245

doorway. He pushes himself off the wall and joins the conversation with a look of intensity.

Shade turns, noting the guard's intent interest at the mention of trees. "Have you heard of something like this?" He asks.

Tyson is nodding and Blair says, "These tree attacks have started happening as of late. I treat injuries from them once or twice a week. We don't know who's doing it but Duke Harvard has some of his men looking into it."

Shade rests his hands on the back of a chair to stop them from shaking. "The others are still out there. They would know to come here but they may not be arriving at the Western Gate. Tyson, can you do anything about this?"

Tyson is already heading out the door. "I will handle it, my lord."

There's several seconds of quiet, the events of the past several hours catching up to them. Then, Dru gives Shade a look, mouthing a teasing, 'My lord?'

He sighs, rubbing his forehead, "Tyson and his men are loyal to the throne. Other guards may not be. He will try to intercept any of our people who may arrive at a different gate." He looks at Ryker's arm, Risa's forehead, and each of their fatigued stances. "Blair, can we get them cleaned and comfortable?"

Blair turns to Liv. With his left hand makes a 'thumbs-up' and places it on the open palm of his right hand. Then he moves both hands in an outward arc towards Shade and his friends. "Help them." He says. He returns his attention to Shade's crew, "There is a shower at the back and plenty of fresh clothing. I will get a pot of stew going. If you are in need of stitching, there isn't a surer hand than Liv's in all the land. I'll be

246

back out to check on you soon, keep resting." He says the last part to Dru who waves a hand almost dismissively, not looking at the healer.

While Liv takes a look at Ryker's arm and Afton's shoulder, Fray goes in search of the bathing room. Risa walks up to Shade. "A word?" She says quietly.

He meets her eyes and something in them tells him it can't wait. He glances at Dru who gives a subtle nod. "I'll show you the fresh clothing." He says. Shade starts down the hallway and leads Risa into one of the side rooms. He begins digging in the chest of drawers.

"Prince," She whispers, in a tone that makes him stop digging. He had found the clothes anyway; they were waiting right on top. But he'd wanted to give off the impression of a search, in case any curious eyes had followed their departure from the living room. It is clear Risa has something important to tell him.

He faces her; she's closed the door slightly, leaving it barely ajar. "What is it?" Shade has yet to see Risa look uncertain; but in this moment, there's a confusion in her eyes that gives him an uneasy feeling. "Risa." He says quietly.

"They attacked us from above," She begins. "Dropping from the trees, like Ryker said. Surrounding us on the road so quickly, we hardly knew it. It was dark, it was difficult to see. Everything was chaos, people shouting, horses running, weapons drawing. I could be wrong." She sounds like she's trying to convince herself more than anything. Her eyes are downcast, making her seem small, even though her 6'2 frame, the same height as Shade, is anything but.

"Risa, what did you see?" He says in a tone he hopes sounds comforting.

"I was at the back of the group. Vision was on the

247

outside to my left. She was hit. Struck down with a sword." Risa explains. She meets his gaze, taking a deep breath, "But it did not come from the trees."

Shade grows tense, his fists clenched, whispers of a traitor playing through his mind. "What did you see?" He repeats in a low voice.

Risa swallows, then sets her gaze on his, as if determining what she saw as truth. "It came from behind her. It came from Afton."

CHAPTER 18

Shade sits in the living room, staring at Afton. Night has fallen and the man is asleep, sprawled out on the couch without a care in the world. Shade's fists clench and unclench as he works over in his mind their next move.

After her confession of what she saw, Shade warned Risa to keep it quiet, tell no one else. If Afton was a traitor, they would catch him in the act; he would slip up again at some point, in the daylight, where everyone could see. And Shade would be there to catch him. He doesn't trust the man after what Risa has said; plus, Shade recalls the man saying, 'I don't sleep,' back in the woods before Yagar. Yet, here he snores.

There's another part of Shade that questions Risa's story. She could be lying, saying it was Afton to throw Shade off her own traitorous scent. But if Risa were a traitor, wouldn't Perez be as well? Fray had said he saw Perez *help* Vision after she fell. Why would Perez help someone he was betraying?

Unless Fray is the one who lied.

Shade drops his head into his hands. He's got to stop this, stop placing the blame on others. The more he asks these questions, the less he trusts any of them. All he can do right now is continue watching their back, like he was doing before, and hope the others arrive. Perhaps, Vision will be able to shed more light on the situation, assuming her injury isn't fatal.

"When's the last time you slept?" Dru asks. She's standing near the entrance to the hallway, having come from the back bedroom. One hand is leaned against the wall, holding a lot of her weight. She is still very weak.

He looks up, hair unkempt and eyes heavy. *Next to Erin*, he thinks to himself. In the woods next to Erin holding her hand. That is the last time he feels he truly rested. He sighs. "I can't sleep. Not until they are safely here." And not until he knows Afton will not try to hurt any of them. Shade looks back at the sleeping man, snoring softly. It'd be relatively easy to end this right now, it wouldn't take much. Shade blinks, horrified with himself at the dark thought of killing someone being an easy action.

Dru wraps the blanket tighter around her shoulders. "You're no good to them like this…a walking zombie. They will find their way to us. Come get some rest." Without another word, she turns and heads back to her room, expecting him to follow.

Shade stands. Risa appears, having snuck down from her room upstairs. She is showered and cleanly dressed. Her dark hair has been re-braided, two braids starting from the crown of her head and trailing down her back. Her eyes have returned to their sharp fervor. She is donned with her weapons. "I will be awake." She says.

Shade knows this means she will keep watch over Afton. Her vivid eyes train on the older man with distaste. He nods his thanks and steps down the hallway. But once in the room he's claimed as his own, he doesn't feel comfortable. So, he picks up the pillow and blanket and walks down to the last room on the left.

Dru's room.

She has already tucked herself under the covers. Her eyes open when he enters, but she says nothing; only smiles when he drops the pillow next to her bed and lies down on the floor.

Shade throws the blanket over top of him and stares at the ceiling, one hand resting on his chest.

"I could scoot over, you know." Dru says.

"Two of us in a twin bed? You know my legs drape off the end, right?" But as he says it, he knows they would fit. Dru is small enough she'd easily fit in the crook of his arm, against the curve of his torso...

He shakes the thought from his mind. What is he doing? He has no time for these kinds of thoughts. Sure, maybe once he's reclaimed the throne and the Renegade threats have been extinguished. But until then, the kingdom requires his utmost attention.

"Suit yourself," Dru says, sounding unbothered. "Enjoy the hard, dusty floor."

"I've slept in worse conditions."

"You? A prince of Zion? I don't believe it."

He smiles in the darkness at her playful banter. "Need I remind you of the past few weeks of my life? And yours, in fact."

"Ah, yes. Well, I'm talking even before we met. My father was always traveling and I would go with him. There aren't many places in Zion I haven't been to." She pauses, "Save Lockwood and a few others. This is new territory." There is silence for a few beats. Then she speaks again. "Do you think the others are okay?"

Shade takes a breath. He sits up, moves to the door, and closes it. When he turns around, he sees Dru's form has sat up in bed.

"What's wrong? What do you know?" She whispers.

He can't see her face but knows it must be intently looking at him in the darkness. He sits on the edge of her bed and tells her about his conversion with Risa.

251

"You're sure Afton can't be trusted?" Dru asks once he's finished.

"Risa is, at least." Shade says. "She seems pretty confident in what she saw. If she's right, the only worry for the others is that they make it back without any more attacks." He lies back down on the ground, propping his head up with the pillow. "I do hope they're okay."

Dru rolls over to face him, "They are. They'll be here by tomorrow." She's asleep within the next few minutes, Shade can tell when her breathing evens out. He follows soon after.

Tomorrow comes and there's still no sign of them.

Dru is getting stronger and able to be up and about more. She, Ryker, and Shade don hoods with face coverings across their eyes and mouth and spend the morning sightseeing. Marv is never far, keeping a close eye on the prince and his lady friend.

Shade knows it's for his own safety. But he can't help wondering if there's a part of these guards who do not fully trust him.

The city is beautiful and lively with countless street vendors and festival-like gatherings. It reminds him of Glimmer and he misses home. One of the vendors beckons for his attention and they spend several minutes admiring his paintings of the nature of Lockwood.

At one point, another vendor has pulled Dru's hood and mask down and is playing with her black hair, twirling and braiding it.

Dru laughs and looks at Shade, shrugging.

The people of Lockwood are welcoming and, he notes, curious; many try getting close to him. Poe manages to keep a safe distance between Shade and anyone else.

By late afternoon, they are back at Blair's place with still no word from the others. Fray has grown impatient and decides he's going to pay a visit to every gate.

"Well, we might as well settle a meeting with any leaders within the city," Ryker says, "Duke Harvard and his wife, Duchess Jane, will likely be strong allies. There are other leaders that I am not so certain of. Does Duchess Brandy still live here?" He asks Blair, who has just entered from the kitchen.

The healer carries a tray of mugs filled to the brim with medicinal tea. "Lady Brandy. She dropped the title after her late husband killed himself."

"Killed himself?" Dru asks, eyebrows raised.

"That's the story." Blair says, not looking entirely convinced. He sets down the tray and begins handing out the teas. Afton and Risa share the couch. Ryker is in one of the armchairs, Dru occupies the other, and Shade stands once more in front of the fireplace.

"*Lady* Brandy would be an unlikely ally. But I can arrange a meeting with her nonetheless." Ryker states. "Any other prominents I'm leaving out?"

Blair considers this. "Sir Reginald and Lady Lilith. If they're not on vacation, they'd be interested in what you've got going here. Duke Flynn, Lady Sprite, Lady Colette. There are many who would find your presence here…intriguing."

Shade catches his choice in words and remembers Bane's warning back in Frostfire: that Lockwood would assuredly present friend *and* foe.

He wonders how long they need to reside here in the city. Greaver's last advice was to get to Lockwood, that there would be ready allies here. Well, he has made it. He is working on a plan to gather forces. Is Lockwood to be their home base? Shade rubs a hand across his eyes, disengaging from the conversation as Ryker continues talking with Blair about potential allies.

Lockwood is big; almost, too big for it to be a centralized base of operations. It has a great security system with every gate in or out heavily guarded. But Tyson has already warned him that there may be guards disloyal to the throne. Shade can't have that. He needs to be certain that everyone on his team can be trusted. Dru overheard individuals speaking of Shade's departure for Lockwood. That means whoever the traitor was talking to, almost certainly knows of his presence here in the city. Not to mention the felled enemy in the woods with the parchment in his pocket. A city like Lockwood, no doubt, has consistent communication with other large, well-off cities like Glimmer. If wind of his arrival goes public, Windenmeyer could know his location in two weeks' time, easily.

What's more, there are far too many innocent people here for it to be the main hub for his revolution. Too many risks of those innocent lives being hurt or lost.

Shade decides it then. They will likely not stay here permanently. It is safer for the city and for he and his team to make allies and then make tracks to some place far more inconspicuous. What of the caravan of wagons Shade saw on his way in? He wonders what Drake has discovered and hopes he is okay.

"I will speak with Tyson," Blair is saying when Shade returns to the conversation, "He will be able to arrange a meeting with Duke Harvard. From there, it's in the duke's hands."

As if on cue, the door opens and in walks Tyson, having heard Blair's last sentence. Fray is right behind him. He must not have made it far before running into Tyson. Shade notes the sharp look in his eyes and stands a little straighter, preparing for whatever news the guard brings them.

"I can certainly arrange a meeting," Tyson says. "But, I'm afraid, that will have to wait. Some guards were doing ride-bys between here and our sister city, Greenbriar, out the Twilight Gate–between the Western and Southern Gates. They came across some interesting folk and brought them in. They're being held at one of the guard station's just inside the city. Could be your folk. One looks like a Viking."

Perez.

Ryker stands, "How many?" Everyone is already in motion. Blair takes the hot mug from Dru's hand before she spills it everywhere. He gives her a look to sit back down, but she ignores him, touching Shade's arm in an attempt to settle her nerves.

There should be six, Shade thinks, *please be six*.

"Five." The guard says and Shade's heart falls. Beside him, Dru shakily returns to her seat on the couch.

"And," Tyson says, his eyes downcast and voice low, "You'll need to see for yourself, but word from Marv is…one of them appears to be dead."

CHAPTER 19

They decide their entire crew should not go galloping through the city, even though that's exactly what each of them wants. Dru still isn't in exact condition to be riding. She puts up a fight, even threatens to slit Shade's throat if he keeps her back, but he knows the threats are empty. Well, he hopes they are, at least. She eventually settles back down on the couch with a grumble. Shade is out the door with his face covered before anyone has the chance to try and force him to stay. A couple of guards are already out there with their horses.

"I'll stay back with Dru." Afton says from the doorway.

Risa is almost to her horse, but comes to a nonchalant stop. With a fleeting glance at Shade, she turns back to the house. "I can stay, they may need your...compassion." She says, then quickly ducks back into the house.

Afton glances back, a question in his eyes, but doesn't argue. He and Ryker climb aboard their horses.

Tyson quickly leads them in a direction Shade has not yet explored. This part of the city is far less populated, less regal, and more quiet and down to earth. The homes and businesses are further spread and the markets less in number. Despite the pit in his stomach, Shade marvels at the beauty of Lockwood. He swallows a knot of fear, readjusts his hood, and rubs Poe's neck. Five...but one of them is dead.

Please, Erin, please, be alive. He doesn't even feel guilty for the thought, knowing that if she lives, it means someone else has died; he doesn't care. He just wants to see Erin's smile, hear her musical laugh. It's his fault she's out here. He got her into this mess back at the castle. He should have told her to stay away from him; to stay with her family.

But Shade also knows that would have meant she'd have been in bondage there at the castle. Just like her family. Just like *his* family.

"Please, Erin," His whisper is caught by the wind and dissipates in the air.

The Twilight Gate is a lot smaller than the Western. He can see it in the distance, nestled between two rock formations. They stop about fifty yards from it, at a steel single-story building with several horses tethered outside of it.

Shade recognizes Yagar horses. He notices one horse, deep brown in color, with a very familiar tan bow attached to the satchel on the horse's back. He takes a deep breath, having to fight the urge to bust down the door and yell for Erin. What will he find? The door is also steel and strangely built; it raises up and tucks away inside the building when Tyson pulls up on the handle at the bottom. Surprisingly, the noise it makes is barely a whisper.

"Some of them need medical attention, but the guards at this gate have been ordered to question first." Tyson says, stopping them before entering. "We answer to Duke Harvard. But the lesser gates have different leaders. This one answers to Lady Brandy. She's pretty ruthless." He leads the way into the station. It's smaller inside because of the three jail cells lining the back wall. Shade barely registers the rest of the layout because he is too busy noting the five bodies that occupy cell number three.

Baron stands against the bars of the cell, yelling

insults at every guard in sight. His voice falters when they enter and recognition registers on his face. He stops talking. Perez leans against the back wall of the cell, seemingly bored.

"Ryker," Trix whispers, scrambling to her feet and joining Baron at the bars.

Ryker stiffens, "Release them." He almost growls.

Shade approaches the cell, counting five bodies; the three he has already mentioned, one lying on the floor of the cell, the other bent over it, facing his direction.

As he draws closer, the figure finally looks up. He wants to fall to his knees, to let out a breath of relief, to reach through the bars and draw Erin to him. But Shade does none of these things. He only stops in front of the bars, drinking in the sight of Erin as she does the same to him. Her breath catches and her eyes shut for a moment in relief. But she is sad, a frown evident in the deep furrow of her brow. They are all sad. Because lying on the cold ground of the cell is Vision; her skin is ashen white and her face slack, rid of any life.

Shade meets Baron's eyes. They must have understood by Shade's shielded appearance that keeping his identity a secret is of utmost concern; none of them say his name or make any sort of royal gesture. Not that Baron ever would have done such a thing anyway. Still, Shade is grateful. He gets the feeling the Twilight Gate is one of those gates Tyson did *not* want Shade's team arriving at. Baron doesn't speak, just shakes his head once with an air of finality.

Vision is dead.

"Release them." Ryker states again, his teeth clenched.

Shade balls his hands into fists. He looks briefly

over his shoulder and back again, almost imperceptibly. Afton is behind him. Directly behind him. If Risa's story is true, that man is to blame for Vision's death. Shade has similar thoughts to those of last night; he can end Afton's life right here, right now. He wants to. Baron is now watching him closely; he glances behind Shade, so quick the prince almost misses it.

Then, just as quickly, the red-head shakes his head again. This time, in warning. They stare one another down, all the while Ryker is demanding their release and Tyson is arguing with the guards.

Does Baron know something?

Finally, Shade comes to his senses. It appears that Baron does know something specifically about Afton. Had Vision warned them? Did she know who struck her down? Further, Afton is not the only traitor; there are likely plenty more he has been communicating with for however long he's been in opposition to the throne. If they are careful, they can use Afton to lead them to other traitors.

Shade takes in their frames, Baron with blood seeping through a hastily tied wrap of gauze around his injured leg; Trix and Perez both sporting cut and bruised faces; and Erin, eyes dark and fatigued, shoulders drooping with the obvious sign of something broken. Suddenly, more than anything, he wants her out of this cage, wants her getting help; wants all of them getting help. These are his people and these guards are treating them like disposable waste.

"What must we do to earn their release?" He asks loudly, above all the voices. It grows quiet as all attention turns to him. "Speak with your master? Perfect, I was planning on meeting with her anyway."

"And what if she doesn't plan on meeting with *you*?" A shrill voice demands from the doorway.

Shade turns. The woman is tall, imposing. She wears thick furs around her shoulders and tall stiletto boots that reach to her thighs. Her accent is typical of other Lockwood residents he has heard, but it's also demanding and firm. Her beauty is harsh. The kind of beauty that you want to look away from, but can't seem to, all angles and hard edges. She's a young widow, perhaps no older than forty. Without having to ask, he knows this to be Lady Brandy. "I can be persuasive."

Lady Brandy's seamless eyebrow lifts in an arc that almost reaches her hairline. She barks out a mocking laugh. "The Lady has far better things to do, darling. She's just caught five, very intriguing individuals in need of interrogation."

"I have a better offer. One I am only willing to present after you release them." Without another word, he lowers the hood and pulls aside the facemask. He is risking a lot here, basically putting his life and the lives of his team into the woman's hands.

Lady Brandy must know this. Because when her guards begin to grumble and reach for their swords, she halts them with a hand. There are several beats of silence, in which Shade questions his decision and begins looking for escape routes if necessary. There are cell keys on the belt loop of the guard to his right. Shade could get to them and have the cell door open before the guard knew what was happening. But getting much further than that would be difficult.

Thankfully, it doesn't come to this. A rueful smile crosses Lady Brandy's lips and she opens her arms wide. "Well...this just might be a better offer. Rufus, release them. Then bring them back to my estate. I'll have the kettle brewing and fire going. I am nothing if not hospitable."

"I trust you are also a woman of integrity." Shade beckons to the cell, "Please, let us bury our friend."

Lady Brandy looks less than happy to do this, but she waves her hand dismissively. "Yes, yes, of course. On your way to my estate. Nothing too long, though. The days are short and the nights are long in a city like Lockwood. I would hate any trouble to cross your path in the dark."

That's a warning to not keep her waiting; or else any deal is off the table. Shade doesn't doubt the woman will turn him over to the enemy in a heartbeat; and without remorse.

The guard to his right unlocks the cell. Lady Brandy calls for a few of the guards to follow her while the others stay, eyeing Shade and the others warily. Trix surges forward into Ryker's arms. Perez comes next. He stares at Shade with little emotion and only says, "Risa?"

"The others are safe." Shade says quietly.

Then Baron is there, explaining in a low voice they were separated from Hagan. "He's still out there. We can go look for him."

Shade nods, a headache forming. They certainly will, but not right now. He is trying to quickly prepare for this impromptu meeting with Lady Brandy. He had hoped to begin with an easy target like Duke Harvard and his wife, almost certain allies. "We will find him, Baron. Drake is out there, too. We will talk later. There is a lot to discuss."

For once, Baron is not haughty or sarcastic. He is serious. And, there's something else. Worry? Fear? The haunted look passes from Baron's eyes and he turns to lift Vision from the ground.

Afton hurries by to aid him and Shade resists the urge to grab him by the neck and throw him against the bars of the cell. Baron stiffens with Afton's presence, but plays it off coolly by cracking his neck and muttering something about needing a mender to tend to his back.

Baron *definitely* knows something about Afton. Fray is nearby and offers help once they carry Vision's body out of the cell.

Then Erin is exiting the cell, one arm gingerly holding the other at the elbow, keeping it tucked against her chest. He thinks her breath catches when he gently touches the small of her back and guides her out the doorway.

She's alive. Shade has never been more grateful for anything in his life.

Outside, he leads her to the horses and stops only when they are out of earshot of any others. "You're alive. Thank Zion you're alive." He can't help it. The words come out in a rush of relieved panic. He lightly touches her elbow. "You're hurt. Collarbone?"

She tries for a laugh, but ends up wincing. "Shattered when I fell off the horse. Can you believe that? *Me*, falling off a horse?"

He shushes her gently, "You need aid. Maybe I can send you to the others with Baron or Perez."

"No," She says firmly, "I am not leaving you. You made it; I knew you would." She touches his cheek lightly, seems to realize what she's doing, and drops it just as quickly. He wants her to put it back. Instead, she looks away, towards Baron and the others coming out of the station. "Something happened out there. Before Vision died. She said something to Baron that has him spooked."

"We will talk later. Right now, I need your help coming up with a speech for Lady Brandy. How am I to convince her to join our cause?" He tries for a light tone, but their situation is anything but light. Oh, how he wishes they were back in the woods outside the castle, riding horses and chasing the sunset. He would enjoy chasing every sunset with her.

Erin smiles at him, "You've always been a better speaker than me. I trip over my words." She has a far off look in her eyes and he wonders if she's thinking back to simpler times as well. She sobers, "Those people who attacked us, they were not like the Renegades we met on the mountain. These people were trained."

"I know," He doesn't want to spend these few stolen moments talking about this, "We can discuss this later."

"Dru," Erin says suddenly, "Is she okay?"

"She's fine. Recovering back at the healer's place. We'll return there after talking with Lady Brandy." Thinking about Dru reminds him of the feverish kiss they shared on the road. He releases Erin from his grip, confused with his own thoughts. Instead, he occupies himself with rubbing Poe's neck, "This guy's incredible."

Erin begins petting him as well, cooing things in his ear.

The others gather around. "Is there a quiet grove on the way to Lady Brandy's?" Ryker asks, as Baron and Afton lay Vision over one of the horses with a bit of effort. "Somewhere the animals like to nest or graze?"

Two of the guards look at each other. One shrugs. "Dom's land. There's not much to it but sometimes the cows are out there." He says. The other turns and tells them all, "We will take you there. But you heard the Lady—no funny business. Get her in the ground and then let's go."

Once again, the anger in Shade rises. So much so that Erin actually places a hand on his hip, warning him to cool it as he turns to face the guard. "Watch your tongue in how you address our friend. It'd be a shame for you to find a place beside her."

Shade thinks he has stepped too far, but his team stands at attention, equal stares of anger piercing the guard in place. The guard glances around, a bit nervous, trying to maintain eye contact. He's intimidated. "Well, just hurry then. We're wasting time." He finally says, before jumping on a horse and leading the way.

Tyson draws up beside Shade. "I will return to Blair's, alert the rest of your group to the situation, then meet you at the Brandy Estate. I don't suspect any foul play. The Lady, albeit conniving, is a woman of her word."

"My people need aid; can I send them with you?"

"I'm afraid not. Lady Brandy expects each of you to show up at her place. Let's not keep her waiting. I'm sure she will have healers on hand."

Shade nods, not happy with this situation. "Thank you, Tyson. We'll see you soon."

He bows his head, "My liege." Then he rides in the direction of Blair's.

"Ooh, my liege, eh?" Erin says, smirking. "That's a new one."

Shade just ducks his head. Between her and Dru, he'd never hear the end of this. They hop aboard horses, Erin moving gingerly with her broken collarbone, and follow after the guard. He notices Erin's wince with every step the horse takes and prays the Brandy Estate isn't far.

"We got separated," Baron says once they're riding. He trots next to Shade, one hand holding the reins, the other pressed to the wound on his thigh. "It appears the others all made it?"

"Risa is back at the healer's with Dru, who wanted to come but is still recovering."

His relief is evident as his shoulders drop and some of the tension leaves his body. "Good. She's okay."

"On my way with her, we came across Drake on the road. There was something I needed him to attend to. I expect him to report back before too long." In mixed company—particularly Afton—Shade does not feel comfortable going into further detail. "Vision...was she killed during the fight?" He looks sadly to where she rides alone, strewn over her horse. Trix rides beside her, holding her horse's reins, a stiff expression on her face.

"Injured," Baron says, his nostrils flared. "She passed in the night, several hours after we'd fled the road and sought safety further south. Hagan was with us at first. He got bogged down amongst two or three attackers. He's still out there." He trails off, eyes canvassing their surroundings as they ride.

"Her injury was too great; she was never going to make it." Perez adds. It might be the longest sentence Shade has ever heard him string together.

"It had to have been a long-sword." Erin says. "The cut across her back was so long and so deep." Her lip trembles a bit, but she swallows back the tears and sits taller in her saddle. Shade is amazed at her strength. Neither of them has ever experienced what they have the past few weeks. But he, more so than her, has been exposed to stresses of war and dealings with death in his time learning strategy from his father. In Shade's lifetime, there has always been peace under the rule of King Bronze. Or, at least, he thought there had always been peace. Now, he realizes the rotting darkness of greed and hatred has been seeping into the minds of individuals across Zion for some time now; the recent attack in the castle has only just been the beginning of a long-standing evil.

No one speaks again until they arrive. It's a small field, with several trees lining one side and a creek running through them. There's an open patch of land next to one tree and several yards away from where the earth dips and the creek flows. Upon arriving, they scare off a few grazing cows and a flock of birds from where they had been resting in the dimming light of the approaching evening. It's a nice place for a burial site. They don't have any shovels, so they have to settle for digging up the earth with Fray's club and Ryker's shield. In the end, many of them use their hands and they finally have a deep enough hole to lay her in. She looks peaceful, resting among the trees, the voices of nature sending her off. Shade wishes he had the privilege of knowing her longer. He looks away from her prone form, realizing her death is on account of his mission; an uneasy feeling in his gut reminds him that she will not be the last to fall for their cause.

After darkness has fallen, they stand in a circle around her grave. Ryker rubs sweat from his brow and breathes out a long sigh. "Vision," He begins, "Many of us have known her our whole lives. To lose her means to lose someone we love."

He continues by sharing personal memories of

266

different occasions he has spent with her. Trix shares another, followed by Fray who mentions something about Vision's keen sense of right and wrong, and how she never failed to make him laugh.

Then, it's Baron's turn and he doesn't look up, only stares hard at her body in the ground. "You didn't deserve this." He says, his voice loud. "I'm sorry."

Shade glances across the way to where Afton is standing. The man, to Shade's relief, has not spoken up. If he did, Shade is certain he wouldn't be able to stop himself from stomping over there and demanding an explanation. Even still, Afton has the audacity to be…crying?

Shade blinks, sure the darkness is playing tricks on his eyes. But no. Afton is most certainly crying. The tears glint off the lamplight one of the guards wields. Shade watches him wipe his face with one hand, the movement drawing his eyes upwards to connect with Shade's. Afton's gaze doesn't waver and, in his face, Shade recognizes something he knows all too well. He saw it in his own reflection in Ryker's shield, when he lifted it off the ground and returned it to its owner. Because Shade is the reason Vision is on this mission, he feels guilty for her death.

It's the same look on Afton's face right now. And in that moment, Shade knows with unexplainable certainty that Afton is guilty of wielding the sword that struck Vision. Afton finally looks away, wiping at his face again.

Shade swallows, returning to Baron's speech, taking a breath to calm the emotions inside himself.

We need him alive; he reminds himself; *he will lead us to other traitors.*

"*Drengs–*" Baron cuts off, having to clear his

throat from the sudden emotion.

"*Drengskuerto.*" Shade says in his place. The red-head glances his way quickly, then nods his thanks, repeating the Old English. "'Honor in death.'" Shade says. He does not feel it right to say much else, because he did not know her like the others did. But he finishes by bowing his head to her form below. "Thank you for your loyalty to Zion. Your sacrifice will never be forgotten."

The others all murmur similar phrases. Then, Fray spits on Vision's body. At first, Shade is taken aback. Where he's from, this is considered a deep insult. But when the others begin spitting as well, he realizes this is honoring Vision as spitting seemed to be a favorite pastime of hers. Shade is the last to do so, but he adds his own saliva to the mix. They begin covering her grave with dirt.

"You've had your time. Now follow me." The guard called Rufus says.

With one last glance at the mounded gravesite, they leave the grove. The ride is quiet and the evening darkness settles across the city like a shadowed blanket.

A few minutes later, they turn off the main road and ride a little further into the trees, down a dirt path that winds its way to a large opening. Before them, behind a gated fence, sits a beautiful white mansion surrounded by lots of land.

"Now, *this* is an estate." Baron whispers in awe.

Rufus takes them to the front where a pristine staircase leads up to the door. Several footmen await their arrival. He whistles for the footmen to take away the horses, then begins climbing the staircase without checking to see if the rest of them are following.

Shade is no stranger to the regal lifestyle. Windenmeyer Castle is easily the grandest, most beautiful castle in all of Zion. It has never been flaunted; it has simply been this way for generations. Windenmeyer is second to none. But when Shade steps over the threshold and into the mansion of Lady Brandy, even his breath is taken away. The sheer size of the chandelier dangling in the entryway is enough to pull a gasp from Trix's lips. The only one who does not appear impressed is Perez. Shade can't decide if that's because nothing impresses the Viking-look-alike or if he's familiar with this lifestyle, confirming Shade's assumption of their royal lineage.

The floor is marble with various sizes of real furs lying about. There's a grand staircase leading upwards to a landing lined with lights and flowers. Separate rooms or hallways branch off on either side of the entrance they just came through. Rufus guides them left and into yet another incredible room, this one the home to a long mahogany table with chairs lining either side, and a larger chair at one end. The table is filled with wonderful looking pastries and steaming bowls of soups, vegetables, and meats. It is in the larger chair where Lady Brandy sits, eyebrows raised upon their arrival.

"Well, go on then," she announces, "Sit! I didn't call up all available servants for nothing."

"Lady Brandy," Shade says, his voice echoing around the quiet dining room. Servants stand at attention against the walls of the room. He is a little caught off guard by the woman's provision of food. This is a big step from the jailhouse to her mansion, not to mention the change in atmosphere—he assumed Lady Brandy to be a hard-nosed prune without a heart.

He remembers Tyson's warning about her and tells himself to be on his toes around her; she may not be as she seems. "I thank you for this meal, which we are looking forward to enjoying. But my people need medical attention. The food will still be here once they've received aid."

Lady Brandy's smile never wavers. And, as if she hasn't heard a word Shade just said, she opens her arms and repeats loudly, "Sit!"

So, they sit.

A servant guides Shade to the chair on the edge, at the right hand of Lady Brandy. He watches them give the other seats away to his group. They don't even occupy half of the long table. Erin is seated diagonally from him, still clutching her arm tight to her chest. He grits his teeth, biting back concern for her so he can speak cordially with Brandy.

The food smells delicious. Like something straight out of Windenmeyer's kitchens. Even still, Shade isn't hungry at the moment. Unfortunately, Lady Brandy seems as carnivorous as a beast from the Silent Sisters. And if Shade hopes to gain her trust and respect as an ally, he'll have to appease her. A part of him wonders if any of this food is poisonous.

Lady Brandy senses the tension. She gives a hearty laugh, one that doesn't reach her eyes, and dumps a spoonful of vegetables on her plate. "Truly, young *hilcipe*, if I wanted to kill you, believe me," her eyes meet his and they glint with a darkness that sends a chill down his spine, "You'd be dead."

After only a moment's hesitation, Shade begins filling his plate. The others take their cue from him and follow suit. Ryker sits directly across from him, nodding slightly. Shade recalls how the Gray at least knows of Lady Brandy and wonders if the two of them have ever officially met.

He also wonders what they are about to get themselves into.

After several minutes of the sounds of chewing, utensils hitting the plates, and glasses being refilled, Lady Brandy finally reclines back in her seat, eyeing them curiously.

"Well, this is something, isn't it?" She eventually says. "The missing prince and his entourage, falling into my lap like a gift." She watches Shade, eyes glinting, "There's quite a bounty on your head. Dead or alive, might I add."

Shade shifts uncomfortably, wishing he knew the Lady's true motives. His fingers tighten around the knife he's using to cut his steak in the event an altercation occurs.

Lady Brandy runs her tongue across her front teeth, then uses one nail to pick unceremoniously at a piece of food wedged between them. "I've never cared much for bounties." She continues, "You see, they never tell the full story." She takes a large bite of pork, chewing with her mouth open, a stark contrast to the elaborate etiquette style around her. "Prince Shade Alwyn. What's your story?"

Shade holds back a cringe at the use of his full name. Only his mother calls him that. Alwyn is a name that has been in his family for generations. It means "loved by all." It has not brought him much luck as of late. "I am innocent."

The words have hardly passed his lips and The Lady is laughing, glancing around at her servants as if they find it funny as well. She pauses long enough to say, "They always are, aren't they?"

271

Shade sets down his utensils but keeps his hands atop the table in case he still has use for the knife. "I did not kill my father. Someone wants the Kingdom for themselves. It is my intention to reclaim the throne. By force, if necessary." Lady Brandy says nothing, only continues stuffing her face, the smile still present. When she begins devouring the rare steak the blood dripping down her chin gives her a carnivorous look. So, Shade continues with slight repulsion. "With strong encouragement from a stable hand named Greaver, I fled the castle for Lockwood in the hopes of gathering reinforcements. I have been informed that you would be quite the ally."

"Ah, the ghost of Greaver Estes haunting the Great Castle?" Lady Brandy says in a sing-song voice. "Lovely. You should know he and I never saw eye to eye."

Shade can hear the gulp Trix gives from beside him. His eyes don't leave Brandy's. "I get the impression you don't see eye to eye with many people."

Lady Brandy stops chewing, seeming to contemplate his statement. Then she bursts into laughter once more, "No, no I don't suppose I do!" Then, as if flipping a switch, her laughter cuts off and she goes very still. "Lift up your sleeves, all of you."

Eyes meet Shade's in question. He finally nods at them, knowing full well what Brandy seeks. They lift their sleeves, even Erin, who although does not bear the mark of loyalty, is the most loyal of all.

"My husband wore that mark proudly. Loyal to the throne, through and through." She says, her face impassive. "It's what got him killed." Her head turns at the snort that arises from the opposite end of the

272

table. Shade's pretty sure it came from Baron. "I hear the rumors," Brandy says, "I know what they say about him. About me. Contrary to popular belief, I did not kill him. Nor did he kill himself. But—suicide, homicide—what does it matter? He's dead." She stares at Shade once more, trapping him in her icy gaze. "I do not bear that mark—it is too easily used as an excuse to act without reason. Senseless wars waged over centuries, many of which have come about because of marks like that one. I prefer to choose my battles, figure out which side benefits me more. Some call this cowardice—I call it wit." She pauses and gains a thoughtful expression, "You say you intend to take the throne. But why does Zion need a throne, anyway? What would happen if *nobody* was in charge?" Her eyes take on a vacant look.

"Anarchy. The demise of our kingdom." Ryker speaks up. "Every village, town, and city would resemble the lost cities of Klepton and Pire. Nowhere would be safe."

"Hm. Perhaps." Brandy blinks and the trance is gone. She resumes cutting her food and filling her mouth. "Rest assured, I do not wish for this. But there are many who do."

"Renegades." Shade nods.

"I used to think that," Brandy says, then shakes her head, "But, no. Renegades are disloyal to the throne because they want to claim it for themselves. *They* want to be in power. No, there's others out there who are loyal to no one. Who do not seek the throne's power, but it's *destruction*. That is anarchy. And that is what I do not want."

Another chill slides down Shade's spine. His eyes flick once to Afton, who sits diagonally from him next

273

to Erin. Afton stares down at his plate, seemingly oblivious to the conversation. "Lady Brandy," Shade says, "Your knowledge of the kingdom, among other things, would be very beneficial towards my cause. I was framed, I did not kill the king." He ignores the tiny voice in the back of his mind, reminding him of Bane's words: *Trust no one without a Loyalty Mark.*

Lady Brandy waves a dismissive hand, "Killed the king, didn't kill the king—I don't care. That is no concern of mine. You could be the kindest prince or as terrible as the Renegades claim and I would still back you. Why? Because, presently, anarchy does not benefit me." She smiles then, almost maniacally, and Shade wonders if there aren't a few screws loose in that head of hers. "You've hardly touched your food!" She exclaims, "Eat! Dessert will be out shortly."

There's almost a collective sigh as everyone returns to their plates. Shade isn't sure if he's relieved or stressed that Brandy has sided with him. He supposes it does help that she's an ally; he would not want to face those eyes on opposite sides of a war.

After dessert, in which some small talk is had amongst most of the party and in which Shade learns Ryker and Brandy actually know each other distantly through a history of family ties, they are dismissed to a common room where Brandy has sent several medics to see to their injuries. Baron, having left a puddle of blood in the chair he was sitting in is seen first. The thigh wound is cleaned, stitched, and wrapped, all while Baron complains loudly. He claims the liquid in his eyes is a piece of dirt from the graveside, but Shade can't hold back a smirk; he won't be letting the Green forget this anytime soon. The others, aside from Erin, have smaller, more manageable injuries that take very little time to help.

Not much can be done for Erin. The medics give her some painkillers and lather her in healing ointments and oils. Other than that, one arm is placed in a sling, and tied tightly against her body. Baron jokes that she and Ryker are "twins," and grins widely at Perez who doesn't smile.

Lady Brandy has disappeared. Which is fine with Shade. He can only take so much of her chilling gaze. "You could have warned me she was crazy." Shade mutters to Ryker as he joins him standing against the wall.

Ryker's eyes watch Trix as she shadows the medics. She's easily one of the best medics there are, but she always prides herself in growth and learning. "The last time I saw Lady Brandy, I was fourteen. And she was married to her second husband at the age of only twenty."

Shade's eyebrows raise, "And her most recent was…?"

"Her fourth." Ryker states grimly, "I do believe she loved each of them. It's unfortunate they never last."

"The marriages?"

"The men."

Shade looks at him then, jaw slack. "No way. You mean…?"

Ryker nods, "They've all died. The first was killed in a hunting accident, the second by a freak house fire, the third during a Renegade attack, and the most recent threw himself off a cliff. Well, supposedly. Lady Brandy seems pretty convinced it was not of his own accord."

Shade feels a bit of sadness for the woman. "No wonder she's a little out of her mind. I'd probably be no different after so much loss."

"She's thick-skinned. And, although she's on our side, I would trust her as far as I can throw her." Ryker says under his breath, "She's in the game for her own vices."

Tyson is suddenly there, walking in from the doorway leading to the dining room. His hair is disheveled from his horse ride. His eyes scan the room until they land on Shade, who has dismantled himself from the wall and is striding toward the guard. "Your Highness, I apologize, I had intended to be here for the meal, but…well, ran into a slight problem."

"What's the issue, Tyson?" The concern in Shade's voice draws the attention of the others. They gather closer curiously.

"A messenger and his friend were at Blair's when I arrived. Marv said he appeared at the Western Gate demanding he knew Greaver, so he brought him to the healer's. Dreads, has a purple hood."

Drake. "And the other guy?" Shade asks.

"Red-head, tall, brooding. Green hood."

"Hagan." Baron says, sounding clearly relieved.

Tyson just nods. "Sure. Anyway, the dreads guy was babbling, acting confused. Saying something about a caravan and a lady in blue. Dru and the Viking girl were attempting to calm him down. They were at a loss. But he kept requesting to speak to you."

New worry settles in Shade's stomach and he makes for the exit. "Then, let's not keep him waiting. We were just on our way out, anyway." He hates to leave without thanking the host, but Lady Brandy is nowhere to be found and he must get to Drake and find out what he knows.

"That isn't all," Tyson says, "He claims he just

276

came from Skarsdale, another large city northwest of here. That's where he ran into trouble."

"What kind of trouble?" Fray demands impatiently.

"Royal guards. From Windenmeyer."

Shade's blood runs cold. Absentmindedly, his gaze locks with Erin's. What are royal guards of Glimmer doing this far east? So far from home? There could only be one explanation. "He's close." Shade says grimly.

Baron glances between Shade and the guard. "Who? Prince Jeb?"

Tyson nods, "*King* Jeb. His coronation was a few weeks ago. The dreads fellow left Skarsdale as soon as he knew. He had to beat him here."

"Beat him *here*?" Erin's voice comes out barely a whisper. Her eyes are wide as she glances between Shade and the guard. Shade grits his teeth and watches Tyson's face as his lips form the dreaded words.

Tyson's frown deepens. "Here. The king is on his way to Lockwood."

CHAPTER 20

Blair's place is swelling with activity by the time they make it back, a ride that took them almost thirty minutes. Outside, townspeople mill about, demanding a closer view of the interior. Guards are posted near the entrance, keeping the crowd at bay. It is well after sunset, yet these people's curiosity has them out of bed and craning their necks at the windows.

Tyson directs them to a back entrance that is far less populated and they duck into the coverage of the building with little resistance. Shade passes the medical wing rooms on his way down the hallway and to the living room. The curtains are drawn over the windows and there's quite a few voices coming from the living room, all talking over each other. When he rounds the corner, the first thing he notices is Drake's darting form, pacing quickly back and forth. The second is Hagan and Dru who speak in raised voices towards one another. It's odd to see Hagan, usually so mild-mannered, with a loud tone and red face. Risa stands nearby, eyes watching the entire scene unfold. Blair and Liv speak to one another using hand gestures that Shade promises, if heard, would be the loudest noise in the room.

"What's the meaning of this?" Shade demands.

The talking and miming ceases and all eyes turn to them. Dru stands, but she gets up too quickly and appears dizzy. It doesn't stop her from exclaiming, "Baron!", before sinking back onto the couch.

Drake rushes to Shade, eyes wild. Shade has never seen the messenger look this way. He appears almost manic, his hands ringing and words tripping over each other. "Prince, I found it. The caravan, the symbol—a blue dress, familiar faces—the king rides close, he's almost here, soldiers with him—"

"Drake! Enough!" Ryker hisses, looking at the man in embarrassment, "Control yourself, man!"

"He can't." Hagan says in a voice that indicates he's been having the same argument for the past hour or more. "He can't form a complete sentence, won't explain what he means about the blue dress or the caravan. I can't get him to sit down long enough to calm down or take a sip of water. After I got separated from the others, I doubled back and found the road that led to the Western Gate. I was nearly here when I ran into Drake," he eyes the messenger almost sadly, "He was already in this state. He's aware enough to recognize us, but beyond that...I don't know what happened to him."

"Many things can cause this," Dru interjects, "But, I'm telling you, it's Cyphur Fever!"

Hagan turns back to her, "Cyphur causes low oxygen intake, not delirium."

"Delirium is a side-effect of the low oxygen intake," Dru says, stamping her foot angrily, "My mother died from this, *I* would *know*." She glares at him indignantly, momentarily forgetting the arrival of the others.

So many confusing thoughts are running through Shade's mind, he can hardly keep them straight. He needs to have a private conversation with Drake about the caravan. But if the messenger is acting out of mind, the first step is to get him aid. And what about all the people outside? They can't hide inside Blair's place forever. Then, there's the whole traitor issue with Afton standing a mere five feet away. And, what of

279

Duke Harvard and the other potential allies Shade still needs to win over? Lady Brandy seems pretty vicious, but one ally in all of Lockwood simply won't do.

Baron starts in on Hagan and the two of them get into their own argument. A proper reunion can't even be enjoyed with all the disagreements taking place. So, Shade steps over to Blair, pulling him aside. "Sir, I thank you for your hospitality. I'm afraid this location has become a little too popular." He beckons out the front doors where prying eyes vie for a peek inside. "Is there somewhere else we could reside that is safe and secluded?"

Blair looks at him, and relief spreads over his features, as if grateful someone is finally willing to listen to him. "Liv and I were just talking about that. She doesn't like my idea, but I believe it to be the best option we've got. I've already sent Marv to make preparations for your arrival."

"Arrival where?"

"I can't promise seclusion, but I can safety. Duke Harvard's estate. When Tyson informed him of your coming to Lockwood, he sent word immediately that his home was open and ready for your stay. The duke has made ill-advised decisions in the past," He's referring to the banishment of Greaver, "but, ultimately, he wants what's best for Zion. He will be able to provide protection that I cannot."

Shade doesn't argue. He trusts the healer. "What of Drake?"

Here, Blair hesitates, eyes observing the Purple's antics, his pacing. "I do believe Miss Dru is correct. This seems to be some form of Cyphur Fever. If this is the case, there isn't much to be done. If you're familiar with it, you know it's only carried through certain

280

types of iron that can be found in mines down south—
I'm uncertain how he even caught it, lest there be
individuals carrying it from the mines. I understand
you spent some time in Yagar?"

At this, Shade nods.

"The General spends a lot of time in the Drysdale
region, it's possible he or one of his men are
unintentional carriers of this illness. Once in the host,
the fever is not contagious. Unfortunately, it acts fast
and has a mortality rate like no other. First his mind
will go, then his eyesight, until, eventually, all of his
organs shut down. There's only been a few cases seen
here since I've been a healer, some forty years."

Shade's heart falls as he glances at Drake.
"*Nothing* to be done?"

Blair just shakes his head. "I give him two days,
maybe three."

Shade turns then, fed up with the arguing. "This
bickering will only tear us apart! Enough!" The noise
dies down, but only after a few moments. Grumbling
can still be heard. "We're all tired. What we need is a
good night's rest and then reconvene in the morning to
discuss recent events. Blair has arranged our stay at a
separate, safer location."

"And why should we trust you?" Hagan is
suddenly back on his feet, glaring at Shade. "Drake has
something to tell you, about a caravan and a woman in
blue, saying you sent him on a separate mission. What
are you hiding from us?"

Shade opens his mouth, stammering. "I'm not
hiding anything from you. That is something we can
discuss in the morning—"

"And what happened on the road?" Hagan turns on
the Grays, "Why didn't we see that attack coming?

Why weren't we more aware? Vision might still be alive."

Fray's face changes and he steps closer to Hagan, "Careful, Greenie." Ryker places a hand on Fray's arm, saying, "Come now, Hagan, that is unfair."

"We all should have been more aware…" Baron says, but trails off in the middle of his sentence. He looks around the room, suddenly desperate. There's fear in his eyes when they finally meet Shade's. He mouths the name, 'Afton.'

Shade's head whips around the room. The Black is nowhere to be found. But Shade knows Afton followed them inside the house, he made sure of it himself.

"He's gone." Risa says, her voice cutting. She is staring down the hallway, out the open back door.

"And you said nothing?" Baron asks, his fists clenched.

Risa only looks at Shade. "He can lead us to whoever he answers to. That must be where he's headed. He's spooked."

There's several moments of silence, until Hagan finally speaks up, "Can someone please tell us what in Zion is going on? Where's Afton?"

Shade nods once to Risa, "Take your brother. Trail him. Report back to me at the duke's," he starts to ask Blair where Harvard's house is located, but Risa passes by with a, "Don't worry, we'll find it." She beckons to Perez who follows her down the hallway and out the door without question.

Shade rubs his brow, suddenly very tired. "Afton is not to be trusted. We have reason to believe he is working with whomever attacked you on the road."

"And what reason is that?" Hagan demands. But the fire in his eyes has died. He's just as tired as the prince and must see arguing right now is pointless.

"Because he killed Vision," Baron says. He sighs and sits down beside Dru, who leans against his arm. "I saw it with my own eyes. When he drew his longsword, I thought it was in defense, that he must have seen a close enemy. But then he turned and just…" He closes his eyes, shaking his head, "She didn't know it was coming. I argued with myself whether what I had seen was actually true. But even she knew who it was. She heard him mumbling apologies as he swung. Then she confirmed it with me in private right before she died."

Mumbling apologies? Shade thinks, confused. "Why would he knowingly deal a death blow while apologizing?"

"I wondered the same." Baron said, "When she spoke with me, Vision seemed to think he didn't want to kill her. That it was more of a *need*." He shakes his head again, "I know this sounds crazy, but she didn't even appear to be upset with what he'd done. As if she knew his thought process in the whole situation."

"You don't think Vision was in on it." Trix says, sounding unconvinced.

"No," Baron and Hagan say at the same time.

Hagan finally looks calmed down. He appears sad, resigned. "No." He repeats. "There's got to be more going on. The twins will find out something. In the meantime," He looks towards Shade but doesn't meet his eyes. "You said something about a safehouse?"

CHAPTER 21

They go out the back. With help from Tyson, they are able to leave without alerting too many of the townspeople. Liv waves goodbye, which is, to Shade's relief, an easy sign to interpret. Through Blair, he tells her he would like to learn more sign language. She smiles, nodding. Blair sends him off with a bow, then presses something into the palm of his hand. It's a rounded object with a slightly raised middle attached to a string; at first, Shade thinks it's some sort of coin. But then in the dim light of one of the passing lamp posts, he realizes it's a necklace. What surprises him most is the engraved symbol.

The Loyalty Mark.

He slips the necklace over his head and tucks the end into his shirt with a newfound respect for Blair.

Unlike Lady Brandy, whose estate is tucked away behind trees and closer to the outskirts of the city, Duke Harvard's place sits up on a hill, looking over a water-filled rock quarry that leads into a relatively small river, bending out of view. From the hill, the town square can clearly be seen, giving Shade the impression that the duke and his family might spend a lot of time watching people. If Brandy's estate is described as breathtaking, then Harvard's is nothing short of captivating. Tall pillars guide a staircase up to the front door. Large glass windows line the entire front side of the mansion, most of them dark.

A large man stands just inside the doorway once they pass through. He is both tall and wide, his large belly hanging low over his belt, his royal clothing tight against his form. A wide smile spreads across his equally wide face. "Greetings!" He exclaims. One arm extends, inviting them further into the house. He recognizes Shade and attempts a bow at the waste, only making it halfway. "Your Highness, it is a pleasure to have you reside in my home. Now, there will be more time for conversation later. I took the liberty of inviting some of Lockwood's greatest leaders to a meeting, I hope you don't mind. I understand it's late, but I have heard a certain royal character is enroute to Lockwood and trust you might greatly benefit from this meeting."

"We're meeting right now?" Ryker speaks, before Shade can really process what the duke has said. "With the other leaders?"

"Most of them," the duke confirms. "Except for Lady Brandy, who sent a messenger informing us she has already had the pleasure of meeting you. And Lady Colette who is feeling a bit under the weather this evening."

Shade fights off a yawn and blinks rapidly, trying to wake up. "Wonderful. Where's the meeting?"

Duke Harvard beams. "Up the stairs in our grand dining room. My wife has already sent the servants home for the night, but she makes a mean coconut cake and has the coffee brewing. You are the last of our guests to arrive."

As much as Shade wishes he could speak with his team and get answers from Drake about the caravan, he knows that will have to wait. He takes a breath and follows the duke up the stairs. Harvard is saying something about some of the tapestries on the walls and the elaborate glass ceiling. Shade is preoccupied with devising a plan to win over more allies while Ryker gives him a whispered crash course on who they're about to meet.

"Duke Harvard is married to Duchess Jane. They have a daughter, Lady Sprite. Duke Flynn Godwin is orphaned, late twenties. His parents were rather well-to-do, sort of celebrities of Lockwood. Spends a majority of his time living in luxury off the millions of dollars his parents left him. But he's wily and we could use money. Sir Reginald Opal and his wife, Lady Lilith, are married, with no children. He owns a messenger company and she either sews or oversees the sewing of half the clothing in the city. There may be a few others present that I do not know much about. Not all may be allies, but it doesn't mean they're enemies. Lockwood, as a whole, has always been loyal to the throne. Duke Harvard maintains a stellar reputation of trusting those he puts in office. These are relatively good people, whether we gain their support or not."

They reach the top of the staircase where one butler stands to greet them. To either side are hallways branching down the length of the house. There are multiple doorways to either side, although the left appears to have less. Duke Harvard turns to face them, arms clasped behind him. "I would advise only bringing a few with you into this meeting. Such a large entourage might make a few of the dignitaries nervous. Waldo, here, will direct the rest of you to your rooms." His arm beckons to the butler and then down the hallway to the right. "You'll find each room comes with its own bathroom. We are well-off enough to have our own indoor plumbing. By that I mean you'll find it's more than just a hole in the floor. There is also a commons room at the very end of the hall with a welcoming fireplace and plenty of lounge seating for everyone. If in need of a drink or a late-night treat, the kitchen is down the left hallway."

"It appears he is no stranger to those," Shade hears Baron mutter to himself, "Late night treats, that is." The Green adds.

Thankfully, the duke doesn't hear and continues looking at Shade expectantly.

Right. He's waiting for Shade to pick some to attend the meeting with him. Ryker is an obvious choice, especially with his knowledge of Lockwood. Hagan might be another, if he hadn't spent the last hour making accusations and acting like a buffoon. "Ryker," Shade says to the Gray, who nods without question. Risa would be his next choice had the Blue been present. Erin or Dru would both be a comforting presence. But one look at the two of them and he knows they need rest more than anything right now. Besides, Dru has been helpful with keeping Drake calm on their ride over and, even now, she whispers soothingly to him and wipes his forehead of sweat while he glances furtively around the room. Instead, he surprises even himself when he says, "Baron."

Baron chokes out a surprised laugh, easily smoothing it over into a cough, then joins Shade at his side. "Let's get this show on the road."

I'm going to regret this, Shade thinks.

Duke Harvard nods, glancing expectantly at the butler, "Show the others to their rooms. Take them some of Jane's cake. Prince Shade, right this way." He turns and waddles down the left hallway. The three of them and Tyson follow.

The guard steps up beside Harvard and asks him about Jeb's arrival. Harvard rubs his double chin thoughtfully. "This changes nothing." He explains, "Merely, speeds things up a bit. Can you send for some

287

of your men and make ready the summer estate?"

Tyson bows his head, nods at Shade, then leaves quickly back down the staircase.

Before they continue walking, Harvard says, "This is a beautiful home, but it is only our winter residence. We have a regular home about a mile from here, still in Lockwood, but up on a giant hill."

Shade recalls seeing this home from afar. He is sure it is even more magnificent up close.

"During the winter, the trek up to it can become treacherous with ice and snow, so we live here to ensure we can still go about our business as needed. That residence is much larger. It is where we will house King Jeb and his entourage." He holds up a hand to stop Ryker from speaking, "I assure you, this is not ideal. Housing these vile men is the last thing I want to do. However, it would appear strange for me not to offer up my home to the king of Zion." He waits for anyone to disagree.

Of course, no one does. Because this makes perfect sense. Shade nods.

The first room on the right they pass is a shower room. They quickly pass the kitchen on their left, which stretches the length of most of the hallway. A few bedrooms line the right side of the hallway, but mainly they appear to be conference rooms or tea rooms. He wonders if there's a library anywhere in the house. It would be beneficial for Shade to read up on some Zion history.

They reach the end of the hallway facing two closed double doors. Low voices can be heard from the other side, but when their footsteps approach, the talking ceases.

Harvard throws open the double doors, smiling

broadly. "Our honored guest has arrived!"

The room contains a long vertical, wooden table with several of the chairs occupied. One woman in a beautiful cream dress and a gray and white furred shawl is pouring coffee in some of the guests' cups. She turns at their arrival, matching Harvard's smile.

This must be Duchess Jane. She is beautiful, with dark hair speckled with gray and a smile that lights up her whole face. She is small, petite, a stark contrast to her husband. "Your Highness," She sets down the coffee pot and curtsies.

Shade's eyes travel the rest of the room, settling on the six other individuals. They all wear pleasant, if guarded, expressions. One young girl smiles tentatively. She can't be much older than him. She stands, bows, and says, "It is an honor to meet you. I'm Lady Sprite. Just Sprite is fine."

Shade sees the resemblance and notes how lucky the girl is to have received her mother's looks. "The honor is mine. Thank you for meeting so late." He takes a seat on the sparse side of the table, Ryker and Baron on either side of him. "I am Prince Shade. These are two of my friends, Ryker and Baron, who hail from Frostfire."

"It would appear you have been through it." An older man, with a large beard and dark hair says, eyeing Ryker's sling and the fading bruises on Shade's face.

So much has happened in the past week, Shade almost forgot about his broken nose. Beside him, Baron shifts uncomfortably, a sheepish look on his face.

The older man continues, "I am Sir Reginald, this is my wife, Lady Lilith. We are intrigued by your presence. Although, I must admit, not surprised. Long ago, Lockwood was an annual visit for your late father."

Shade is slightly caught off guard. His father never mentioned Lockwood beyond its trade value, let alone visiting it consistently. "You knew my father?"

Reginald nods, his deep eyes warm. "Indeed. But truly, it was for your mother's sake. Queen Rose used to have family that resided here. An old aunt and some cousins. After her aunt died and her cousins moved, the king and queen didn't visit as much. Still, we knew them."

Shade recognizes that old look of familiarity. "You were friends." He says, suddenly missing his parents with a fervor he'd been avoiding since fleeing the castle.

Lady Lilith speaks up then, her voice quiet, sweet. "Your mother was always so kind, so welcoming. Is she…?"

Shade swallows. "I haven't heard anything of her or my sister since I left. I hope for the best, but can't help fearing the worst. King Jeb is reportedly on his way here. I assume he will be here by morning, if not sooner. There is a bounty on my head and, presumably, any who aid me. I understand if there are any of you who wish not to get involved."

"This is our kingdom, no?" A young man, with a brash voice and handsome features speaks up. His blonde hair makes a large swoop over his forehead and falls into his eyes. He shakes his head to flip it out of his face. "It would appear we are already involved, whether we wish it or not."

"Duke Flynn." Duke Harvard introduces the orphan with a sweep of his arm.

Flynn raises an eyebrow in greeting.

Two other people sit around the table, neither of which appear to be dressed like the others. In fact, Shade believes them to be regular townspeople, not leaders of the city at all. Curiously, he looks their way. The woman is stiff, shoulders back against the high chair. Her gray hair is pulled into a tight bun. The man is more relaxed, wearing a toothy grin and spectacles. Both are older and, by the rings on their clasped hands, seem to be married.

"Mr. and Mrs. Wolf." Harvard says.

"I'm Alaric, this is Helen," the man says, "We knew your parents. We're blacksmiths and create a lot of weaponry and armor you see around Lockwood. When your parents would visit, your father would spend a lot of time in our neck of the woods and a lot of money for our efforts."

"He would bring it back to Glimmer?"

"Some of it," Helen says, "But most of it went to arm Lockwood and other cities loyal to the throne. Even back then, your father knew some cities would rebel against his rule. He was making alliances long before you. Many of which you will now gain because of him. We knew your parents. And we loved them." She shares a look with Alaric, who nods.

"You have our support," he says, "And our steel and iron."

"How many allies do you have thus far?" Sir Reginald asks.

Shade clears his throat. "Honestly, not many. But I have to start somewhere. The village of Frostfire, several of which have made the journey here with me. General Saipan and Yagar, Lady Brandy, the guards of the Western Gate, the healers, Blair and Liv." As he says it, he realizes how small his group of allies really is. He tries to swallow the lump in his throat. "Not enough. But more than I had yesterday. And less than I'll have tomorrow. Our mission is to retake the throne. Not now, maybe not even soon, but someday. Every ally I make brings me closer to that moment."

Duke Flynn throws back his steaming cup of coffee. If it burns going down, he doesn't show it. "Well," He says, after loudly setting the cup back onto the table, "I, for one, enjoy a good fight." He grins at Lady Sprite, "What do you say, *mi frimor*?"

"Me free-more." Baron sounds out next to him. "My love." He translates. Shade tries not to look annoyed when he waves a hand at him under the table. Now is not the time for translations.

Sprite looks away from Flynn, rolling her eyes at the duke. "I do not like wars." She states matter of factly, "But I believe those currently in power do *not* have the best interests of the people at heart—on the contrary, they only serve themselves. I do not like wars, but I like inequality even less."

Shade thinks that means she's on board.

Sir Reginald leans forward, setting his coffee mug down and clasping his hands together on the table. "It's interesting that Lady Brandy sides with you. It makes me think she is aware of something else at play."

Shade shares a glance with Baron, "Some of us were attacked on the road to Lockwood and it would appear they were better trained than what we have known Renegades to be. Lady Brandy believes there is another party out there who seeks only anarchy."

Lady Lilith breathes in a slight gasp, "Anarchy? In *Zion*?"

Understanding dawns in Reginald's eyes,

"Anarchy would not bode well for a woman like Brandy who has made too many enemies over the years." He looks once more at Shade, "We side with you, as well. My messengers are at your disposal. King Jeb is on his way here, what preparations need to be done?"

At this, Duke Harvard steps forward, his belly bumping the edge of the table. "Nothing for me, for now. I am preparing our other home for his stay. I assume he has been informed of Prince Shade's supposed sighting. He could also be interested in Lockwood's Harvard Ball. That approaches in just three days." He looks at Shade and his companions, "It's an annual party my wife and I throw. Invitation only, of course. But folks from near and far come to celebrate the close of another year and the beginning of the next! It's quite a time, I must say."

Shade has no interest in a ball. There isn't time for such festivities.

Small talk begins amongst Baron and Duke Flynn, who is particularly interested in the Green's vibrant hair. Shade decides he likes the orphaned duke when he asks Baron if he has to dye his eyebrows. Baron's smile is more forced after that.

Reginald and his wife say their goodbyes and make for the door.

"Sir," Shade says, stepping towards them before they can leave.

"My friends call me Reg." He says with a smile, Lilith's arm wrapped in his. "What can I do for you, Prince Shade?"

"Reg," Shade says with a nod. "Thank you for your support. Lord Bane of Frostfire is expecting a message from me, alerting him of our arrival in Lockwood.

Unfortunately, my messenger is currently in a bit of duress. I fear he is incapable of completing the task. Can you spare a messenger to deliver my letter?"

"Of course! Have the letter ready in an hour and I'll send my best man to pick it up. He'll be at Frostfire within four days—my messengers are very fast." The couple bow their heads and leave.

Shade turns with a tired sigh. Thankfully, his mission is beginning to prove worth it. Already, he is feeling better about his chances at succeeding with the few allies he's made.

Duchess Jane is in front of him, offering up a slice of coconut cake. "It's still warm, Your Highness. And it's made with little sugar, so it won't keep you up."

Shade smiles ruefully, "I'm afraid very little would keep me up at this point." He takes the plate, "Thank you. For everything."

"Breakfast will be first thing in the morning. Our staff will be present and they go all out with meals. You will not leave the table hungry." She smiles at him, genuine, if a little sad. "The weight of the kingdom can be a very heavy thing. You do not have to carry it alone. Rest well, knowing you are in safe hands here."

The tightness around his chest lessens slightly. "Do you have a pen and paper I can use?"

The duchess steps away, opens the drawer of a nearby desk, and produces what he has asked. She hands the items to him. "There is plenty more if needed."

Shade nods his thanks. Now, onto other matters. He needs to have a conversation with Drake. He bids farewell to the other royals in the room. Ryker finishes his coconut cake, shakes Harvard's hand, then follows

Shade out the door. Baron is still stuck in a conversation with Flynn and his eyes plead for Shade to rescue him.

Shade hides a smirk and leaves him to it.

When they reach the commons room at the opposite end of the hall, everyone is still awake. Most are sitting quietly on various couches and lounge chairs. Hagan stands next to the fireplace, his elbow leaning against the mantle. Drake talks to himself, wringing his hands. Everyone turns at their arrival.

"He's going on about a caravan and a woman. Explain yourself." Hagan mutters, clearly still upset about not being chosen.

Shade doesn't sit. He stands in front of everyone and recounts the events that occurred on his way into Lockwood. Shade realizes Drake, although definitely in his right mind at that time, was battling the illness at that point. The deep effects of the sickness must have taken hold of him sometime after that encounter. When Shade gets to the part about Drake returning days later, the messenger finally speaks loud enough for all to hear.

His eyes are scrunched in concentration, as if aware of his illness and the effects it is having on him. "I'm trying." He says. "So many thoughts. Trying to separate."

"Take your time." Dru says soothingly. She pats his knee where it bounces up and down continually.

Eventually, he begins again. "Caravan with symbol. Tattoo symbol."

"The Loyalty Mark." Fray says, "Yes, you've already said that."

"Give him time. The sickness causes great confusion." Dru snaps, her eyes narrowed. It must be bringing back upsetting thoughts about her mother, who she lost not all that long ago to this same fever. Shade gives her an encouraging nod.

"Inside," Drake picks back up, "A woman. Wearing blue. Familiar. Very familiar, very strange. Not alone."

Shade begins working this out in his mind. So, there was more than one person in the caravan and the woman wearing blue was familiar to him.

Drake looks at him and Shade nods for him to continue. "Another woman, older than the first. Familiar but not very."

Familiar, just like the first girl, but not very. Perhaps the first is one he knows and the second, one he has only heard of? "Do you know the woman in blue?" Shade asks.

Drake nods, then shakes his head. "Not a woman. Girl, young. Seen her, not know."

"Okay," Shade says encouragingly, "So the young girl in blue is someone you have seen before. In person?"

He shakes his head.

"In a portrait?"

He nods.

"The other woman is older than the girl in blue. What was she wearing?"

Here, Drake looks confused and he begins muttering again.

"That's not important," Dru explains. "Part of the sickness is that it causes the host to recall only necessary facts about situations. Ask something else."

Shade thinks. It matters to Drake what the first girl was wearing, for some reason; but not the second. The second woman is older and appeared familiar but not heavily so. "Do you know the second woman?"

He hesitates, then answers, "Yes and no."

What in Zion does that mean? "Have you seen her before in person?"

"Yes and no."

Okay, new strategy. "Was anyone else in the wagon?"

He shakes his head.

"Did you speak with them?"

"Tried. Heavily guarded. Too close to the king."

So, he tried getting in contact with the caravan, but Jeb must have been close by. Perhaps, even talking with them already. Why would Jeb be speaking to someone in a caravan containing the Loyalty Mark? Unless he wasn't aware of the symbol on the wagon. Or, unless Jeb himself is disloyal to those who have placed him in charge. Shade rubs his face. This has only been more confusing.

Drake seems to pick up on this, because he stands now, desperate to help them understand. He rubs his chin, thinking, his eyes somewhat crazed. He looks around the room, then frowns, as if not seeing what he hoped for. "Girl in blue, scared." He acts out hiding his eyes. "Scared."

"What was she scared of?" Shade asks.

Drake points at him.

"Me?"

Drake shakes his head and starts waving his finger.

If this had been a game of charades, Shade might think this meant to keep guessing because he was on the right track. "Scared of someone like me? Scared of royalty? Scared of Jeb?"

Drake jumps, "That!"

"Scared of Jeb." Shade says again and Drake nods

297

in confirmation. "Did you see them talking?"

Another nod. "Yelling. Him. She…" He mimes tears falling down his cheeks. "Older girl also yelling."

"Yelling at the girl in blue?"

"At him."

Okay, so there was some sort of fight between Jeb and this older woman that Drake saw. Jeb was yelling at the girl in blue and, perhaps, the older woman was defending her. "Did Jeb know them?"

Drake nods. Once again, he points at Shade.

"Do I know them?"

He nods excitedly, then stops. Shakes his head. He holds up one finger.

"I know one of them?"

Drake, excited again, nods. "They are all coming. Here."

Just then, footsteps approach the door and it opens to reveal the butler. Behind him are Risa and Perez.

"I hope you bring some sort of news. We are getting nowhere here." Fray says, he exits the room, clearly frustrated. Shade has yet to see the bald man display patience.

The twins enter.

Dru sighs, "Maybe Drake should rest. He's expending a lot of energy just by standing, let alone trying to form thoughts and words."

Ryker turns to the twins, who are standing at attention just inside the doorway, always ready for action. "Did you find him?" Ryker asks.

Risa nods, "Oh, we found him alright. They're holed up just inside the Northern Gate, at an old windmill. We couldn't tell how many there were, but when Afton went inside, there was a lot of yelling."

"Did you catch anything else? Useful information?

Names?" Ryker asks. He has taken a seat on the arm of the chair Trix is sitting in. She places a comforting hand on his back.

Perez shrugs, "I heard the name 'Storg.' But am unfamiliar with it."

Shade freezes. In his peripheral vision, he sees Dru and Erin look his way. He speaks up. "When we left Frostfire, I was made aware of a potential traitor getting in contact with a man named Storg. This is now being confirmed."

"You've known about this since we *left*?" Hagan is angry again. His fists clench and unclench from their position on the mantle. He speaks with his back to the room. Shade brushes aside the thought that he wishes Hagan were the traitor so he could run him through.

"Come now, Hagan. Did you expect him to tell us? He didn't know who he could trust." Ryker says, sounding perturbed. "Take a seat and calm down. Enough of this."

"Afton told them about King Jeb. They acted surprised by this news." Risa continues. Perhaps they really are an anarchist group, like Lady Brandy was saying. She goes on, saying,

"Then Afton asked about his family. I got the impression this Storg fellow was holding them captive."

"Which would explain why Vision was understanding towards Afton when he attacked her. She said he kept muttering something and apologizing. Maybe he told her they had his family." Baron speaks from the doorway. He must have finally escaped Flynn and his incredibly long story. The Green looks worn, dark circles evident under his eyes.

Risa continues. "We were too cautious to stick

around for long. There were people milling about nearby, getting closer to our hiding spot. So, we bolted back to the horses, ran into Tyson, and he pointed us here."

"Thank you," Shade says, his mind working in overdrive. He glances at the sundial hanging on the wall. It shows the time to be about two in the morning, well past their need for rest. "Perhaps, we would all do well to get some sleep."

But Drake starts talking again, words that don't make sense. Shade wonders if now he's speaking in the Old English of Zion. Drake hurries closer to the twins, who eye him warily, and even a little startled. He points at them, then looks back at Shade. "Older woman! Older woman!"

Shade shakes his head, "Drake, I'm sorry, I don't…" It's near impossible to understand the Purple. Shade watches him sadly, wishing desperately that there was some way he could help Drake.

"Older woman. Not very familiar." He reiterates.

Shade considers this again. Okay, the older woman was not very familiar to Drake. So that means she was *somewhat* familiar? When Shade asked if Drake had seen her before, he replied with 'Yes and no.'

"Do they look like them or something?" Erin asks quietly, not wanting to interrupt Drake's gibberish in case it causes him confusion. She's standing, arms crossed, a thoughtful expression on her face.

Shade stares at her and her words echo in his head. The older woman looked like *them*. *That's it*, Shade thinks suddenly. He grasps Drake by the shoulders and gently faces him. "Drake, you said 'not very familiar.' Was she dressed like them?"

His eyebrows scrunch together, "No."

"So, she *looks* like them? Does her face look like theirs?" Shade points at the twins, who, to their credit, stand there with patient, bored expressions, waiting for an explanation.

Drake nods.

Shade looks at Risa, "How old was your sister when she was taken?"

Her face starts and she glowers at him, "I told you that in confidence." Her accusatory eyes flit around the room.

The prince ignores her, "Risa, how old? Ten? Eleven?"

"She was thirteen." Risa says through gritted teeth. "What is the meaning of this, *hilcipe*?"

"She was taken seven years ago," Shade remembers. He turns back to Drake, "How old was the older woman? Twenty?" This whole time, Shade has been assuming 'older' means fifty or above. That isn't at all what Drake's saying. He just means older than the young girl in blue.

Drake nods at his question, "Older, but young. Looks like them. Familiar, but not very."

"Drake," Shade refrains from shaking the messenger by the shoulders, "Could she be their sister?" When Drake nods, Shade drops his hands from Drake's shoulders and turns to the twins in wonder.

Risa's mouth is slightly parted as varying emotions of anger, confusion, and something else…hope, perhaps, flash across her face. Perez says nothing, but his eyes watch the scene with an intensity Shade has not yet seen in the warrior.

"It can't be." Risa says, not allowing a fraction of hope inside. "Impossible. He is mistaken." She looks the Purple up and down, nostrils flared.

"I don't know if it's true. But he's describing a woman, around the age of twenty, who looks like you two." Shade shrugs, "It could be your sister. It could be one of your people. Who knows for certain?"

"Me!" Drake exclaims. Annoyance crosses his features and his eyes look relatively sane for the first time since Shade's been back in his presence. "She was almost an exact replica, just younger." He shakes his head, "I'm sorry. My mind won't...function. I can feel it starting to slip back away." He shuts his eyes tight, voice shaking with fatigue and emotion. "And the girl in blue. Never met her, but I see her in portraits because she's...she's..." But when his eyes open, they are once again dazed and out of focus, confused.

"That will happen often." Dru says in the silence that follows. Drake had just had a moment of sanity in the midst of the illness. But, no more; he's once more under the Cyphur's vicious grip.

Shade steps closer to Drake once more, lifting an encouraging hand to his arm again. "She's what? Who is she?" He asks gently. "The older woman is their sister, who is the young girl?"

Drake looks at him then, one final moment of clarity surfacing. "She's yours." Then he's quiet, wringing his hands, uncertain eyes never focusing on any certain thing.

"She's..." Shade lets out a breath he didn't realize he's been holding. It escapes his lips as quickly as the tightness returns to his chest. "Mine? She's my sister. You saw Amberle?" It would explain how Jeb knew her and why he would be yelling at her. It would explain Drake's hyperfocus on the color of blue, seeing how it is the primary color of the Alwyn family crest. Drake begins babbling nonsense again and Trix guides

302

him to a seating position, where she starts checking his blood pressure. Shade looks at Erin, wondering if the stricken look on her face mirrors his own.

He has to get to Amberle. He has to keep her safe. But if there's one thing he's learned over the past few weeks, it's that those in his presence are so incredibly far from safe.

"I know what you're thinking and I'm here to advise against it." Ryker says plainly. "Making a move to get her would be stupid. King Jeb likely expects it. Whether he has truly gone Renegade or not, the safest place for her to be right now is with the king. Because if he's bad, she's leverage. And if he's good, he loves her and, therefore, will do anything to keep her safe."

He knows the Gray is right. "But, why is she here?" Shade asks no one in particular. "Why isn't she with my mother?" The haunting thought of something having happened to his mother crosses his mind. He throws it out, along with any illogical thought of storming Lockwood in search of his sister tonight. Those are not the thoughts and actions of a future king; it would only do to put more of them in harm's way. "This is a lot to process. We should sleep on it and reconvene in the morning."

"Speak for yourself," Perez says, his cool voice always so surprising, "If that mutt has my sister, I'll kill him and get her back before morning."

Shade starts to repeat Ryker's advice and warn him against such actions, but, to his surprise, Risa beats him to it. "That is unwise, Perez." She says, a hand on his arm, "*If* it's really her, we will act when the time is right."

"Correct, and right now, the time is right for me to fall into bed." Baron says, yawning loudly. His arms stretch above his head. "Oh, and guess what. Harvey's throwing a ball! This weekend. Isn't that great? I haven't been to a ball since..." He pretends to do some math before shrugging happily, "Ever!"

"We're going to a ball?" Dru asks, some excitement sounding in her voice.

"We're not going to a ball." Hagan mutters.

"King Jeb will be there." Ryker says, shaking his head in agreement with Hagan.

When Harvard first shared the idea, Shade shot it down without a second thought. But knowing his sister is involved changes everything. "It might be a good opportunity to gather information, gain new sources, and leave an impression on the king himself."

"Risky." Ryker says.

"But..." Trix looks up from her patient, "The prince is right. It might be worth it."

The group looks around, passing glances to each other.

Eventually, Hagan's head drops and he sighs. "We can talk."

Baron pumps the air with his fist. "We're going to a ball." He holds out his hand and Dru slaps it with her own. Then he walks out of the room with an air of finality.

The butler still stands at his position by the door. He turns to Shade, "I will show you to your room, Your Highness."

Shade nods. "Thank you. Goodnight, everyone." They all begin shuffling out to their various rooms. On his way, Shade realizes he's lost his coconut cake somewhere. He must have set it down in the commons room without realizing it. The butler takes him a short walk to a room on his left.

"Your bath has already been drawn. Clean, suitable clothes are hanging in the closet for the morning. Nightwear is in the bottom drawer of the chest set." Waldo, the butler says.

"Um, thanks." Of course, Shade is used to servants and butlers waiting on him. This is normal within the castle. But Shade hasn't heard these words in a while. And those that wait on him in the castle have learned that Shade prefers to do things on his own. They don't ever "draw his baths" or pick out his clothing. He rarely even lets them call him "prince" and "your highness." Shade enters the room, shutting it behind him. He thinks about locking it, but decides against it. Ryker and Hagan had remained in the commons room. It is likely they plan on splitting the watch for the night and Shade is happy to let them do it. Duchess Jane's words echo in his head and something tells Shade he really is safe here. At least, for tonight.

The room is about the size of Dru's entire house back in the village where she's from. Thinking of that reminds him of her father and Juliett who are currently being held captive somewhere. He sighs tiredly, before continuing further into the room. He passes the bathroom on his right and pokes his head inside. The butler, true to his word, has the bathtub full with steaming water. There's a separate shower next to this, one toilet, and a large wooden counter area with a sink and a mirror hanging above.

Yikes. It'd been a while since he saw himself in a mirror. Since he fled the castle, actually. His hair is longer now, dark and unkempt. It falls a couple of inches past his shoulders and Shade is pretty certain this is the longest it's ever been. He knew about the fading bruises under his eyes and around his nose, but

305

the stubble on his face and chin is becoming too much. It makes him look much older and more like his father who he can't afford to think about right now. He steps inside the bathroom and begins rummaging in the cabinet drawers. He takes out a knife and finds some soap and makes quick work of the stubble. There, he looks more like himself.

The haunted look is still in his eyes. Shade may only be eighteen and true, only a month or so has passed since leaving Glimmer, but he still looks as if he's aged a few years. The hair will have to stay the same for now. Besides, he kind of digs the longer length.

He leaves the bathroom and explores the rest of the room. A king-sized bed with a navy blue blanket and four fluffy pillows occupies a majority of it. Then there's one chest of drawers, a walk-in closet, and a large desk with a rolling chair sitting in the opposite corner. Along the far wall is a window that faces out the front of Harvard's mansion, looking out over Lockwood. He steps closer to the window and opens it slightly, letting in a cool winter breeze.

He sits in the rolling chair, pulls the pen and paper from his shirt pocket, and sets them on the desk to begin his letter to Lord Bane. Shade trusts Sir Reginald to be a man of his word, but he's uncertain how many eyes might read the letter before it reaches Frostfire. He decides to keep it brief, unassuming.

Destination reached. Traitor found—family whereabouts unknown. Two dead. In spite of loss, the mission is proving successful. Windenmeyer is close. Reinforcements appreciated. —S

Perhaps Afton's family is missing from Frostfire; Lord Bane can then not only know who the traitor is, but can find a way to get the innocent family back. And

306

Drake will likely be gone by the time this letter reaches Bane, which is why Shade included the second death. By mentioning the proximity of the castle, Shade hopes Lord Bane understands that he means Jeb is in Lockwood. He adds the last sentence because any help is welcome. Having a leader like Lord Bane nearby would greatly increase morale, especially Shade's.

As an afterthought, Shade adds a rather crude, but recognizable drawing of the Loyalty Mark. He rolls up the piece of parchment carefully, finds a string of floss in the bathroom, then ties it up nice and neat like a scroll.

He returns to the rolling chair and unlaces his boots, setting them to the side. He leans back in the chair, closes his eyes, and sits quietly for a moment, listening to the soft noises of Lockwood city life coming in through the window.

The serene moment is interrupted by someone knocking.

Immediately, he's on edge. But he reaffirms that he is safe for the moment. And is further relieved when he opens the door to find it's Ryker.

The Gray bows his head, "Hagan, Risa, and I are taking shifts for tonight. I just wanted to reassure you that you can rest easy."

"Thank you, Ryker. Be sure you all get some rest as well."

Ryker nods, "Of course. Sir Reginald's messenger is also here to collect the letter. He's downstairs, I can take it to him."

Shade retrieves the letter from the desk and hands it to Ryker, "Read it. I tried to remain as impassive as possible. I would like to trust this messenger, but I've learned you can never be too careful."

Ryker unties the letter and reads it quickly. When he finishes, he ties the floss around it, smiling a little at Shade's choice of string. "I think that's fine. Lord Bane is, no doubt, itching for any reason to join us." He turns to leave, but then pauses with one more look his way, "You have earned Risa's trust. As someone who has grown up directly with her, gaining the trust of Risa is not an easy feat. You are doing well, Your Highness."

"If that be so, Ryker, please, refer to me as you would a friend. You are a man of respect, but I assure you, it is no disrespect when it's my preference."

Ryker nods, then says, "Very well. Goodnight...my friend." He disappears down the hall.

Shade chuckles to himself. He closes the door and returns to the bathroom. He lets the water drain out of the tub, then takes a shower, preferring to be in and out quickly so he can sleep. Afterwards, he doesn't bother with the nightwear, opting to simply slip on a clean pair of underwear and then hop in bed.

He's asleep the moment his eyes shut. However, it doesn't last long. At some point in the night, he hears a noise, like the sound of a door being opened. It only takes a moment later for him to realize it is a door being opened. Specifically, the door to his room. He's on his feet and against the wall within a moment. Whoever's coming in will likely suspect the prince to still be in bed; when they step inside the room and a few feet later, past the wall, he will be waiting.

It opens quietly. He hears someone step inside and the door close. Seconds pass in silence. The light from the full moon shines brightly into the room and his eyes have adjusted to any darkness that's left. Shade holds his breath, waiting. Waiting.

And then, "Shade?" Comes a whispered voice.

He straightens and rounds the corner with a sigh. "Not the time to be breaking into rooms, Erin."

Erin stands there, looking sheepish. Her arms are crossed, hands rubbing them against the chill of his room. She's in a night shirt and pants and her hair is ruffled from lying in bed. "Sorry." She mumbles. "I couldn't sleep. So, I…" She sighs, "Sorry, I didn't mean to wake you. I'll leave—"

"No." Shade says quickly. Truthfully, he feels better having her close. At that moment, he suddenly remembered he's in only his underwear. Erin seems to notice as well and she looks at the floor. "I couldn't sleep, either." He lies. He holds out an arm, trying for a comforting smile. "Take the bed, I'll take the chair."

One side of her mouth lifts. "Please, prince. We've shared beds before."

Yeah, when we were eight, Shade thinks.

"You take one side; I'll take the other. As long as you don't fight in your sleep like you used to, we'll be fine." She walks past him and climbs in the bed closest to the bathroom wall without another word.

Shade feels along the floor, finds his shirt and slips it on over his head. He doesn't want Erin feeling any sort of discomfort. Then, he climbs in bed on the other side. After several minutes of quiet, he wonders if she's asleep.

But then she says, "Thank you. It just feels nice to be near you."

He swallows, letting out a breath. "I agree." Fatigue drags at his eyes. "Goodnight, Erin." He mumbles out through a yawn.

Her chuckle comes softly. "Goodnight, Shade."

CHAPTER 22

A knock on his door is the next thing he knows.

"Rise and shine, Prince Charming; breakfast is served!"

How is it that even when Shade gets a room to himself, Baron's obnoxious voice is still the thing to awaken him?

He cracks one eye, staring at the window, still open from the night before. Daylight streams in through the slightly drawn curtains. The room is freezing, but the cool air helps to bring him to his senses. He suddenly recalls Erin sneaking into his room last night and glances quickly across the bed. She's gone; not even a wrinkle left as evidence she was ever there at all.

Shade begrudgingly drags himself out of bed and opens the closet door. Hanging there are two options for a shirt. Both are long-sleeved tunics, but one is a crimson velvet fabric and the other a cream cotton fabric. He chooses the cotton shirt and clothes himself with it and the only pair of breeches, a forest green color. He ties his boots back on and makes his way to the bathroom. There isn't much to be done about his fatigued appearance, so he just ties half of his hair back with more floss string he found in a cabinet drawer, brushes his teeth, and leaves the room.

The door is hardly open before the delicious scents permeate his nostrils.

Baron separates from the wall where he'd been leaning, wearing something similar to Shade's own outfit. "Bout time. Get a haircut while you were in there, too?"

Shade doesn't admit he considered it. "Is everyone

else already up?"

"Hagan's still sleeping off his last shift. Everyone else is either in the dining hall or heading there. Some people thought you deserved a little more rest." They begin walking down the hallway.

"What time is it?"

"Almost noon"

"*What*?"

"I'm just kidding. I don't know, man, I just woke up, too. Barely sat down at the table and Ryker tells me to come drag your sorry butt out of bed. He didn't say it quite like that. I think the sundial on the windowsill outside my bedroom window read just after eight. Something like that."

The door to their right opens and Dru joins them. She's wearing a light pink tunic with frilly sleeves and brown breeches. Her dark hair is wild, surrounding her face in waves. "Is your bed as comfy as mine or did I just get really lucky?"

"Slept like a babe," Baron replies, winking at her.

"My head already misses that pillow," Shade says, "Surely there's a better system of waking up that *doesn't* involve Baron."

Baron pretends to consider this, "Eh, sounds lame."

The dining room where he met with the leaders the night before is filled with bustling people. The servants are mainly the bustling ones, while most of Shade's crew is seated around the table that is filled with a seemingly endless supply of breakfast items. Many of them look a little overwhelmed, not familiar with the idea of being served. Erin sits at the feet of Risa, the Blue braiding Erin's blonde hair. Shade finds the scene peculiar and can't help smiling. Risa catches his eye

311

and remains stoic, daring him to say something.

Shade doesn't, but Baron has never been good at keeping his mouth shut. "I didn't know a Viking princess braided other people's hair. Do you also enjoy painting nails and doing each other's make-up?"

"The only thing I do with nails is rip them out as I torture my victims." Risa says, unflinching. Her fiery eyes flit to Baron's, "Are you volunteering?"

A slight shudder passes through Baron and a distant smile settles on his face, "That's kind of sexy."

Dru snorts and sits beside Erin, "Me next, please? Look at this mess." She holds up her hands to indicate her hair.

"Well, I wasn't going to say anything…" Shade teases.

She lashes out at him with one boot and he dodges it deftly.

Breakfast passes uneventfully. Afterwards, Hagan insists they get back into a daily routine of training. Lord Harvard, who is currently at his other home with his wife, was sure to insist they use his training room in the basement. Shade doubts Harvard has ever set foot in that training room, but is grateful for his hospitality nonetheless. They train for several hours, switching between weight lifting, running, and agility. Towards the end, they practice some hand-to-hand combat and sword fighting.

By the look on Erin's face, Shade can tell she wants to join the fray, but she and Ryker are forced to simply watch, their arms' in slings. The training room is large, stretching the entire length of the house, with rubber lining the floor to protect one from any hard falls. After what seems like endless hours, they take a break. Duchess Jane makes an appearance, joining some servants as they bring them water and refreshing lemonade. She insists each of Shade's crew stand for measurements, "You can't very well go to the ball dressed like that." She also brings them news of the king. Duke Harvard has been tied down with entertaining him and the entourage he has brought with him. For the moment, the king appears to be unconcerned with the rumors of Prince Shade being in Lockwood. Jane says many soldiers have made the journey with Jeb, she guesses around thirty total. Princess Amberle is also among them, as well as another woman of whom Jane did not recognize.

"But she could very well be related to the two of you." Duchess Jane says, eyeing the twins, "You do have very similar features." She blinks, "Almost identical, in fact. I saw her very briefly in passing, but there is no doubting the resemblance."

Risa and Perez share a concerned look. Risa turns to Shade, "Permission to locate her under the coverage of darkness this evening? Not retrieve, just lay eyes on her."

Shade understands their longing, and it hasn't even been seven years since he last saw his own sister. But he cannot justify them going. "I'm afraid that's too risky. I'm sorry." He addresses Jane, "Duchess, will you please keep an eye on them? Make sure they're being taken care of?"

Duchess Jane's eyes are wide with genuine concern, "Of course. You have my word." She leaves soon after with some of her ladies, returning to her other home.

As the day goes on, Drake becomes weaker and weaker. He can no longer stand for more than a few minutes at a time, and any hopes of translating his conversation have evaporated. They take turns watching him, making him comfortable, and providing him with food and drink.

That afternoon, Lady Colette pays them a visit. She's a young, stern looking woman, with high cheekbones and dark, silky hair that's currently piled in an eccentric braid atop her head. In her lilting, seductive voice, she apologizes for being too sick to visit the night before. Shade studies her, intrigued. There is something strangely familiar about the woman, but Shade can't quite put his finger on it. She isn't a beautiful woman; but it would be a great injustice to call her ugly. Her appearance is most definitely striking. He notices Baron giving her second and third glances and narrows his eyes at him to be polite. Honestly, did no one teach this red-head manners?

"I am the city's biggest fundraiser," She tells them, as she runs a nail-file over her perfectly manicured fingernails. "Because of this, I am on the road often, gone for up to weeks at a time. I meet with sponsors and potential prospects from other cities, near and far, in the hopes they will invest in *something* of Lockwood's. Whether that be our food industry, horses, land, etcetera."

"Do you have much luck with that?" Ryker asks at one point.

Lady Colette grins mischievously, a look that gives Shade an eerie feeling. "Why seek luck when charm or deceit works just fine? Lockwood doesn't need sponsors. It is quite successful on its own. But our sponsors don't need to know that."

Nobody says anything in response to that for several moments. Until Baron lets out a forced laugh

314

and says, "Of course." His laughter eventually dies off and he clears his throat awkwardly.

Needless to say, nobody is disappointed when Lady Colette looks at the time and insists she must return to her duties elsewhere. She leaves without saying whether or not she will join their cause and Shade doesn't ask, worried it would involve her sticking around longer than necessary.

After intense boredom, Shade decides to explore the rest of the house. Downstairs is a large living room with a massive fireplace, the main kitchen, a washroom, and an elegant closed door he assumes must be the master suite. It takes up a third of the downstairs. Most of the rooms on the second floor are bedrooms, the occasional sitting room, the two kitchens, the dining room, and the commons room. There is a separate cubby with a skinny hallway that leads to stairs whose only direction is up. Shade finds himself at the bottom of these stairs, looking upwards in curiosity. He turns to see Dru standing behind him, her eyes alight with mischief.

She grins. "After you, my *lord*."

He leads the way up the stairs, which wind in a circle up, up, up until finally ending at a closed wooden door. He looks over his shoulder at Dru, a smile on the edge of his lips. "A secret dungeon for traitors to the throne." He teases.

She slaps him softly. Being a couple of steps down from him and already short enough as she is, her hand hits him on his lower back, just above his butt. He mocks surprise, "Dru, I never."

Her face turns red and she shoves him this time, with enough force to knock him up the next step. He laughs and has to put his hands against the door to stay upright. It must not have been closed well enough because it swings open and he braces himself against the door frame so he doesn't fall. He starts to jokingly complain about the women in his life always pushing him around, but the sight beyond the door takes his breath away.

It's a library. A beautiful, majestic library that must stretch the entire length of the house because it's so big. The ceiling is high and in the center of it is a large circle window; it's completely glass, looking up to the sky which is currently changing colors with the setting sun. Streaks of blue, orange, red, purple, and pink jut across the sky beyond the glass. Stacks of books create rows on shelves all across the large room. There are multiple areas for sitting, lounging, and reading. Several tables are spread throughout the room and the natural light from the outside world casts the room in a warm glow.

Dru lets out a breath. "Holy Zion." She whispers. "This is amazing."

Shade nods. "Lockwood's greatest treasure." He says. He looks at her out of the corner of his eye and she does the same. They smile at each other. Shade admires her quaint beauty for several seconds. Long enough for her smile to fade and her eyes to take on something different, something curious. There is no time to question it further because the door opens behind them and Erin traipses in.

She pauses, seeing their locked eyes, but Shade turns away before anything more can come of it. He grins cheekily at Erin, "Look at this place."

Her eyes are narrowed. But then she begins looking around and fascination crosses her features. She starts walking, exploring the glorious library. Loud footsteps sound up the steps and Baron comes into view, pretending to be winded. "Did they have to include so many stairs?" He stops, one hand on the wall, head ducked, sucking in deep breaths. "Is anyone else dizzy?"

For the next hour, they explore the wonder of the library. Granted, Shade has never been one who enjoys reading or even listening to someone reading. However, he wishes now he had paid better attention in his history and language classes. Perhaps, he would have learned more about Zion and the people within it. Besides, he can't argue with the library's captivating beauty. Baron finds the rolling ladders on one of the stacks on the far wall and spends several minutes pushing off with a running start and riding it around the outer wall of the room. Dru and Erin find interesting books and sit down in the comfy chairs to read them. Shade searches for books on the Old English of Zion.

He finds a rather thick one and is pursuing through its pages when Baron says, "You know, if you want language lessons, I could just teach you."

Shade's eyes settle on the word he'd been looking for. He tries it out, uncertain if he's pronouncing it correctly. "*Kronidiota*." He must pronounce it correctly because Baron steps back, one hand on his chest as if injured.

"I am not an idiot." He says with mock hurt.

"The literal translation is 'as stupid as you can get.'"

He opens his mouth, pauses, grins, "Well, now, that is fairly accurate, isn't it?" He laughs. "But truly, I am a fairly good teacher. And, seeing as you are to be," He clears his throat, "*king*, one day, it might come in handy for you to know more of the old language."

Shade straightens, closing the book. He looks at Baron and folds his arms across his chest, "You're being serious."

"I try not to be but sometimes it just happens."

Shade nods in approval. Perhaps he will take the Green up on this offer at some point.

Later that evening, after they have rejoined everyone else, they spend hours talking and even laughing in the commons room. Shade is reminded that even in this difficult time, it is important to find joy. Baron takes out a deck of cards he brought from home and they play games until many start to yawn and turn in for the night. By ten, it's only Shade, Baron, Dru, and Erin, reminding him of how most of the days in Frostfire ended.

Dru yawns, "Aye, I need to head to bed. I'm definitely still recovering from that sickness."

"If only it hadn't taken our prince, here, so long to get you aid." Baron says, shaking his head. "They should have sent me. Poe would've listened eventually."

That horse listens to no one except Shade, now, much to his surprise. He ignores Baron's jab and leans back against the couch, closing his eyes. He is thankful for slow nights like this; especially since he knows they are few and far between.

"Yeah, right. Poe can't even stand the smell of you." Dru says. "That horse is a champ. I'm thankful Shade had him; cause Zion knows I was absolutely no help."

"Were you out the whole time?" Erin asks.

Baron laughs, "Oh, I'm sure. Out like a light."

"Not the whole time, but I was so out of my mind."

Dru laughs, "What was I saying Shade?"

Shade smiles, eyes still closed as he recalls the conversation he had with Dru on the road, her voice full of delirium and fever. "*Before* or *after* you tried punching me in the face?"

"Nice," Baron says.

Shade goes on, "Hmm, you said something about Baron acting a big game about not trusting me but that he actually thinks I'm the best leader he's ever met. Trusts me more than his own father. Pretty sure that's what you said."

"Liar." Baron says over the girls' laughter.

"Honestly, I think it was something to that effect, but not quite that dramatic." Dru admits, "I'm telling you I was so out of it. Shade, did we kiss or am I just making that up?"

Shade's eyes snap open.

Dru's laughter sounds in the room, but it's the only one. Shade sits up. He feels Erin's eyes on him, but can't bring himself to look at her. Instead, he finds Baron, who sits there with a surprised expression, eyebrows raised. "You kissed her?" He asks, voice sounding somewhat higher than usual. Or maybe that's just in Shade's head.

"Technically, I kissed him." Dru says after a moment. She's no longer laughing, but still smiles. Shade wonders if she can feel the sudden tension in the room as strongly as he can. "I blacked out again after that. The next thing I knew, I was in a stranger's house and everything felt foggy, even in my waking."

Shade clears his throat once, mind scrambling for the words to say. He had not intended for anyone to ever find out about that kiss. For multiple reasons. One reason being the current look on Erin's face: a mix

319

between confusion, hurt, and anger. Another being Baron's incessant nagging and joking; although, strangely, the Green appears to be rendered speechless. And the final reason being Shade's own combination of mixed emotions. The kiss had been in the heat of the moment; quite literally, the heat from Dru's fever lips. It's true, Dru had kissed him first, but he had most definitely kissed back. If he is honest with himself, he didn't exactly mind it. In fact, part of him enjoyed the kiss and has even thought about it multiple times since then. Dru is a pretty girl and fun to be around. She makes Shade laugh and, in a rather short time, has become one of his greatest friends. Kissing her wasn't so bad.

Yet, he can't shake the awkward, torn feeling he's experiencing right now. He finally looks up, attempting a smile, "A pretty girl goes to kiss you, you going to resist?" He regrets the words as soon as they pass his lips and silently berates himself.

The words are meant for Baron, and it has the intended effect, for the Green smiles slyly and his eyebrows wiggle. "Ne'er have you spoken truer words, my prince."

But Erin's wide eyes knock the breath from Shade's lungs like a punch in the gut. Then, just as quickly, a new look crosses her features. One Shade has never seen. His eyes find her, trying to decipher what it means. Erin makes a disgusted face at Dru, "Ugh, that must have been horrible. It's okay, Dru, you don't have to pretend you enjoyed that. These boys will never let you hear the end of it!"

Dru snorts out a laugh in return. "It *was* a bit sloppy."

Erin laughs and they stand together. "You're right,

though. It's time for bed. Night, you two. Don't worry, I'm sure there's two damsels in distress somewhere out there, in need of your rescue. You'll find her someday." She turns to the door, patting Baron on the shoulder.

Shade is sure she will walk past him without a second glance. But she pats him on the shoulder as well, looking him in the eyes, which is somehow much worse than if she had ignored him completely.

"Night, prince." She says, following Dru out the door.

Shade finally recognizes the look on her face. Resolution. All his life, Erin had been someone he could read like a book. But when they had met eyes, all he saw was a beautiful, unreadable face.

Once they've left, Baron lets out a low whistle. "You and Dru, eh? I'm not going to lie, I thought you and Erin had a thing when we first met. But, hey, if she's available…" He wags his eyebrows again.

No, thanks. Shade is not about to talk relationships with Baron. "I do not have a thing with anyone. There's no time for that."

Baron cocks his head. "Come on, man. All work, no play? That's how it's going to be?" He actually manages to look a little sad. "That's no fun."

"Yeah, well, fun is not my goal." Shade says, frustration leaking into his voice.

Baron sighs. He finally stands and stops next to the couch where Shade sits. "Let's make a deal. Dru's right. As much as I hate to admit it," His brows draw together, "And as much pride as I'm having to swallow down right now to say this… I *do* trust you. Teach me how to be the type of person people want to follow, and I'll teach you how to relax, have fun, let your hair down, even in the midst of leading. Deal?"

Shade has to scrutinize his face to be sure he isn't joking. But Baron wears the same look as earlier when he offered to teach him Old English. "Fine." Shade says.

"Wonderful. Okay, I'm first watch tonight. Going to grab me some grub from the kitchen. Want anything?"

"No. Thanks."

Baron leaves, whistling all the way down the hallway to the kitchen. A door opens up somewhere, followed by an annoyed 'Shut up!' to which Baron replies, 'Sheesh, uptight much?' Shade's pretty sure it was Trix.

He rubs his forehead, a headache forming from that last conversation. Wanting to be gone before Baron returns, Shade stands and heads to his room.

It takes him a little longer to fall asleep, this time. Partially due to the sick feeling that that final conversation left him with. Partially due to the fact that he waits for over an hour, eyes wide, staring at the ceiling, hoping against hope...

But Erin never shows.

CHAPTER 23

The next day is similar to the last. The only ones who venture off the campus of Harvard's winter home, are the twins who go in search of more information regarding Afton and this Storg character. Their mission proves futile as the building they previously tracked Afton to was vacant. And, not wanting to risk a run-in with King Jeb or any of his lackeys, they decided to come straight back to Harvard's estate. All of them endure training with Hagan, eat several delicious meals, and talk strategy about the ball. Shade desires to learn more of Afton and whomever it is he is working for. But without being able to explore the city and seek answers, for the time being, there is nothing to be done about that situation. At around one, Sir Reginald arrives with a letter from Yagar.

Shade opens it. He reads it and then shares the information with the rest. "General Saipan has found allies further south, in some of the desert regions. He also mentions some naysayers of whom he claims 'won't be a problem anymore.'"

Baron makes a cutting motion across his neck.

Shade is not very fond of that method. The one that is "kill any who disagree." But he doesn't doubt this to be a motto someone like Saipan lives by.

"Well, this is relatively good news." Hagan says. He hasn't spoken to Shade much in the past two days. He hasn't spoken to anyone, really, except to boss them around on the training mat. "Any word from Frostfire?"

Reginald shakes his head, "My messenger should be arriving there any day now. He really is the best,"

He assures Shade. "I must be going. I wanted to see this letter made it to you myself."

Shade thanks him and before he leaves, asks, "Will you be attending the ball tomorrow night?"

Sir Reginald smiles, "I'm not much of a dancer, but I don't miss any of Harvard's parties. They are never *boring*, to say the least. Has he informed you of the slight change in dress code this year?"

"Duke Harvard has been very busy with the king. He hasn't been by the house since the other night." Ryker explains.

Reginald nods. "It's more for your sake, Prince Shade, than anyone else's. This year's ball is a masquerade. My wife is already sewing a mask for each of you; she's through with about half of them. I assume none of you have proper outfits for such an occasion, so we will be providing those for you as well. I'll have it all delivered sometime tomorrow before the ball." He bows and takes his leave.

"A masquerade." Dru barely hides her squeal. "How *exciting*."

"Truly." Risa says without emotion.

Drake takes a turn for the worse that evening. He's officially bed-ridden and servants enter and exit his room, always carrying new rags and various medical supplies. Trix assures us he isn't suffering, but it makes it no less difficult to see him lying there, immobile. Besides, how can one not be suffering if their organs are slowly shutting down?

Shade can't believe this is the same man who, just days before, was lively and sane, going about his business. What a terrible disease Cyphur Fever is, more so than even Green Ghoul, what Dru is still recovering from. Shade hates seeing his people suffer.

He hates even more that the walls of Windenmeyer kept him from seeing and knowing his people for so long.

"It makes you question your entire upbringing." Erin says to him later, as people are beginning to trickle off to bed for the evening. "We have lived in luxury, safe behind those castle barricades for all of our life. I only knew about Cyphur Fever from the books we read in history class. Meanwhile, the rest of Zion lives this kind of life daily."

Shade nods, her words mirroring his own thoughts. "We can't fault ourselves, though. We didn't know. Now that we do, we can strive every day to make a difference." They're sitting beside each other on the couch in the commons room. Shade is grateful that, since the strange conversation last night, nothing has seemed too out of the ordinary between them; even if Erin is a bit withdrawn. There are a few others in the room, but they are either engaged in conversation or asleep. Still, Shade lowers his voice, "I plan on talking to him tomorrow."

Her head turns his way slightly, lips barely moving as she says, "That's a stupid idea even for you."

"It could prove very informative." He continues, "I have to know if he's really changed, if he's chosen a different path than how we were raised. If we plan it well enough, we could even get him alone. He's my brother, he wouldn't try to hurt me."

Erin snorts in disbelief, "How can you know that for sure? No, Shade. It's too dangerous."

"What's too dangerous?" Baron asks as he steps by and takes a seat in the armchair across the way. His hair is not in its usual low ponytail, instead framing his face in such a way it resembles a lion's mane. His face is flushed from the cold night air outside. He and Dru have just returned from exploring the rock quarry down by the river. Earlier, Shade and Erin had joined them as well. After dinner, they wanted to go further into the caves down below, but Erin wanted to shower and Shade hadn't been up for it.

Dru joins them, plopping down at Baron's feet, a huge smile on her face. "There's one cave that goes down so far, we had to retreat for fear of being lost in the darkness forever. We need to take torches next time we go. Honestly, that'd be an *incredible* hideout if we ever needed to get away." She seems to notice they've interrupted something. Her eyes flit between the two, before settling on Shade. "What is it?"

"Erin was just saying how dangerous something would be." Baron prompts, eyebrows raised. "Come on, don't get shy on me now."

Erin glares at him. It's the first time Shade has seen her look at Baron in that way. "I wasn't talking to you. Can't you mind your own business for once?"

Baron shrugs, looking unoffended. "No." He says truthfully.

Shade decides he might as well tell them. It's important for everyone to be on the same page. "I'm going to find a moment to speak with my brother tomorrow night at the ball." Shade expects Baron to laugh in his face and tell him what a horrible idea that is. But the red-head only nods, as if having already known this news.

"Of course, you are. I'd do the same. I'd even get in a quick brawl, see who's stronger—"

"Did I just hear what I think I heard?" Hagan asks from across the room. His eyes are lighter than recent days. Perhaps he has been able to get more rest and is, therefore, in a better mood. "You're wanting to meet with the king?" He stands and Shade can almost see the gears turning in his head. "Let's call a meeting. There are clearly many things about tomorrow to discuss."

Five minutes later, a majority of their crew are gathered in the commons room. Save Drake, who's bed-ridden and Trix, who's staying by his side.

"I think the prince has something he'd like to share with us." Says Hagan, a challenge in his eyes.

Shade grounds his teeth, biting back a smart aleck retort. He stands and addresses the room. "I believe it is in our best interest if I find a way to speak with my brother tomorrow night. Before you object," He says when several voices start to speak at once, "Hear me out."

Ryker closes his open mouth.

"For one, he's my brother. Believe what you will about him, I still hold to the hope that he is simply in the wrong place at the wrong time. I am ready to accept the potential truth that he has turned from good, but again, I do not believe that to be the case. Gaining this knowledge of whether or not Jeb is to be trusted can influence how we choose to proceed with this rebellion."

"How so?" Fray asks in the middle of Shade's pause.

"If he's working with the Renegades, I will no longer be distracted by wondering which side my brother is on. I can move on and we can strike back at the castle harder than ever." This isn't entirely true. Shade would never give up on his brother, no matter the circumstance. But his face remains impassive as he continues. "If he remains loyal to the kingdom my

327

father was building, then we've got a powerful man on the inside."

Fray scrutinizes him, then looks away, 'hmphing.' "The boy presents a fair point."

"Further, he needs to know I mean business. Daring to pull him aside in the midst of a party in a large city in which he has heard I may be hiding…It's a power move." Here, Shade grins, enthralled with the guts of it all. His stomach twists with excitement, despite the dangerous circumstance.

Dru raises her eyebrows, "Are you—" she looks incredulously at Erin beside her, "Is he—" and back to Shade, "You're kidding me; you find this plan *enjoyable*?"

The grin only increases, "Who doesn't love an aggressive act of dominance? What's *enjoyable* is the fact that I am not alone and, therefore, can gain some momentum in this fight for the kingdom." He looks at some of the others. "Jeb believes us to be in hiding. Essentially, we have been. We've been laying low and gathering forces, neither of which are wrong. In fact, it's exactly what I intend to continue doing…*after* tomorrow night. The ball can be the first time we're on the offensive, for once. No one will expect it." He can see he's starting to convince some of the others that this plan could work.

Baron's grin matches his own, and he nods each time Shade pauses.

"The masks will disguise our faces. Mine and Erin's are the only recognizable ones, anyway. We use the festivities of the party as a distraction to get the king alone. Get in, get out. It's simple."

Ryker blows out a puff of air. He scratches his jaw, eyeing the prince warily. "So many things could go wrong."

"But, they won't. Because we will all be there." Baron insists.

Hagan has been silent, listening. But now he speaks, watching Shade. "Too many gathered around you will draw attention we can't afford. We will all be in the crowd, but only a couple of us will be close enough to you if anything goes wrong." He sighs. "I understand you can take care of yourself; I am not challenging that." Another sigh. "I know my behavior has been rather unbecoming the past couple of days. You do not make following orders easy, Prince Shade."

Fray grunts, "Hard-headed. *Obstiballr*." He pronounces it obe-stee-bi-yar.

Shade can guess that one probably means something along the lines of 'stubborn.'

"Duke Harvard sent word today that we are all on the pass list." Ryker says, wielding a letter he pulled from his coat pocket. "He's given us all interesting aliases." Ryker opens the letter, "Hagan will be acting as Sir Baldwin of Fleet, a town northeast of here. Myself and Trix are servants, working in the Harvard household. Erin is a lady in waiting for a soon to be bride in Sparkston. Fray is a father from here in Lockwood, bringing his daughter, played by the lovely Dru, to her first ball."

"Aye," Fray throws up his hands, exasperated. "How old do I look?" The bald head doesn't help his case, although the spiderweb tattoo stretched across it still makes him rather intimidating.

Dru laughs. She doesn't seem bothered by the alias at all. She links her arm with Fray's and leans her head on his shoulder. "My first ball! Thank you, thank you!"

Shade marvels at her infectious attitude.

Ryker goes on, "Risa and Perez are royal, well, twins from some northern village I cannot pronounce. Baron and the prince are the great nephews of a wizened duchess who is simply too old and tired to attend." He looks up from the letter.

Baron grins cheekily and elbows Shade, "We'll act out the part of two young bachelors, out for a good time."

"Oh, that shouldn't be too hard." Dru says drily.

"We should arrive at different times." Hagan says, speaking as if he's already thought this plan through. Which he likely has. "I will go first as a scout. I suggest Erin be with me. Keeping the two of you separate reduces the chances of you being recognized." Erin nods at him. There's a fire in her eyes that can only mean she's a little excited as well. "Prince Shade, you and Baron should arrive somewhere in the middle of us. The rest of the order doesn't matter, as long as someone always has eyes on the prince. How do you plan on getting King Jeb alone?"

Shade glances at Baron, "I was hoping you could help me out with that, seeing as how you're always looking for a fight."

Baron's eyes widen with curiosity, "As you say, dear prince!" He claps Shade on the back.

"It also helps that you will be a servant," Shade says to Ryker, "I have an idea for that."

Ryker inclines his head in a nod.

"What about our sister?" Perez interjects coldly, his lilting accent heavy in the air. "I will not leave this place without her." He narrows his eyes at Shade, "And, you. What about *your* sister?"

Of course, Shade has thought of this. Amberle is

the only one he's been able to think about the last couple of days. If his sister is at the party, Shade will most definitely find a way to speak with her. This isn't something he's going to share with the others. He still believes that Jeb would never do anything to hurt her; that doesn't mean others wouldn't. What is she doing out here, away from the castle? And where's the queen? Surely, Jeb hasn't done something too terrible to even imagine.

"We don't know that it's truly her." Risa says. It isn't often the twins disagree. Seeing them at odds is strange for everyone. "We have the word of one feverish man? No offense," she says to each of them, "But, I'll have to lay eyes on her myself before I believe it." She looks back at Perez, "*If* it's her, we will handle that when the time comes, brother."

"Amberle may be young, but she can handle herself." Shade says, sounding more confident than he feels. "I stand by what was said earlier—she's safer with the castle guards than she would be with me right now. I will make no move to retrieve her. For now." Despite knowing this is the best decision, he feels a tug of heartache knowing there isn't much he can do for his sister at the moment.

"It's settled, then." Baron states, looking content. "Tomorrow night's ball shall be one to remember. Get in, gather information about the Windenmeyer royals, enjoy the evening's revelries, get out. Piece of cake."

"We are not going for enjoyment." Hagan reminds him.

"But we must act the part, yes?" Baron says, holding up a finger. When no one speaks, he nods. "Indeed. Well, I'll be off to the washroom, then." On his way out the door, he pauses with a sly look at Risa.

"Care to join me?"

She raises a fist but Baron ducks out of the room before she can take a swing. His laughter can be heard down the hall.

* * * * *

Drake takes a turn for the worst that evening.

The sundial, which Shade finds can be read at night permitting that the moon is bright enough, reads just past three in the morning when there's a light knock on Shade's door. He's grown accustomed to the need for being a light sleeper, so he's on his feet within the next moment, pulling his shirt over his head.

It's Trix, looking somber. Her hands are clasped together in front of her and the bags under her eyes speak of tiring work and sleepless nights. "He's asking for you."

Shade follows without another word. He doesn't bother to slip on shoes and the patter of his bare feet echo softly off the long hallway walls. Trix leads him to Drake's room, only a couple of doors down from his own. The smell of oils, herbs, and ointments is apparent upon entering the room, mixed with another, sickly smell.

Illness.

Drake lays on the bed atop the covers, sweating profusely. He mutters to himself, his eyes moving rapidly behind his closed eyelids.

Trix sighs. She sits down at the chair next to the bed and points to another chair sitting idly a few feet away. Shade pulls it up and sits next to her. "He's been in and out of consciousness for several hours now. I am preparing to gather the others to say their goodbyes. But he insisted on seeing you first. He wants to tell you something himself. I've been trying to decipher his words, but..." Another sigh, "It's difficult. Maybe you'll have better luck. He should wake back up in a few minutes. It's actually fairly regular, his waking and sleeping."

Shade watches the Purple sadly. This man, once strong and determined, now looks death in the face. He reaches out a hand and sets it on Drake's shin, closing his eyes. Softly, he whispers, "Drengskerto."

It's quiet for a moment. Then, Trix speaks. "It's '*drengskuerto*.' The 'k' and 'u' make the 'squa' sound. Like 'square.'"

Shade opens his eyes. "Right. Sorry, still learning these things."

Trix is watching him for several long seconds. Finally, she nods. "I know. And I know you truly desire to learn, to know more about your kingdom. That's admirable."

He studies the scar running down across her eye. Realizing he's staring, he looks away quickly, back to Drake's prone form.

Trix chuckles then. An empty noise, without humor. "Go ahead. Ask me."

Shade opens his mouth in surprise and a bit of embarrassment. "My apologies, I didn't mean to...I don't mean any offense." When she doesn't say anything, he says, "What happened?"

"How well did you know your father?"

Shade is a bit taken back by this question. On impulse, he starts to say that, of course, he knew his father very well; they spent nearly every day together, especially in later years. They talked and laughed and joked together, spent hours talking battle strategy and riding horses, took entire days to go fishing and sailing. Shade would consider his father one of his best friends.

But then he thinks about the times he would go days on end without seeing him; Shade was always told at these times that the king was busy or on a business trip. He also thinks about the times the king had to suddenly leave recreation for various business deals or meetings. Shade remembers the times he'd catch his parents whispering in the corridor or see the many unreadable expressions on their faces. Perhaps, there was more his father didn't tell him than Shade thought.

Trix must read the epiphany on his face, because she continues. "That's what I thought. He knew of the Renegade rebellion fairly soon after it began, some fifteen or so years ago. He then designated individuals from every loyal town, village, or city within Zion to act as ambassadors of sorts. My parents were such individuals. They traveled often, meeting with fellow ambassadors of the king, discussing the latest Renegade movements, new information, potential crises, etcetera. Sometimes, they would even be called upon as extra protection for the king whenever he would take certain business trips." She looks straight ahead at the wall, her eyes unfocused. Almost subconsciously, she traces one finger across the edge of her scar. "Sometimes, they would be gone months at a time. So, they would take me with them. I was thirteen. We were in northern Zion. Klepton."

Shade's concern spikes. First, his father had a secret group of guards, and now he learns he spent time at a criminal dump like Klepton? "That's not possible."

"Klepton wasn't always the hell-hole it is now." Trix says, her eyes flicking his direction. "No more interrupting, please." There's the attitude he saw back on the mountain. She goes on, "Dad was a healer, Mom was a warrior. Together, they were two of King

334

Bronze's most lethal ambassadors. There were already disloyal figures in Klepton and your father was there trying to keep the peace, to shut down any rebellion before it could get started." She sighs, shaking her head. "It was late, I was supposed to be in bed but I had begged to go with them to a late night meeting your father had called with Klepton's governess. We had barely left the lobby of the hostel when there was a massive explosion. Mom must have sensed something was wrong, because just before, she shouted for me to hide and she took off sprinting towards the king. That's the last image I have of my mother. The explosion was caused by a bomb strategically hidden in the commons room of the hostel. The force of it hit me hard, knocked me off my feet. It was only after I came to that I realized my face was hurting and I couldn't see. A piece of debris had sliced above my brow, shredded my eyelid, and dug into my cheek."

Shade just listens intently. He can't help himself from studying the scar, white and slightly raised against her olive skin.

"I don't remember much more after that, other than Dad appearing before me and getting me aid. Through sobs, he tells me mom is dead, having thrown herself over the bomb and taking most of the hit, saving the rest of us. The loss made Dad physically sick and a couple of months later he, too, passed. The only illness he's never successfully treated: his own." Trix turns to face the prince. "I know that's more than you asked for. But I figure it may be insightful. Your father was a good man, a smart man. He surrounded himself with loyal people who loved him, who were even willing to die for him. So, I say this with all due respect...it's curious he was brought down by a measly bottle of poison."

Shade finally speaks up. His eyebrows raise. "Curious?"

"It's just, when I knew him, he was so intuitive. He was easily the most perceptive person in any room. That's what my parents told me, but even my young eyes picked up on something like that. I just wonder…well, I don't know."

"Wonder what?"

She shrugs, "I wonder if there's more to his death than meets the eye. Clearly, we know and trust that you were framed. But for someone to supposedly sneak poison into his drink, *without* his suspicion?" She shakes her head, unconvinced, "No, there's more to the story. Got to be."

She's implying that in order for someone to have poisoned the king, he would have known about it first. But that would mean King Bronze was aware of his coming death. Not only that, but that he was even willing to allow it to happen. Before Shade can press the matter further, Drake awakens with a startled moan. Trix grips his arm and whispers soothing words. His crazed eyes find Shade. "Prince. I'm sorry." He says. His eyes roll back, but he's still conscious because he continues speaking. "Wish I could…serve you. You…warm."

"I'm…warm?" Shade asks, giving Trix a quizzical look.

"Kind, welcoming." She translates with an irritated sigh at Shade. "Keep up."

Drake's eyes snap open again. "Girl in blue."

"Yes, Amberle, my sister."

"Unhappy, scared. Older woman comforts her. They," He stumbles over his words for a moment, then

336

says, "travel together."

"They were traveling in the caravan together." Shade says.

Drake shakes his head, "Yes, but…*live* together. Am-Amb…Amb…"

"Amberle and the woman live together?" That doesn't make sense. "Amberle lives in the Windenmeyer Castle with Jeb and my mother. She lives in Glimmer."

But Drake shakes his head.

"He's been saying this for a while, but I couldn't get him to elaborate much further." Trix explains sadly. "He's so confused. It's difficult to watch someone you've grown up with suffer like this."

When Shade watched his father at the dining room table, struggling to breathe, fall out of his chair, stare vacantly at the world, the pain he felt in his stomach was a feeling he'd never felt before. But that had been a quick, sudden death. This prolonged suffering can tear away at the mind, the heart, the soul, bit by bit. He hopes he never has to experience someone he loves going through this type of suffering. It's hard enough watching his newfound friend in Drake slowly dying.

"No more. New home."

Shade blinks, sitting straighter in the chair. "New home? On whose orders?" There's only one person who could order a royal out of the castle and that's the highest royal himself. "Did Jeb send Amberle away from Windenmeyer?"

Drake nods.

Shade takes a deep breath and lets it out slowly. There's no way he goes to the ball tomorrow night and doesn't try his best to speak with his sister. Jeb has sent Amberle away from the castle and, according to Drake, she is living with the older woman who, also according to Drake, is the sister to Risa and Perez. Where in the world does she fit into all of this? He suddenly thinks to ask, "Drake, what about the symbol? On their caravan was the Loyalty Mark, engraved into the wood."

Drake's brow furrows, "Thought so. Closer, just scratches."

Upon closer look it was just scratches. That doesn't make sense either. Shade is certain of what he saw. He decides to broach the subject further at a later date. Drake doesn't have much time left and he should spend these last few moments with the people he cares about. Shade grasps the man's hand. "Thank you, Drake. For your great service to this kingdom. I only wish I could have known you more."

Drake's eyes soften slightly, fighting against the crazed expression. "Honor." He points at his chest.

"He said this earlier. I think he means it has been an honor to serve you for the time that he could." Trix says.

Shade swallows down a lump of grief. He smiles at the man, "The honor is mine." He squeezes Drake's hand once, then stands. "I'll go get the others. They will want to be here." He excuses himself from the room. Out in the hallway, several are already gathered, awaiting their turn to wish the Purple goodbye.

No words are spoken in that hallway. Just silent nods of understanding and heartache. This is the second fallen comrade on this journey. Each of them knew the risks, knew that pain and, even death, were likely outcomes. It doesn't make it any less difficult to experience.

Drake passes quietly in the early morning,

338

sometime after 4:00. Waldo the butler insists he be buried at the beautiful pass between two caves at the bottom of the rock quarry. It's a small plot of land, mainly sand and a bit of grass, but it is a nice enough place for a burial.

So, in the growing light of the rising sun, they lay the messenger to rest.

Ryker shares a few sentimental words, the butler plays a harp, and, similarly to Vision's ceremony, they all perform something specific to Drake's personality. They each write a letter to him and deliver it to his graveside, leaving it with him in the ground. Shade writes something similar to his last words he had shared with Drake, seals it, and drops it on his frame, six feet below. He watches as the parchment letters float down to land softly on his body. Then, they cover the hole and return to the house.

The mood for several hours is somber. Eventually, Baron makes a comment about how Drake would not want them wallowing in grief. If he were still alive, he would want them focused on tonight and the overall mission.

Around three in the afternoon, Lady Lilith arrives with an entourage of ladies and servants. They bring in loads of covered material that can only be dresses and other various outfits, as well as large trunks, containing who knows what. Sir Reginald comes in last, carrying the largest trunk and looking a little sheepish as his wife bosses him around along with the servants. He grins, "What can I say? She wears the breeches in the family."

"Those are trunks for the women, obviously." Dru says at Shade's blank stare. She rolls her eyes, "You know, make-up, ribbons, bows, all the things to doll a woman up."

"I have never seen one of those in my life, Peanut." Shade replies. His sister and mother, no doubt, own at least twelve of these trunks; but before today, he couldn't have told you what was in it. "I have a closet. With a shoe rack."

"The masquerade is tonight at 7:00. We will separate the items and then begin preparation." Lilith says, once all the trunks and bags have made it to the top of the stairs. She is somewhat out of breath, her hair falling into her eyes. She beckons one of her lady servants closer, then eyes the large bag she is holding. "This is Trix's," she calls. Trix raises her hand tentatively and Lady Lilith smiles at her, "Wonderful. When I call out your name, please, direct my servants to your rooms so they can prepare your outfits." She claps her hands and does a little hop, "How exciting!"

"Is it? Is that what this is called?" Risa asks, sounding unconvinced.

Shade rubs a hand across his face. He has been to many balls in his lifetime, all at Windenmeyer. Duke Harvard might know how to throw a ball, but Shade's mom could definitely give him a run for his money. Typically, Shade enjoys these parties; it's always a time for mischief and fun. He wishes now there was another way he could speak with his brother without it having to be at a ball.

"I'm probably biased, but Lilith is an incredible seamstress." Reginald says to them as Lilith commands around the servants. "She put careful thought into each of your outfits. I think you're going to like them."

"Prince Shade?" Lady Lilith calls. When Shade turns, she bows, straightens, and smiles, "Your outfit,

Your Highness." A male servant steps forward, holding an outfit hidden from view in a bag.

Shade inclines his head, "Right this way."

CHAPTER 24

A few hours later, Shade stands in front of the mirror, admiring his outfit. It's true, Lady Lilith really has outdone herself. Shade is impressed. He's wearing breeches that stop just above his calves. A sleeveless vest covers his torso. A separate overcoat stretches nearly to his knees, the vest underneath exposed. The sleeves, edges of the coat, the bottom band of the breeches, and his vest are all interlaced with a subtle gold trim. But his favorite part is the color (that *and* the hidden inside pocket of the coat, allowing for a concealed knife). Royal blue, the color of his family crest. The necklace he received from Blair is around his neck and tucked under his shirt. For the first time in what seems like ages, he looks the part of a royal. He just hopes the mask will hide enough of his identity for them to succeed in their mission tonight.

"Would you like to try on the mask, Your Highness?" The servant asks from the doorway, his head poking in. He had respectfully obeyed when Shade declined needing help at getting dressed and had waited just outside the door.

Shade looks at him and nods. "What would you suggest for the hair? Kind of a mess, eh?"

The servant steps inside and smiles tentatively, nervous in the prince's presence. Shade hopes he isn't afraid of him. "I've seen worse. I like the half-back, it suits you."

Shade nods at himself in the mirror, pleased with the servant's response. He rather likes the style he's going with right now, too. It's pulled away from his face, but still frames it in a regal way. The way his curls spread across the top of his shoulders give him a look that is both dashing and intriguing. At least, he thinks so. He has been known to be wrong before. He flashes back to a memory several years before, when he showed up to family portraits with what he thought was well-kempt hair.

"Good Zion, who did that to you?" The queen remarks, her lips parted in a silent gasp, one hand held up to them in concern. "And what are you wearing?"

Shade glances down at his bright red tunic and wiggles his toes in his house slippers. "Wait—will our feet be seen?" He licks his hand and rubs it several times over his hair. "I thought I looked dashing."

"The boy looks fine, Rose, quit nagging." King Bronze states, distracted with listening to the artist as she tells him where to sit.

His mother sighs, a look of motherly disappointment on her face. "He looks scraggly. That hair…is the barber working today?" She tsks disapprovingly. But when the artist insisted they get into position, she just pulled Shade closer, running her hands through his hair in an attempt to tame it. "You see Jeb's hair? That's what you should go for."

Jeb, nose stuck in the air triumphantly, winks at him.

Queen Rose finishes tousling Shade's unruly hair, kisses his forehead, and turns him to face the woman, "At least, smile."

The memory fades and Shade is left standing there with the ghost of a smile on his face. The family portraits had been horrible that year, largely due to Shade, his mop of hair, and his slippers. Which, by the way, were most definitely seen.

"Sure, let's try on the mask." Shade says. The

343

servant steps closer, pulling the mask from its protective box.

He holds it up to his face. It's a thick plastic material and is the same gold color as the trim on his outfit. It's a half mask, covering all of his face save his mouth and down. Not many at this ball will know him well enough to recognize him from his mouth and chin alone. His eyes are exposed, shining a bright blue through the golden mask. Still, Shade believes this will be a sufficient disguise.

"When you are ready to wear it, simply peel the thin layer off the back. Its slightly sticky underside will stick to your face without issue. And without leaving a residue once you decide to remove it." The servant explains.

"Thank you." Shade looks once more at his appearance, shrugs, then makes for the door. "When are we leaving?" He pulls open the door as the servant says, "Within the hour."

There, greeting him on the other side of the door, is Baron, hands in his coat pockets. He's wearing the same type of outfit as Shade, but his is green with gray trim. His red locks are loose, hanging freely around his face. Baron grins, "Aye, you *can* clean up nicely. Come on, everyone else is in the commons room."

The commons room is buzzing with activity. But when he walks in, everyone stops. They stare at the prince with various looks of respect. One by one they turn and bow. He returns the bow, smiling when he rises back to full height. "You all know I wish you would stop doing that."

"You are a prince, yes?" Ryker says, repeating a phrase he said back on the mountain. He's dressed as a servant, wearing long pants that bunch up at his ankles, pointy-toed shoes, and a long sleeve, cream, linen tunic. The only item to indicate he serves royalty is the golden tassel tied around his waist. His blonde dreads are tied back in a high ponytail. Beside him, Trix is similarly dressed in creme, but she's wearing a dress and looks non-to-pleased to be doing so. Her arms are crossed and her jagged hair tousled.

Shade takes a look around the room. Most of their clothing is a far stretch from their normal gear of comfortably fitting breeches and tunics, meant for agility purposes.

The twins look nearly the same as usual, dressed in furs and purple linen. Risa's dress is form fitting from her feet to her neck. Her shoulders are bare, showing off their toned strength, and a fur shawl hangs loosely across them, wrapping around her arms. Shade admits, his eyes subconsciously linger a bit. Perez wears a suit that is mostly purple with silver undertones. There's fur cuffing each sleeve and pant leg and lining his collar. Both of their long, dark hair is braided intricately. Risa's hair stretches down her back; Perez only has half of it braided and pulled back against the portion that is loose. Hagan wears long-sleeved chainmail on his torso, his chest covered by a gray and blue vest. The lower portion of his vest stretches down to his knees, almost like a kilt. Stockings cover the remainder of his legs.

He, too, appears miffed. Shade looks comically from his stockings to his face.

Hagan sighs, "Apparently, Sir Baldwin is a knight."

"Soldier," Baron corrects gently, "No one says 'knight' anymore." He nods at his cousin as if to say, 'It's okay, you didn't know.'

Fray looks surprisingly dapper. His bald head is covered by a black and red chaperon, a bowl-like hat often worn by wealthy men. His suit, also black and red, stretches to his knees, with solid black tights covering his legs. His "daughter" compliments his outfit with a burgundy one of her own.

Dru is beautiful. More beautiful than normal. Half of her black hair is braided back and around her head, disappearing in the folds of the reminder of her loose hair that all hangs on one side. Her dress fluffs out until it reaches her waist, which then tightens to fit her form all the way to the swoop of the collar across her collarbone. Her sleeves are three-quarter length and she wears white gloves to top off the outfit. Shade has never seen Dru wear make-up; it somehow manages to accentuate her natural beauty.

"Eh," Baron whispers, "Eyes up, mister." Shade really hopes no one else hears him say that. He clears his throat dismissively at the Green.

But then he sees Erin and it's like there's nobody else in the room. Her dress is somewhat poofy from the waist down, like Dru's. But where Dru's is bright and welcoming, Erin's is dark and mysterious. It's charcoal gray, with peach intermingling with the gray on her long sleeves, across the fabric on her collarbone, and down the form fitting blouse covering her torso. Like Ryker, her arm is not in a sling for tonight; she had told Shade earlier that she wasn't wearing that 'hideous, constricting thing' to the ball, she'd brave the pain for the evening. Her blonde hair, standing out strikingly against the dark dress, is completely pulled up, intricately woven like braids into a bun. Strands of it have fallen out of the bun, perhaps purposefully, and frame her face in that familiar way Shade's used to seeing. The makeup she wears is darker shades to match her dress.

Dru is beautiful, but Erin is stunning.

She meets his eyes, then looks away quickly, cheeks reddening. Shade thinks his mouth might be hanging open.

Baron gives a low whistle, his eyes lingering amongst the ladies in the room. "We *all* clean up nicely." He winks at Risa and says, "Save me a dance, eh?" Knowing it will annoy her.

Sir Reginald stands to the side with his wife who seems to be glowing. "We will be leaving shortly for the ball. Myself, Tyson, and a few other soldiers will dismiss you a few at a time and guide you to Harvard's other estate." He looks at Shade, "All of your allies will be present at the ball, nothing will happen without one of us knowing. Finalize last moment details and plans, I'm going to check on the horses and then we will leave." He and his wife exit the room, Lady Lilith blowing all of them a kiss with a flourish of her arm.

The room buzzes with low conversation.

"Are you sure about this? There's still time to back out." Ryker asks Shade, genuine concern across his features. "There is no shame in laying low for now."

Shade grips the man's shoulder, smiling, "Tonight will go as planned, Ryker. With you all by my side, there is little to fear. Apart from the embarrassment this one will, no doubt, cause me." He jerks his head towards Baron, who's dramatically greeting each of the ladies.

"Baron is annoying and immature, but he can be trusted to have your back." Hagan says, "He provides a strong cover for you, a haughty bachelor just there for a good time. If we play our cards right, we might make it out of this alive." He adds, still soundly annoyed that they are participating in this party.

Ryker and Hagan step away to chat with Tyson, who has just come in the doorway.

"Wow," A voice breathes behind Shade.

He turns, already smiling. "You must be referring to my hair. Dashing, right?"

Even in her boots, Dru still barely comes up to his chest. She grins at him, not even trying to hide the fact that she's looking him up and down. "I'm referring to all of it. You really are *Kiertunyazi*, then?"

"You aren't so bad yourself."

Her eyes twinkle.

Then Erin walks up, a frown on her face. "I can barely move in this thing." She stretches her arms, tries lifting one leg. Nothing budges and she stops moving, sighing. "Sure hope there's no need for me to run tonight. Or, you know, breathe deeply."

Shade smiles at her, praying the blush doesn't show on his neck. She is breathtaking. "You look beautiful, Erin. Both of you do. I must admit, I didn't realize you knew what a dress was." He says to Erin. "You always wore pantsuits at our parties."

"For good reason." She mumbles. She beckons to him, with one hand, the other resting sassily on her hip. "You look nice, too."

Shade leans in, "Tell me, does my hair look scraggly?"

Her bright green eyes flit around his face, taking in the hair. She smiles, a soft thing that causes Shade's chest to constrict and he wonders if this is what a heart attack feels like. Her smile turns into a smirk, "If I said yes would you honestly go and fix it any differently?"

"Probably not."

"It looks great, prince." She states dryly.

At that moment, Tyson speaks up loudly. "Alright, people, it's go time. I've got the first pair of riders. Is there a Sir Baldwin in the room?"

Hagen steps forward. He gives Erin a look.

"That's my cue," Erin gives both Dru and Shade a nod, "See you there," she says, before stepping up beside Hagan. Shade watches her leave, longing to be the one beside her.

A few minutes later, a separate guard comes to collect Ryker and Trix.

"We will be intermingled with Harvard's other servants. He's already informed them he's hired two new servants to help with tonight's festivities. We will be watching, Prince Shade. If there's anything amiss, you will be the first to know." Ryker tells him. Then, he and Trix leave with the guard.

Sir Reginald comes up a couple of minutes after that and collects Shade, Baron, and the father/daughter combo. They bid the others ado and walk out into the fresh, evening air. A carriage pulled by two horses waits for them at the bottom of Harvard's massive front door staircase. Behind them are two more horses, these for Dru and Fray.

"When we get to the main street of Lockwood, we will simply blend in to the many travelers on their way to the ball. You two," Sir Reginald points at Fray, "Fall in line a little behind the prince. You don't know each other." He turns to Shade and Baron, "Your great aunt," He says, a look of amusement on his face, "Has sent you to the ball with her very best wagon. Take care of it. My soldier, Creed, is here to take you." He winks at them, "Enjoy the festivities."

Baron waggles his eyebrows at Shade. They mount

349

the covered wagon and disappear inside. The wagon has curtains pulled over the open windows. Shade keeps them covered, but pulls the curtain aside to glance outside as they leave the estate.

"Nervous?" Baron asks. He sits across the way, one leg crossed over the other, arms stretched out across the seat back.

Shade shrugs. He isn't exactly sure what he is right now. There is a bit of nerves, mainly for what he will learn when he meets Jeb. He's a little worried for his crew; there's always the reality that something could go seriously wrong. Then, there's the concern for his sister and this mysterious older woman of whom he believes to be Risa's sister. "More anxious, I suppose."

"Remember what I said. Let's try and have a little fun tonight, relax, go with the flow."

"I'm not sure now is one of those times, Baron." Shade mutters. The outside world is dark, but the streets are lined with lanterns. They turn off of Harvard's driveway and onto a side street. Before too long, they are nearing the main street and the noise of many horses and low murmuring voices can be heard.

"Come on, man, it's a ball. Their only purpose is to be fun."

"Not this one. We have a mission."

Baron shrugs. Sighs. Then nods. "Yes, you're right. Perhaps, there will be more parties like this in our future."

The wagon slows, then lurches slightly as it turns onto what must be the busy main street. The noise of the crowd is loud. Shade keeps the curtain fully closed now, not daring to look out without his mask on. In the darkness, he can barely see the shine of Baron's grinning teeth.

"I get the feeling this will be a night to remember." He says.

"Is this your first ball?" Shade asks.

"First, but Zion willing, not the last. We've had parties and dances in Frostfire, but nothing to this scale. We took dance classes in school. So, if you're thinking you're about to show me up on the dance floor, think again, my protege."

They ride the rest of the way in silence after that and Shade thinks Baron is a bit more nervous than he lets on. Eventually, they rise up an incline and come to a stop at the top of a hill. They hear Creed speaking with servants who have come to greet the guests entering the Harvard Ball, telling them the practiced lie about the great aunt, the baroness.

Light shines in through the crack of the curtain and Shade sees Baron slip his mask over his face. Other than the hunter green color to match his outfit, it looks identical to Shade's. Shade peels the thin layer off the back, lines the mask up with his eyes, and presses it gently to his face. It sticks without issue, and comfortably so. The carriage door opens. It's a servant, dressed exactly like Trix and Ryker were. He bows slightly and extends an arm outward. "This way, my lords."

Baron exits first, cockiness emitting from every pore of his body. He steps down from the wagon and straightens his uniform coat, a smirk on his face. "Gee-gee said this was a party. Well, then, where are the *ladies*?"

Shade can only assume "Gee-gee" to be Baron's fake great aunt. He follows Baron, running a hand through his hair and plastering a cool smile across his lips. He nods at the servant, who responds with a, "Just

351

inside, my lord," to Baron's question. Before them is a scene Shade hasn't seen in years. A red carpet is laid out, stretching from their covered carriage, up a slight incline, further up many steps, and into a large entryway, doors wide open. The walk up to the stairs is lined with arches covered in flowers and dangling lanterns. Behind them, their carriage leaves and another one quickly replaces it.

The servant clears his throat, not wanting to be rude but clearly wanting them to move on.

Shade begins walking and Baron falls in step beside him. When they reach the staircase, they are greeted by more servants who beckon them upwards. The red carpet continues all the way up the stairs. Now, instead of flowers lining their walk, it's open and free, allowing the chilly winter air to lightly breeze through. Without a word, they advance up the stairs until they come to the mighty, open double doors. There's a doorkeeper in front of them, checking his parchment paper and identification cards to match.

Shade feels for the card in his coat pocket, his fingers brush the cold steel of the knife resting in the pocket against his ribs. It's comforting; he knows he is not weaponless should a fight occur. He pulls the small ID card from his pocket. On it is his name, date of birth, and description of his appearance. All fake, of course.

A couple enters the mansion ahead of them, laughing with each other about something one of them says. Baron steps up to the doorkeeper. He flippantly shows him his identification card, all while craning his neck past him, looking further into the ball. "Hurry up, would you? I see a pretty girl in need of a dance." Shade notices he does a skilled job of hiding his thick Gargantuan accent.

The doorkeeper doesn't appear affected by Baron's tone. He takes the card, scans it boredly, glances back at Baron, then passes him through. "Next." He says in a monotone.

Shade steps forward and hands the man his card. The doorkeeper scans it, checks it with his parchment, and looks back at Shade. He stares a little longer than he had at Baron, but then passes him through as well. "Enjoy the ball." His voice indicates that he could care less whether anyone enjoys the ball at all.

They pass through the doorway and the classical music, sounds of violins and pianos, becomes so loud he has to lean in to hear what Baron is saying. "Keep your eyes peeled for the royal man. And don't try anything stupid, *hilcipe.*"

The entryway is large and white, a massive chandelier hangs above it all. Lanterns line the walls. There is not a staircase leading upwards, like Harvard's winter home; instead, there are 3 hallways, branching off to the left, right, and straight ahead. The one directly ahead is where the music is coming from. Servants bustle in and out of the room from the various hallways carrying some trays with glass drinks and others containing various delicacies such as prestigious types of cheese and meat.

He sees several individuals enjoying the party's festivities down the right hallway. He recognizes one of them as Lady Colette, the mysterious fundraiser. She is speaking closely with a man of average height and close-cropped hair. And, of course, she isn't wearing a mask, flying in the face of what's expected of her. Shade's curiosity gets the best of him and he taps Baron lightly on the shoulder, then approaches the two without checking to see if the Green follows.

Lady Colette sees his approach and offers a friendly nod without smiling. But her eyebrows raise with familiarity and she speaks, "Good evening, young lords. Tell me, why is it the baroness did not care to attend this year? Not feeling ill these days, I hope."

The man turns at her greeting and Shade catches dark eyes hidden behind even darker, bushy eyebrows.

Without waiting for their response, Lady Colette beckons to the man, "Gentlemen, meet Sir Quinton of Greenbriar. He's one of my most reliable customers in trade. Sir, this is Baroness Lee's great nephew, Lord Grom and his friend, Lord Anson."

A moment passes in which Shade is trying not to scoff at learning Baron's fake name. But he recovers seamlessly and bows his head slightly, "A pleasure to meet you, Sir Quinton."

"I didn't realize the Baroness had a great nephew." Sir Quinton eyes the two of them suspiciously.

Baron sticks out a hand and shakes it with the man, clapping him on the back. "Strange, I've heard so much about you. My dear, great Aunt speaks highly of your significant trade efforts in Greenbriar."

Quinton blinks, his mouth opening with surprise.

Lady Colette's nostrils flare slightly and Shade thinks Baron has stumbled into a mistake.

But thankfully, Quinton's face takes on a pleased look and he shakes Baron's hand back just as enthusiastically. "I thought she hated me. This is good to hear."

Baron laughs heartily. "No worries. She comes across cold-blooded to everyone. It took Lord Anson, here, eleven months to earn her good graces. And, even still, she never lets him sit on the ballroom's upholstery." He looks ready to drop Quinton's hand

354

but the man is still shaking it, so Baron throws Shade a quick look that only the prince catches.

Shade clears his throat and steps closer to Colette. "My lady, I was hoping to discuss a potential trade opportunity with you." He glances sideways at Quinton and then back at the woman.

She appears slightly perturbed but wishes Sir Quinton well and then steps further down the hallway. Shade bows at Quinton and follows Lady Colette. Baron has a difficult time extricating himself from the man's grip but soon falls in step beside them. They walk to the end of the hallway where an open door empties out into a beautiful, lantern-filled garden. Several party guests mill about or are seated in different benches throughout the garden.

"What is it that you want?" Lady Colette asks without preamble. "I find it difficult to believe you would have a trade that interests a powerful woman such as myself. You nor any of your kind."

Shade ignores the jab. Clearly, Lady Colette is not much of a fan of the royal family. "So, it is power that you seek."

Colette comes to a quick halt, eyeing him darkly. "I do not seek that which I already have, *Lord*." She takes a breath, seemingly to calm herself down. Shade's words must have triggered something. He recalls Ryker mentioning Colette's interesting upbringing which involved a ruthless father, a mother who died early on, and a lifestyle of deceit. Shade thinks she must have had countless dealings with people who discredited her or preyed on her weaknesses. Perhaps, to the point that she no longer has any.

He steels his nerves and, in a clipped tone, says,

"You never gave us your answer."

The hard look she gives him almost breaks his resolve, but he sets his feet and doesn't back down. He hadn't realized it before but, this woman, although much shorter, is scarier than Lady Brandy. "And the answer to what question, *pray tell*, would that be?"

Shade glances at Baron who nods and does a rapid sweep of the area. After circling around them once, he returns Shade's gaze and nods again. Even still, Shade leans in close in case any unseen ear resides nearby. "We seek to regain the keys to Zion, to right the wrongs of this trembling kingdom. If you are not with us, I will assume you cannot be trusted. And, therefore, your presence at this party will no longer be required."

Lady Colette stares at him, then at Baron, and back at the prince. She looks like she wants to laugh. "You mock me, surely. Are *you* threatening *me*? Do you know who I am?"

Shade wants to turn that very question on her but can't before she's letting out another deep breath and her eyes lose some of their anger.

"I do apologize for my tone." She says, some of the tension leaving her shoulders. "But there is something you must understand. I am Lockwood's greatest tradeswoman, yes. But my work goes far beyond Lockwood and her neighboring cities." Her eyes alight with victory as Shade listens, "Yes, *prince*," she whispers, "I frequent the halls of your beloved Windenmeyer Castle. I am spokesperson for every major city, minor city, town, village, wagon, or hut within this kingdom. I am *Zion's* greatest tradeswoman."

A heavy weight seems to settle in Shade's stomach.

"I make dealings with every leader. *Including* the

late king, your father. And," Here, she looks down and it now appears as if she is the one who has to steel her nerves. But when she meets Shade's eyes again, they are stone. "Including the current king."

Suddenly, Shade remembers why Lady Colette seemed so familiar when she arrived at Duke Harvard's to meet them. She visits the castle often. Shade vaguely recalls seeing her traipse proudly beside his father, deep in conversation about trades Shade cared nothing about. Now, Shade takes a step back, eyes searching the shadows for any sign of danger. Baron, having heard everything, has slipped further away, searching for danger as well.

But Lady Colette isn't finished. She grips Shade's wrist tightly, her voice low and sure. "I cannot join your cause. I cannot know your comings or your goings. Because if I do, I am no longer helping Zion, I am her greatest threat. I am *your* greatest threat."

Realization dawns on Shade. Because she visits the king so often, she is under far more scrutiny than most people. If she were to be caught with information regarding Shade and his rebellion, her life and the lives of all those involved would be in grave danger and the rebellion would be found and snuffed out. She must have deniability.

Voices approach their position. Shade knows how this must look, a man towering over an angry woman. Quickly and without thinking, he grips her around the waist with one arm and plants a kiss straight on her mouth.

It's like kissing a rose bush, her scent sweet yet sharp. At first, he's afraid she'll shank him in the gut with a knife she's, no doubt, concealing somewhere in that bust. But, instead, she wraps one finely manicured hand around the nape of his neck and deepens the kiss.

The voices, belonging to two ruckus men, come around the corner, falter slightly at the scene, then chuckle to themselves and continue on without a second glance. Once they're out of earshot and eyesight, Shade breaks off the kiss, wiping his mouth with the back of one hand.

Lady Colette pulls away, but keeps the hand on the back of his neck. "I have friends in high places. And in low places. They know never to talk or it'll be the last thing they do. If you're ever in a bind, tell them you work for Collie."

Shade nods.

Lady Colette leans in close again, "If you're caught, I will deny *everything*. You understand? You will not have my protection. You *can't*. For the good of the kingdom."

Shade understands completely. When he looks into her eyes, he sees how serious she is. Lady Colette will not waste a moment's time on protecting or defending him if he's unable to do it for himself. She won't risk any of it. In a lot of ways Colette and Lady Brandy are very similar—both are selfishly looking out for themselves first. Everything else is second.

Still, Shade is grateful for this small tidbit of information about this terrifying woman. There's at least some part of her that loves Zion and wants to see it restored to its former glory; some part of her that wants Shade to succeed.

She just isn't choosing to be a part of it.

Shade nods once and drops her waist. He bows slightly, spots Baron several yards away and walks towards him.

"Oh, and Lord Anson," Colette calls just before

he's out of earshot. Shade turns slightly and looks over his shoulder. She grins wickedly. "They're right, what they say about you."

Shade glances once at Baron, unsure of her meaning. Baron shrugs, eyes wide with all the new knowledge they've learned. The prince looks at Lady Colette once more.

"You are *quite* the kisser." She winks seductively, before disappearing further into the garden.

CHAPTER 25

Shade and Baron make their way back to the main entrance, Baron muttering some nonsense about being a good kisser himself. Shade is only half listening, his mind still stuck on his conversation with Colette.

When they enter back through the hallway and find themselves in the entry corridor, the Ball sounds to be in full swing. Shade's certain most, if not all, of the rest of their party has surely entered the ballroom and are likely curious as to the prince's whereabouts. He plasters on a jovial face, matching Baron's and prepares to enter.

Shade, fully buying into the bachelor part, saunters towards the Grand Ballroom's double doors with Baron. The music is loud and the ballroom is large with a high ceiling and several hanging chandeliers. They are all only half lit so that the room is doused in a mood of mystery. The ceiling is covered with a beautiful design of swirls and shapes. The walls are magnificent wood; the hardwood flooring is occupied with dancers, and drinkers, and talkers. A few circular, clothed tables line either side of the ballroom, but only a couple of the chairs are occupied as many people have already taken to the dance floor and many others have yet to arrive. At the far end of the ballroom are several prestigious looking chairs, facing the ballroom. Shade assumes these must be for King Jeb and other lesser royals who might make an appearance at Harvard's ball. Behind those chairs is an orchestra with about twenty members, playing various types of instruments

As his eyes scan the ballroom, they land on a familiar face. Or, rather, a familiar outfit, hair, and body language. Even with most of her face covered, Shade would recognize Erin anywhere. She stands near one of the tables by the wall. When they meet eyes, she raises one hand nonchalantly, then looks away, perusing the rest of the room. Her mask covers the upper half of her face, with one side of it stretching down to wrap halfway around her chin. It's not the plastic material like Shade's, it's more of a beautiful charcoal gray lace. The top of the mask fans upwards and meets with her hair in a beautiful fashion. Hagan stands at the edge of the dance floor in an apparent deep conversation with a random lady.

Duke Harvard passes by without a second glance. His wife nods once to be polite, but nothing gives away the fact that they know one another. He sees Sir Reginald perusing the dessert table and Duke Flynn chatting it up with a bored looking Lady Sprite. A loud voice booms over the sound of the orchestra and he turns to see Lady Brandy making her entry. She grins devilishly at them as she parades past.

"Think you can manage on your own for a bit?" Baron asks, his eyes watching a group of girls at one of the tables.

Shade doesn't even answer before Baron's gone. Of course, Shade knows he isn't really alone. Baron is more attentive than he's letting on at the moment. And, as Shade begins settling into the vibes of the ball, he notices when a member of their crew joins the continuous influx of party-goers entering, or when they quietly walk past him.

He also notices a woman wearing a tight, ruby dress watching him. She's standing in the shadows, near a side wall, a drink in her hand. Her mask is exotic, with feathers stretching upwards. Her dress drops to her ankles but is so low cut, that it doesn't leave much to the imagination. There is something familiar about her and Shade is pretty certain he knows what.

He came to this ball to gather information. His time with Colette proved rather successful. Time to see what more digging can do.

"Truffle, sir?" A servant appears before him, wielding a tray. It's Ryker. None of the servants wear a mask.

Shade hardly glances his way, waving a dismissive hand. He gently pushes him aside and starts for the woman in ruby. Ryker, ever the dutiful servant, steps aside without complaint and moves on to the next customer.

The woman shifts from her position against the wall as he approaches and sets her drink down on the table. The drink tips slightly and a stream of clear liquid spills onto the tablecloth. Shade takes note of it quickly. It appears he and his team aren't the only ones staying away from alcoholic beverages. There are many vigilant individuals at the Harvard Ball tonight. A coy smile plays at the woman's lips, nearly the only visible part of her face. Her caramel eyes are piercing against her mask, the same color as her dress.

Shade stares hard at her. He steps closer and leans in, until his mouth barely touches her ear. "You've had eyes for me since the moment I walked in." He shifts back and holds up a hand, "Care for a dance?"

She takes it without a word. The twitch of her mouth gives away a slight smile. Shade leads her out to the dance floor, where several couples move to the beat. He catches several of his people watching his progress onto the floor; but they are rehearsed enough to not draw any sort of attention beyond that. The song the orchestra plays is slow, almost haunting. Perfect for what Shade is about to do.

They reach a certain point of the wooden floor and Shade turns, drawing the woman to him and stepping into an easy rhythm of swaying and turning. He recalls from culture class that this type of dance is called the rumba. They dance together, their heads close.

"Awful forward of you, don't you think?" The woman says. She smiles coolly. But Shade can see past her guarded eyes.

"Not forward. Wary." He says, getting right to the point. "It is curious." He watches over his shoulder, appearing unperturbed by the beautiful woman in his grasp.

"What's curious?" She asks, her eyes wide, still feigning innocence.

"You're here. You're originally from up north, yes? Traveled south with the family. Ended up at the top of a mountain."

As he speaks, the smile on her face slowly drops, until there's a barely contained glare.

He stares her fully in the eyes. "How's that for forward?" He whispers.

She plasters on a fake smile. "You have me mistaken for someone else, I'm sure, *sir*." Her tone implies she does not believe him to be a mere "sir" at all. Perhaps, she has caught on to him as well.

"I disagree." Shade says with finality. The woman is shorter than him by a few inches. Over her head, he sees the twins enter through the doorway. It doesn't take them long to find Shade and his partner in the middle of the sparse dancing crowd. Shade can see the tension in their frames as they stiffen with realization.

He turns until he and the woman can both see the doorway. "I'm willing to bet they would as well."

She glances sideways, then back at him quickly. There's suddenly a warning in her eyes, mixed with fear. "What are they doing here? They weren't supposed to be here."

"And to think, here *I* was under the impression *you* were in the wrong place." Shade says, turning them in a slow circle once more. He slides his arm along her waist and she falls into the dip naturally. He lifts her back to standing position and they continue the dance. "You resemble them quite well. As the night goes on, I doubt I'll be the only one to notice. I would tread carefully."

Her mouth is a hard line. "That's laughable, considering I recognized you the moment you stepped from the carriage."

Alarm spikes in his chest but his demeanor remains impassive, "Oh, I'm sure you've learned a lot from our double agent. How is Afton doing? Planning anymore tree attacks?"

Here, she looks genuinely confused. But it's overshadowed by whatever fear she's feeling related to her siblings. "I don't know what you're talking about. I was told what you look like by…someone I've spent a great deal of time with lately."

Shade's hand tightens around hers with a crack. It takes him a moment to realize he's popped the girl's knuckles. To his surprise, she matches his strength with her own. "Where is she?" He asks tightly.

The smirk returns to her lips. "Whomever do you mean?"

Shade takes a deep breath, letting it out slowly. This woman, Risa's sister, has been with Amberle.

Why? Why has Jeb brought their sister along? Shade watches Baron lead a girl onto the dance floor, notes the way he says something to her, but glances swiftly at his surroundings when she closes her eyes with laughter. He thinks he hears Dru's loud storytelling voice from somewhere to his right. He can't find any of the others, but the crowd is becoming denser by the moment. "Why are you here?" He asks, growing tired of the dance. "Risa tells me you were kidnapped seven years ago. Where have you been? Why show up now, here? Why not go home?" He doesn't miss her flinch at the mention of her sister's name.

"That's a long story."

"Great, I've got time. Starting with, why is the Loyalty Mark on the side of your wagon?"

She starts, "That was supposed to have been scratched off before I returned to the king."

"It was." He says, recalling how Drake mentioned that close up, there was no mark, only scratches. "But why was it there in the first place? Did you put it there?"

She sighs, eyes flitting around the ballroom as if she has somewhere better to be. "No, I didn't. But that wagon came from Glimmer, so it's no surprise the Loyalty Mark was there."

This catches Shade off guard. How had that wagon made it this far?

"I scratched out the mark because it's what was expected of me. By both of my bosses."

"Both?"

She's said too much and she knows it. Her eyes meet his fiercely and the hand on his shoulder digs in. "There is so much you don't know. My choices, decisions, even actions are not my own. I…" She sighs,

365

"You should not be here. None of you should be."

"Which side are you on? That will tell me everything I need to know."

She shakes her head. "It's not that simple. There's more than just good and bad, right and wrong. There's everything in between." She glances away and her eyes narrow, "I need to go." She looks back at him and whispers, "There are more than just two sides, prince."

Shade grips her tighter, not ready to end their conversation. "We aren't done here. Where's my sister?"

Her eyes soften. "Amberle is safe. I will take care of her, I promise you."

"Forgive me if I don't put much stock in your promises."

She hisses in annoyance. "I don't have time for this. Take your posse and leave, you do not want to be here tonight." She starts to pull away but Shade presses her closer. She glares at him, "Amberle is *me*, you hear? Your brother wants her trained like I was when I was stolen away from my home. He's sending her with my former handler." She hesitates, "Also my current handler. I *will* keep her safe." She sighs, "I am not your enemy, prince. We will meet again."

And then she disappears in the crowd. Former handler? What is Jeb up to? Who is this mysterious handler? The music changes from slow to fast and Shade is caught up in a frenzy of twirling and dancing. He searches the dance floor, but to no avail. There is no sign of the girl in the ruby dress.

There is sign, however, of her furious-eyed sister. Risa appears before him. She grips Shade's hands as they join in with the upbeat dance. "It *is* Sif. Where did she go? What did she say?"

366

Shade can hardly think straight, his mind whirring almost as quickly as his feet. "She disappeared. Said we needed to leave. Said something about a handler. I think she's working for someone against her will. Perhaps, two someones."

Risa mutters something unintelligible and then she's gone as well. A random girl becomes his new dance partner and he puts on a fake smile, all while stealing glances around the room. It doesn't appear that King Jeb has shown up, yet. Shade feels as if everyone would have noticed if that had been the case. He looks for a young girl in blue, maybe Amberle is nearby. But she, too, is nowhere to be seen.

The tune switches again, alerting everyone to switch partners. Shade turns and finds Dru in his arms. She's smiling wide, without a care in the world. "I have no idea what I'm doing." She says excitedly, "But we have *got* to do this more often!"

Shade can't help smiling, even in the midst of everything. He twirls her out and in, her back against his chest. She laughs and it's so contagious that he laughs as well.

"Soldiers off the ballroom, through those doors." She says when she's close enough. Shade follows her nod to closed double doors behind some of the tables. "Fray thinks they're Jeb's men."

Shade nods, pulls her close, grins at the catch of her breath. "Thank you." The beat skips, he releases her, and she shifts to the next dancer. Shade isn't sure when it happened, but Baron is next to him in the crowd. Baron takes Dru's hand and she throws her head back and laughs at something he says. Shade wishes he could feel calm enough to enjoy himself right now. Instead, he's feverishly checking all corners of the room for potential dangers, he's spinning ladies and replacing them with the next, and he hears Sif's urgent warning in his mind:

"Take your posse and leave, you do not want to be here tonight."

The melody switches to something slow. Dancers break apart, laughter fills the hall, and new members join the floor for a slow dance with a partner of their choice. Shade is about to excuse himself from the fun, and find a shadowed seat to simply watch, when a hand catches his wrist, turning him back around.

"You didn't think you'd get off that easy?" Erin says, her face a mask, even beyond the physical one. Her eyes appear just as guarded as Sif's had. But there's still that smile; that beautiful, comforting smile Shade has known for a long time. "Got a dance left for me?"

The fist around his heart loosens slightly. "Always." He takes her in his arms; one hand at her waist, the other holding a hand of her own. She places her free hand on his shoulder and looks up at him. She's taller than Dru, but shorter than Sif.

Green. Beautiful green eyes. It takes a moment for him to realize he's just staring and they haven't moved. They're standing still in the middle of the dance floor with gently swaying bodies all around them. Shade clears his throat and covers up the fumble with a, "Sorry, lot on my mind."

Erin sighs. She touches the side of his neck gently, then rests it back on his shoulder. "I know. It seems strange to think it's only been a couple of months since we left Glimmer. I feel like you've aged years."

Shade scoffs, "I look that bad? You said I didn't look scraggly."

She playfully punches his shoulder, "That's not what I meant." They begin swaying to the music. "Any news?" She leans closer so her ear is near his mouth.

He breathes in her sweet fragrance, something like lemon and cookie dough. Her hair tickles his cheek but he doesn't mind. "Spoke with Sif, Risa's sister. She was a joy." Shade says without humor. His eyes flit around the room. Jeb's guards are still near the same double doors, awaiting his arrival.

"I saw that, who's she with?"

"She wouldn't say. But she did tell me there's more going on than I realize, and that we don't want to be here tonight. It was a warning—something's going down."

She pauses for a breadth of a moment, then continues swaying. "Something bad?"

"I'm not sure. But I have every intention of finding out."

She's quiet for a moment. The situation would be peaceful if Shade wasn't hyper aware of their current situation. Suddenly, Erin wraps her arm around his neck and pulls him closer. Shade's mind goes blank with shock; she's going to kiss him! But then her mouth is at his ear and she's whispering, "The king is making his entrance. He isn't alone. Don't do anything stupid—"

At that moment, the music shifts dramatically to fast tempo, loud trumpets and cymbals. The orchestrator jerks with quick movements, then silences the band. The dance floor becomes still, everyone glancing around.

"Attention!"

Shade turns towards the voice, coming from the double-doors along the far wall. The doors Dru pointed out to him earlier with a number of guards near it. A bard stands there with a goofy looking hat and his hands behind his back. The annoying voice has come from him. He beckons to the double doors and they fly open from the inside.

"Attention!" The bard repeats, "His Majesty, the king!"

First, two soldiers step through, their hands resting casually on their hilts, their helmets off, eyes scrutinizing every inch of the ballroom. Then, Jeb steps through the doorway.

And, wow, he looks terrible. Has it really only been about two months since Shade last saw him? His brother has changed drastically since then. Jeb's eyes appear sunken, his hair is the literal definition of 'scraggly.' He's skinnier than Shade remembers, unhealthily so. The crown is too big for his head. Even now, it slips down over his ears a bit so that Jeb has to lift a finger and gingerly slide it back up.

But Jeb's frightening appearance isn't the worst of it.

No. The worst of it is the woman he carries on his arm. Shade sees the dirty blonde hair, cascading beautifully around her shoulders. He sees the crown, slightly smaller than Jeb's, atop her head. But he doesn't have to see her face to know.

"Mom."

CHAPTER 26

It comes out as a strangled whisper, so quiet no one but Erin hears. Still, she buries her face in his shoulder, shushing him quietly, her fingers near his lips.

The Queen faces the crowd, head held high. Her eyes are dark, but not sunken like Jeb's. Her shoulders are back, her gait is proud, and she doesn't appear to have been treated cruelly. She looks similar to how she did during Shade's last conversation with her, many days ago. She wears a gray dress so dark it's almost black and Shade assumes she is still in mourning. It is customary to wear dark colors for three months after the death of a royal. And, although she technically is no longer Queen, she will keep the title without the power as long as there is no other queen to replace her. Jeb, however, wears royal blue, flying in the face of customary rules; and his grip on Mother's arm is possessive. As if he's afraid he will lose her at any moment. Shade is frozen in place. He can only watch, powerless to go to his mother's aid.

"And, Her Majesty, Queen Rose!"

There is then great applause for the royals, the loud noise reverberating throughout the tall ceiling of the ballroom.

"Hagan was doing some recon earlier and found out about your mother. Amberle is here, too, but not at the ball. She's somewhere in the mansion." Erin says, "Hagan gathers that they are both here against their will, but they aren't being harmed."

Shade makes a noise in his throat, further indicating his feeling of helplessness. "Erin."

"I know," She whispers. "You can't do anything

371

for them right now. Please, Shade." Her eyes plead with him to listen. She faces him, her body pressed tightly against his, her eyes searching his face. He clenches his teeth, breathing slowly.

The royals are directed to the end of the ballroom where the high-backed chairs sit. The orchestra begins a soft melody and conversation resumes. Shade counts seven guards with Jeb, all armed. Jeb and his mother sit down in the chairs while servants come by carrying food and drink.

"He looks bad." Erin whispers.

"Ugly as sin, that one." Baron says, not even trying to hide the look of disgust shown in the way he turns down his mouth.

There's more activity near the double doors and several guards lead in two more prestigious royals; lesser than the king and queen. Shade does a double take. Yes, the blonde hair, the lean frame, the beautiful face…

It's Duchess Sansa, Erin's mother. And on her left arm is Eleazar, Erin's twelve-year old brother. He's pale and frowning, eyes glancing uneasily around the ballroom.

It's Erin's turn to panic. Her legs wobble and she grips Shade's arm to steady herself. He holds her, shifting smoothly into a dance as the music picks back up.

"They're here." She whispers. Her eyes follow her mother and brother to the other high back chairs next to Shade's family. "But where are the others?"

Shade is wondering the same thing. Eleazar has a twin sister. Where is Eliza? And where is the youngest, Edith? "What are they doing here?"

Erin's mouth works. Finally, she says, "It's

customary for lesser royals to travel with the king and queen."

"Yes," Shade agrees, "But, in light of recent events and for safety concerns, I would think most customs would be put on hold for a while." He spins Erin again to get a better view of the royals. None of them appear happy. Eleazar is seated beside his mother. As he looks out across the ballroom, his frown only deepens. His eyes land on Shade, who turns again, quickly out of the young boy's sight. "We mustn't be together for too long." He says to Erin. Their chances of being recognized have just increased immensely.

Erin takes one last longing look towards the far end of the ballroom, then back at Shade. Her eyes ask a thousand questions; all of which Shade so wishes he could answer. "Be careful." She whispers. She squeezes his hand and then she leaves. Shade already misses her steady presence.

Baron tugs at Shade's sleeve, pulling him away from the dance floor and to one of the round tables against the wall, opposite the side of the room Jeb and the others had just entered. Baron sits at the table, but Shade is too on edge for that. He knows it isn't time, but he wants to go ahead with the plan. He wants to speak with Jeb right *now*.

"I know what you're thinking." Baron says, "Patience. It's a virtue, you know."

Shade grits his teeth. He watches the royals, itching to get to his mother and Erin's family. A servant comes by with a drink of water. He starts to wave it away, until he realizes it's Trix and there's a thin piece of parchment under the glass on the tray she's holding. Shade picks both the glass and the paper up. He meets Trix's eyes for a split second, and then she's gone.

"No drink for me, eh?" Baron calls after her. "Rude." He mutters.

Shade sits down, now, fingers already pulling open the paper.

Got your message in Yagar. Traitor family unaccounted for. Tracking Windenmeyer, staying masked. Reinforcements available. —B

Bane was already on the way and ran into Reginald's messenger in Yagar. He must have discovered who the traitor was before leaving Frostfire because Afton's family was nowhere to be found; figuring out the traitor may have been the reason he decided to leave before receiving a message from Shade saying they had made it to Lockwood. Either he is tracking Jeb's progress or he has someone else doing it.

"Staying masked?" Baron asks, also reading the message. "Does that mean they're staying hidden or is he saying he'll be here at the ball?"

Shade thinks the latter, but doesn't have time to discuss it any further. Because a loud shout interrupts the night's fun. Through the open double doors across the way, a man bursts through, screaming loudly.

"He's not *my* king!" The man hollers, anger rippling off him like the spit flying from his mouth as he shouts. "Zion needs no king!" He draws his sword.

Baron and Shade are on their feet in a moment.

"Anarchist?" Baron asks. Shade grunts in agreement.

Four of Jeb's guards hurry towards him, drawing their weapons as well. A small brawl ensues, as many of Harvard's party-goers scream and scramble out of the way. The dance floor clears.

"Looks like you're getting your wish after all, prince." Baron says, "Permission to initiate Project

374

King?"

This isn't how it was supposed to go. Project King was supposed to start with Baron initiating a fight with Hagan, drawing the attention of the guards. But this is even better. Shade's already in motion, "Permission granted." He hopes the others are in place. He slinks along the outer wall, eyes watching the royals as they stare with concern at the guards grappling with the crazy man.

Behind, Baron clears his throat and stomps onto the dance floor, eyes blazing. He points at the guards and shouts, "Unhand him, you despicable blighters!"

That might be a bit over the top, but Shade doesn't slow. He continues along the wall.

Baron breaks into a run, straight towards the four guards and their captive, of whom they've managed to disarm and tackle to the floor. He's met in the center of the dance floor by two more guards. He ducks under their arms and makes a big show of egging them on.

Jeb is out of his seat and Queen Rose sits there with a hand covering her mouth. Eleazar is on his feet, standing in front of his mother. Shade notes how the boy has grown in the past couple of months. All servants have fled the area, taking cover like everyone else, along the walls and out the main doors.

All the servants, except for two. Who, unbeknownst to everyone else, are quietly making their way past the royals.

Except, one of them--Ryker—*accidentally* trips just as he's passing the king and the tray of jelly-filled scones he had been holding flies out of his hands and hits the king of Zion directly in the chest. One scone even bounces off his face.

The lone guard, only a foot from the king, pounces

on Ryker immediately, who has fallen to the ground, pleading for forgiveness. Ryker falls with a cry of pain and Shade thinks some of it might be real due to the Gray's previous injury. Trix is also on the ground, sputtering apologies; because when Ryker tripped, he *accidentally* hit Trix who *accidentally* flung her tray of juice-filled glasses all over Jeb.

Scone jelly and grape juice drip from Jeb's torso. He watches the entire situation with a mouth slightly open. Shade expects him to be angry, but there's hardly any emotion at all. While the guard is busy with Ryker, Trix stands and beckons for Jeb to follow. "Please, let me help you get cleaned up. I'm so sorry."

The rest of the ballroom is too occupied with the two separate fights occurring to notice the drama with the king. But the guard won't let Jeb go alone. He pins Ryker to the ground, orders two other guards to detain him, then stands to quickly guide Jeb towards a side door.

Towards the side Shade is quietly sneaking. He reaches one of the doors along the wall and ducks inside. The other side is a long stretch of dark hallway with separate rooms and galleries on either side. Shade picks a room and waits.

The double doors open and voices enter the hallway; Trix, still apologizing; the soldier, commanding her to stand down and return to the party. Their voices draw closer. Closer. Closer.

Shade jumps out of the room and onto the back of the soldier. The man is bigger than him, but Shade is able to wrap his arm around the man's throat and squeeze. At the same time, Trix kicks Jeb in the back of the knee and holds a kitchen knife to his throat when he lands on his knees.

The soldier flails wildly, reaching over his head and landing a punch to Shade's face. But he doesn't let go. After several long seconds, the soldier stops struggling, goes still, and then drops to the floor, unconscious.

Breathing heavy, Shade pulls the knife from his jacket pocket, nods at Trix, and drags Jeb into the room. Trix closes the door, leaving them alone. Shade knows she's just standing guard outside.

"You'll hang for this." Jeb growls.

Shade slings him into the center of the room, lit by only one lamp. Jeb stays on his feet, turning with a look of hatred. He stops in his tracks.

Shade's mask hangs loosely in his hand.

Jeb blinks. But if he's surprised, he hides it well. "I wondered when you might show up. You dare show your face in my presence?" His features are, again, devoid of emotion. The only signs of feeling are the clenched fists at his side.

Meanwhile, Shade is filled with an influx of emotions ranging from confusion and anger to joy at the sight of his brother. "Why are you here?"

"You do not get to ask the questions."

Shade holds up the knife. "I do when I've got the upper hand."

Jeb eyes the knife coldly, then looks back at Shade. "You would harm your own brother?" He scoffs, "Oh, I forget, you are not above killing loved ones."

Shade's brow furrows, the image of his poisoned father flashing through his mind. He grips the knife harder and takes a step forward. "I did not kill Father, Jeb. You know that. I was set up. Framed by someone."

At this, something flashes in Jeb's eyes.

Shade swallows. "I'm here to find out if that

377

someone was you. Are you working with the Renegades, Jeb? All these years I thought you were learning and training to take the place of Father at the right moment, when you were actually planning to kill him and overthrow the throne yourself?"

He pauses, eyes calculating. Then, he asks quietly, "You think so little of me?"

And suddenly, the ghoulish man before Shade isn't scary at all, but tired. Lonely. Shade lowers the knife. "No." He says. "Everyone told me not to trust you, that Renegades had turned you against the kingdom. I didn't want to believe it. But if I didn't kill Father and you didn't kill Father, then who did?"

He sighs and sits down on the arm of a nearby chair. With the droop of his shoulders and the haunted look in his eyes, this man doesn't look the part of king at all. "That's what I've been trying to find out. Just as you have presumed, I have come to the conclusion that it must have been the doing of the Renegades. How they penetrated the castle walls, I have yet to discover." He looks up at him, "I am not against the kingdom, Shade. But I am against the throne."

Shade's skin prickles and he slowly lifts the knife again, "You're an Anarchist."

Jeb continues resting there, his hands on his knees. "That's what I hear them calling us. But I prefer the term 'Freedom Fighter.' Resisting the rules of a monarchy, building a resistance up against it. But there are true factions of anarchy. The man out there," he points in the direction of the ballroom, "The one who came through the doors screaming, he's not with us. Neither is the second man with the red hair."

"He's with me." Shade says, "The red-head."

Jeb's eyebrows raise. "Impressive fighter." He

says genuinely.

"I tell you that so you know me and my people are not powerless. We are many and we do not intend to see the downfall of Zion."

"Neither do we, Shade. We intend to see it reborn, strengthened under the ruling of many. Not just the ruling of one."

"And, yet, you had no problem accepting the crown."

As if on cue, the crown slips down over the tips of his ears. He sighs heavily, brings up his hands, and lifts it from his head. "This thing is heavier than it looks." Jeb stares at it sadly, his thumbs caressing its gold frame.

Shade gets the feeling he means that in more ways than one. "Why have you brought Mom and Amberle? Erin's family? And where are the others—Eleazar and Edith?"

Jeb breaks from his staring stance. "Lockwood is heavy with past supporters of Father. I came here to meet with them, hoping to make them see the benefits of a council-led kingdom. I felt our family would be better protected with me than left behind at the castle. Erin's family, too. It is customary for lesser royals to—"

"Travel with the king and queen, yes I know." Shade says in irritation. He remembers what Sif said earlier about Amberle being trained as she had been. How does that fit in here?

Jeb goes on, "Whoever killed the king and his right-hand duke is still out there."

"Is it possible you brought them along? One of your guards?"

Jeb shakes his head, "I've done countless

background checks. I trust my soldiers with everything. No, whoever did it went into hiding. For what it's worth, I never believed it to be you, either."

Shade doesn't show it, but that does actually mean a lot. Although he knows their relationship may never return to what it once was, Shade misses and loves his brother. "Do you trust Sif?"

Here, Jeb looks up in a bit of surprise. He hadn't expected Shade to know about her. "I have my misgivings, but she has proved trustworthy so far. She seems to care for Amberle like a sister."

What kind of misgivings, Shade wonders. Sif warned him to leave the ball. Why? Did it have something to do with the anarchists? If so, Jeb does not appear to be aware of anything exciting to happen tonight; and, if he is, he isn't showing it. Sif alluded to having two bosses. Could the other have something to do with the Renegades? She was unaware of Afton; so whichever side he's involved with has nothing to do with Sif. Very little is making sense at the moment. He and Jeb are not enemies; and yet, they want different things for the kingdom. Shade has spent the last months preparing himself to one day retake the throne and lead Zion. Jeb wants Zion to be free of a monarchy, he wants a democracy. Shade admits, that doesn't seem like such a bad thing. But with the other anarchist factions, it is difficult to truly know which ones want equality and which ones seek destruction. "Jeb," He says, "You can stop this madness. Return to the castle, build your following, and seek to change the course of Zion through other means; not as a freedom fighter. Develop a board to help you vote on laws and seek counsel from lords and ladies of Zion's cities. You can create a democracy without abolishing the throne."

"When there is democracy, there is no need for a throne." He counters.

Shade sighs in frustration. "You are only adding to the chaos."

"If chaos is what it takes…" He doesn't have to finish the sentence for Shade to know Jeb will do anything to have his way.

Shade shakes his head. "What you are doing is worse than anarchy. You know it is wrong and yet still go through with it."

Jeb stands then, placing the crown back on his head. His face has returned to the cold mask it was before. The creepy ghoul is back. "I do not want to be your enemy, Shade. Do not force my hand."

The door behind Shade bursts open. It's Trix. Her eyes are wide. "The ballroom, something's happening!" Down the hall, they hear heavy sounds of fighting.

Shade glares at Jeb, "What did you do?"

"I was about to ask you the same thing." He growls as they both turn and sprint after Trix. They sprint down the hall and bust through the ballroom doors.

What greets them on the other side is complete mayhem. Yelling, fighting, the sounds of metal on metal. A battle has broken loose at the Harvard ball.

There are soldiers and guards grappling all across the dance floor. Some of them appear to be fighting each other. This must be what Sif was referring to. Shade searches the ballroom, but doesn't see the ruby dress anywhere. He spots many of his friends caught up in the battle. Baron, a slight cut above one eyebrow, has his fists up and is going toe-to-toe with two sword-wielding individuals who are not in guard's uniforms. On the contrary, they appear to be wearing normal clothing; pants and a long-sleeve shirt, obviously not originally on the guest list. Further down, the twins engage in a similar situation; at least, they have short swords of their own that they probably swiped off of fallen warriors. To Shade's dismay, there appear to be a lot of them. He prays he doesn't see any familiar faces.

Beside him, Trix lets out a sudden gasp and takes off into the fray. After several feet, she stops and turns back to Shade, her eyes a mask of fear. She's torn on whether to leave Shade or not. Beyond her, Shade spots Ryker warding off a large man with a club. The Gray doesn't appear to be faring too well.

"Go!" Shade yells without a second thought. Trix nods once, then runs to Ryker's aid.

"What is the meaning of this?" Jeb screams at one of his guards who, seeing him, takes a defiant stand at his side.

"Stay back, Your Highness!" Then, upon seeing Shade, the guard does a double take. "Erm, Your Highness?" He seems to fully realize who he's seeing and turns the sword on Shade, "King Jeb, look out!"

Stupidly, Shade had dropped his mask in his hurry to the ballroom. He raises his knife, preparing to warn the man against any attempt to disarm him.

But Jeb takes a hand and knocks down the guard's arm, "Not now, Julian! There are clearly more dire things at hand! What's going on?"

The guard, temporarily shocked at the king's chastisement, finally says between breaths, "These people attacked out of nowhere, storming the mansion. I think it's the anarchists. Or Renegades. Or...I don't know."

"What do they want?" Jeb asks, ducking a little

382

behind the guard.

"You!" A man screams, appearing in front of them, his eyes crazed. It's the same man that had burst into the ballroom earlier. In the chaos, he must have escaped from the guards. In one movement, the man lifts the sword high and brings it down in a striking arc.

Shade acts fast. He throws himself in front of Jeb, lifting his knife for protection. The sword loudly strikes the knife, slides down the blade, and rests against its handle. The blow drives Shade to his knees, but he doesn't waver, glowering up at the man. They share equal stares of animosity. Then, the man is tackled from the side. His sword clatters to the floor, knocked from his grip. Shade stands, lifting the newfound sword into his hand; he deposits his knife back into the fold of his jacket.

Baron stands, winded from the tackle. He grins at the man, groaning on the floor. "Not on my watch, *anarchist*."

Shade glances around at the chaos, the question not even past his lips when Baron says, "Escape now, talk later." Shade nods. He glances once at Jeb, who's watching him with a torn look. The guard beside Jeb is talking to him, asking him for orders. But Jeb's mouth moves without sound.

So, Shade turns away and takes after Baron, through the bustling crowd of brawls. He has more important matters to attend to right now. Like escaping. He's halfway across the dance floor when he feels the air shift, and narrowly dodges a flying knife. It skims his arm, tearing through fabric and nicking flesh. He turns, brings up his sword in time to block the second one aimed for his head. It ricochets to the ground. Before him stands a gangly fellow with stringy hair and a red welp on his neck. Shade recognizes the mark. It's the same one as the man in the forest, the one Erin killed. Hagan had said he must have been a northern Renegade.

Anarchists, Renegades, Freedom Fighters...who else was invited to this ball?

The man grins and whips out four more knives, two in each hand. "You look an awful lot like someone whose face is plastered on papers all over Zion."

"And you just look terrible." Shade retorts. He raises the sword and sprints towards the man.

Taken by surprise, the man can only release two knives, both of which Shade blocks easily, before Shade is upon him. He trips the man with one swipe of the sword and he lands on his back on the hard floor. Shade turns in time to block the sword of a different man and then it's all swings and parries for the next several minutes.

Every time he fends off one enemy, another is there to replace him. Or her. He notes there are a lot more women Renegades than he thought. It's difficult to tell the Renegades apart from the Anarchists; unless, of course, they are northern Renegades, all of which have a similar burn mark on their neck. His sword gets knocked out of his hand and then its fist against fist between him and the current man he fights. Shade lands a hard kick to the man's kneecap, earning a satisfying crunch. The man screams and drops.

Someone hits Shade hard from behind and the two of them go to the floor, grappling for a handhold. Shade's on his back and the girl glowers at him, her ruby dress ripped up the seam from where she's straddling him, his arms pinned between her legs and the floor. "I told you to *leave*." One hand squeezes his throat, closing it off from receiving oxygen. He's too shocked by their current position to put up much of a fight. Her teeth are gritted and her eyes blaze almost as brightly as her dress. "The man I work for cannot be trusted. He's playing all sides, orchestrating this very attack tonight. My mission was to befriend the king, become one of his trusted allies, and be a spy for Storg."

Shade's eyes bulge at the mention of that name. Sif's head tilts to the side, "You know him." She releases ever-so-slightly on his throat. He takes the moment to buck upwards, sending her over his head. He grabs her wrists before she can topple head-first onto the dance floor and she lands on her side. He pulls her to a sitting position and kneels down beside her.

"I know *of* him." Shade corrects. "He's been tracking me since Frostfire. Maybe even before. If you are mixed up with him, you are most definitely my enemy." His grip on her wrists tightens and he drags her to her feet.

She hardly bats an eye, "Working for him has never been my *choice*. It's been my only hope for *survival*. Spying on the king was only meant to be another job." Her eyes soften and she bites her lip. "But then I met Amberle. And your mother. They are good people. They have inspired me to fight back, even without knowing it." She goes to pull away.

"Where are they? Safe?" Shade asks, still holding tight.

"For now." Says a cool voice behind him. Sif glances over his shoulder and her eyes widen. He releases her and turns.

Sif gasps and quickly curtsies, an odd sight in the midst of a battle. But, for Shade, it's as if the battle has paused around him. Everything seems to move slowly.

Queen Rose stands there, ten feet away, a pillar of serene in the heat of war. Swords and arrows and battle cries sound around her, yet she stands immobile; her hands casually clutched in front of her voluminous dress. Her beautiful hair and crown catch the light, dazzling the world around her. Her eyes glance between Sif and Shade.

"Your Highness, I—" Sif is at a loss for words, her eyes downcast in shame at the queen learning of her original intentions. "I apologize, I wish you no ill-will or harm. You must believe me–"

"I *must* do nothing of the sort." The queen retorts, her tone clipped in such a way that even Shade flinches and he feels like he's five years old all over again. "We will speak of this later," she continues, nodding once at the girl. "Go. Find Amberle."

Sif nods gratefully. She gives Shade a passing glance, then jumps back into the chaos.

Queen Rose turns her attention to her son, several fleeting emotions crossing her face; the most pronounced being relief at the sight of her healthy son. "You are well?"

Shade nods. "As I can be. And you?"

She nods, her eyes searching his. "You have grown. Matured."

He swallows, "I didn't have much of a choice. Mother, you and Amberle should come with me. I can protect you." Even as he says it, he knows it isn't true. They are safer behind the castle walls; even in the hands of someone seeking to ban monarchy. "I didn't kill Father."

She smiles sadly. "I know, my son. I warned him there were only so many times he could cheat death.

He knew the risks."

And then he wants nothing more than to fall into her arms and not let go. He swallows down a wave of emotion, fists clenched. "I miss you." Is all he says.

"Your Highness!" A guard rushes to her, one hand holding a bloody stomach. He recognizes Shade and points the tip of his sword at him. "Stand down, traitor!"

Baron reappears then, grasping Shade's arm, breathless and bloody. He blinks away the red liquid, squinting at Shade with one eye. "Get lost, did you?" He realizes the situation and eyes the Queen warily. Then, after a moment of indecision, he bows his head. "My lady." He tugs at Shade's arm. "The cavalry's coming, prince. Time to go."

"Go." The Queen whispers. The soldier looks at her dubiously, "Your...Highness?"

Shade stares at her hard, one last time. "I'll fix this." He assures her. Then, he picks up the sword from where it had fallen in his scuffle with Sif and follows Baron, uncertain if he will ever see his mother again.

They don't make it very far before they're thrown back into the frenzy of battle.

"Good Zion, how big is this dance floor?" Baron gripes as they stand back-to-back and take on foes.

In the back of his mind, Shade is desperate to find the others. There's no time to take a breath and glance around the room for Erin or Ryker or any of his other friends. The current man he battles is tall and wide and can wield a sword with the best of them. He is giving Shade just about all he can handle. The man knocks the sword from Shade's hand, so he ducks under the man's arm and has enough foresight to roll out of the way of the approaching blade. The sword slices into the floor

387

and sticks in the wood. In the reflection of its blade, Shade spots someone behind him, getting ready to deal a death blow. All Shade can do is turn.

It's Afton. His eyes are all agony and terror, as if he does not wish to commit this heinous crime. But his hand is ever sure and the longsword continues its dangerous arc towards the prince. An arrow zips past Shade, nailing Afton in the shoulder. It lands solidly, digging deep into the flesh between his armor. The force of it knocks Afton's aim off just enough that the blade misses Shade by a mere hairsbreadth. Afton shouts, now with a face of pain and shuffles sideways.

Shade stands to his feet just as Erin joins him at his side, a bow in her hand. If looks could kill, Afton would be dead four times over. Her hair has half fallen from its eccentric bun and one hand has her skirts bunched up at the hip to free her feet. "Where'd you get the bow?" He asks, smiling crookedly. It's good to see her.

She blows a strand of hair out of her face, still glaring at Afton's retreating form. "How dare he show his face here. How dare he raise a *single finger* at you—" A loud trumpet sound cuts her off. They look around wildly as people begin retreating, escaping through doorways and out windows.

"I know that sound." Baron says. He grasps Erin's hand and pulls on Shade's arm. "Hurry, some of the others are around back, horses at the ready." He glances around as if searching for someone.

Shade searches the crowd for Afton but the man is lost in the chaos.

"Dru already made it out," Erin shouts as they run towards the same hallway as Afton. Shade recognizes has the one Jeb entered through only a little while before. "I saw her come this way a few minutes back."

But that isn't who Baron is looking for, because his eyes never stop scanning. They run into a group of fleeing party guests, mainly women, all weepy-eyed and scared. It is in this moment of annoyance, in which they're trying to shove through the crowd of individuals, that Shade turns to the main entrance and sees Lord Bane barreling through, a conch horn at his lips. Its sound echoes through the ballroom once more.

"Baron, it's your dad!" Erin exclaims.

There's a proud gleam in Baron's eye and a smile spreads across his face. "I knew it. Come on, he's buying us time."

"Buying us time for what?" Shade asks, "What's going on?" It has become evident to him that they know more about the situation than he does. Someone has prepared horses for their escape. Bane's message had been more literal than Shade realized, seeing as the Lord of Frostfire is currently leading a regime of warriors into the ballroom.

"When you disappeared from the ballroom and all chaos broke loose, Hagan and Ryker made a plan for escape. Tyson was nearby and he and Hagan went to get the horses."

"I don't need rescuing."

Baron gives him a look over his shoulder, "He says as I pull his slow butt out the door."

"He says as I save his life with a bow and arrow." Erin adds.

"While you were off talking with the king, I received word from one of our Frostfire messengers. I knew my dad was nearby. They had gotten wind of a potential crisis at the Harvard household this evening."

"Potential?" Erin mutters, eyeing the bodies strewn

389

about the room.

They weren't noticeable at first, but now that the ballroom is largely clearing out, death is evident everywhere. They've reached the doorway when Shade sees Perez, lying in a pool of his own blood. He's alive, but without help, he won't be for long. He lies on his side, one hand clutching his chest as blood seeps through. His bloodied teeth are grit and his eyes somehow find Shade's across the room.

Shade begins to turn back, but stops short. Perez has lifted a hand towards Shade, palm up and steady. He's telling Shade not to come. He is surrounded by Renegades. Or anarchists. It doesn't matter, they're all starting to look the same and they're all enemies of Zion, so what's it matter anyway? The enemies approach Perez, weapons drawn. He lies there, one hand clutching his side, a dire look of pain on his face. The enemies draw ever closer.

Shade watches him helplessly. No, this isn't right. He has to go help; he will not allow another friend to die for him. He takes one step back inside the ballroom, but a hand wraps around his midsection.

"I don't think so, prince." Baron says, grimacing. There's a resolved look in his eyes. "I want to help him, too." He says quietly, "But, that isn't the mission."

Shade can't tear his eyes away from the Blue.

"Get him out of here!" A voice shouts. Shade vaguely recognizes it as belonging to Bane, who has ventured further into the ballroom, disposing of any enemies who try his hand. The Lord of Frostfire is slowly making his way to Perez.

There's no way he makes it in time, Shade thinks. "Baron, he'll die."

"He knew the risks." Baron says, adamantly dragging Shade deeper down the hall.

He knew the risks. The same words his mother had just spoken only minutes before. How many more would have to die knowing the risk it takes to fight for Zion? Before they are too far down the hallway and Perez is fully out of sight, Shade is just barely able to read his lips. One word, uttered in the face of death.

Kiertunyazi.

CHAPTER 27

The hallway seems to drag on. Shade can't get the sight of Perez, in a pool of his own blood, out of his head. He blinks it away and continues after Baron and Erin. Then, his sights set on a lumbering form, several doors ahead of them.

Afton.

Shade's eyes narrow and he picks up speed, Baron right beside him.

Erin deposits the bow and uses both free hands to hike her skirts and run more freely. "I *knew* we'd be running." She trails off, muttering something about at least having the forethought to wear trousers underneath.

Erin's arrow to his shoulder has caused Afton's gait to be labored. He runs off balanced, one hand clutching the spot where the arrow had once been. He hears their footsteps and looks back at them in alarm, just as both Shade and Baron close the distance with identical flying tackles.

Shade draws his sword, rolling to his feet. Erin kicks Afton's sword out of his reach and the three of them surround him menacingly. He stays on his knees, hands raised, eyes downcast. Tears spring from his eyes and drip down his face.

"*Why?*" Baron spits, his voice thick with emotion. "She loved you like a brother."

Afton's eyes squeeze shut and he bows his head to the floor, quietly sobbing.

Coward.

Baron grabs him by the hair and lifts his head so he has to look them in the eye. Afton cries out in pain.

"*Coward*." He says, voicing Shade's exact thoughts. "Have you no loyalty? Have you no shame? Your tears mean *nothing*."

"He has my boy!" Afton cries, and Baron stills. Erin and Shade share a passing glance. "He has my wife."

Baron lets go of his hair and Afton nearly falls face down again. He lifts his head just enough to say, "Storg. He threatened to kill them if I didn't do everything he said. I was told to betray you all and kill any who got in the way." He sobs again, then continues, "Vision was getting too close, asking too many questions. I warned her to just stop, to shut up, to mind her own business. I didn't want to kill her." He looks up at Shade, "And, then, he told me to kill you."

Erin scoffs at this, "Fat chance at that." She growls. Shade kind of likes this protective side of her.

Baron straightens, staring sadly at the brutish man. "You could have told us. Asked for help."

"I didn't know how. I was scared." He places his forehead to the floor again. "I'm sorry. I'm so sorry." Then he trails off into tears again.

And Shade realizes in that moment that Afton may have been scared, but he isn't a coward; he's just a very, very broken man. He steps back, sheathing his sword. "You can choose a different path, Afton."

He sits there, shoulders slumped. "I can't. Not while he has my family."

Shade finds that he can't argue with this. Afton sees no other option while his family is in the clutches of this evil man and Shade can't blame him. "We're going to stop him. And, I'll do everything in my power to save your family."

At this, Afton says nothing.

So, Erin grips Shade's arm and the three of them take off running down the hallway once more, leaving the broken man behind. Baron's face is shadowed, resolved. Shade is honestly a bit surprised the Green didn't try to kill the man.

They've almost reached the end of the hallway when Baron ducks to the right. They find themselves in a short outlet hallway of about twenty feet with a large open window at the end of it. Shade reaches the window and looks down. Multiple pieces of fabric, curtains it looks like, have been tied together to create a rope leading down the side of the mansion wall, to the ground four stories below. They look out on the back of the mansion grounds where a beautiful garden, four times the size of the one from earlier, sits bathed in moonlight and starshine. Since the mansion is on a hill, the ground slopes down, away from the mansion. Towards the bottom of the hill await several horses with riders already atop them, their forms nearly shrouded by tree coverage and shadows.

Baron eyes the curtains dubiously. "Why does this give me freshman year vibes?"

Schooling in the castle isn't given such names, but Shade knows Baron must be talking about his teenage years in school.

There's the loud clatter of others entering the hallway from the ballroom and the sound of pounding footsteps and shouts. "They went this way, after them!" Someone yells.

Baron sighs, shrugging. "Down the rope it is. Not a huge fan of heights but who's asking, right?" He tries for a smile, swallows, then lifts a leg out the window. He grasps the curtain rope so tightly his knuckles turn white. With an unsteady smile, he begins his descent down the mansion wall.

They watch his descent; the smile has completely vanished from Baron's face. Shade places a hand on Erin's back and urges her forward. "You next. I'll be right behind you."

"You've ruined your coat." She says beckoning to his jacket, one side of it shredded. Blood seeps through a cut over his ribs that he hadn't realized was there. She has the audacity to appear annoyed with him.

"Really, Erin? *Now*? Can't we discuss this later?"

She follows Baron out the window. Once she's several yards down, Shade grasps the curtain and lowers himself over the edge of the window. Below, Baron is about halfway to the ground and Erin is somewhere between them. Squinting towards the horses at the bottom of the hill, he spots Hagan's impatient urge for them to hurry.

Five soldiers round the corner, spot him, and one begins shouting orders. He recognizes the Windenmeyer symbol on their armor. So, Jeb has decided to send men after him anyway. He tries not to let that bother him as he scrambles down the makeshift rope, hand over hand, feet bouncing rapidly off the stone wall. He's several feet down when the guards reach the window. One of them has a crossbow and aims it their way.

"Arrow!" Shade shouts. He turns away, meeting eyes with Erin. She tenses and shifts to her right as an arrow glides past Shade, barely missing Erin's hanging form. It embeds itself in the ground below. Baron reaches the first flight and drops the rest of the way to the ground.

From the bottom of the hill comes return fire. One arrow finds its mark, and a soldier topples out the open window. "Look out!" Erin screams, but it's to no avail. The body slams into Shade, causing him to lose grip of the curtain with one hand. The trajectory of the body changes after hitting him and it falls harmlessly the rest of the way to the ground, landing with a sickening sound. Shade slides down the curtain, only gripping with one hand. Gravity drags him down until he's able to tighten his grip, his hand burning with the friction. He rights himself and regrasps the rope with both hands.

He looks up. One of the soldiers has joined them on the rope, clearly lacking the agility to efficiently maneuver down the curtain like Shade and the others. Arrows still fly from the hill, finding marks. There are more soldiers to replace those hit; Shade starts to realize that not all of them are Jeb's men. Some of them wear Renegade or Anarchist clothing. It seems everyone wants a piece of the traitor prince.

Baron shouts at them to hurry. Shade has an idea; but there's Erin to consider. He can't risk her getting hurt. He looks back up towards the window. One of the soldiers lifts a sword, readying to bring it down on the curtain and sever it from the window. Another stops the blade, yelling, "No! He'll get away!"

Shade glances back down. He's at the second story; right now, the fall would be somewhere around twenty feet. Erin has reached the first floor. Shade makes a decision. "Let go!" He yells. Erin gives him an incredulous look.

"Do it!" Baron says. He holds out his arms, preparing to catch her.

She glances once more at Shade, then lets go of the curtain. A small squeak escapes her lips, but then Baron is catching her and setting her on her feet and

Shade can go forth with his plan. With one hand, he pulls the knife from his coat pocket. He looks up at the window, grins, then slices through the curtain, just above the part he's holding. The drop is a bit further than he expected, and his stomach flies to his throat as he watches the ground draw closer. He clutches the knife, holding it away from his body so as not to accidentally impale himself. Then his bent legs are hitting the ground and he rolls to absorb the impact safely, flipping deftly to his feet and letting his momentum take him down the hill in pursuit of Baron and Erin. Shouts follow after him, but now they're only empty threats. He reaches the others and finds it is Ryker who has a bow trained at the guards in the window; Shade assumes it's one he found in the battle, as it is not cobalt gray like his normal weapon of choice.

He nods his thanks at him and glances around quickly. Hagan, Ryker, Dru, and Risa are all there. "Where are the others?"

Ryker appears stricken. "I lost sight of Trix and I haven't seen Fray since the fight began." He stares up towards the mansion, clearly wanting to go back and find her.

"Perhaps they are with my father." Baron says.

Understanding dawns and Hagan says, "Of course. The horn."

"And Perez, then, too?" Risa asks.

Shade can't look at her. So, he jumps atop Poe and they begin riding away from the mansion. "Perhaps." He says, then asks, "Where to, now? All our supplies are back at the house."

They trot away from the mansion, Hagan leading the way. "Back to Harvard's estate. Tyson returned to prepare for our departure. We are leaving Lockwood tonight. It's too dangerous right now to stay. You appear to have *many* enemies, Your Highness."

So much for considering Lockwood a potential home base for their endeavors. But he knows Hagan is right. The best present course of action is to leave with their lives; live to fight another day, per say. He avoids Risa's gaze as they ride, but he still feels it boring into his back. She suspects something and he doesn't have the heart to tell her.

They take side streets and hidden allies to avoid notice. Most of the city is indoors for the evening, as it is no doubt nearly midnight. Harvard's other estate is dark and a bit ominous looking when they arrive. He wishes he could go back to three days ago when they were all gathered inside, enjoying each other's company. True, they've been in hiding. But at least they were relatively safe in those moments. Shade isn't surprised when they don't go inside, it's likely Tyson has already gathered any supplies they will need; he hopes Greaver's cloak is included in that. Instead, Hagan leads them around the back of the house and down the steep slope that takes them to the rock quarry. The horses neigh with indignation, but ride the slope without trouble.

At the bottom, near the edge of the creek, wait a host of people. Among them are multiple boxes and crates, some of which look to be carrying food and various supplies. Shade spots Blair and his aid, Liv. And there's Tyson the guard. He sees many of their newfound allies, including Lady Sprite and Sir Reginald Opal. Tyson is the first to approach them. "All of your weapons and attire are stored for travel. The servants have readied meals for the next several weeks. You will be well taken care of." He bows at Shade, straightens, and appears sad. "It is an honor to serve you. I hope we meet again."

Shade dismounts, looking Tyson in the eye. The good one; truthfully, the vacant, glossy one gives him an eerie feeling as it stares off into empty space. "We will, Tyson." He clasps the other man's hand and gives one hard shake. Looking past him, Shade sees an unexpected sight.

It's General Saipan and some of his men. The general grunts at him and says, "You said reinforcements, so here we are. I've brought a couple of my men; trustworthy, hearty individuals." He looks away, "But, honestly, I'm just here to collect the horses."

"Horses?" Shade asks, looking between the general and Tyson. His grip tightens on Poe's reins as he realizes he will actually miss the big guy.

"Yes," Hagan says, handing off his horse to one of Saipan's men. "We will no longer be needing them. Tyson, where is he?"

Tyson glances over his shoulder at the dark water, "Oh, he should be around shortly. Had plenty of time to prepare the sails."

As if on cue, something large comes from the left, floating into view from around the bend of the creek. It's a boat; a rather large boat; large in comparison to the creek it's riding in, at least. It looks like an ominous dark, terrifying object; if it weren't for the moon glinting off its masts, Shade would wonder what creature glides before him. The boat is at least twenty-five yards long and he guesses about ten feet wide. Its sails are currently folded in and the boat moves silently and effortlessly through the shallow waters. It comes to a smooth stop in front of them. A ramp slides down from the side; a figure appears and slips down it, stopping before Shade and his crew.

Duke Flynn crosses his arms and flashes a wide grin. "Captain Flynn, at your service! This is *Loretta*. Beauty, isn't she?" He sighs contentedly and smiles up at the ship.

"Wait," Dru says, "This is, we're—" her eyes glance between the ship and Shade, "We're *riding* this thing?"

Shade turns to Hagan, "*This* is the plan?"

"Where did you even keep this thing?" Baron asks, amazed. Flynn turns to him and begins discussing how his parents left him a lot of land with a large hangar built over the water in which *Loretta* has been quite safe and cared for.

Hagan sighs, "There are a great many allies still to be found, away from the mainland. So, yes, this is the plan. For now." He shakes Tyson's hand, thanking him for the quick preparations.

Ryker and Risa begin helping some of the servants load items on board the ship. Erin admires the boat, her hand resting on its wood as she cranes her head up to take it all in. General Saipan taps his foot impatiently, holding out his hands for the reins. He sizes Shade up thoughtfully, "I take it you and Poe were able to get along?"

Shade reluctantly hands over the reins, giving Poe a rub down his nose. "Eventually." He says, "He's a rather interesting horse, that one."

Saipan stares at the horse in wonder, eyes gleaming. "My pride and joy." The horse whinnies and nuzzles the man's chest. "Good, boy." The general grunts at Shade, who assumes that must be his version

400

of a goodbye.

Blair and Liv approach Shade. He can't help gripping each one of them in hugs. They have helped him far more than they may ever realize. "Thank you for everything." He says. He brings one hand up to his mouth, fingers together, and lowers it towards Liv, palm facing in. She smiles and nods at his thanks.

"There is a lot of danger out there, Your Highness." Blair says, "Be careful. I do hope we meet again."

"I trust we will." Shade says, fighting back the sudden emotion he's feeling. "Will you be safe here?"

Blair smiles, "There is no need for you to worry. We will be fine. We will pick up the pieces of what has happened at the Harvard ball tonight. We'll regroup and continue seeking allies for Zion."

Shade is still trying to figure out everything that happened at the ball, as well. "Sir, I'm not sure who's even left. There were so many dead."

Blair holds up a hand. "Again, that is not a worry of yours. You have a greater duty to uphold. For the kingdom."

"Indeed," Sir Reginald says, walking up behind Blair and clapping the man on the back. "You do, Prince Shade. I am sending two of my messengers with you, their names are Friga and Sten. They will serve you well. I was only at the ball for a brief time and missed all of the action, but I hear our friends from Frostfire made an appearance."

Shade nods. "Lord Bane is a good man. He will be of great use towards our mission."

"I have no doubt. Godspeed, young man." Reginald says, gripping Shade's shoulder. "You have many who believe in you. Who believe in Zion. Be safe." Then, he leaves to speak with some others in the crew.

Liv takes her hand and touches the tip of her middle finger—bent forward at the knuckle—to her chin, then twists the hand towards the front in one fluid motion.

"Good luck." Blair translates. "Although, if things go our way, you won't need it." Blair and Liv take their leave. Shade watches them go, a tiny void already filling his soul. He can't tell if it's because he will miss these sweet people, or if it's because things rarely go his way.

Shade sees Ryker then, looking up towards the mansion, his eyes desperate. He realizes the man is looking for Trix. "Knowing her, she's safe." Shade reassures.

Ryker glances at him, looks once more at the top of the cliff, then turns back to Shade with a nod of finality. He smiles, but it doesn't reach his eyes. "Oh, I know. She's a tough one." He sighs, looking saddened, "But, we really need to leave, enemies could very well be on their way to our location as we speak. And, I was just hoping Trix would be coming with us."

It dawns on Shade, then. Ryker is planning on leaving Trix behind to get Shade safely out of Lockwood. It's a brave and difficult decision to leave the one he loves, indefinitely, for the betterment of the kingdom. Immediately, Shade feels a pang in his chest; he can't imagine doing such a thing, although he knows at some point, he very well might have to. He makes a decision then, certain of himself. He hugs Ryker, tightly, pats him hard on the back. "We will have to make sacrifices on this journey for the throne. But," He pulls away, looking into the Gray's eyes. "This is not one of them for you."

Ryker stares at him, slack-jawed. "Absolutely not,

402

Your Highness. If you think I will simply let you leave without my assistance, you are sorely mistaken."

"I make many mistakes," Shade says with a laugh, "But, this is also not one of them." He repeats. "Permission to stay behind and rally troops in the mainland cities granted."

Ryker opens his mouth to object.

"No, not granted." Shade says, "*Ordered*. Ryker, I know you are torn between defending me and staying with Trix. I am making the choice for you. Look around," He beckons to their friends, "I have many qualified warriors going with me. The good people here, in Lockwood, need someone like you to lead and defend them."

Ryker's eyes glisten in the moonlight. He swallows, steps back, and bows in respect, lingering a bit longer than normally. When he rises, his eyes are clear of any tears and Shade wonders if they were ever there at all. "As you say, Kiertunyazi." And then they hug again. "I will miss you, Shade."

"As will I." Shade says in return. "Give Bane my regards."

They separate. "Of course." Ryker says, "We will meet again. Until then, stay safe. The waters can be…unkind. Don't do anything I wouldn't."

Shade only grins. Ryker smiles, but it fades as he steps away to say goodbye to the others. Shade takes a deep breath and turns when Hagan says, "It's time we leave. While we still can."

Most of the cargo has been loaded onto the boat. No more than five minutes has passed since they arrived at the creek side. Shade thanks Tyson and starts to follow the others up the ramp, when he notices someone standing to the side.

"Ladies first." Shade says, holding an arm out at the ramp.

But Risa doesn't smile. She stands there with almost a blank look. She fists her hand, holds it over her chest, and bows. "I'm afraid I cannot make this part of the journey with you." She says to the ground.

Shade is taken aback. He did not expect this. "Risa…" He trails off when she looks him in the eye and he sees the truth there. She knows. She knows about her brother.

To further confirm it, she says. "You saw something in the ballroom and I intend to discover it on my own. I must see it for myself. For my family. Besides, Sif is out there. Somewhere. It is my duty as the older sister to protect her, whether she wants it or not." She goes still, her eyes unfocused. "I failed her years ago. I will not fail her again."

Of course, Shade understands. How often in the last couple of days has he had that very thought? It took all of his willpower to turn away from his mother and his sister, to trust them in the hands of an anarchist, freedom fighter, whatever he's calling himself. But, oh how he does not like this; he does not like saying goodbye to newfound allies and friends. First, Ryker. Now, Risa. He straightens and follows her lead, placing a fist over his heart. Then, he reaches out a hand and they grasp arms. "As you say, Risa. Or, is it, *Lady* Risa?"

Her eyes flash in surprise.

"I'm not as daft as I look. You must reign from some royal lineage. In a northern city of Pire or Klepton, perhaps, before they went rogue?"

At this, a smile plays at the corner of her lips and she gives him a coy look. "You speak too soon, young prince, for you are still rather daft. I do hail from a line of royals." She leans in closer to whisper, "But it was much further north than the rogue cities. And they did not call me lady." Her lips brush his ear, "They called me princess." She pulls away.

It is Shade's turn to look surprised. There are no cities north of Pire or Klepton. Only frozen tundra that stretches to the Glacial Sea. Unless she is implying there are more cities, more lands in which he is unaware of. He doesn't have time to ask her, because she pulls away, her smile fading.

"All futile titles, now." She says, repeating a similar phrase to one she had spoken back in the woods before they ever reached Lockwood. "All that remains of my lineage is me and my siblings." She clears her throat, "And even that is in danger."

"Sif thinks highly of my sister, Amberle, and our mother. I gathered that from our brief conversation. And Erin's family…"

Risa can already tell where he is headed and she nods, "I will search for them as well."

Shade grips her arm softly, "If you do find them, promise me you will keep them safe."

She inclines her head then thoughtfully, "I do not make promises, hilcipe. I let my yes be yes and my no be no." She pauses, her eyes softening, "Yes—if I find them, I will keep them safe. I hope you survive this war, Prince Shade. You might make Zion a greater kingdom, yet." She turns and walks away.

"Thank you," He says to her back. She looks over her shoulder and he adds, "Until next time."

One nod and then she's disappeared into the darkness and Shade knows she's on her way back to the ballroom. He hopes, somehow, Perez is alive; but the amount of red seeping onto the floor did not appear very promising. Her words linger in his mind.

I let my yes be yes and my no be no. Sometimes, promises are only empty sayings. Lies given to make someone feel better. He trusts that Risa truly means what she is saying. Her very word is her bond, no oath required. If she says she will do it, then she will. Shade tucks this into his mind; he will let his yes be yes and his no be no. He stares once more into the darkness but can't see her anymore.

He has only taken one step onto the ramp when there's the sound of approaching hooves and an entourage of several individuals comes riding down the hill on horseback. Shade jumps down from the ramp, immediately poised for a fight. But Tyson holds up an arm to call him off. "It's only The Lady."

Lady Brandy stops her horse mere feet from Shade's form, and gracefully dismounts. Her tall, imposing frame nearly blocks out the entire moon as she stands, smiling darkly.

"You're late." Hagan says, his voice low.

Lady Brandy scoffs. "A woman is never late. Everyone else got the time wrong. Come." She claps her hands and three of the guards who came with her jump into action, unloading supplies from different horses and carrying them up the ramp. Lady Brandy throws Shade a demeaning look, then follows after her men, her high-heeled combat boots (almost a contradiction of themselves) clomping loudly with each step.

From the deck of the boat, Dru's mouth falls open in surprise.

Shade is not particularly happy about this arrangement either. He turns to Hagan expectantly, but the Green speaks before him. "It's out of my hands. I was able to speak with Duke Harvard before the disastrous ball fell apart. He insisted Brandy come along. Her powerful influence apparently stretches far and wide. It was either her or Lady Colette." He adds at Shade's doubtful look.

Shade pictures the deceptive smile and seductive, lilting voice of Colette and shudders involuntarily. "Right. Any more surprises?" He asks, somewhat testily.

Hagan doesn't appear perturbed by his tone and says, "Not if I can help it."

They climb aboard, then, with those staying behind waving their goodbyes. Tyson has already left, taking some of his men to guard Harvard's territory in case any enemies have found them. General Saipan waves once and then turns away, barking for someone to get him a tall glass of something—the words are drowned out by the sound of the boat releasing from the shore, into deeper water. Flynn is at the helm, expertly spinning the steering wheel.

"Compared to other vessels, *Loretta* is rather small. But unfortunately, this creek isn't designed to withstand too much of even her." He grunts in effort as the bottom of the ship gets snagged on the creek bed. "So, it might be a bit bumpy to start."

Shade stands by the railing, gripping it tightly. Several others do the same. Duke Harvard's estate disappears around another bend, but the homes and lights of Lockwood are still very much present. They pass beautiful homes built on the edge of the creek and hear the sounds of music and laughter emanating from nearby taverns and bars. Shade wishes he had more time to fully discover the city, and without having to hide. They wind their way through the city and, after a few minutes, the creek begins to widen.

"Where are we?" He asks no one in particular.

"We will be passing near the Southern Gate shortly." Lady Brandy speaks from directly to his right. "Then it's down through the barren lands and out to the sea. I assume that's where we're headed." She looks at him plainly, "To sea. It's the most logical answer at this time, clearly. Safer, too. If they aren't with you, then they're trying to kill you." She beckons at the city, seemingly annoyed with all the action.

Shade hopes she is with him. Something catches his eye in the distance. A mansion up on a hill, brightly lit.

Wait. No.

His grip tightens on the railing and he sucks in a breath. "Is that Harvard's ball?"

"Can't be." Erin whispers. He hadn't realized she was next to him.

"It's on fire." Baron states, in both awe and horror.

Yes, it is on fire. Up on that hill, beautifully, brilliantly, horrifically bathed in the light of a raging inferno. "We have to go back." Shade says. "People could be hurt. Our people!" He turns to Flynn.

The young duke's eyes are sad. But his jaw is set and he stares southward, away from the city. "We can't."

For several long seconds, everyone watches the terrifying sight of that burning mansion, before it's no longer visible as they dip around another bend.

"Ah, well," Lady Brandy waves dismissively, "Buildings can be rebuilt and Harvard has plenty of money to do it." She catches her words and stands straighter, "That is, if he's still alive to do it." She

408

doesn't seem too concerned. She turns away from the edge. "Wake me up when we're there." Then, she and her guard, Shade remembers his name being Rufus, disappear down a hatch in the floor of the boat.

With the widening of the creek, they are able to pick up more speed. Flynn begins giving out orders about masts and sails and mooring lines to various people. Friga and Sten, Reginald's two messengers, seem to know their way around a boat and begin obeying his commands. Saipan's men have somewhat of an idea and jump into action as well. Hagan is standing next to Flynn at the helm, looking as if he wants to take over steering *Loretta*. Shade is almost certain the Green doesn't know how to sail a ship; but it's simply in their nature to desire control.

Baron leans his elbows onto the railing and lets out a long sigh. For once, he doesn't say anything and Shade is grateful.

What really is to be said about their current predicament? Separated from their allies, uncertain if they are still alive, and on the run once again. For the next several minutes, he watches the lights of Lockwood fade and, eventually, disappear altogether as they head south, away from the beautiful city. He doesn't know where they are headed, but Flynn seems to know what he's doing, so Shade decides to trust him for the time being.

A shoulder bumps into him. It's Erin. She's watching his face carefully, scrutinizing his expression. "Are you hurt?" She asks, her voice like a velvet blanket, enveloping him in safety.

He takes a breath. She is his lifeline, his anchor in the surrounding storm. "Not physically." She pulls aside his coat jacket and raises an eyebrow at the cut along his ribs. He shrugs because it hardly hurts. "Not physically." He repeats. The cut isn't deep anyway, it's already stopped bleeding.

She nods, looks away. He misses her eyes. "I know what you mean." She says. The four of them, Baron, Dru, Shade, and Erin lean against the railing, watching the trees go by. The moment is surreal. And, if not for the fact that they're running for their lives, Shade might even say peaceful. Although winter is basically upon them, tonight is not as cold as others. And the light breeze mixed with the dreamy stars overhead only add to its beauty.

The moment ends when Baron opens his mouth.

"Who knew the twins' sister was a total babe, right? I mean, come *on*." The last word comes out as almost a growl.

"Of *course*, you were mesmerized." Dru says ruefully, "Was it her cascading midnight locks or the dress cut down to her navel?"

As the two of them begin bickering back and forth, Erin turns to Shade with a sigh. Her hair is completely down, having fallen from the bun sometime between the ball and the boat. She so rarely leaves it out of a braid that it's a nice change. "Do you know where we're going?"

He looks over his shoulder at Flynn, whose eyes are still glued to the water ahead. The duke's face is calm and his hands unwavering on the wheel. Shade returns his attention to Erin. "No. But Ryker trusts him, so I do, too." He feels a pang of loss at the thought of leaving some of their group behind.

Erin must read it in his face, because she places a hand over his on the railing and squeezes it, saying, "We will see him again. All of them. For now, their duty is on the mainland and ours…" she shrugs, "Well…isn't." She cocks her head, thoughtfully, "I do wonder what could possibly be at sea worth our time. Surely, we aren't just heading away from the mainland to go into hiding."

Shade has to replay her words over in his mind several times before responding. He's been staring at her hand. Finally, he comes back to himself and clears his throat. "Hagan made it sound like there are allies somewhere out there. Maybe distant islands?"

"I never knew Zion had islands."

"Yeah, unfortunately, there's many things we didn't know about Zion."

She pauses and they can still hear Baron and Dru arguing.

"How many times must I tell you, my crossbow is just as strong as your long bow. Stronger, probably." Dru is saying. Baron laughs loudly, bending over the railing dramatically. "You are *deranged*!" He exclaims.

Erin looks back at Shade, almost shyly. "I'm sorry, I missed it." There's something in her eyes, remorse perhaps, even sadness.

"Missed what?" He asks.

"Your birthday."

Oh. Right. That had happened, hadn't it? Several days ago. It never even crossed his mind. He shrugs, "I genuinely could not care less. To be honest, I'd forgotten it myself."

She smiles at him, "Everyone deserves to be appreciated on their birthday. I know I'm late, but happy birthday. I appreciate you." There's a pause, then she adds, "Even if no one else does." They laugh together.

411

"And, there's at least one thing we *do* know about Zion." Erin says, "We know that it's worth fighting for."

Shade thinks about the miles they've traveled, the people they've encountered, the friends they've made. He considers the beautiful scenery they've experienced and the memories they've created. It has been a difficult month and a half since fleeing Glimmer. But it has also been beneficial and eye opening. It has managed to further inspire Shade to protect Zion and all of her inhabitants.

He smiles. "Yes. It's worth fighting for." He turns his palm into Erin's and squeezes.

And he will fight with every breath to save his kingdom from the ravaging of Renegades and the destructive forces of anarchy. He will not rest until he has regained the throne and restored every city to its former glory. He won't rest until every child, like the ones of Yagar, go to bed with full stomachs and joyful hearts. He won't rest until he's able to live up to that humbling title, born from the hearts of loyalists of old and passed on through the mouths of loyalists still today. That one title, that one word, uttered only an hour ago past the dying lips of a powerful, fallen warrior.

Kiertunyazi.
True King.

ACKNOWLEDGMENTS

The idea for this book started 8 years ago, when I was sitting in 12th grade Creative Writing class. For a while, there was excitement—I had this cool storyline with an endearing, aloof character who had a strong desire to do what's right. Life happened, things got busy, and my focus shifted away from the storyline; until one day something else sparked another idea and I returned to Prince Shade's story and began typing away once more. This irregular pattern continued over the next 8 years; until I finally set my feet and decided something for myself:

I didn't want to teach forever.

I graduated from Welch College in 2018 with a degree in English Secondary Education and have been teaching ever since. Now, don't get me wrong, I love the opportunities the world of education has provided me with. I get to meet new people—especially young people—and teach them discipline and what good character looks like. I get to show them Jesus through my actions and words, and I can care for them in a way that most of them have never experienced. Again, I love the opportunities teaching has given me. However, teaching itself just isn't my passion.

So, I returned to the keyboard, typing away furiously while visions of book signings and summers free of professional development danced in my head.

For 8 years, this manuscript has been known quite simply as "Prince Shade." Here I was, nearing the end, and it still needed a name. I bounced around several different titles of my own, asked close confidants for their suggestions, even searched up one of those

413

random name generators online and refreshed that through a couple of times. Nothing was sticking out to me.

Until, one day, it dawned on me. There was no need to create a name; I already had the perfect one. I mean, if it ain't broke, right? Therefore, without further ado, "Prince Shade" became *Prince Shade.*

It's important my readers know that the Old English language of Zion is not, in and of itself, a real language. However, its roots are drawn from words within the Spanish and Norse languages; both beautiful dialects worthy of Zion.

I have my manuscript, I have my title, and now I have my printed copy of my first book. All of my dreams packaged into 370 pages of hard work and wonderful, fun-filled hours of imagination. These dreams, however, would not have become reality without some very important people who deserve the utmost acknowledgement.

Not to be a cliché first-time author…but where do I begin?

First and foremost, the only reason this book was ever possible is because of the Lord and His unfathomable grace. He has blessed me with the gift of writing and He will receive all the praise for it. I thank You, Lord, that Your mercies are new every morning (Lamentations 3).

To all of my family, grandparents, aunts and uncles, cousins, and loving co-workers and friends; your kind words and gentle encouragements mean more than you realize. I love you.

Mom and Dad, thank you for always believing in me and for humoring ALL of my crazy stories. You have read my writings throughout the years and have seen me through so many writing phases (Remember the Sacketts phase? I'm sure Louis L'Amour would not have appreciated me plagiarizing his material). But, beyond that, you have raised my siblings and me to serve the Lord and to serve others. Because you first gave me over to God, and I discovered His mercy for myself, I will spend eternity in His presence. There is no higher calling. Mom, the first one to read *Prince Shade* in its entirety, you are amazing. Words can't describe how grateful I am for your constant support and your wise counsel. Dad, you make me smile. And, yes, despite your best efforts, I am just like you. It's one of my best traits.

Kendal, Olivia, & Jack—three of my most favorite people in the world. Being your sister is a blessing I will never deserve. You've provided me many laughs and have been the inspiration behind several of my characters; you even tried helping with a title (I'm sorry, A Glimmer of Shade didn't make the cut, Liv…haha). There have been countless times I've called to talk with each of you about a potential plot idea or character arc. *'What if he did this here?'* Or, *'Does this part here make sense?'* Or, this one: *'Is Shade too mushy?'* Thank you for listening, loving, & guiding me through the highs and lows of not only my writing career, but through life as well. God knew I needed you.

To my best friends, Katie and Morgan, thank you for your consistent reassurance. And for the ice cream parties when celebrating my successes and when mourning my failures alike. You put up with my long moments of creativity when all I could do was type madly and stare at the screen, unable to respond to anything you said or asked; multitasking has never

415

been my strong suit. Katie, you read my book all the way from its beginning—the very, very rough draft—to the final copy. You listened to my incessant questions about narrative fidelity and character development; and offered advice I really needed to hear. I was so relieved when you assured me the book was, in fact, engaging and exciting. At least, now I knew I wasn't the only one who thought so. Morgan, thank you for being the incredible, Enneagram 7 friend that you are. You can have all the copies you want for your classroom library (it'll only cost you a lifetime provision of Cotton Candy Blizzards).

My cousins, Kaitlen and Claiborne: You two kept me writing when I experienced one of my many, many times of writer's block. Kaitlen, Trix owes her entire backstory to you. Claiborne, that 'Future Bestselling Author' mug you gifted me hits a little different now. And, bestselling or not, the author part is finally true. No worries, I'll fly you both to New Zealand myself if this somehow becomes a major-motion picture. My cousin, Michal: You were the inspiration behind my very first published book. You will always be my Bye-Bye.

I know it's your given name, but since Aunt Marianne looks really strange typed out on my computer screen, I'm going to continue calling you Bubba—a name given to you years ago when Marianne was a mouthful. Aunt Bubba, you were calling me an author before I even believed it fully myself. You wanted every little piece of writing I created sent your way, finished or not. The couple of years I lived in the house next to you were precious times I will never forget; times of fear and sadness, joy and peace, and learning and growth. I had always loved you as my aunt, but that's when I also grew to love you as one of my dearest friends.

Jen: When I asked you to edit this book, it was because I knew you wouldn't hold back. Thank you for your honesty and friendship. If Shade's story had no business being told, you would have been the person to tell me. When you called to say it had promise, that was the final motivation I needed to see this project to its finish.

Mr. Mays: My high school English teacher, who was the first person—outside of family—to tell me I could write. I still remember the day you signed me a copy of a short story of your own with the comment: "I know one day you will be signing one of your books for me." You were right. Here you are, Mr. Mays, your very own signed copy. I've never stopped creating.

Of course, this final project would not have been possible without Trevor James and my incredible team at Amazon Pro Hub for the hours of editing, formatting, and designing they put into making this story real.

And, finally, to my readers: you are as much a contributor to Shade's success as I am. Without you, the story doesn't live.

Once again, from the bottom of my heart, I thank you all. And Prince Shade does, too.

All glory to God; He is worthy.

Never stop creating.

ABOUT THE AUTHOR

Maredith Ryan lives in the Nashville, Tennessee area. She is a middle school English teacher and enjoys spending time with family and friends, as well as staying consistently involved in athletics. Ryan's self-care includes slow Saturday mornings with coffee, time spent in activity, and doing puzzles. Her faith is very important to her and she knows any talent in writing is only because The Lord has graciously blessed her with it. This is Ryan's first published chapter book; she knew she wanted to be a writer at an early age and, taking the advice of her high school English teacher, has "Never stopped creating." It is largely because of the countless worlds she's experienced, adventures she's embarked on, and individuals she's met through the incredible act of reading, that she now creates worlds of her own. Ryan now encourages fellow writers with that very same mantra from her early years of writing: Never stop creating.

Made in United States
Orlando, FL
07 September 2022

22077482R00255